W9-DEV-628

"THE FUTURE IS BULLSHIT."
-SOME GUY

IMAGE COMICS, INC. • **Robert Kirkman:** Chief Operating Officer • **Erik Larsen:** Chief Financial Officer • **Todd McFarlane:** President • **Marc Silvestri:** Chief Executive Officer • **Jim Valentino:** Vice President • **Eric Stephenson:** Publisher / Chief Creative Officer • **Nicole Lapalme:** Controller • **Leanna Caunter:** Accounting Analyst • **Sue Korpela:** Accounting & HR Manager • **Marla Eizik:** Talent Liaison • **Jeff Boison:** Director of Sales & Publishing Planning • **Lorelei Bunjes:** Director of Digital Services • **Dirk Wood:** Director of International Sales & Licensing • **Alex Cox:** Director of Direct Market Sales • **Chloe Ramos:** Book Market & Library Sales Manager • **Emilio Bautista:** Digital Sales Coordinator • **Jon Schlaffman:** Specialty Sales Coordinator • **Kat Salazar:** Director of PR & Marketing • **Drew Fitzgerald:** Marketing Content Associate • **Heather Doornink:** Production Director • **Drew Gill:** Art Director • **Hilary DiLoreto:** Print Manager • **Tricia Ramos:** Traffic Manager • **Melissa Gifford:** Content Manager • **Erika Schnatz:** Senior Production Artist • **Ryan Brewer:** Production Artist • **Deanna Phelps:** Production Artist • **IMAGECOMICS.COM**

VOLUME THREE
CUTTING-EDGE DESOLATION

CHRISTOPHER SEBELA
::.SCRIPT + DESIGN.::

RO STEIN + TED BRANDT
::.LINE ART.::

TRIONA FARRELL // DIANA SOUSA
CH. 13-15 ::.COLORS.:: CH. 16-17

CARDINAL RAE
::.LETTERS.::

JULIETTE CAPRA
::.EDITS.::

DYLAN TODD
::.LOGO.::

ALIVÓN ORTÍZ // HOLLEY MCKEND
JOEL BARTLETT // RICHEL // NYLESHIA DAVIS
::.COLOR FLATTING.::

::.CREATED BY SEBELA, STEIN, BRANDT, FARRELL, RAE & CAPRA.::

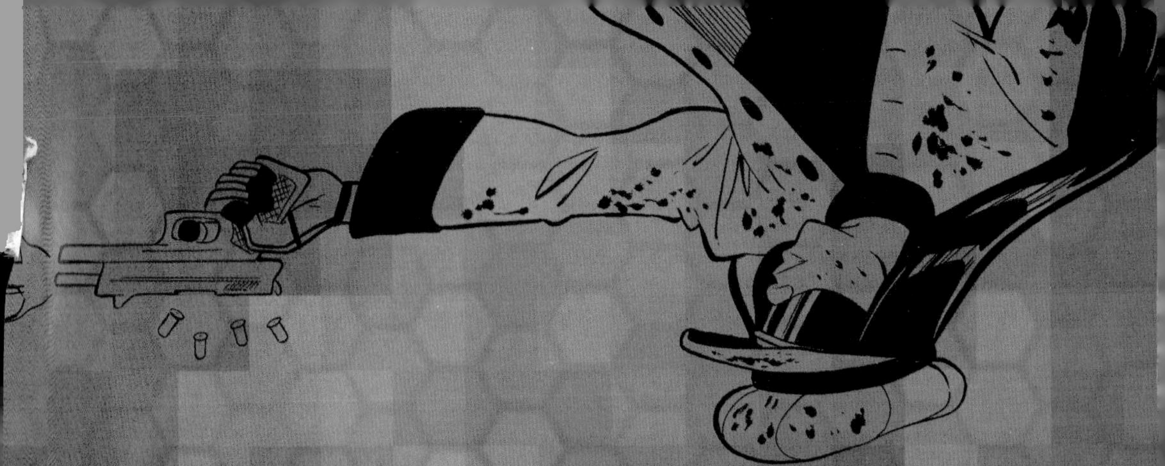

CHAPTER THIRTEEN

STRONG HAND

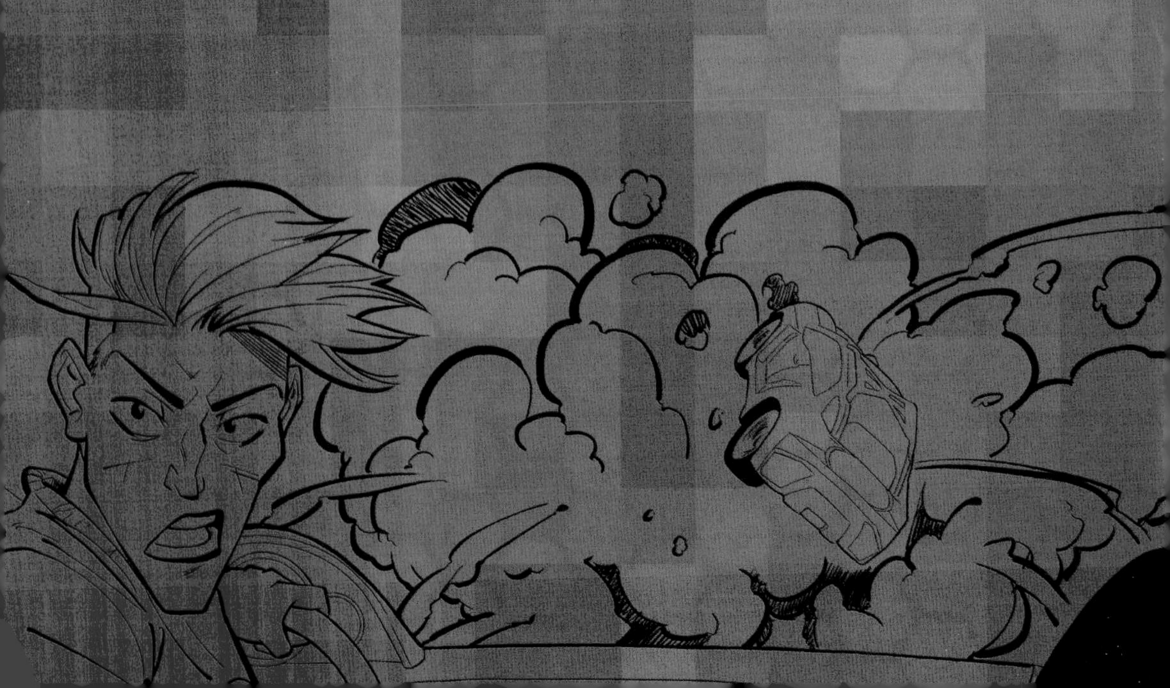

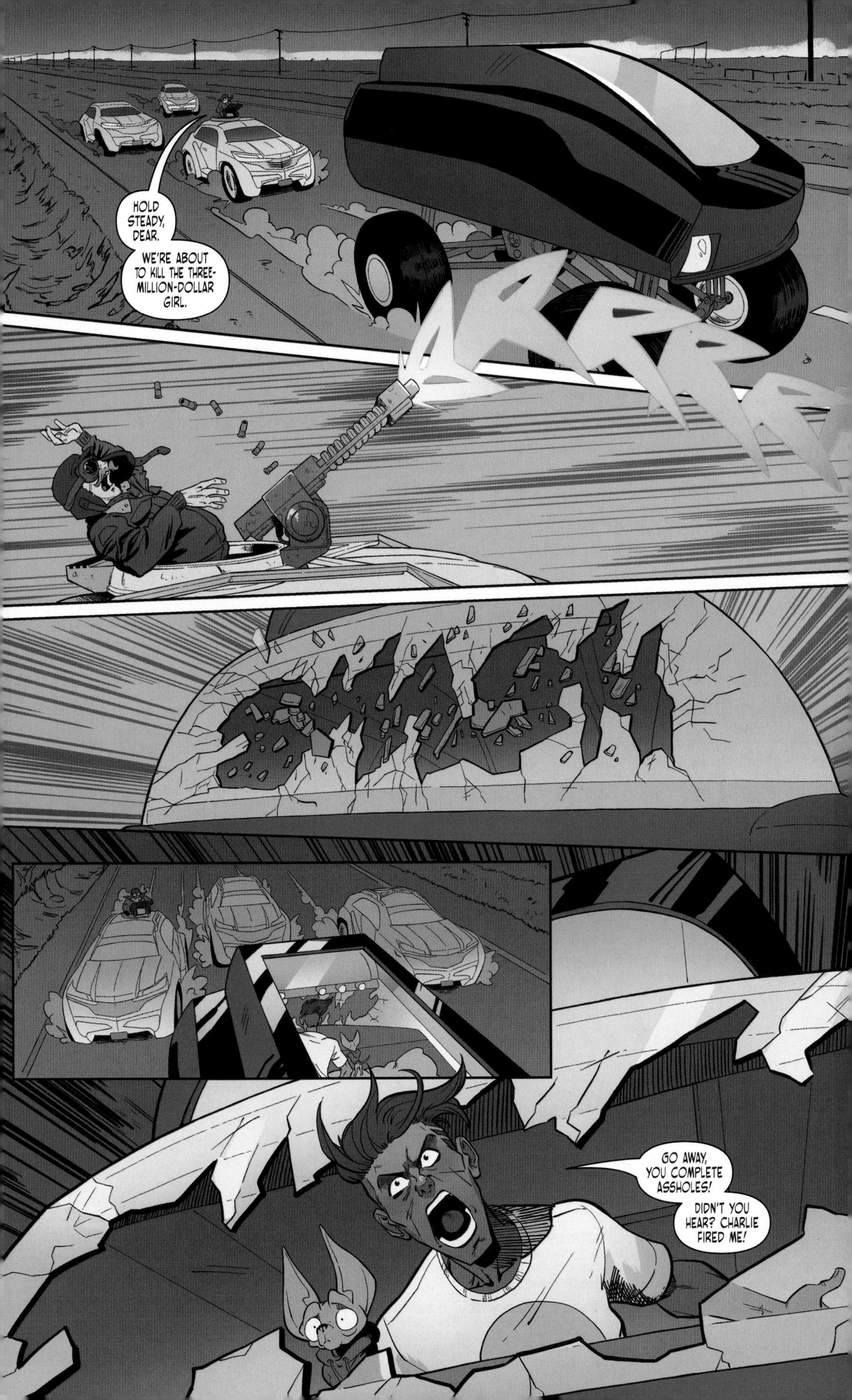
HOLD STEADY, DEAR.
WE'RE ABOUT TO KILL THE THREE-MILLION-DOLLAR GIRL.
GO AWAY, YOU COMPLETE ASSHOLES!
DIDN'T YOU HEAR? CHARLIE FIRED ME!

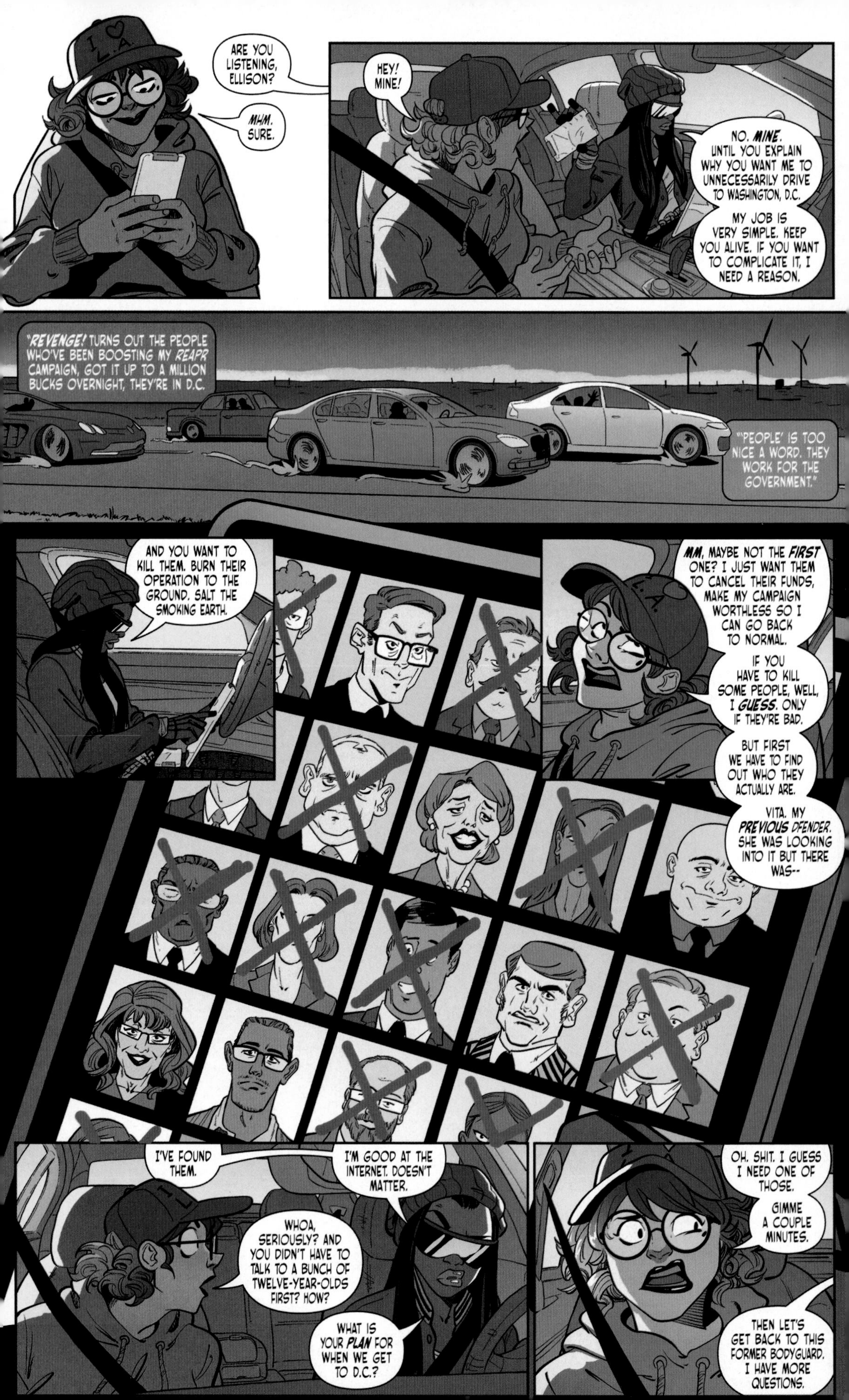

ARE YOU LISTENING, ELLISON?
MHM. SURE.
HEY! MINE!
NO. MINE. UNTIL YOU EXPLAIN WHY YOU WANT ME TO UNNECESSARILY DRIVE TO WASHINGTON, D.C.
MY JOB IS VERY SIMPLE. KEEP YOU ALIVE. IF YOU WANT TO COMPLICATE IT, I NEED A REASON.
"REVENGE! TURNS OUT THE PEOPLE WHO'VE BEEN BOOSTING MY REAPR CAMPAIGN, GOT IT UP TO A MILLION BUCKS OVERNIGHT, THEY'RE IN D.C.
"'PEOPLE' IS TOO NICE A WORD. THEY WORK FOR THE GOVERNMENT."
AND YOU WANT TO KILL THEM. BURN THEIR OPERATION TO THE GROUND. SALT THE SMOKING EARTH.
MM, MAYBE NOT THE FIRST ONE? I JUST WANT THEM TO CANCEL THEIR FUNDS, MAKE MY CAMPAIGN WORTHLESS SO I CAN GO BACK TO NORMAL.
IF YOU HAVE TO KILL SOME PEOPLE, WELL, I GUESS. ONLY IF THEY'RE BAD.
BUT FIRST WE HAVE TO FIND OUT WHO THEY ACTUALLY ARE.
VITA. MY PREVIOUS DFENDER. SHE WAS LOOKING INTO IT BUT THERE WAS--
I'VE FOUND THEM.
I'M GOOD AT THE INTERNET. DOESN'T MATTER.
WHOA, SERIOUSLY? AND YOU DIDN'T HAVE TO TALK TO A BUNCH OF TWELVE-YEAR-OLDS FIRST? HOW?
WHAT IS YOUR PLAN FOR WHEN WE GET TO D.C.?
OH. SHIT. I GUESS I NEED ONE OF THOSE.
GIMME A COUPLE MINUTES.
THEN LET'S GET BACK TO THIS FORMER BODYGUARD. I HAVE MORE QUESTIONS.

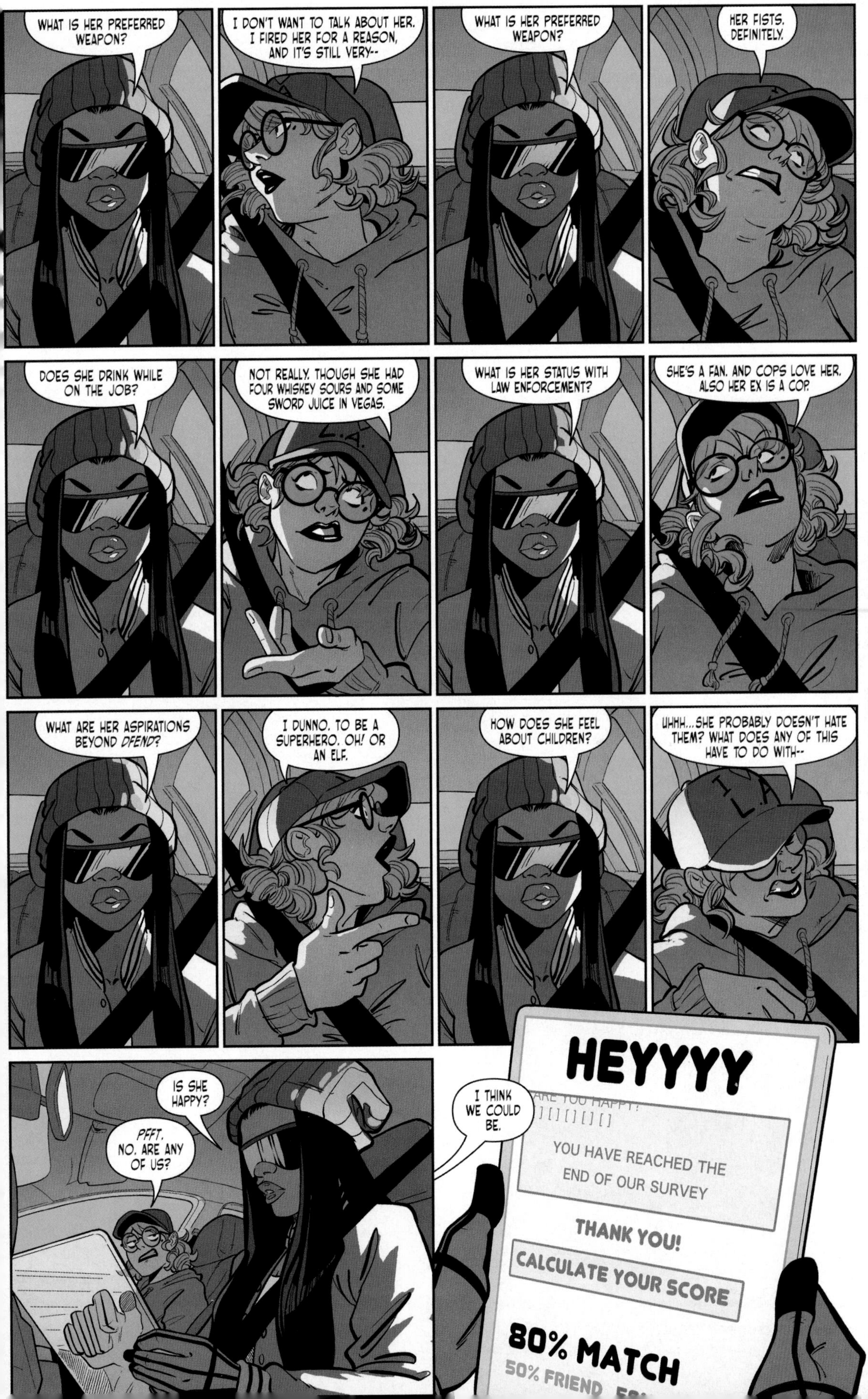
WHAT IS HER PREFERRED WEAPON?
I DON'T WANT TO TALK ABOUT HER. I FIRED HER FOR A REASON, AND IT'S STILL VERY--
WHAT IS HER PREFERRED WEAPON?
HER FISTS. DEFINITELY.
DOES SHE DRINK WHILE ON THE JOB?
NOT REALLY. THOUGH SHE HAD FOUR WHISKEY SOURS AND SOME SWORD JUICE IN VEGAS.
WHAT IS HER STATUS WITH LAW ENFORCEMENT?
SHE'S A FAN. AND COPS LOVE HER. ALSO HER EX IS A COP.
WHAT ARE HER ASPIRATIONS BEYOND *DFEND*?
I DUNNO. TO BE A SUPERHERO. OH! OR AN ELF.
HOW DOES SHE FEEL ABOUT CHILDREN?
UHHH...SHE PROBABLY DOESN'T HATE THEM? WHAT DOES ANY OF THIS HAVE TO DO WITH--
IS SHE HAPPY?
PFFT. NO. ARE ANY OF US?
I THINK WE COULD BE.
HEYYYY
YOU HAVE REACHED THE END OF OUR SURVEY
THANK YOU!
CALCULATE YOUR SCORE
80% MATCH

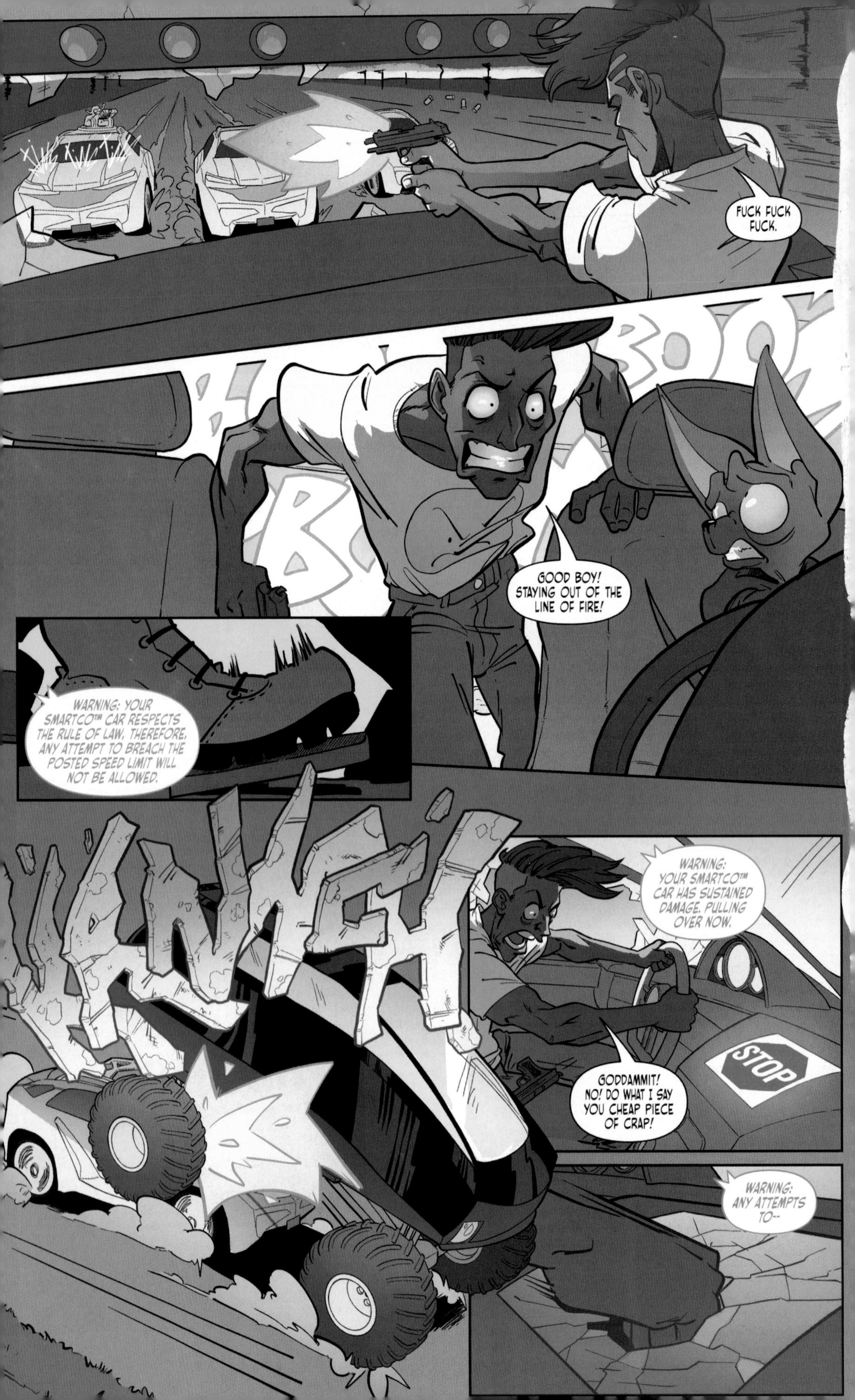
FUCK FUCK FUCK.
GOOD BOY! STAYING OUT OF THE LINE OF FIRE!
WARNING: YOUR SMARTCO™ CAR RESPECTS THE RULE OF LAW. THEREFORE, ANY ATTEMPT TO BREACH THE POSTED SPEED LIMIT WILL NOT BE ALLOWED.
WARNING: YOUR SMARTCO™ CAR HAS SUSTAINED DAMAGE. PULLING OVER NOW.
GODDAMMIT! NO! DO WHAT I SAY YOU CHEAP PIECE OF CRAP!
STOP
WARNING: ANY ATTEMPTS TO--

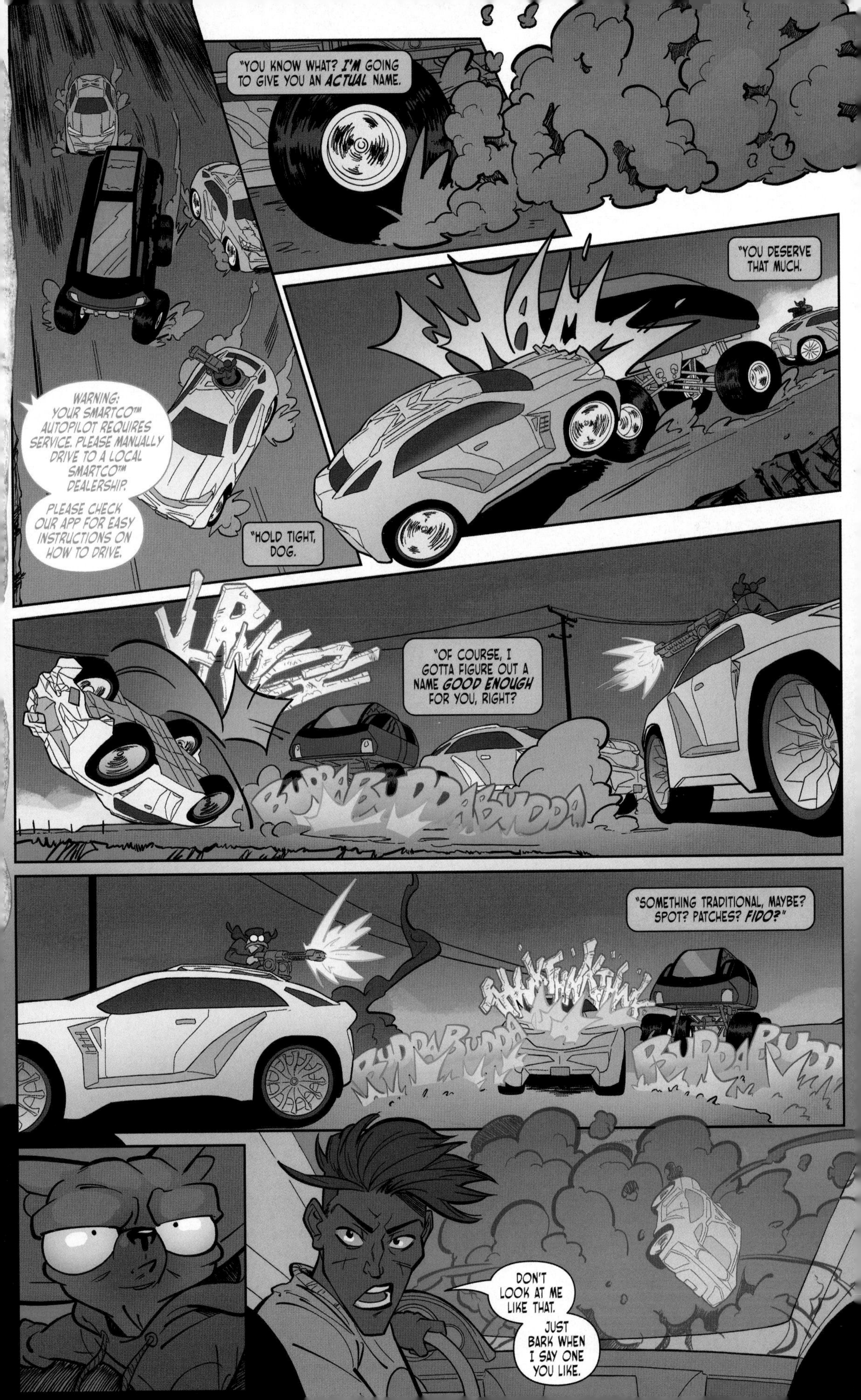
"YOU KNOW WHAT? I'M GOING TO GIVE YOU AN ACTUAL NAME.
"YOU DESERVE THAT MUCH.
WARNING: YOUR SMARTCO™ AUTOPILOT REQUIRES SERVICE. PLEASE MANUALLY DRIVE TO A LOCAL SMARTCO™ DEALERSHIP.
PLEASE CHECK OUR APP FOR EASY INSTRUCTIONS ON HOW TO DRIVE.
"HOLD TIGHT, DOG.
"OF COURSE, I GOTTA FIGURE OUT A NAME GOOD ENOUGH FOR YOU, RIGHT?
BUDDABUDDABUDDA
"SOMETHING TRADITIONAL, MAYBE? SPOT? PATCHES? FIDO?"
DON'T LOOK AT ME LIKE THAT.
JUST BARK WHEN I SAY ONE YOU LIKE.

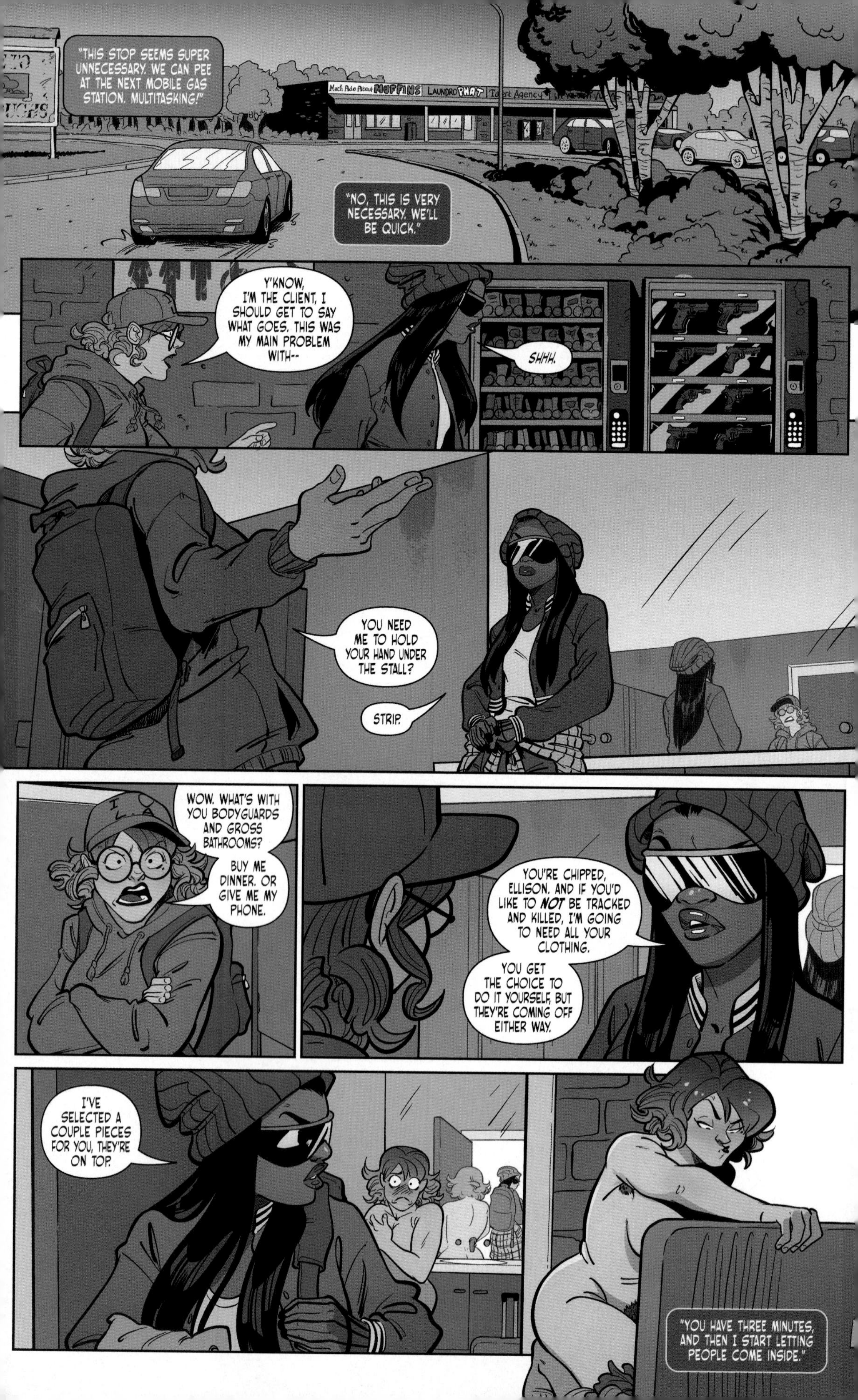

"THIS STOP SEEMS SUPER UNNECESSARY. WE CAN PEE AT THE NEXT MOBILE GAS STATION. MULTITASKING!"
Much Ado About MUFFINS
LAUNDROPHAT
Talent Agency
"NO, THIS IS VERY NECESSARY. WE'LL BE QUICK."
Y'KNOW, I'M THE CLIENT, I SHOULD GET TO SAY WHAT GOES. THIS WAS MY MAIN PROBLEM WITH--
SHHH.
YOU NEED ME TO HOLD YOUR HAND UNDER THE STALL?
STRIP.
WOW. WHAT'S WITH YOU BODYGUARDS AND GROSS BATHROOMS?
BUY ME DINNER. OR GIVE ME MY PHONE.
YOU'RE CHIPPED, ELLISON. AND IF YOU'D LIKE TO *NOT* BE TRACKED AND KILLED, I'M GOING TO NEED ALL YOUR CLOTHING.
YOU GET THE CHOICE TO DO IT YOURSELF, BUT THEY'RE COMING OFF EITHER WAY.
I'VE SELECTED A COUPLE PIECES FOR YOU, THEY'RE ON TOP.
"YOU HAVE THREE MINUTES, AND THEN I START LETTING PEOPLE COME INSIDE."

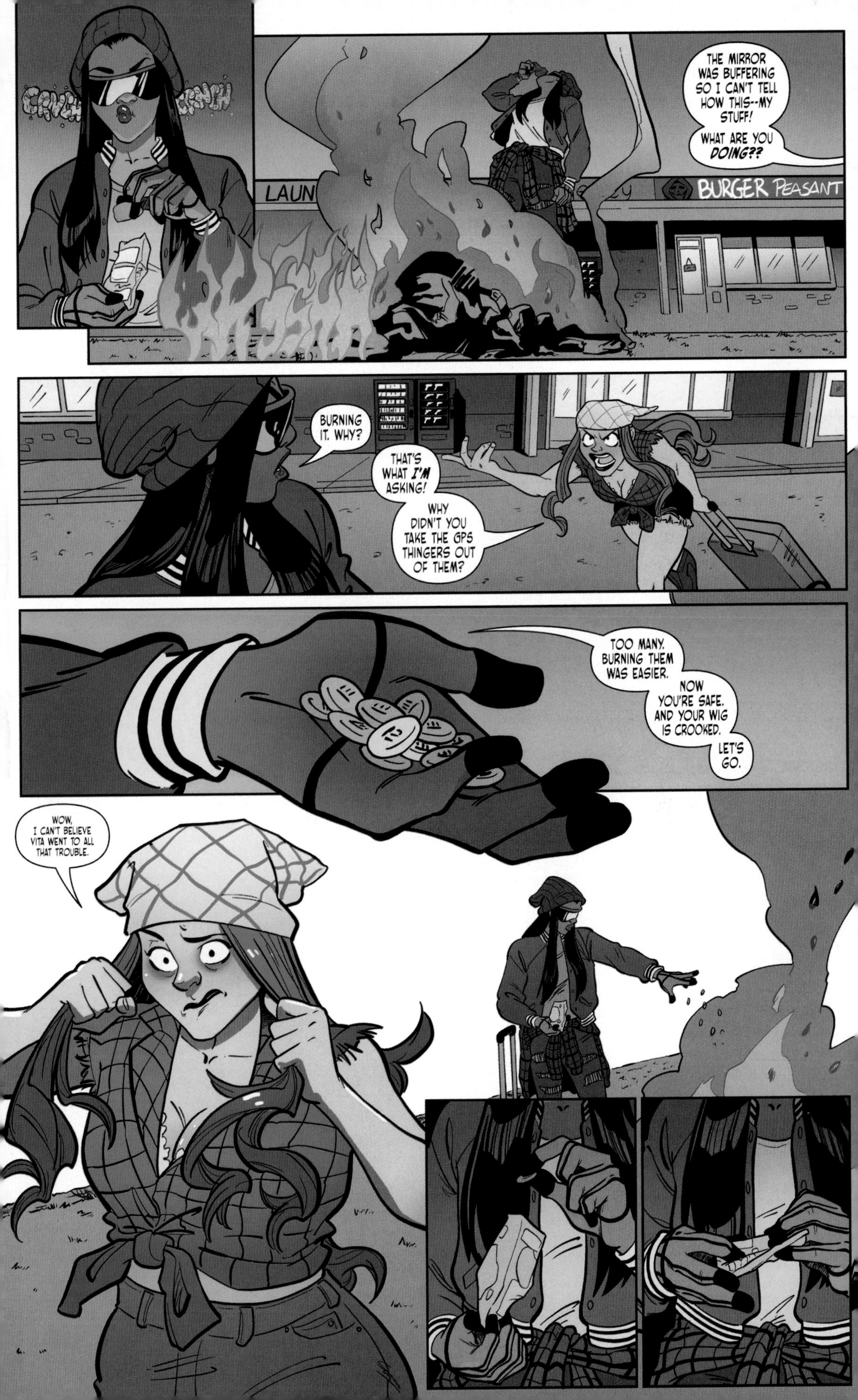
CRNCH CRNCH
THE MIRROR WAS BUFFERING SO I CAN'T TELL HOW THIS--MY STUFF!
WHAT ARE YOU DOING??
LAUN
BURGER PEASANT
BURNING IT. WHY?
THAT'S WHAT I'M ASKING!
WHY DIDN'T YOU TAKE THE GPS THINGERS OUT OF THEM?
TOO MANY. BURNING THEM WAS EASIER.
NOW YOU'RE SAFE. AND YOUR WIG IS CROOKED.
LET'S GO.
WOW, I CAN'T BELIEVE VITA WENT TO ALL THAT TROUBLE.

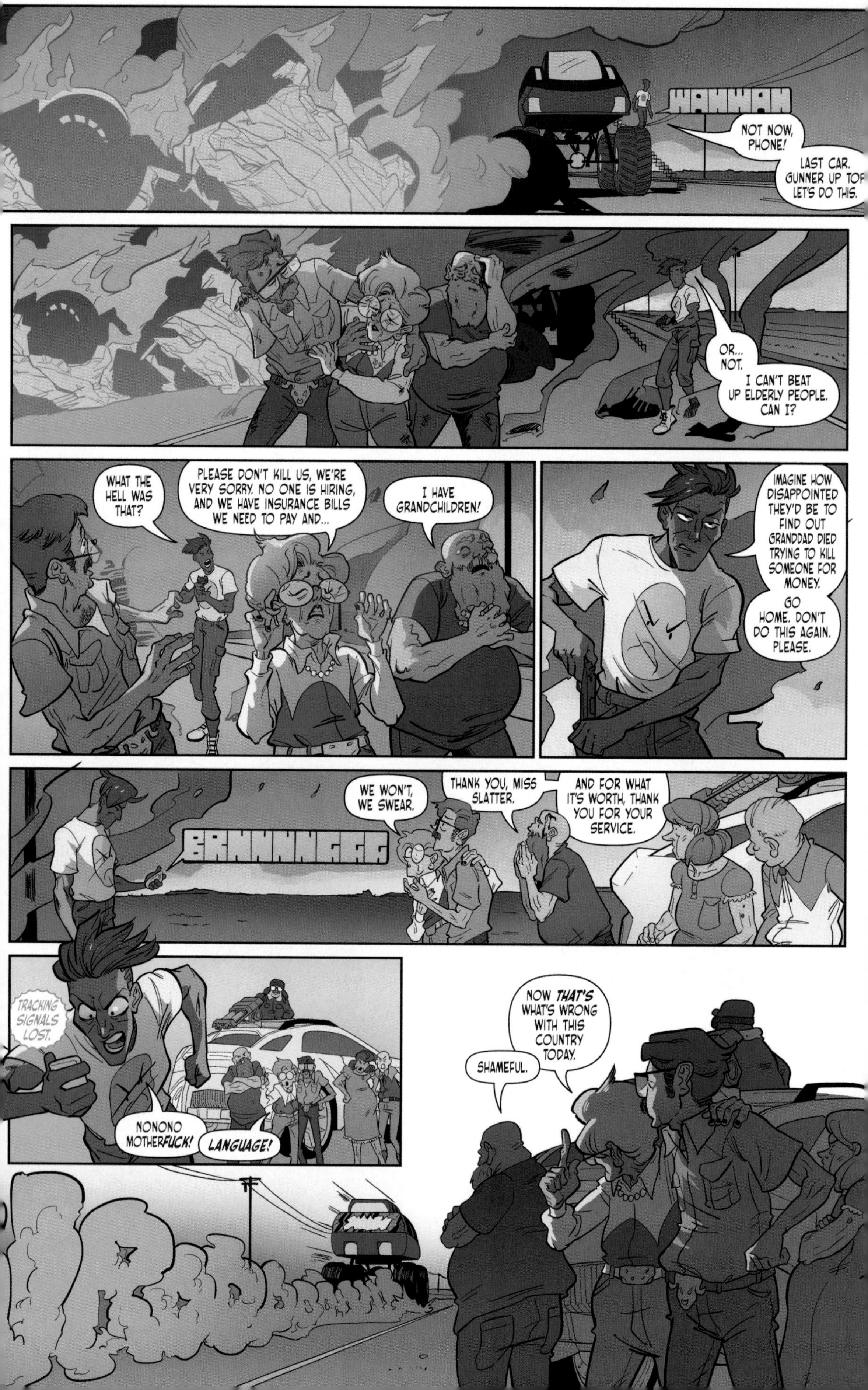
WAHWAH
NOT NOW, PHONE!
LAST CAR. GUNNER UP TOP. LET'S DO THIS.
OR... NOT.
I CAN'T BEAT UP ELDERLY PEOPLE. CAN I?
WHAT THE HELL WAS THAT?
PLEASE DON'T KILL US, WE'RE VERY SORRY. NO ONE IS HIRING, AND WE HAVE INSURANCE BILLS WE NEED TO PAY AND...
I HAVE GRANDCHILDREN!
IMAGINE HOW DISAPPOINTED THEY'D BE TO FIND OUT GRANDDAD DIED TRYING TO KILL SOMEONE FOR MONEY.
GO HOME. DON'T DO THIS AGAIN. PLEASE.
BRNNNNGGG
WE WON'T, WE SWEAR.
THANK YOU, MISS SLATTER.
AND FOR WHAT IT'S WORTH, THANK YOU FOR YOUR SERVICE.
TRACKING SIGNALS LOST.
NONONO MOTHER*FUCK!*
LANGUAGE!
NOW *THAT'S* WHAT'S WRONG WITH THIS COUNTRY TODAY.
SHAMEFUL.

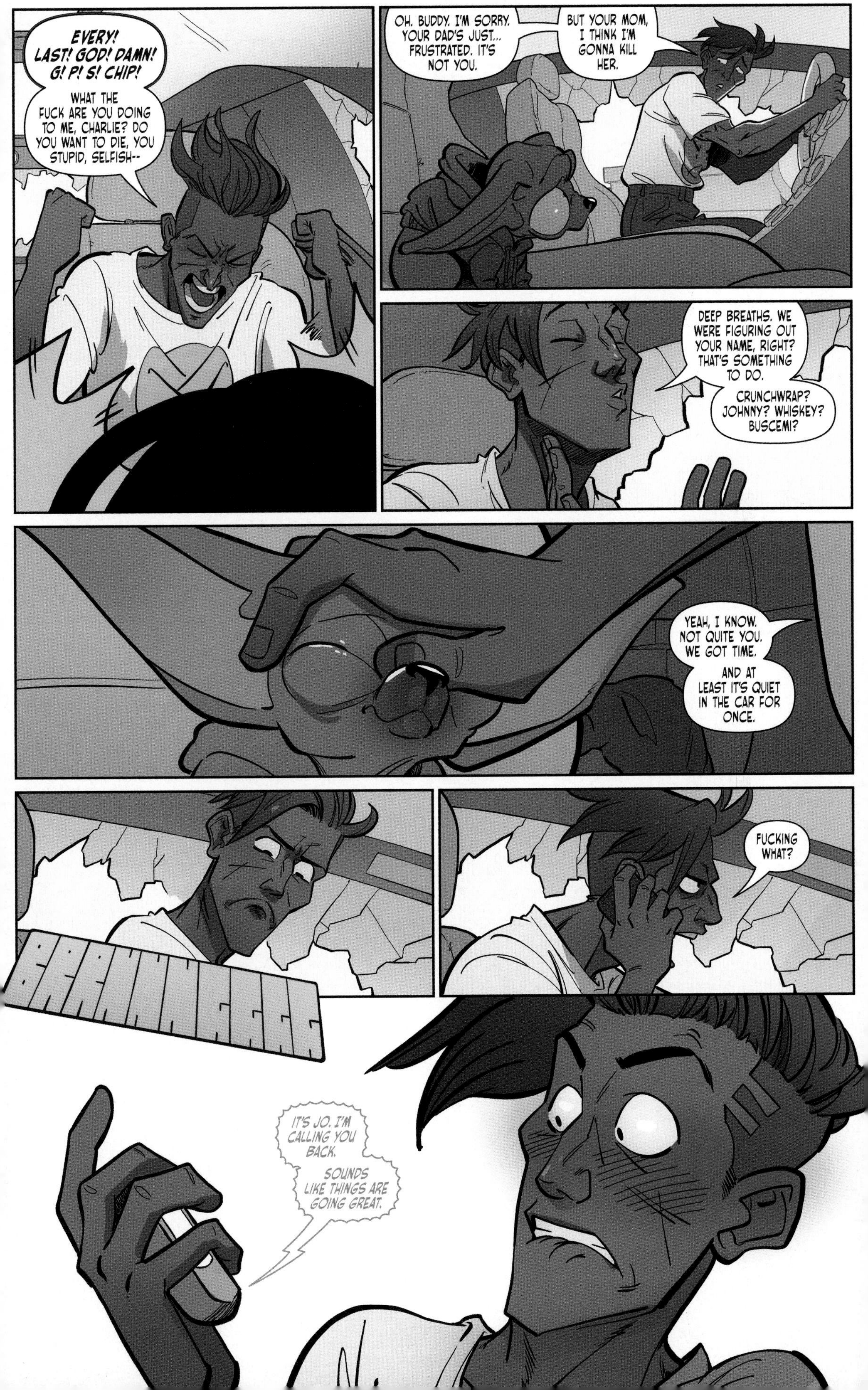
EVERY! LAST! GOD! DAMN! G! P! S! CHIP!
WHAT THE FUCK ARE YOU DOING TO ME, CHARLIE? DO YOU WANT TO DIE, YOU STUPID, SELFISH--
OH, BUDDY, I'M SORRY. YOUR DAD'S JUST... FRUSTRATED. IT'S NOT YOU.
BUT YOUR MOM, I THINK I'M GONNA KILL HER.
DEEP BREATHS. WE WERE FIGURING OUT YOUR NAME, RIGHT? THAT'S SOMETHING TO DO.
CRUNCHWRAP? JOHNNY? WHISKEY? BUSCEMI?
YEAH, I KNOW. NOT QUITE YOU. WE GOT TIME.
AND AT LEAST IT'S QUIET IN THE CAR FOR ONCE.
FUCKING WHAT?
IT'S JO. I'M CALLING YOU BACK.
SOUNDS LIKE THINGS ARE GOING GREAT.

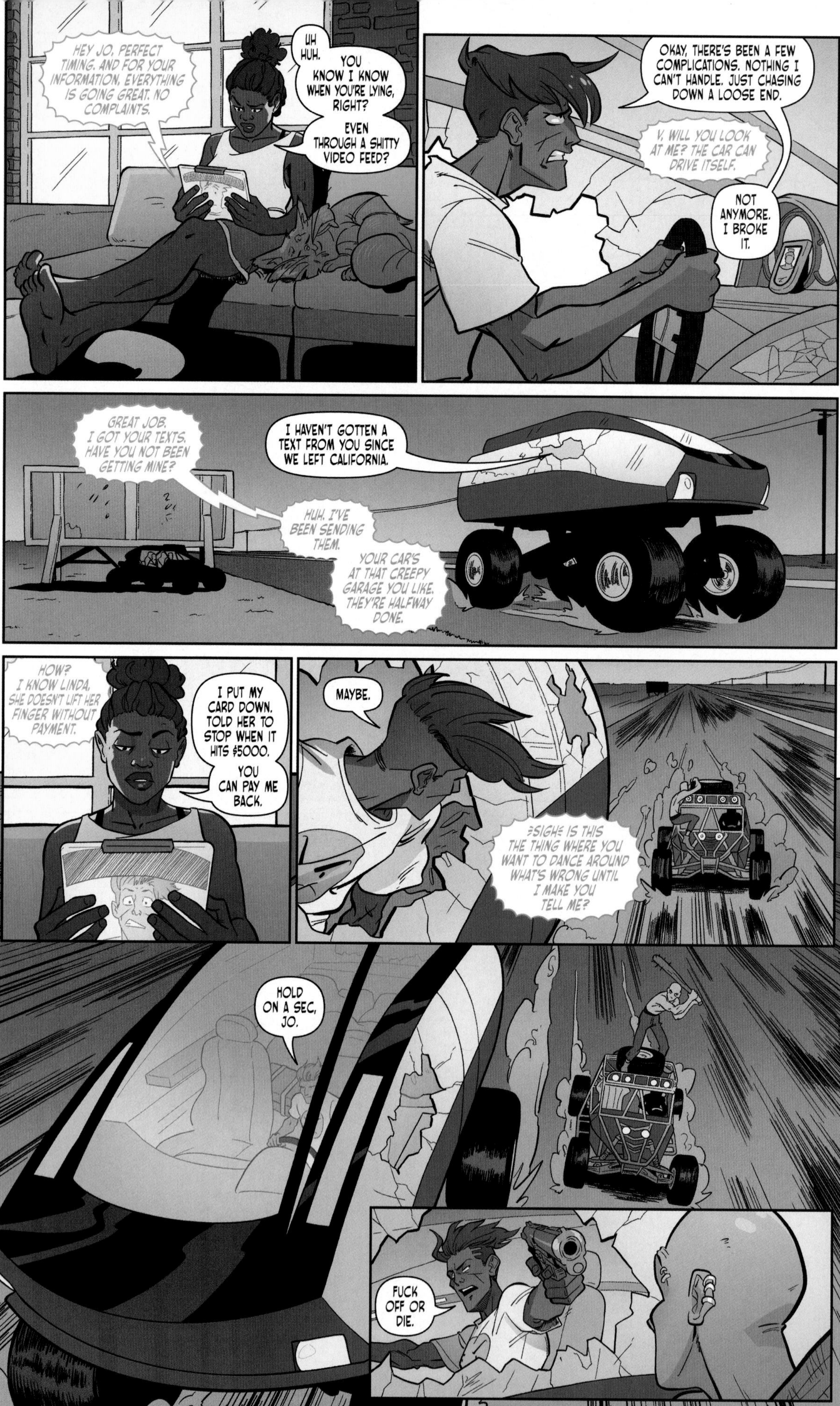
HEY JO. PERFECT TIMING. AND FOR YOUR INFORMATION, EVERYTHING IS GOING GREAT. NO COMPLAINTS.
UH HUH.
YOU KNOW I KNOW WHEN YOU'RE LYING, RIGHT?
EVEN THROUGH A SHITTY VIDEO FEED?
OKAY, THERE'S BEEN A FEW COMPLICATIONS. NOTHING I CAN'T HANDLE. JUST CHASING DOWN A LOOSE END.
V, WILL YOU LOOK AT ME? THE CAR CAN DRIVE ITSELF.
NOT ANYMORE. I BROKE IT.
GREAT JOB. I GOT YOUR TEXTS. HAVE YOU NOT BEEN GETTING MINE?
I HAVEN'T GOTTEN A TEXT FROM YOU SINCE WE LEFT CALIFORNIA.
HUH. I'VE BEEN SENDING THEM.
YOUR CAR'S AT THAT CREEPY GARAGE YOU LIKE. THEY'RE HALFWAY DONE.
HOW? I KNOW LINDA. SHE DOESN'T LIFT HER FINGER WITHOUT PAYMENT.
I PUT MY CARD DOWN. TOLD HER TO STOP WHEN IT HITS $5000.
YOU CAN PAY ME BACK.
MAYBE.
SIGH IS THIS THE THING WHERE YOU WANT TO DANCE AROUND WHAT'S WRONG UNTIL I MAKE YOU TELL ME?
HOLD ON A SEC, JO.
FUCK OFF OR DIE.

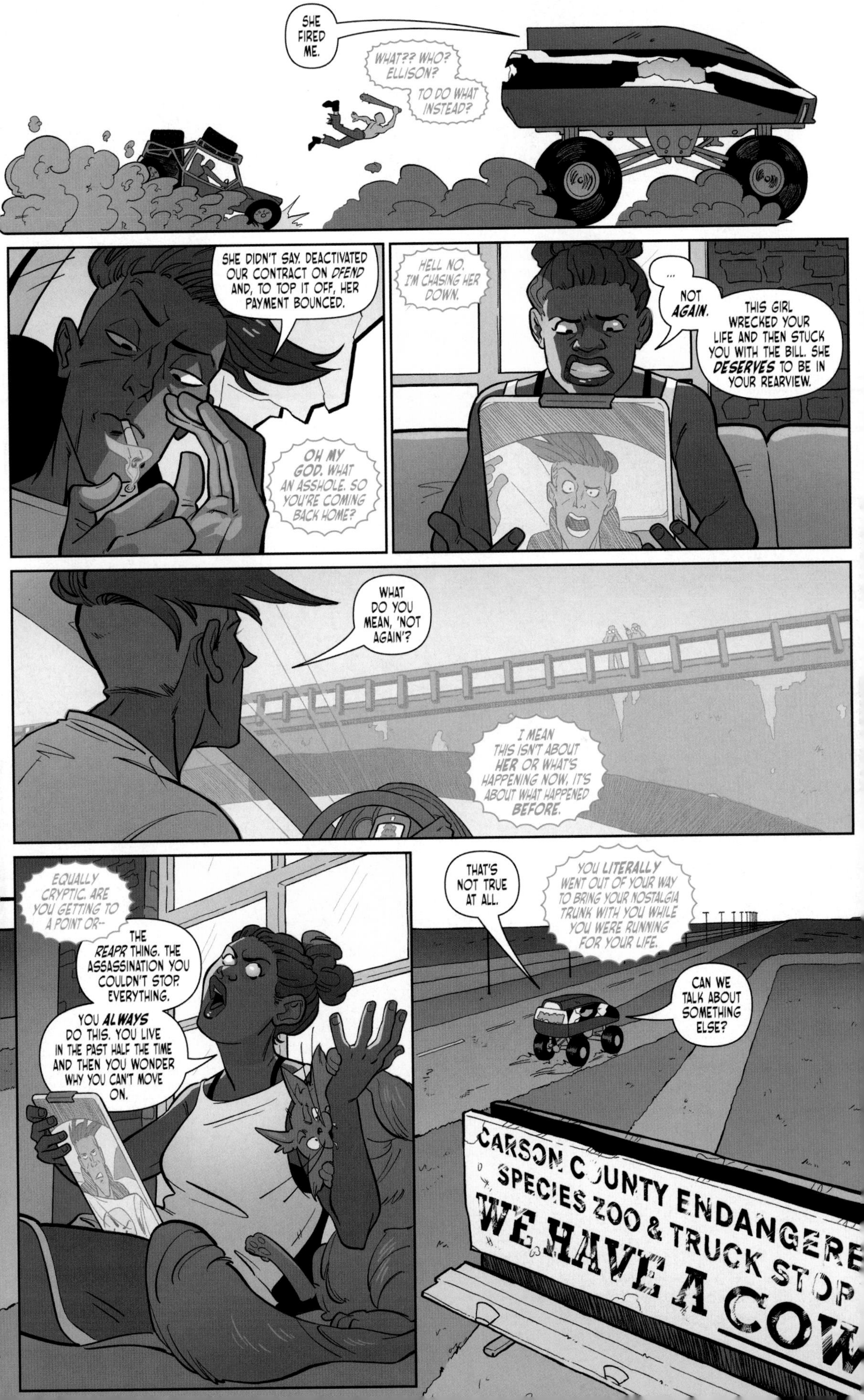

SHE FIRED ME.
WHAT?? WHO? ELLISON?
TO DO WHAT INSTEAD?
SHE DIDN'T SAY. DEACTIVATED OUR CONTRACT ON DFEND AND, TO TOP IT OFF, HER PAYMENT BOUNCED.
OH MY GOD. WHAT AN ASSHOLE. SO YOU'RE COMING BACK HOME?
HELL NO. I'M CHASING HER DOWN.
...
NOT AGAIN.
THIS GIRL WRECKED YOUR LIFE AND THEN STUCK YOU WITH THE BILL. SHE DESERVES TO BE IN YOUR REARVIEW.
WHAT DO YOU MEAN, 'NOT AGAIN'?
I MEAN THIS ISN'T ABOUT HER OR WHAT'S HAPPENING NOW. IT'S ABOUT WHAT HAPPENED BEFORE.
EQUALLY CRYPTIC. ARE YOU GETTING TO A POINT OR--
THE REAPR THING. THE ASSASSINATION YOU COULDN'T STOP. EVERYTHING.
YOU ALWAYS DO THIS. YOU LIVE IN THE PAST HALF THE TIME AND THEN YOU WONDER WHY YOU CAN'T MOVE ON.
THAT'S NOT TRUE AT ALL.
YOU LITERALLY WENT OUT OF YOUR WAY TO BRING YOUR NOSTALGIA TRUNK WITH YOU WHILE YOU WERE RUNNING FOR YOUR LIFE.
CAN WE TALK ABOUT SOMETHING ELSE?
CARSON C UNTY ENDANGERE
SPECIES ZOO & TRUCK STOP
WE HAVE A COW

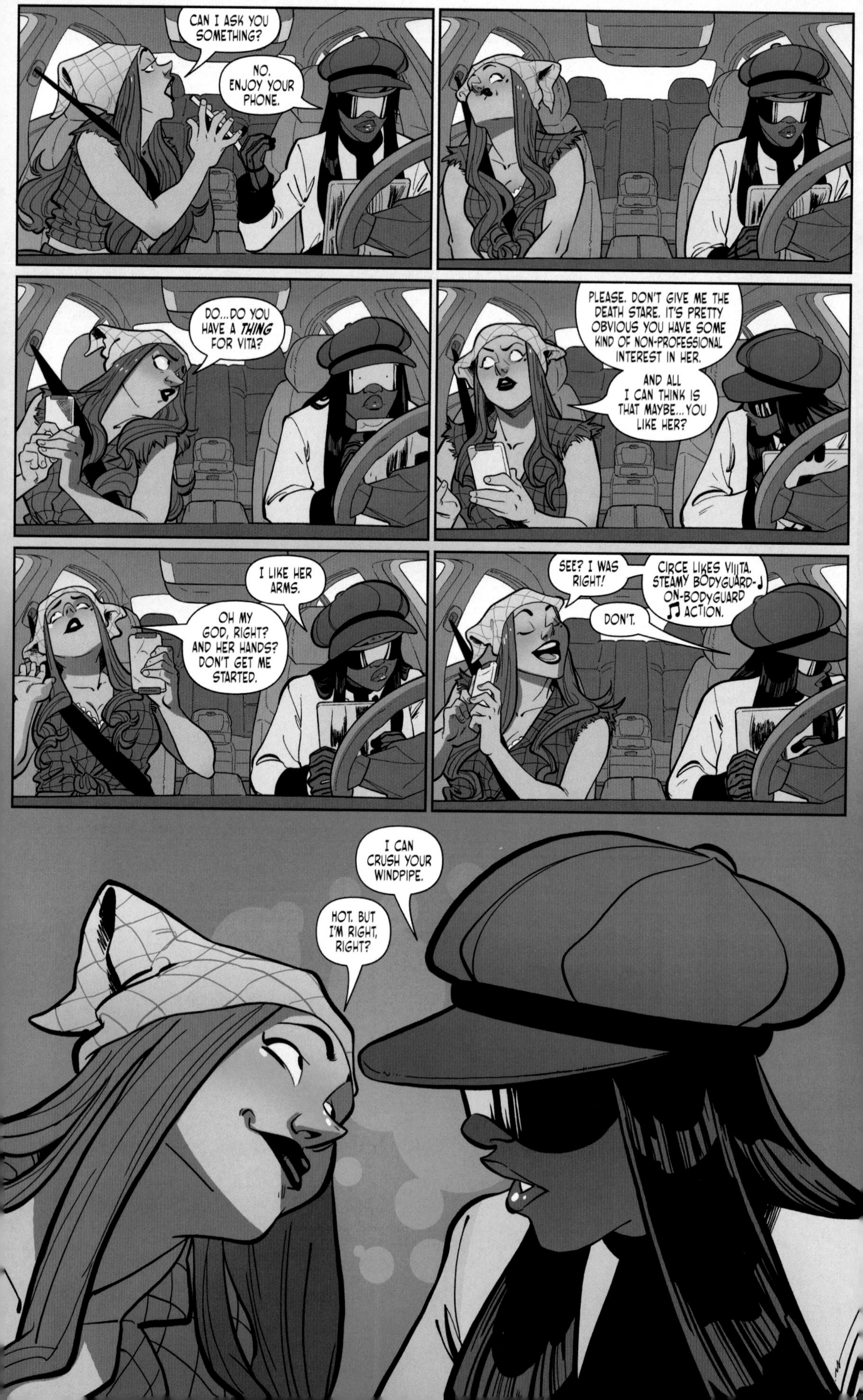
CAN I ASK YOU SOMETHING?
NO. ENJOY YOUR PHONE.
DO...DO YOU HAVE A *THING* FOR VITA?
PLEASE. DON'T GIVE ME THE DEATH STARE. IT'S PRETTY OBVIOUS YOU HAVE SOME KIND OF NON-PROFESSIONAL INTEREST IN HER.
AND ALL I CAN THINK IS THAT MAYBE...YOU LIKE HER?
I LIKE HER ARMS.
OH MY GOD, RIGHT? AND HER HANDS? DON'T GET ME STARTED.
SEE? I WAS RIGHT!
CIRCE LIKES VIIITA. STEAMY BODYGUARD-♩ ON-BODYGUARD ♫ ACTION.
DON'T.
I CAN CRUSH YOUR WINDPIPE.
HOT. BUT I'M RIGHT, RIGHT?

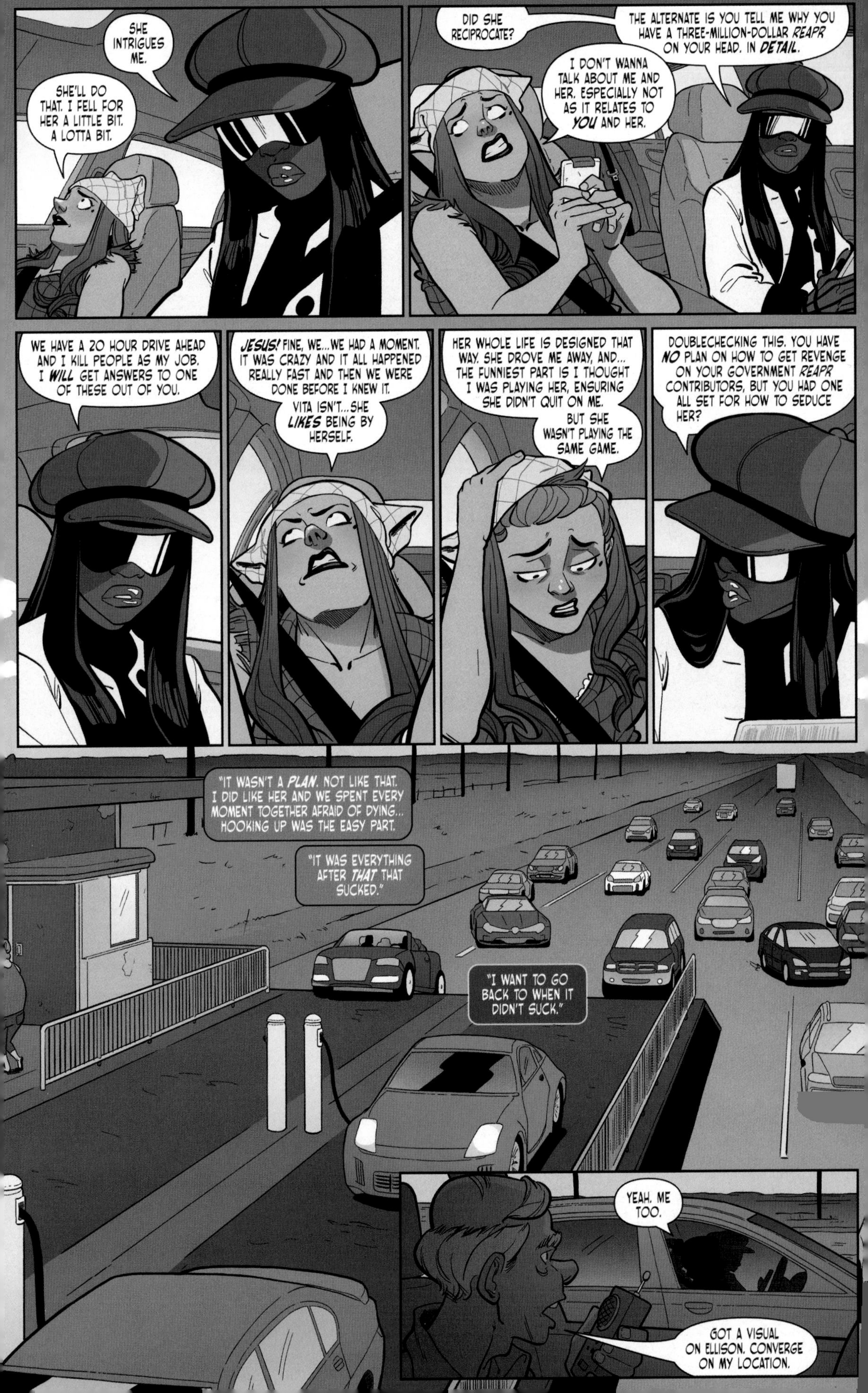

SHE INTRIGUES ME.
SHE'LL DO THAT. I FELL FOR HER A LITTLE BIT. A LOTTA BIT.
DID SHE RECIPROCATE?
I DON'T WANNA TALK ABOUT ME AND HER. ESPECIALLY NOT AS IT RELATES TO YOU AND HER.
THE ALTERNATE IS YOU TELL ME WHY YOU HAVE A THREE-MILLION-DOLLAR REAPR ON YOUR HEAD. IN DETAIL.
WE HAVE A 20 HOUR DRIVE AHEAD AND I KILL PEOPLE AS MY JOB. I WILL GET ANSWERS TO ONE OF THESE OUT OF YOU.
JESUS! FINE, WE...WE HAD A MOMENT. IT WAS CRAZY AND IT ALL HAPPENED REALLY FAST AND THEN WE WERE DONE BEFORE I KNEW IT.
VITA ISN'T...SHE LIKES BEING BY HERSELF.
HER WHOLE LIFE IS DESIGNED THAT WAY. SHE DROVE ME AWAY, AND... THE FUNNIEST PART IS I THOUGHT I WAS PLAYING HER, ENSURING SHE DIDN'T QUIT ON ME.
BUT SHE WASN'T PLAYING THE SAME GAME.
DOUBLECHECKING THIS. YOU HAVE NO PLAN ON HOW TO GET REVENGE ON YOUR GOVERNMENT REAPR CONTRIBUTORS, BUT YOU HAD ONE ALL SET FOR HOW TO SEDUCE HER?
"IT WASN'T A PLAN. NOT LIKE THAT. I DID LIKE HER AND WE SPENT EVERY MOMENT TOGETHER AFRAID OF DYING... HOOKING UP WAS THE EASY PART.
"IT WAS EVERYTHING AFTER THAT THAT SUCKED."
"I WANT TO GO BACK TO WHEN IT DIDN'T SUCK."
YEAH. ME TOO.
GOT A VISUAL ON ELLISON. CONVERGE ON MY LOCATION.

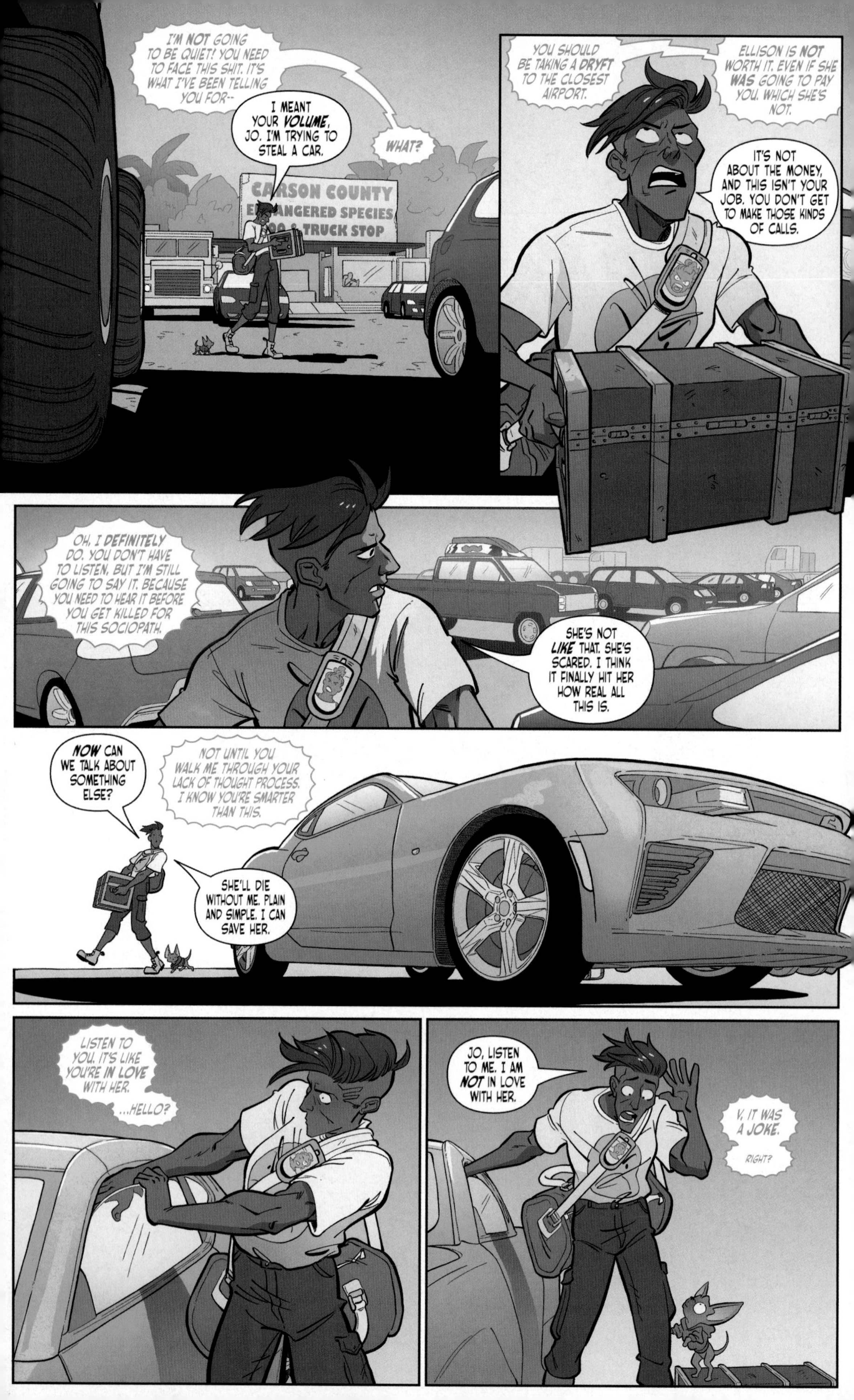
I'M NOT GOING TO BE QUIET! YOU NEED TO FACE THIS SHIT. IT'S WHAT I'VE BEEN TELLING YOU FOR--
I MEANT YOUR VOLUME, JO. I'M TRYING TO STEAL A CAR.
WHAT?
CARSON COUNTY
ENDANGERED SPECIES
ZOO & TRUCK STOP
YOU SHOULD BE TAKING A DRYFT TO THE CLOSEST AIRPORT.
ELLISON IS NOT WORTH IT. EVEN IF SHE WAS GOING TO PAY YOU. WHICH SHE'S NOT.
IT'S NOT ABOUT THE MONEY, AND THIS ISN'T YOUR JOB. YOU DON'T GET TO MAKE THOSE KINDS OF CALLS.
OH, I DEFINITELY DO. YOU DON'T HAVE TO LISTEN, BUT I'M STILL GOING TO SAY IT. BECAUSE YOU NEED TO HEAR IT BEFORE YOU GET KILLED FOR THIS SOCIOPATH.
SHE'S NOT LIKE THAT. SHE'S SCARED. I THINK IT FINALLY HIT HER HOW REAL ALL THIS IS.
NOW CAN WE TALK ABOUT SOMETHING ELSE?
NOT UNTIL YOU WALK ME THROUGH YOUR LACK OF THOUGHT PROCESS. I KNOW YOU'RE SMARTER THAN THIS.
SHE'LL DIE WITHOUT ME. PLAIN AND SIMPLE. I CAN SAVE HER.
LISTEN TO YOU. IT'S LIKE YOU'RE IN LOVE WITH HER.
...HELLO?
JO, LISTEN TO ME. I AM NOT IN LOVE WITH HER.
V, IT WAS A JOKE.
RIGHT?

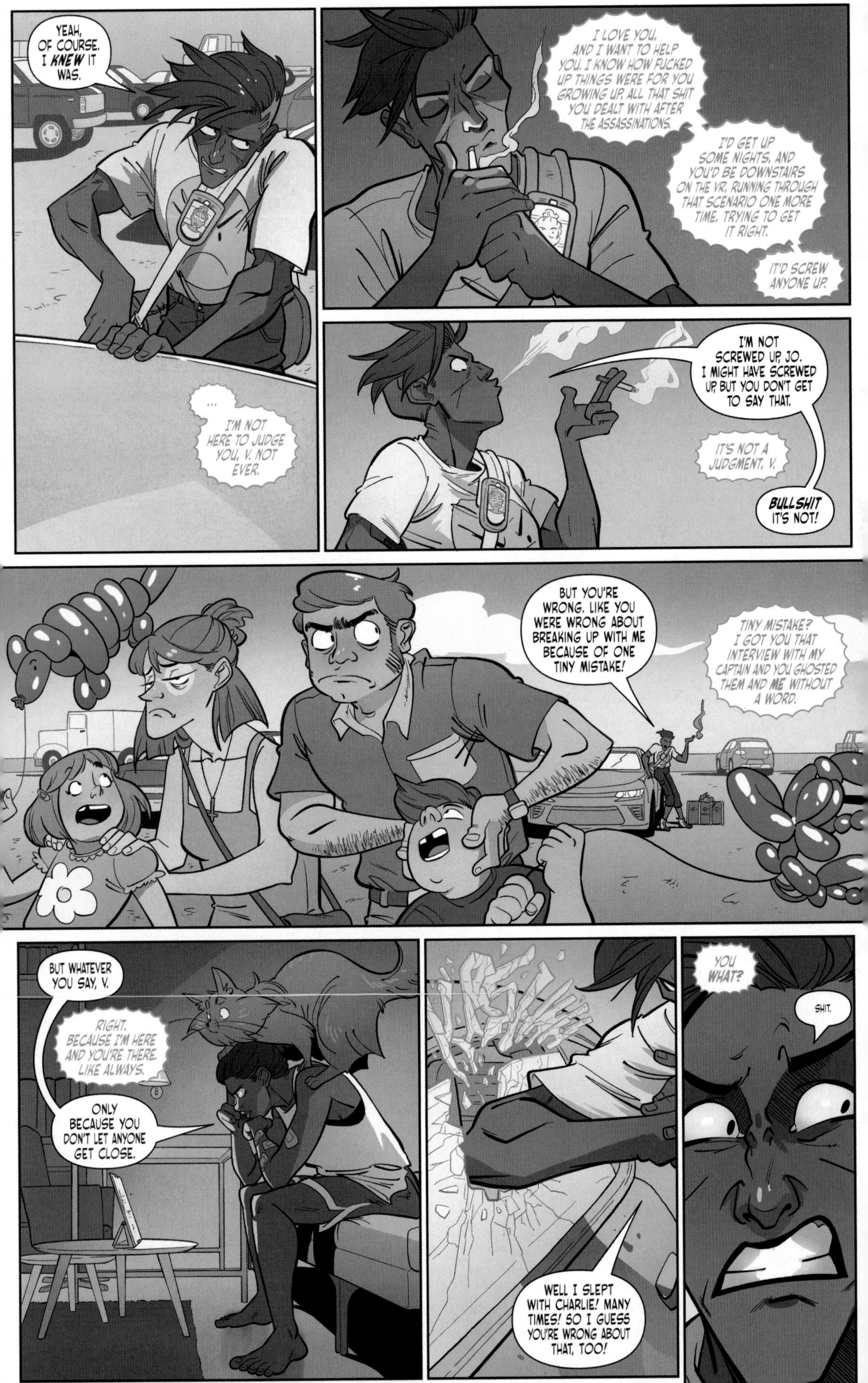
YEAH, OF COURSE. I KNEW IT WAS.
I LOVE YOU, AND I WANT TO HELP YOU. I KNOW HOW FUCKED UP THINGS WERE FOR YOU GROWING UP, ALL THAT SHIT YOU DEALT WITH AFTER THE ASSASSINATIONS.
I'D GET UP SOME NIGHTS, AND YOU'D BE DOWNSTAIRS ON THE VR, RUNNING THROUGH THAT SCENARIO ONE MORE TIME, TRYING TO GET IT RIGHT.
IT'D SCREW ANYONE UP.
... I'M NOT HERE TO JUDGE YOU, V. NOT EVER.
I'M NOT SCREWED UP, JO. I MIGHT HAVE SCREWED UP, BUT YOU DON'T GET TO SAY THAT.
IT'S NOT A JUDGMENT, V.
BULLSHIT IT'S NOT!
BUT YOU'RE WRONG. LIKE YOU WERE WRONG ABOUT BREAKING UP WITH ME BECAUSE OF ONE TINY MISTAKE!
TINY MISTAKE? I GOT YOU THAT INTERVIEW WITH MY CAPTAIN AND YOU GHOSTED THEM AND ME WITHOUT A WORD.
BUT WHATEVER YOU SAY, V.
RIGHT. BECAUSE I'M HERE AND YOU'RE THERE. LIKE ALWAYS.
ONLY BECAUSE YOU DON'T LET ANYONE GET CLOSE.
WELL I SLEPT WITH CHARLIE! MANY TIMES! SO I GUESS YOU'RE WRONG ABOUT THAT, TOO!
YOU WHAT?
SHIT.

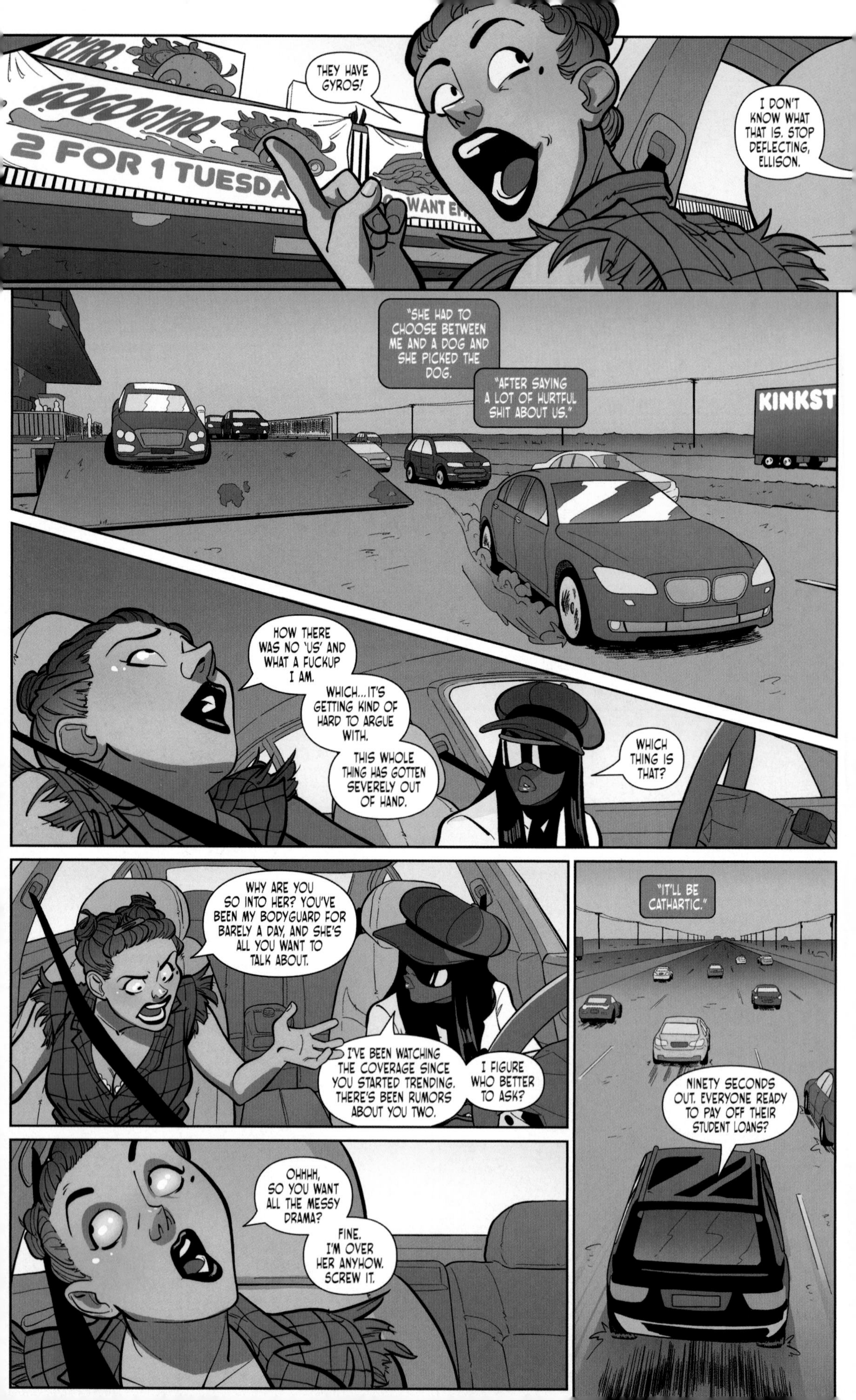
GYRO
GOGOGYRO
2 FOR 1 TUESDA
WANT EM
THEY HAVE GYROS!
I DON'T KNOW WHAT THAT IS. STOP DEFLECTING, ELLISON.
"SHE HAD TO CHOOSE BETWEEN ME AND A DOG AND SHE PICKED THE DOG.
"AFTER SAYING A LOT OF HURTFUL SHIT ABOUT US."
KINKST
HOW THERE WAS NO 'US' AND WHAT A FUCKUP I AM.
WHICH...IT'S GETTING KIND OF HARD TO ARGUE WITH.
THIS WHOLE THING HAS GOTTEN SEVERELY OUT OF HAND.
WHICH THING IS THAT?
WHY ARE YOU SO INTO HER? YOU'VE BEEN MY BODYGUARD FOR BARELY A DAY, AND SHE'S ALL YOU WANT TO TALK ABOUT.
I'VE BEEN WATCHING THE COVERAGE SINCE YOU STARTED TRENDING. THERE'S BEEN RUMORS ABOUT YOU TWO.
I FIGURE WHO BETTER TO ASK?
OHHHH, SO YOU WANT ALL THE MESSY DRAMA?
FINE. I'M OVER HER ANYHOW. SCREW IT.
"IT'LL BE CATHARTIC."
NINETY SECONDS OUT. EVERYONE READY TO PAY OFF THEIR STUDENT LOANS?

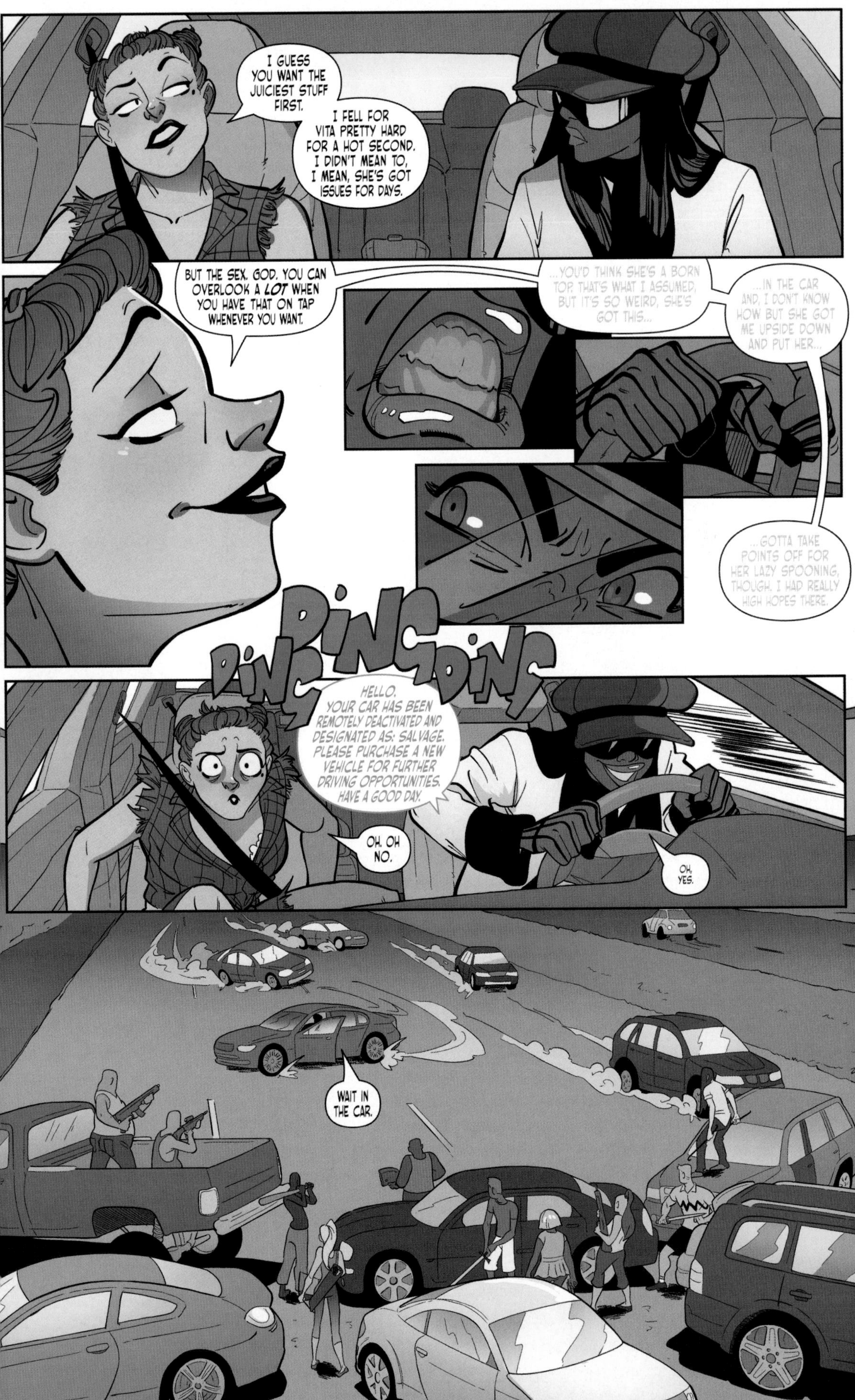
I GUESS YOU WANT THE JUICIEST STUFF FIRST.
I FELL FOR VITA PRETTY HARD FOR A HOT SECOND. I DIDN'T MEAN TO, I MEAN, SHE'S GOT ISSUES FOR DAYS.
BUT THE SEX. GOD. YOU CAN OVERLOOK A *LOT* WHEN YOU HAVE THAT ON TAP WHENEVER YOU WANT.
...YOU'D THINK SHE'S A BORN TOP. THAT'S WHAT I ASSUMED, BUT IT'S SO WEIRD, SHE'S GOT THIS...
...IN THE CAR AND, I DON'T KNOW HOW BUT SHE GOT ME UPSIDE DOWN AND PUT HER...
...GOTTA TAKE POINTS OFF FOR HER LAZY SPOONING, THOUGH. I HAD REALLY HIGH HOPES THERE.
DING DING DING DING
HELLO. YOUR CAR HAS BEEN REMOTELY DEACTIVATED AND DESIGNATED AS: SALVAGE. PLEASE PURCHASE A NEW VEHICLE FOR FURTHER DRIVING OPPORTUNITIES. HAVE A GOOD DAY.
OH. OH NO.
OH, YES.
WAIT IN THE CAR.

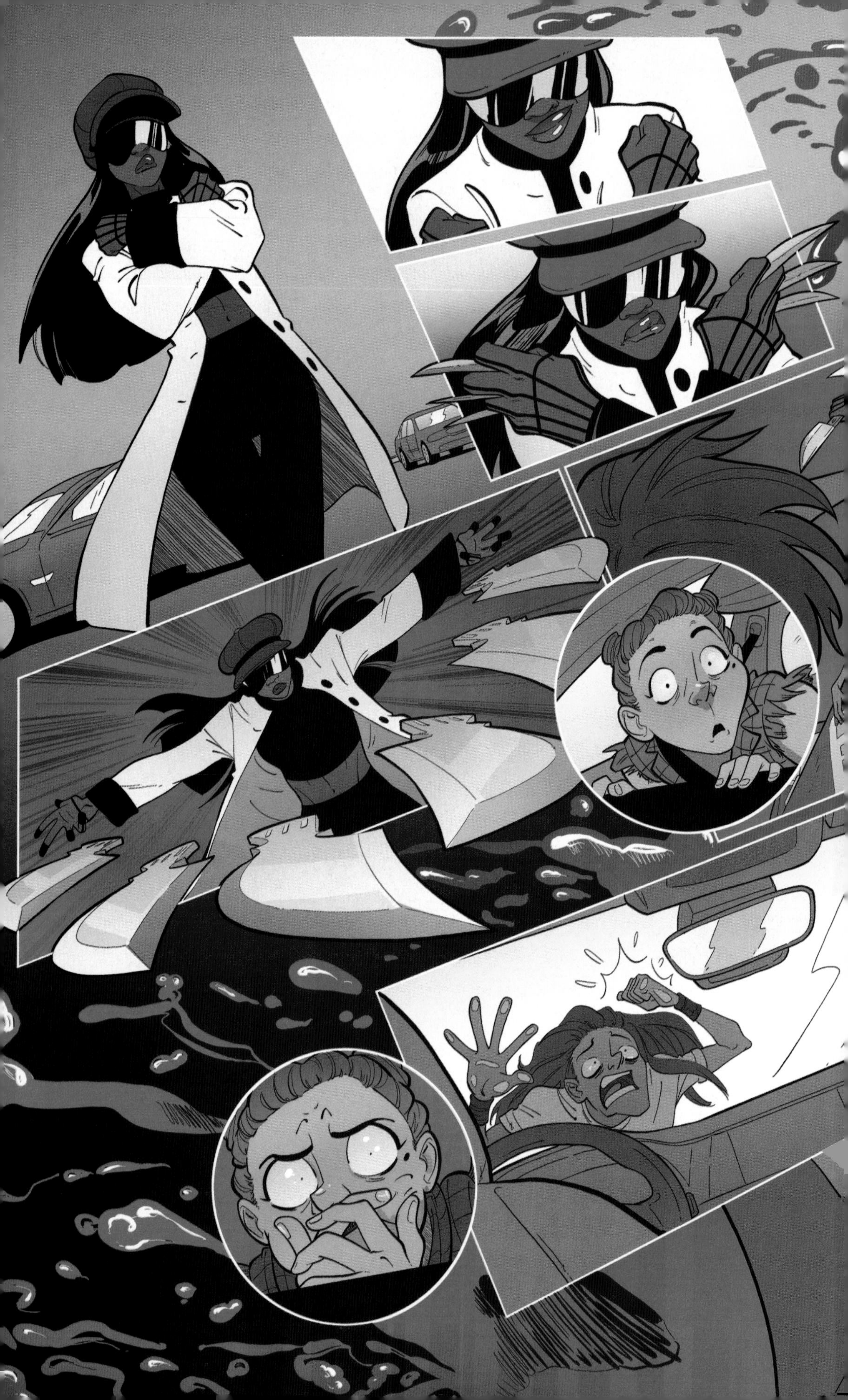

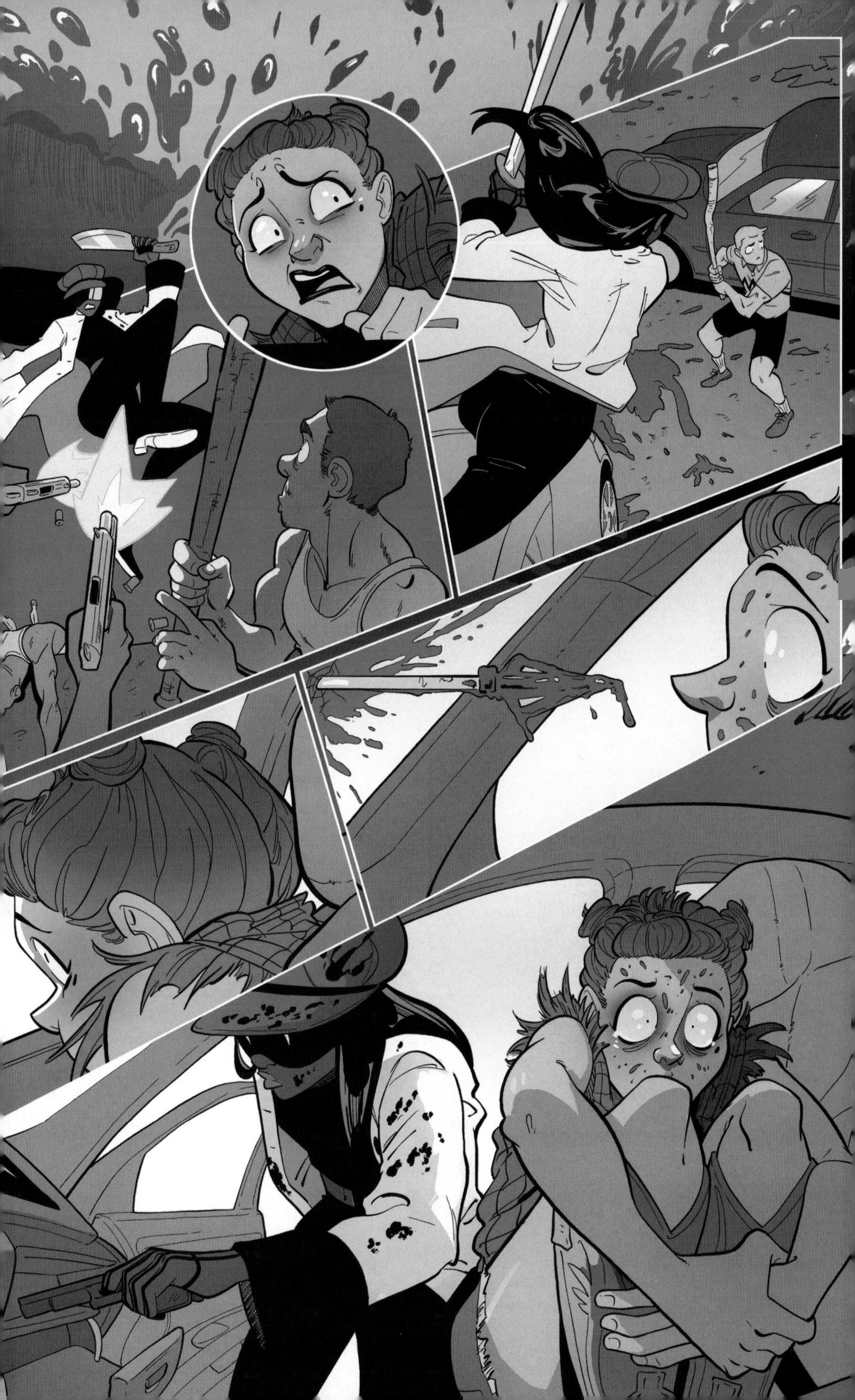

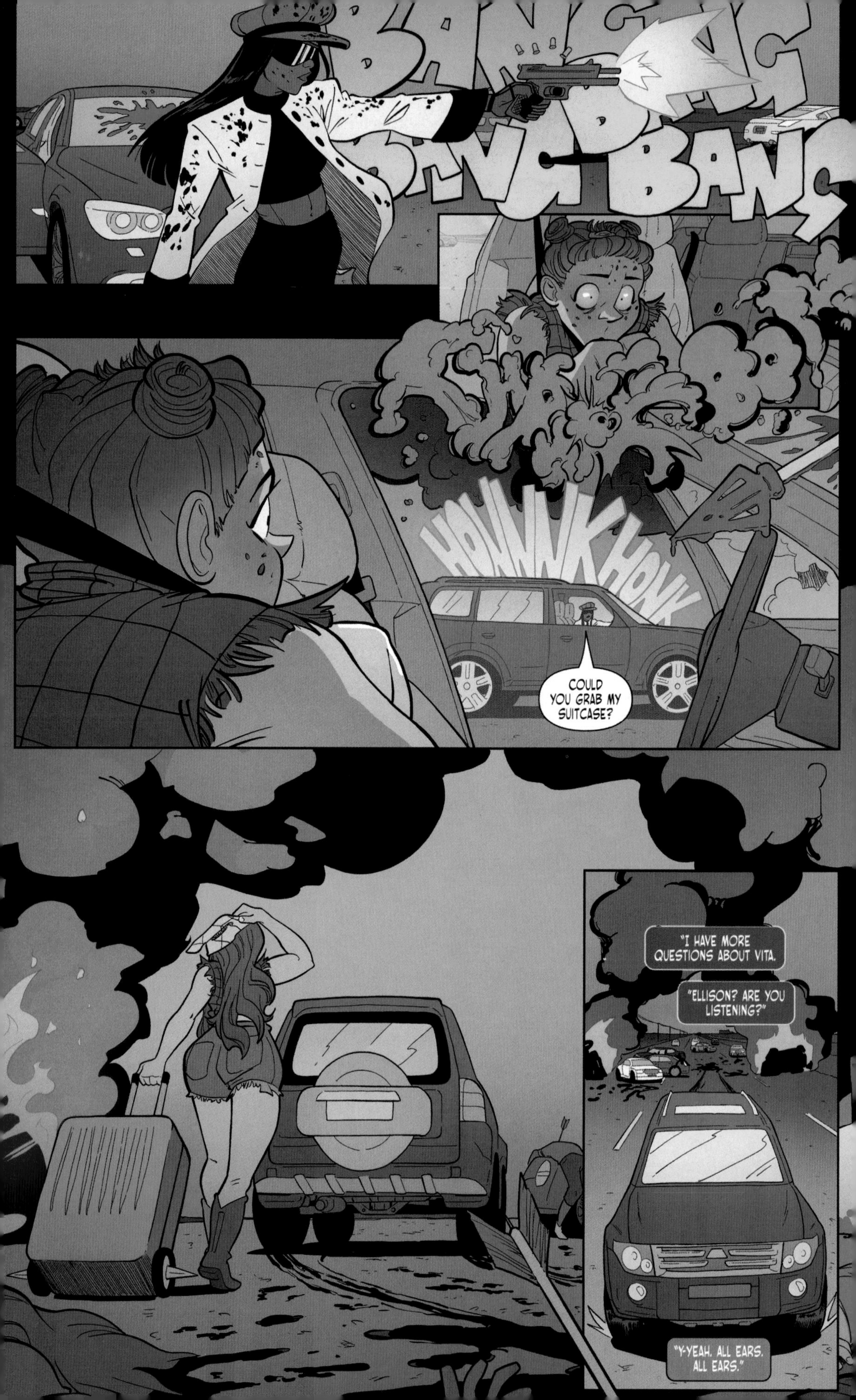
COULD YOU GRAB MY SUITCASE?
"I HAVE MORE QUESTIONS ABOUT VITA.
"ELLISON? ARE YOU LISTENING?"
"Y-YEAH. ALL EARS. ALL EARS."

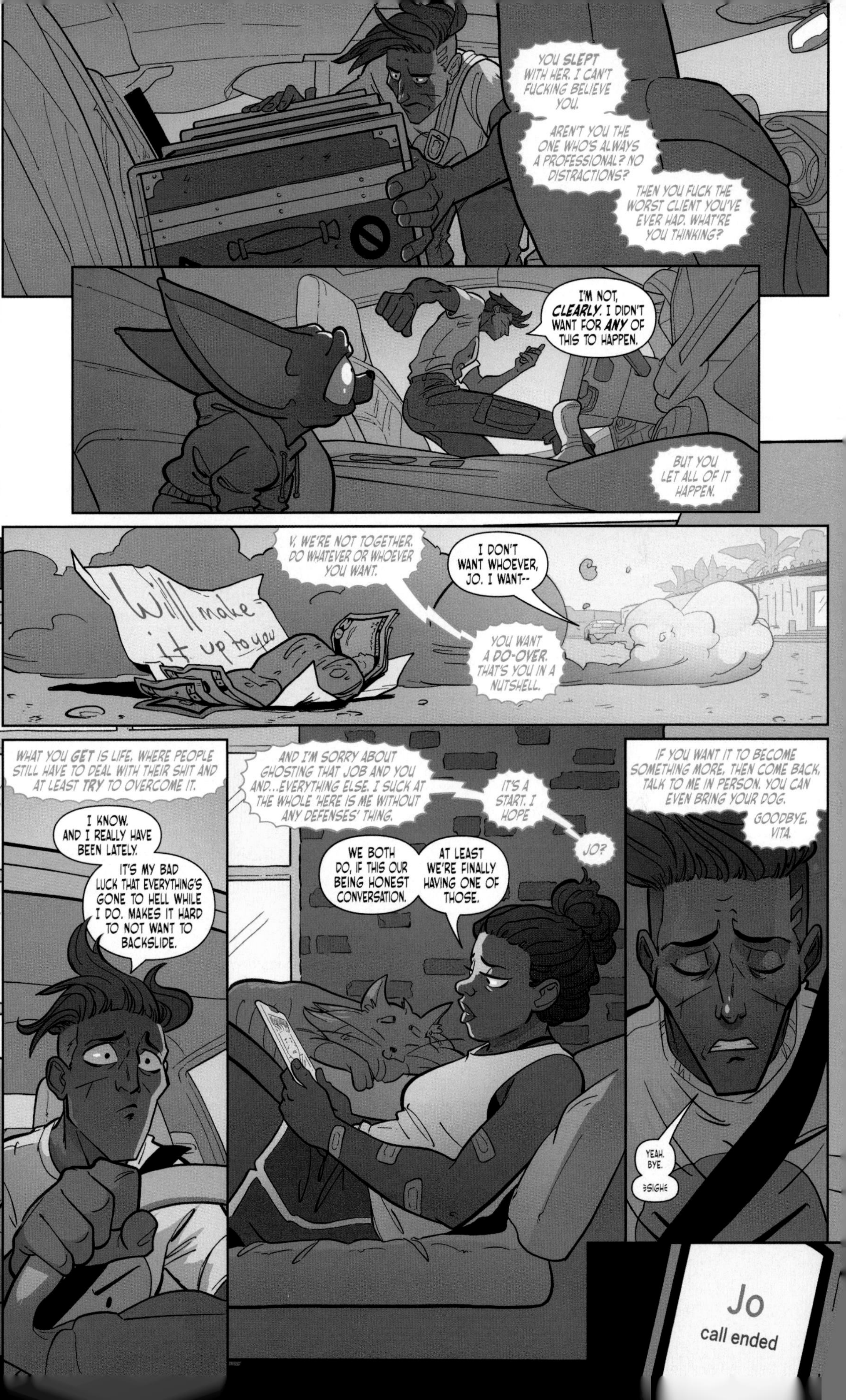

YOU SLEPT WITH HER. I CAN'T FUCKING BELIEVE YOU.
AREN'T YOU THE ONE WHO'S ALWAYS A PROFESSIONAL? NO DISTRACTIONS?
THEN YOU FUCK THE WORST CLIENT YOU'VE EVER HAD. WHAT'RE YOU THINKING?
I'M NOT, CLEARLY. I DIDN'T WANT FOR ANY OF THIS TO HAPPEN.
BUT YOU LET ALL OF IT HAPPEN.
Will make it up to you
V, WE'RE NOT TOGETHER. DO WHATEVER OR WHOEVER YOU WANT.
I DON'T WANT WHOEVER, JO. I WANT--
YOU WANT A DO-OVER. THAT'S YOU IN A NUTSHELL.
WHAT YOU GET IS LIFE, WHERE PEOPLE STILL HAVE TO DEAL WITH THEIR SHIT AND AT LEAST TRY TO OVERCOME IT.
I KNOW. AND I REALLY HAVE BEEN LATELY.
IT'S MY BAD LUCK THAT EVERYTHING'S GONE TO HELL WHILE I DO. MAKES IT HARD TO NOT WANT TO BACKSLIDE.
AND I'M SORRY ABOUT GHOSTING THAT JOB AND YOU AND...EVERYTHING ELSE. I SUCK AT THE WHOLE 'HERE IS ME WITHOUT ANY DEFENSES' THING.
WE BOTH DO, IF THIS OUR BEING HONEST CONVERSATION.
AT LEAST WE'RE FINALLY HAVING ONE OF THOSE.
IT'S A START. I HOPE
JO?
IF YOU WANT IT TO BECOME SOMETHING MORE, THEN COME BACK. TALK TO ME IN PERSON. YOU CAN EVEN BRING YOUR DOG.
GOODBYE, VITA.
YEAH. BYE.
SIGH
Jo
call ended

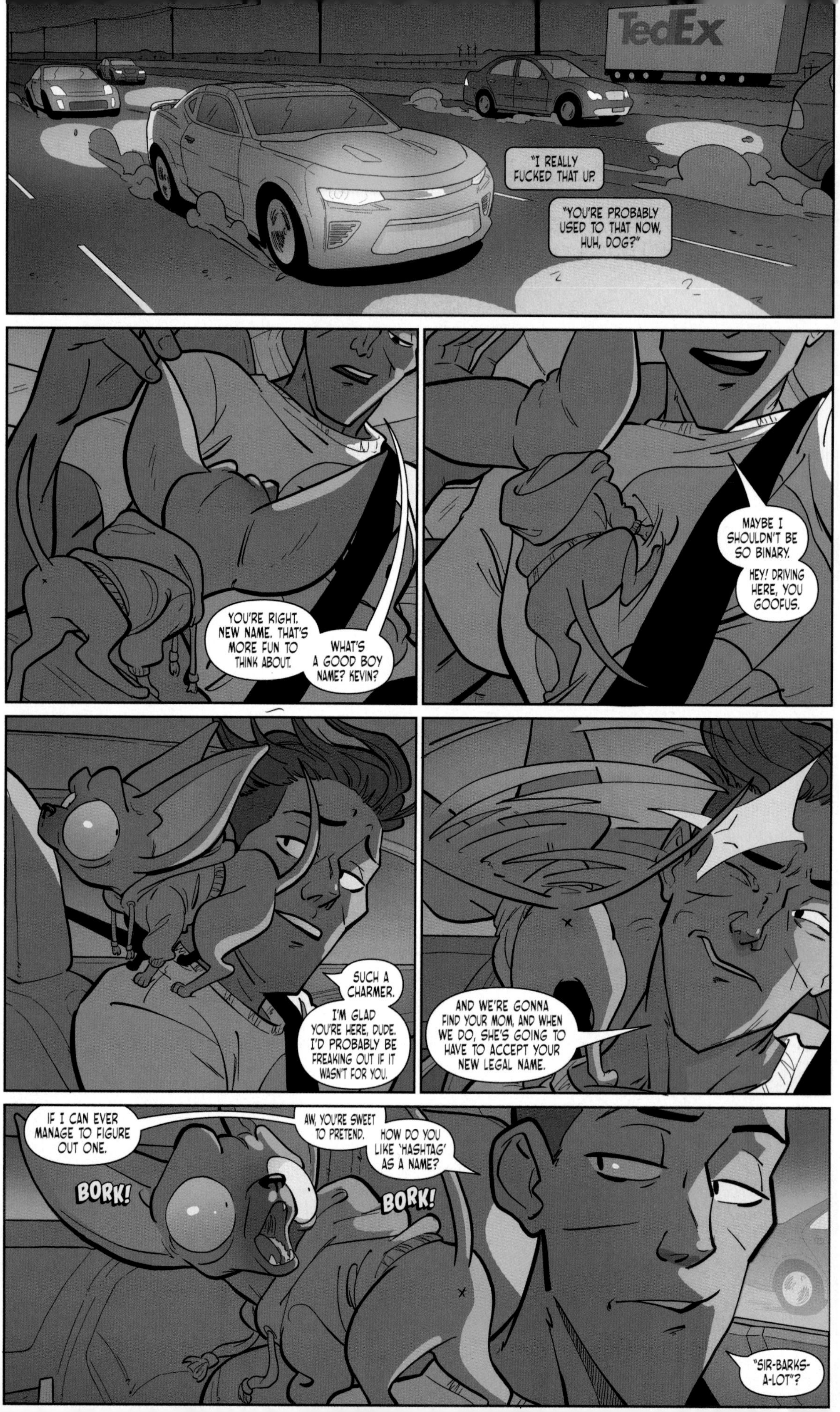

TedEx
"I REALLY FUCKED THAT UP.
"YOU'RE PROBABLY USED TO THAT NOW, HUH, DOG?"
YOU'RE RIGHT. NEW NAME. THAT'S MORE FUN TO THINK ABOUT.
WHAT'S A GOOD BOY NAME? KEVIN?
MAYBE I SHOULDN'T BE SO BINARY.
HEY! DRIVING HERE, YOU GOOFUS.
SUCH A CHARMER.
I'M GLAD YOU'RE HERE, DUDE. I'D PROBABLY BE FREAKING OUT IF IT WASN'T FOR YOU.
AND WE'RE GONNA FIND YOUR MOM, AND WHEN WE DO, SHE'S GOING TO HAVE TO ACCEPT YOUR NEW LEGAL NAME.
IF I CAN EVER MANAGE TO FIGURE OUT ONE.
AW, YOU'RE SWEET TO PRETEND.
HOW DO YOU LIKE 'HASHTAG' AS A NAME?
BORK!
BORK!
"SIR-BARKS-A-LOT"?

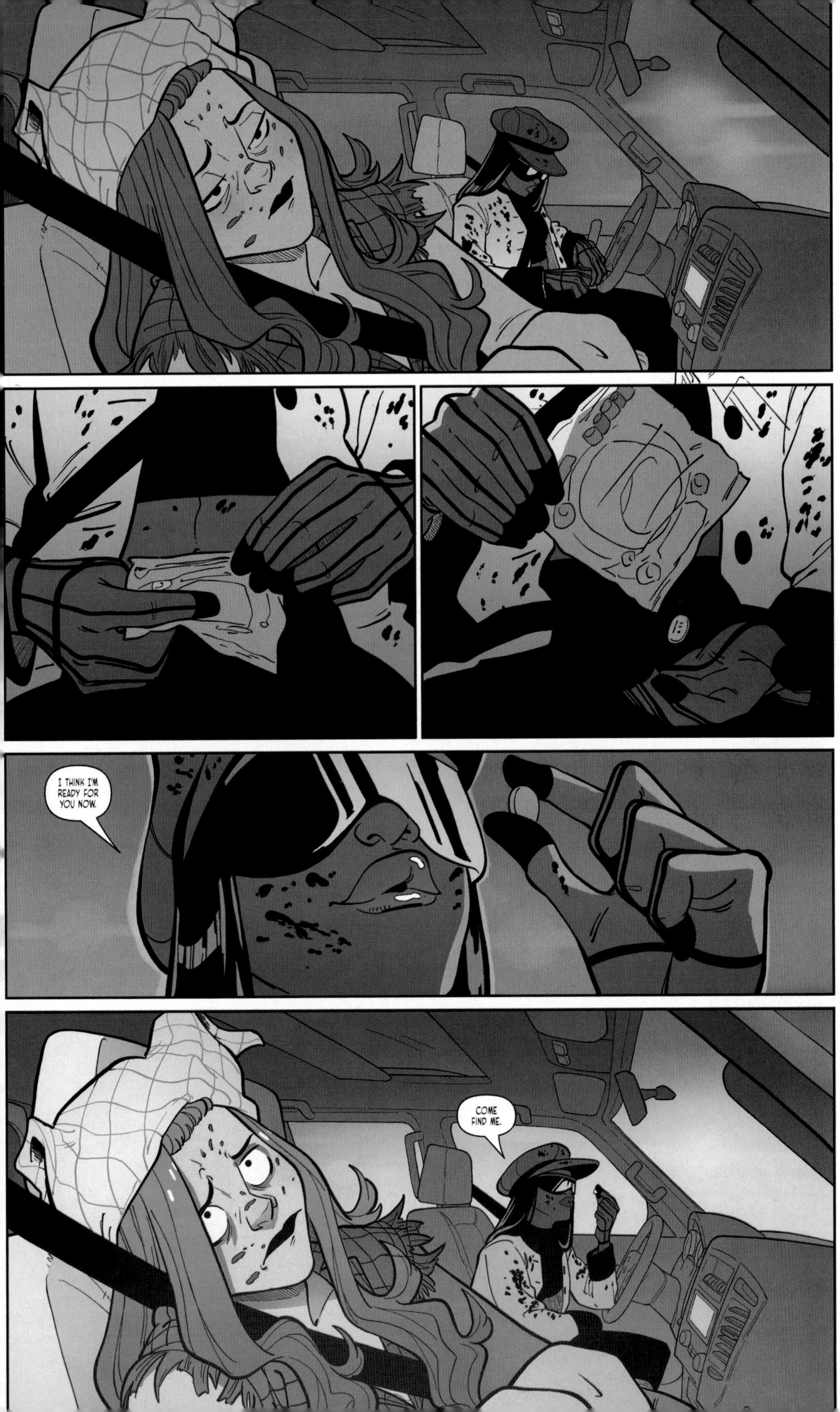
I THINK I'M READY FOR YOU NOW.
COME FIND ME.

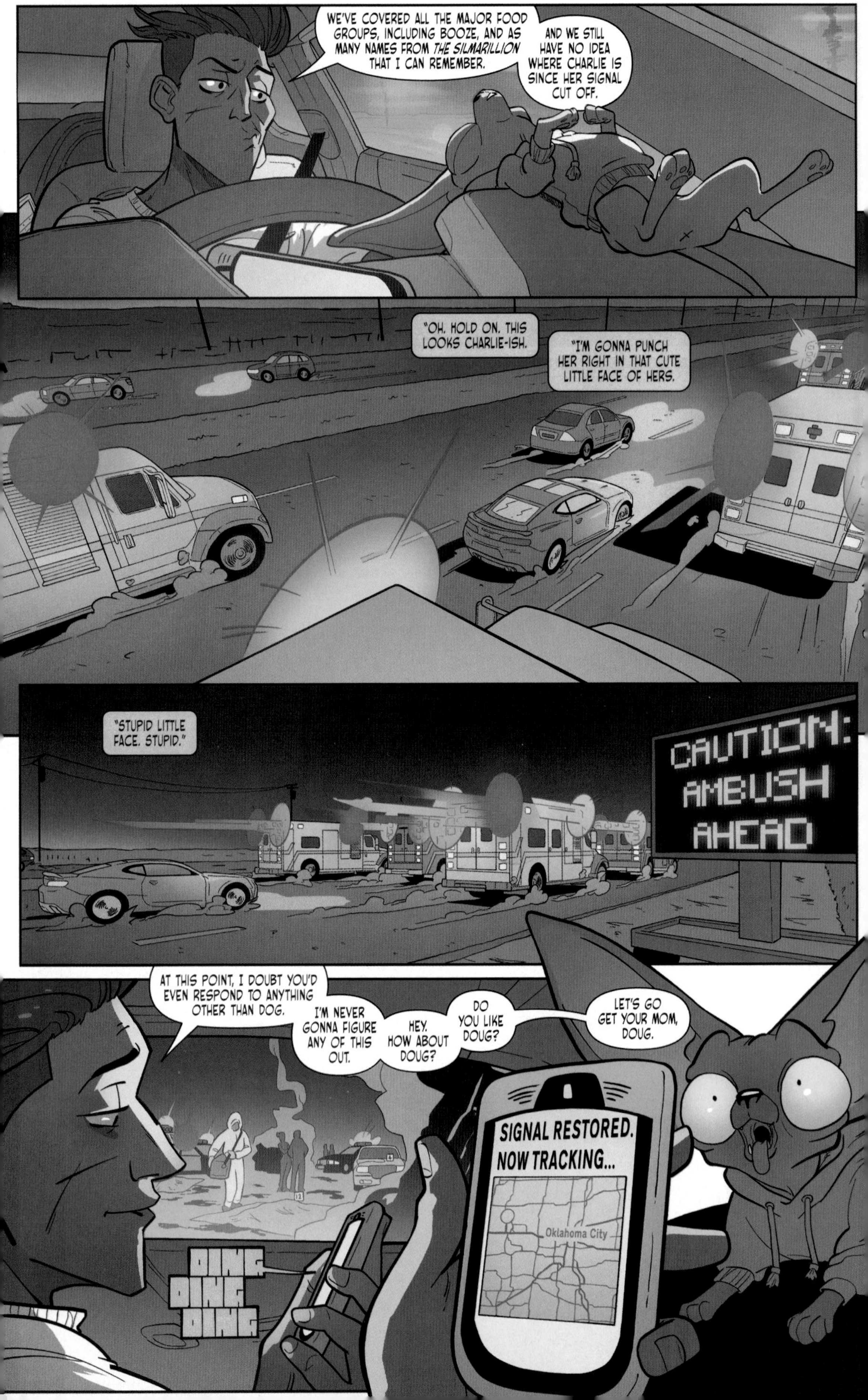
WE'VE COVERED ALL THE MAJOR FOOD GROUPS, INCLUDING BOOZE, AND AS MANY NAMES FROM *THE SILMARILLION* THAT I CAN REMEMBER.
AND WE STILL HAVE NO IDEA WHERE CHARLIE IS SINCE HER SIGNAL CUT OFF.
"OH. HOLD ON. THIS LOOKS CHARLIE-ISH.
"I'M GONNA PUNCH HER RIGHT IN THAT CUTE LITTLE FACE OF HERS.
"STUPID LITTLE FACE. STUPID."
CAUTION: AMBUSH AHEAD
AT THIS POINT, I DOUBT YOU'D EVEN RESPOND TO ANYTHING OTHER THAN DOG.
I'M NEVER GONNA FIGURE ANY OF THIS OUT.
HEY. HOW ABOUT DOUG?
DO YOU LIKE DOUG?
LET'S GO GET YOUR MOM, DOUG.
DING DING DING
SIGNAL RESTORED. NOW TRACKING...
Oklahoma City

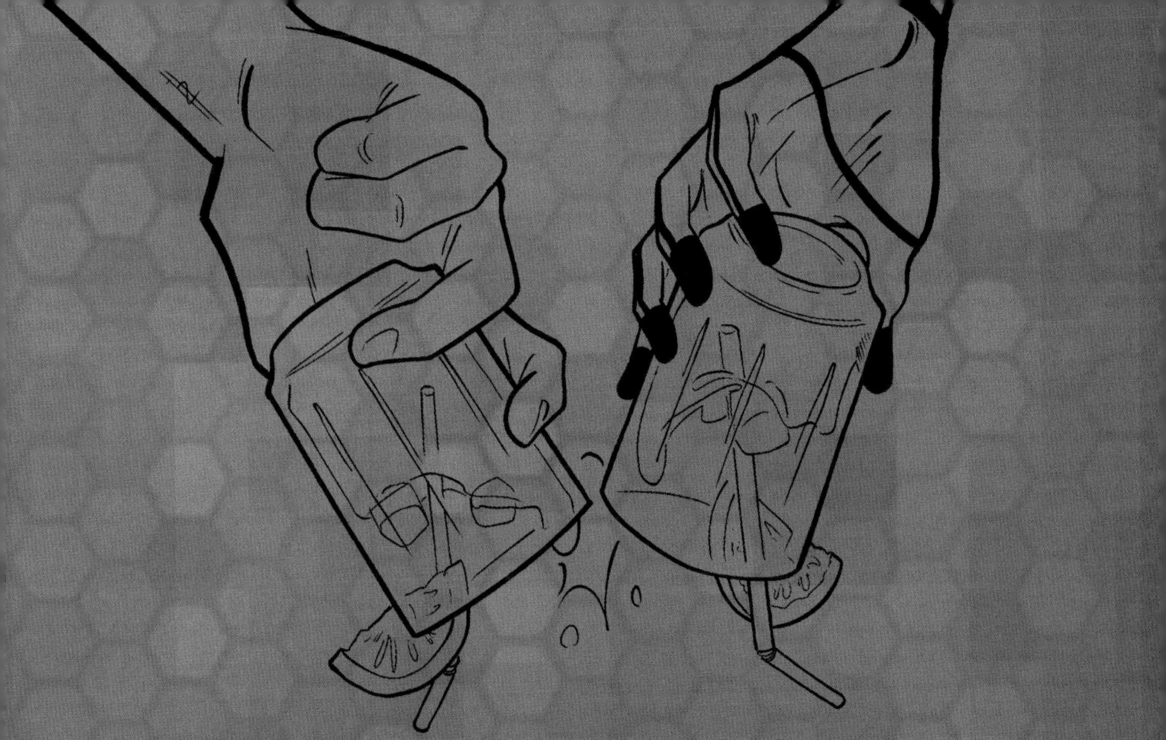

CHAPTER FOURTEEN

DANCING ON MY OWN

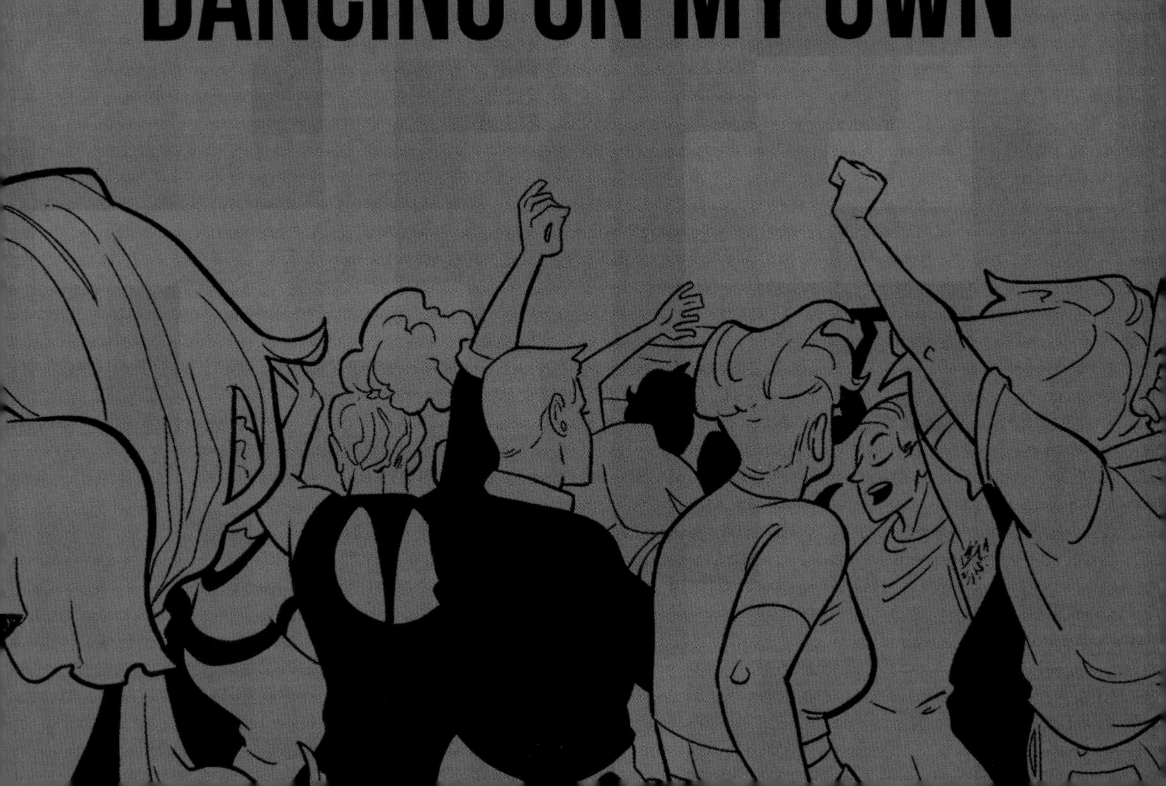

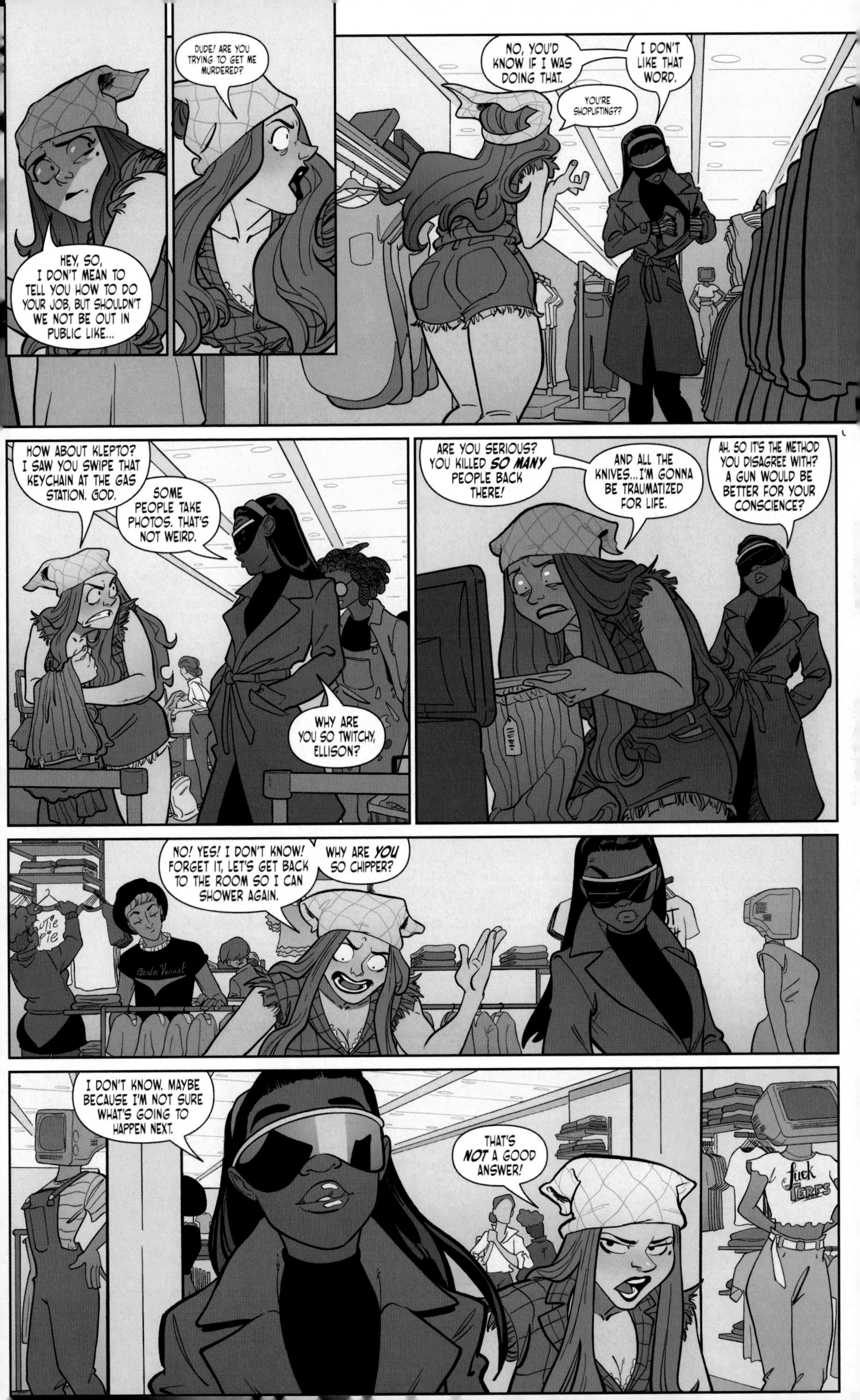
HEY, SO, I DON'T MEAN TO TELL YOU HOW TO DO YOUR JOB, BUT SHOULDN'T WE NOT BE OUT IN PUBLIC LIKE...
DUDE! ARE YOU TRYING TO GET ME MURDERED?
NO, YOU'D KNOW IF I WAS DOING THAT.
YOU'RE SHOPLIFTING??
I DON'T LIKE THAT WORD.
HOW ABOUT KLEPTO? I SAW YOU SWIPE THAT KEYCHAIN AT THE GAS STATION. GOD.
SOME PEOPLE TAKE PHOTOS. THAT'S NOT WEIRD.
WHY ARE YOU SO TWITCHY, ELLISON?
ARE YOU SERIOUS? YOU KILLED SO MANY PEOPLE BACK THERE!
AND ALL THE KNIVES...I'M GONNA BE TRAUMATIZED FOR LIFE.
AH. SO IT'S THE METHOD YOU DISAGREE WITH? A GUN WOULD BE BETTER FOR YOUR CONSCIENCE?
NO! YES! I DON'T KNOW! FORGET IT, LET'S GET BACK TO THE ROOM SO I CAN SHOWER AGAIN.
WHY ARE YOU SO CHIPPER?
Gender Variant
I DON'T KNOW. MAYBE BECAUSE I'M NOT SURE WHAT'S GOING TO HAPPEN NEXT.
THAT'S NOT A GOOD ANSWER!
Fuck TERFS

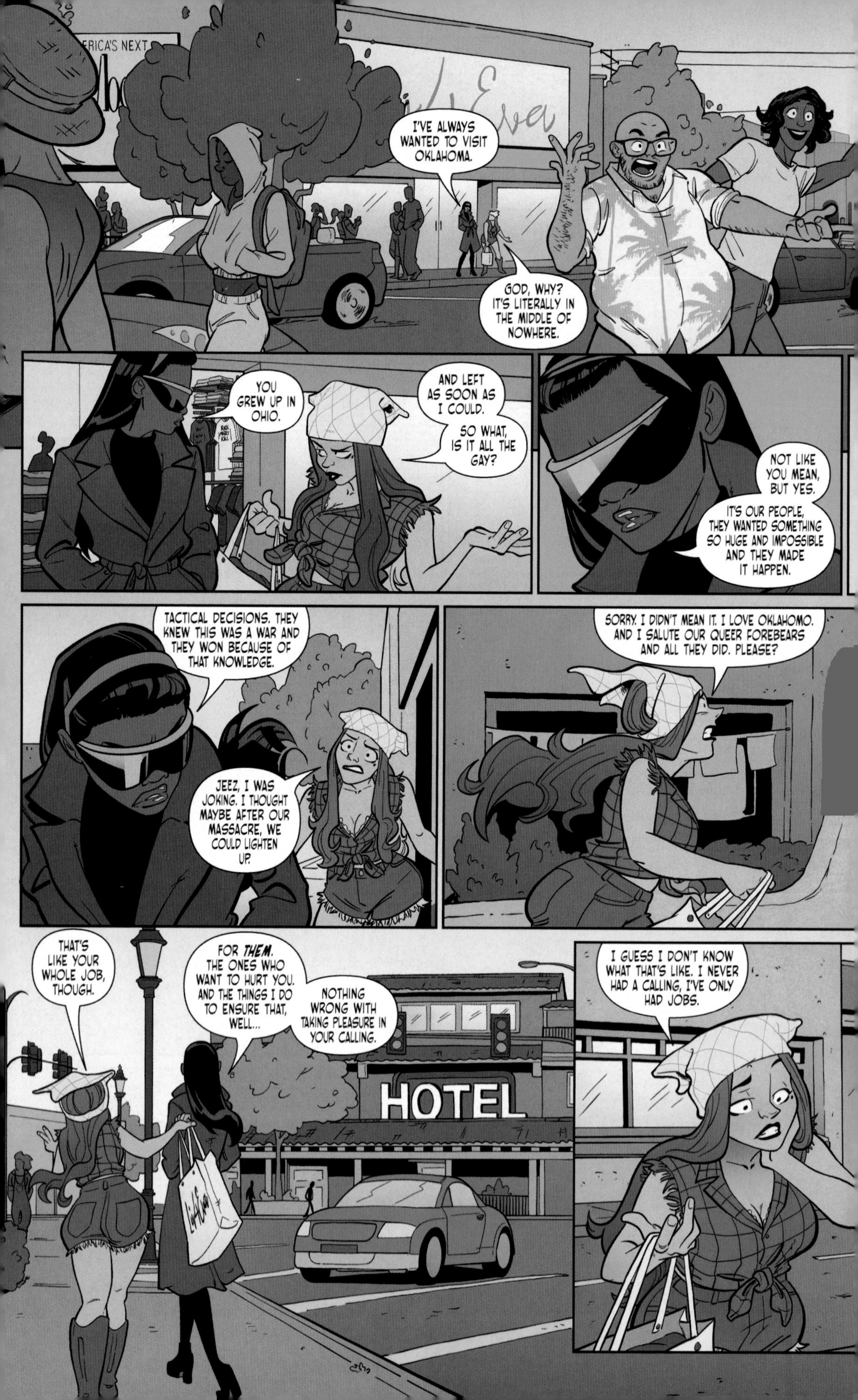
I'VE ALWAYS WANTED TO VISIT OKLAHOMA.
GOD, WHY? IT'S LITERALLY IN THE MIDDLE OF NOWHERE.
YOU GREW UP IN OHIO.
AND LEFT AS SOON AS I COULD.
SO WHAT, IS IT ALL THE GAY?
NOT LIKE YOU MEAN, BUT YES.
IT'S OUR PEOPLE, THEY WANTED SOMETHING SO HUGE AND IMPOSSIBLE AND THEY MADE IT HAPPEN.
TACTICAL DECISIONS. THEY KNEW THIS WAS A WAR AND THEY WON BECAUSE OF THAT KNOWLEDGE.
JEEZ, I WAS JOKING. I THOUGHT MAYBE AFTER OUR MASSACRE, WE COULD LIGHTEN UP.
SORRY. I DIDN'T MEAN IT. I LOVE OKLAHOMO. AND I SALUTE OUR QUEER FOREBEARS AND ALL THEY DID. PLEASE?
THAT'S LIKE YOUR WHOLE JOB, THOUGH.
FOR *THEM*. THE ONES WHO WANT TO HURT YOU. AND THE THINGS I DO TO ENSURE THAT, WELL...
NOTHING WRONG WITH TAKING PLEASURE IN YOUR CALLING.
HOTEL
I GUESS I DON'T KNOW WHAT THAT'S LIKE. I NEVER HAD A CALLING, I'VE ONLY HAD JOBS.

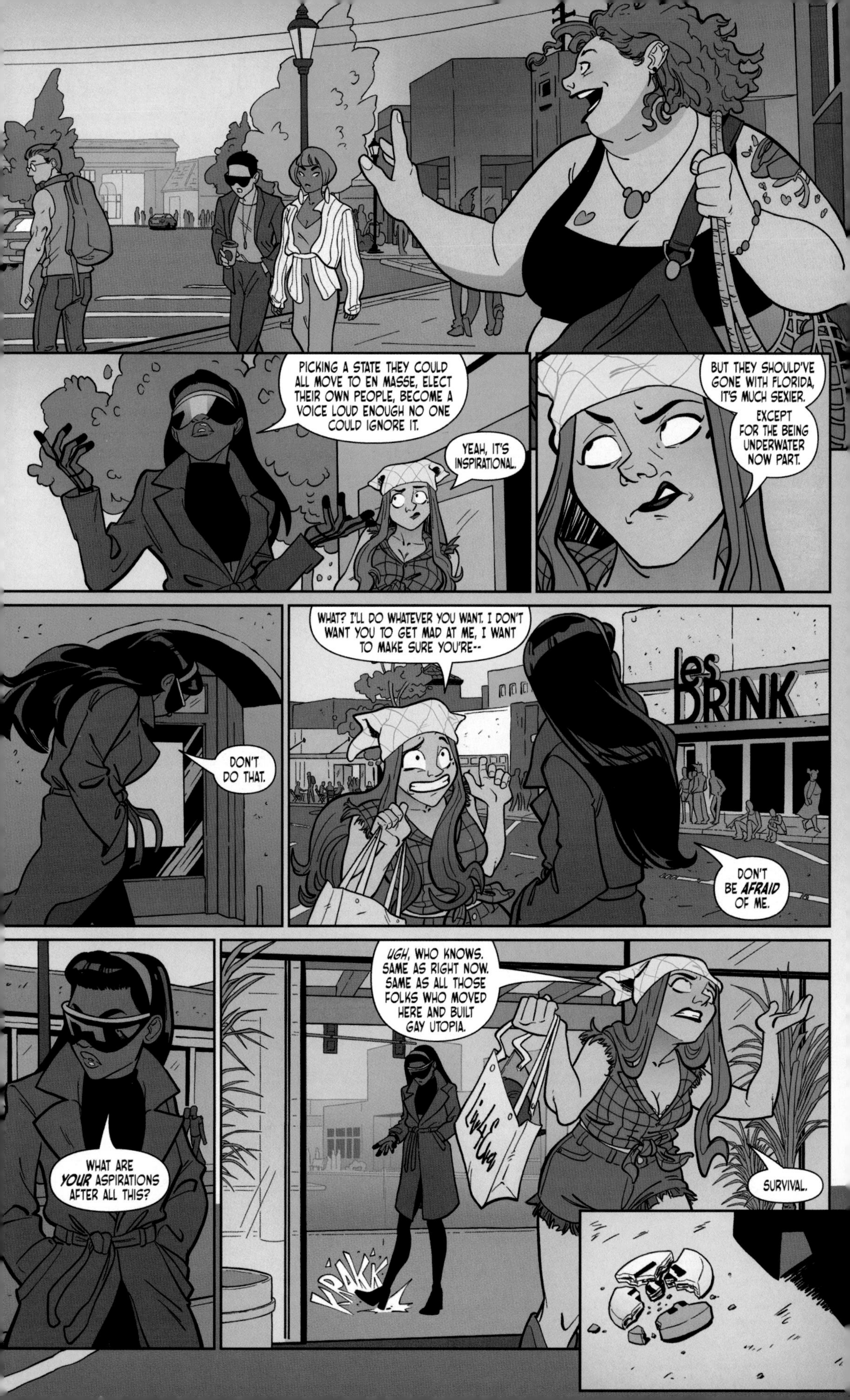
PICKING A STATE THEY COULD ALL MOVE TO EN MASSE, ELECT THEIR OWN PEOPLE, BECOME A VOICE LOUD ENOUGH NO ONE COULD IGNORE IT.
YEAH, IT'S INSPIRATIONAL.
BUT THEY SHOULD'VE GONE WITH FLORIDA, IT'S MUCH SEXIER.
EXCEPT FOR THE BEING UNDERWATER NOW PART.
DON'T DO THAT.
WHAT? I'LL DO WHATEVER YOU WANT. I DON'T WANT YOU TO GET MAD AT ME, I WANT TO MAKE SURE YOU'RE--
les DRINK
DON'T BE *AFRAID* OF ME.
WHAT ARE *YOUR* ASPIRATIONS AFTER ALL THIS?
UGH, WHO KNOWS. SAME AS RIGHT NOW. SAME AS ALL THOSE FOLKS WHO MOVED HERE AND BUILT GAY UTOPIA.
SURVIVAL.
KRAKK

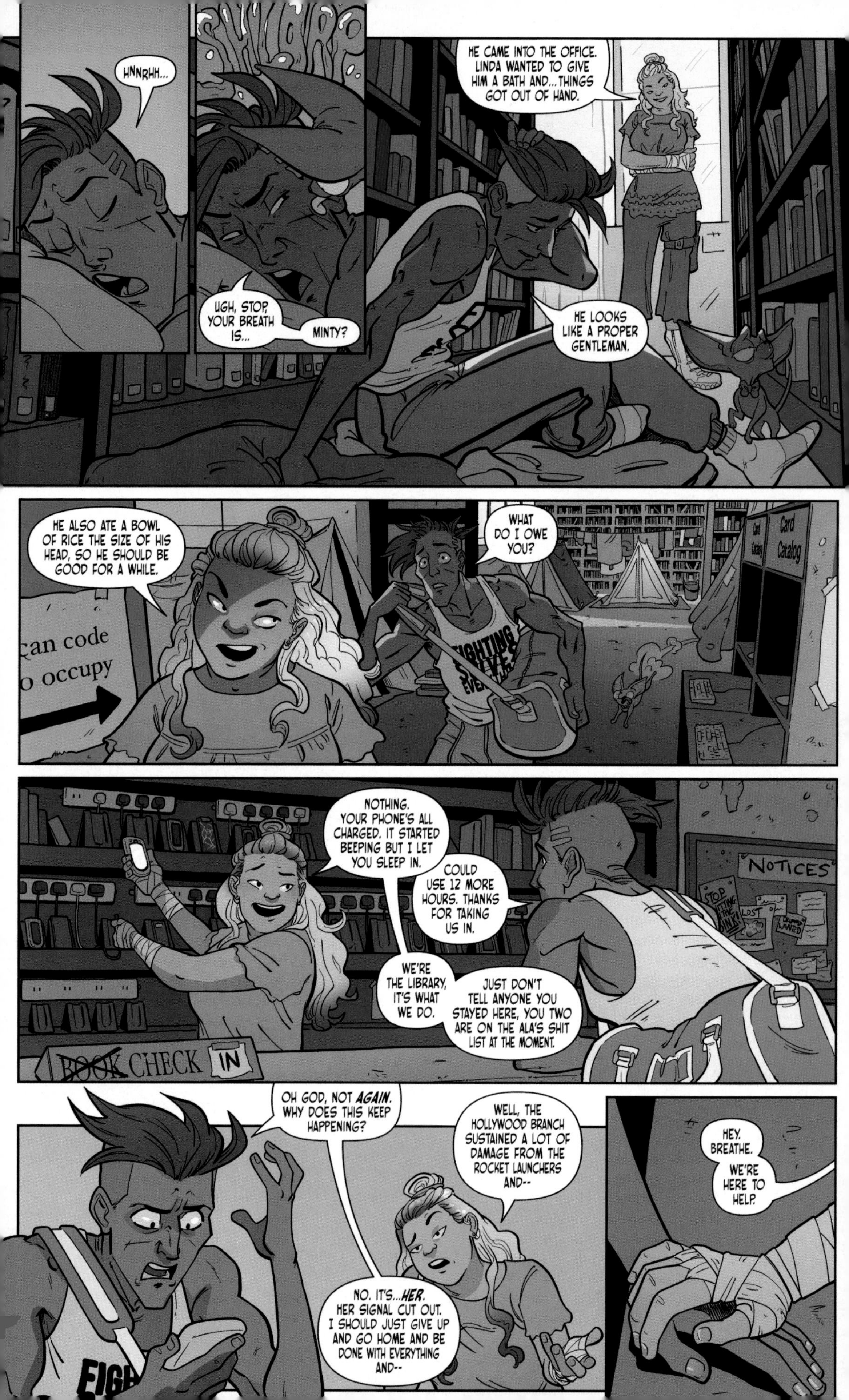
HNNRHH...
SHLURP
UGH, STOP, YOUR BREATH IS...
MINTY?
HE CAME INTO THE OFFICE. LINDA WANTED TO GIVE HIM A BATH AND... THINGS GOT OUT OF HAND.
HE LOOKS LIKE A PROPER GENTLEMAN.
HE ALSO ATE A BOWL OF RICE THE SIZE OF HIS HEAD, SO HE SHOULD BE GOOD FOR A WHILE.
WHAT DO I OWE YOU?
can code
o occupy
Card Catalog
NOTHING. YOUR PHONE'S ALL CHARGED. IT STARTED BEEPING BUT I LET YOU SLEEP IN.
COULD USE 12 MORE HOURS. THANKS FOR TAKING US IN.
WE'RE THE LIBRARY, IT'S WHAT WE DO.
JUST DON'T TELL ANYONE YOU STAYED HERE, YOU TWO ARE ON THE ALA'S SHIT LIST AT THE MOMENT.
NOTICES
BOOK CHECK IN
OH GOD, NOT AGAIN. WHY DOES THIS KEEP HAPPENING?
WELL, THE HOLLYWOOD BRANCH SUSTAINED A LOT OF DAMAGE FROM THE ROCKET LAUNCHERS AND--
NO. IT'S...HER. HER SIGNAL CUT OUT. I SHOULD JUST GIVE UP AND GO HOME AND BE DONE WITH EVERYTHING AND--
HEY. BREATHE.
WE'RE HERE TO HELP.

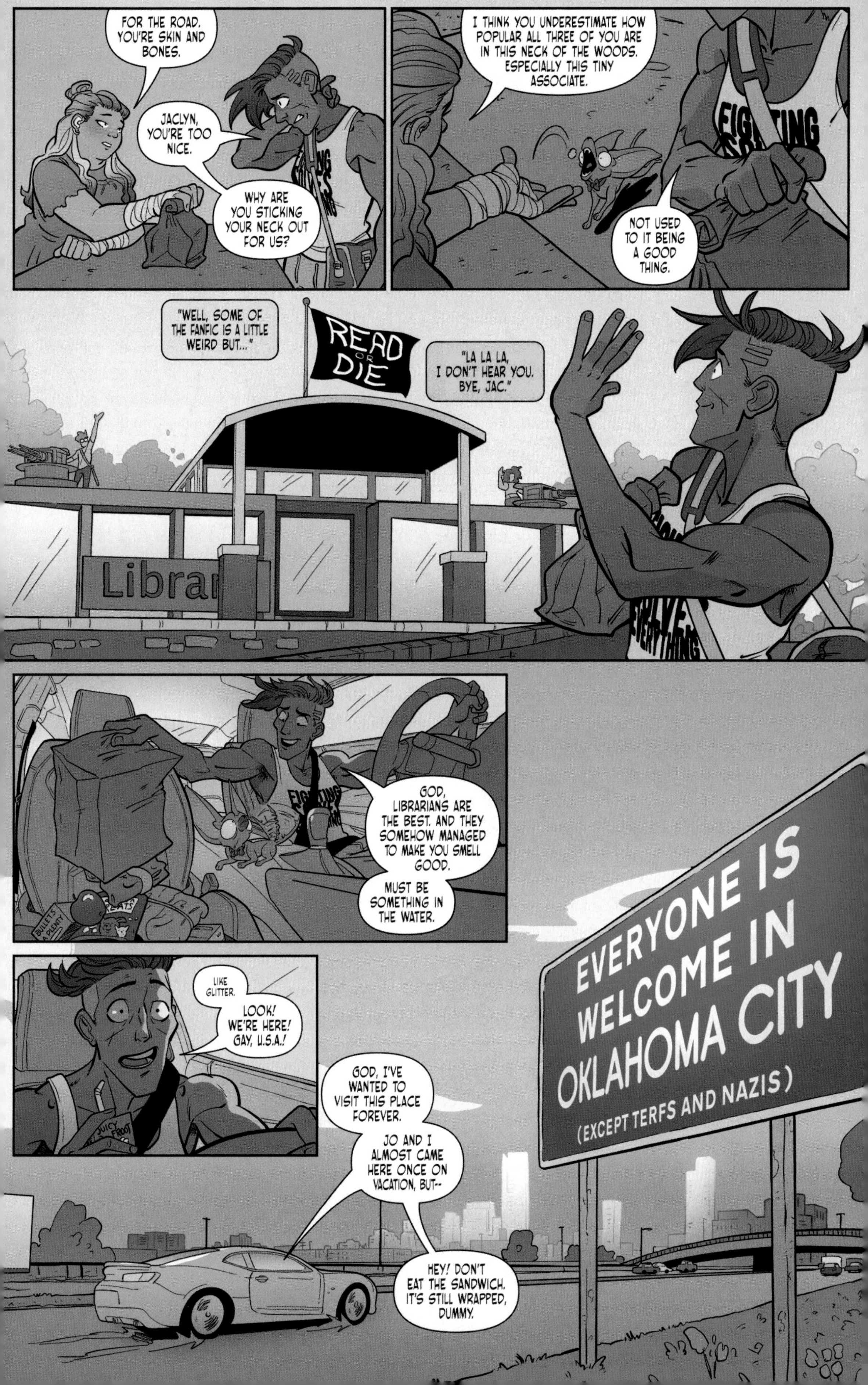
FOR THE ROAD. YOU'RE SKIN AND BONES.
JACLYN, YOU'RE TOO NICE.
WHY ARE YOU STICKING YOUR NECK OUT FOR US?
I THINK YOU UNDERESTIMATE HOW POPULAR ALL THREE OF YOU ARE IN THIS NECK OF THE WOODS. ESPECIALLY THIS TINY ASSOCIATE.
NOT USED TO IT BEING A GOOD THING.
"WELL, SOME OF THE FANFIC IS A LITTLE WEIRD BUT..."
READ OR DIE
"LA LA LA, I DON'T HEAR YOU. BYE, JAC."
Librar
GOD, LIBRARIANS ARE THE BEST. AND THEY SOMEHOW MANAGED TO MAKE YOU SMELL GOOD.
MUST BE SOMETHING IN THE WATER.
BULLETS A PLENTY
LIKE GLITTER.
LOOK! WE'RE HERE! GAY, U.S.A.!
JUICY FROOT
EVERYONE IS WELCOME IN OKLAHOMA CITY (EXCEPT TERFS AND NAZIS)
GOD, I'VE WANTED TO VISIT THIS PLACE FOREVER.
JO AND I ALMOST CAME HERE ONCE ON VACATION, BUT--
HEY! DON'T EAT THE SANDWICH. IT'S STILL WRAPPED, DUMMY.

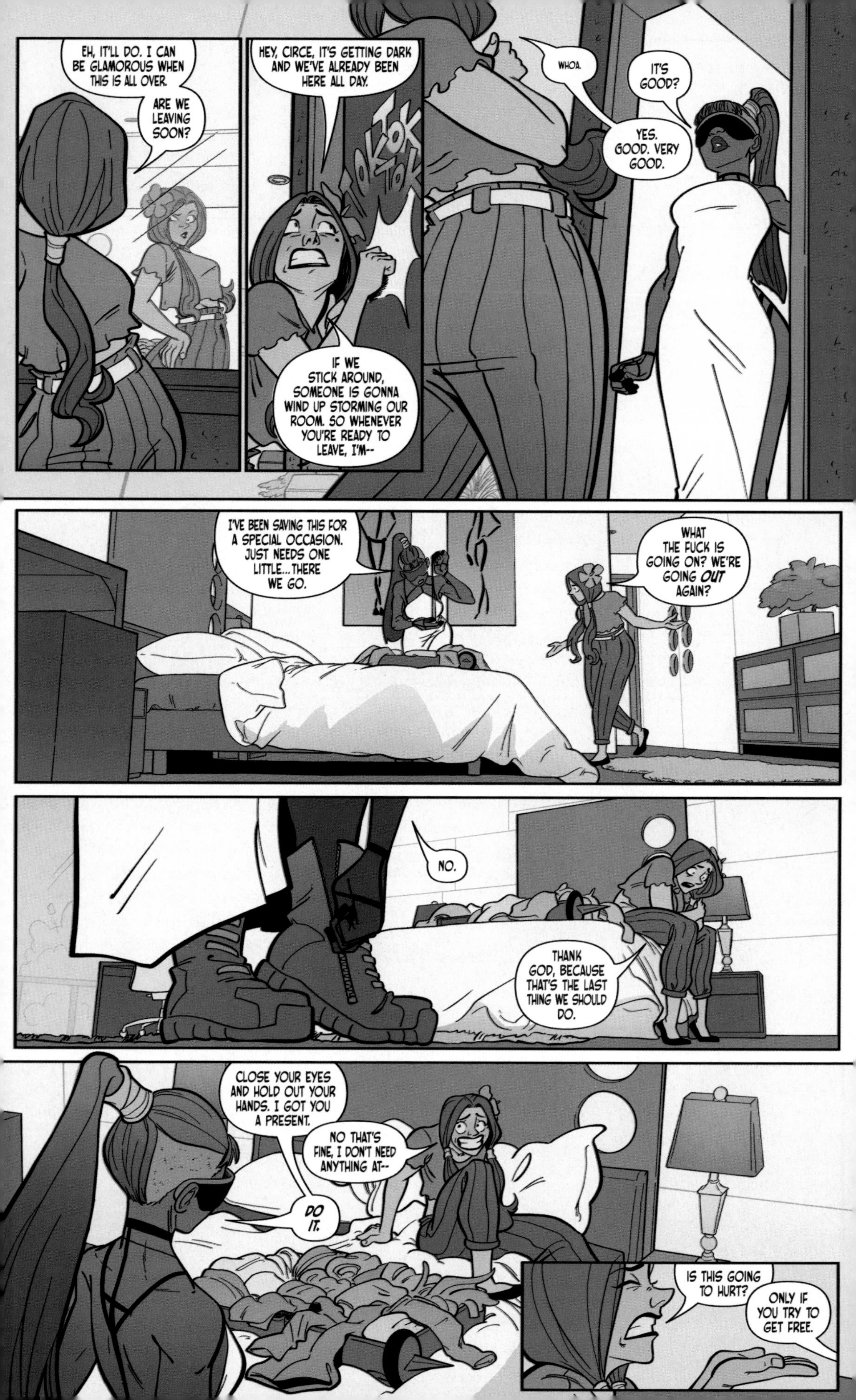

EH, IT'LL DO. I CAN BE GLAMOROUS WHEN THIS IS ALL OVER.
ARE WE LEAVING SOON?
HEY, CIRCE, IT'S GETTING DARK AND WE'VE ALREADY BEEN HERE ALL DAY.
TOK TOK TOK
IF WE STICK AROUND, SOMEONE IS GONNA WIND UP STORMING OUR ROOM. SO WHENEVER YOU'RE READY TO LEAVE, I'M--
WHOA.
IT'S GOOD?
YES. GOOD. VERY GOOD.
I'VE BEEN SAVING THIS FOR A SPECIAL OCCASION. JUST NEEDS ONE LITTLE...THERE WE GO.
WHAT THE FUCK IS GOING ON? WE'RE GOING *OUT* AGAIN?
NO.
THANK GOD, BECAUSE THAT'S THE LAST THING WE SHOULD DO.
CLOSE YOUR EYES AND HOLD OUT YOUR HANDS. I GOT YOU A PRESENT.
NO THAT'S FINE, I DON'T NEED ANYTHING AT--
DO IT.
IS THIS GOING TO HURT?
ONLY IF YOU TRY TO GET FREE.

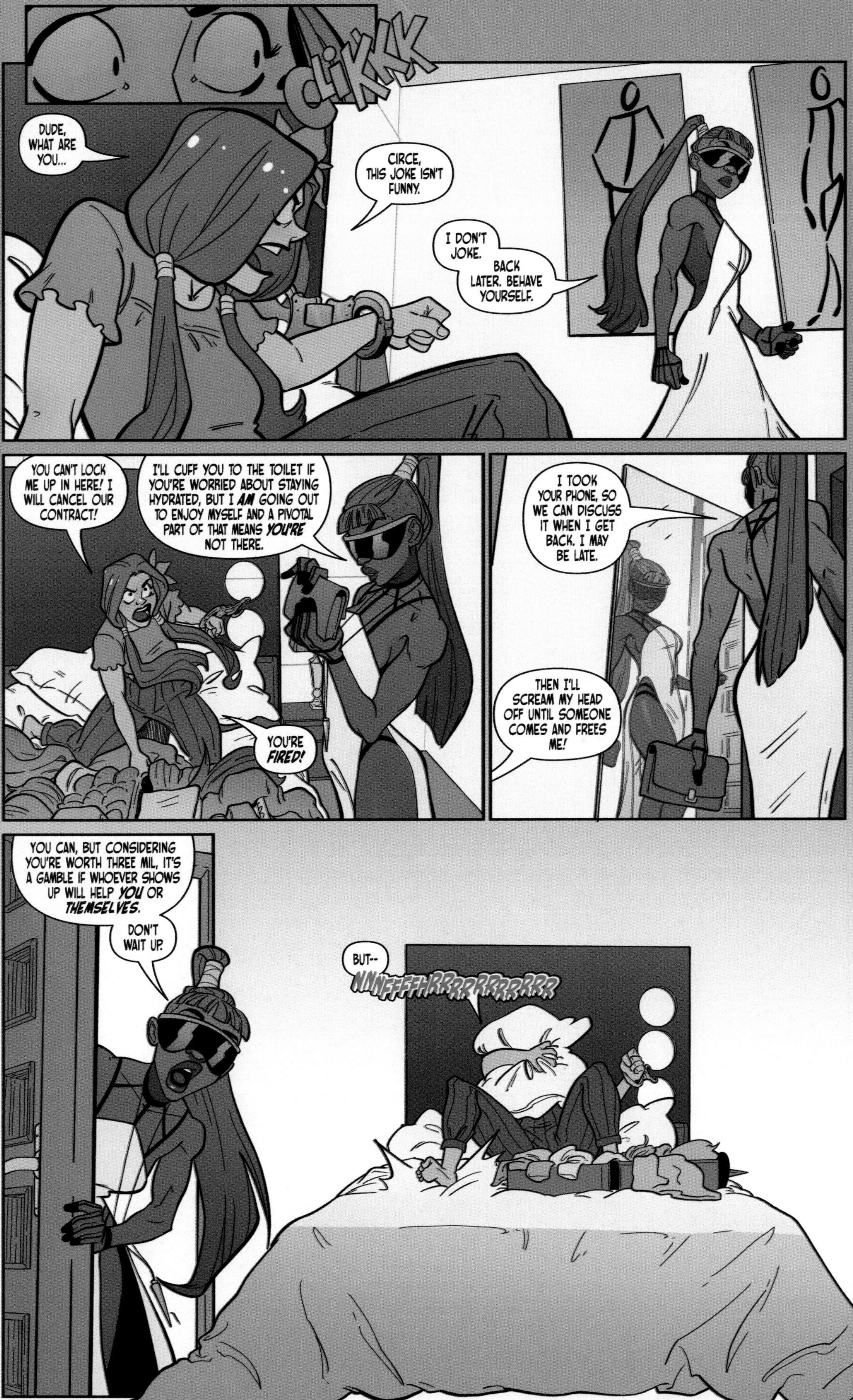
CLIKKK
DUDE, WHAT ARE YOU...
CIRCE, THIS JOKE ISN'T FUNNY.
I DON'T JOKE.
BACK LATER. BEHAVE YOURSELF.
YOU CAN'T LOCK ME UP IN HERE! I WILL CANCEL OUR CONTRACT!
I'LL CUFF YOU TO THE TOILET IF YOU'RE WORRIED ABOUT STAYING HYDRATED, BUT I AM GOING OUT TO ENJOY MYSELF AND A PIVOTAL PART OF THAT MEANS YOU'RE NOT THERE.
YOU'RE FIRED!
I TOOK YOUR PHONE, SO WE CAN DISCUSS IT WHEN I GET BACK. I MAY BE LATE.
THEN I'LL SCREAM MY HEAD OFF UNTIL SOMEONE COMES AND FREES ME!
YOU CAN, BUT CONSIDERING YOU'RE WORTH THREE MIL, IT'S A GAMBLE IF WHOEVER SHOWS UP WILL HELP YOU OR THEMSELVES.
DON'T WAIT UP.
BUT--
NNNFFFFHRRRRRRRRRR

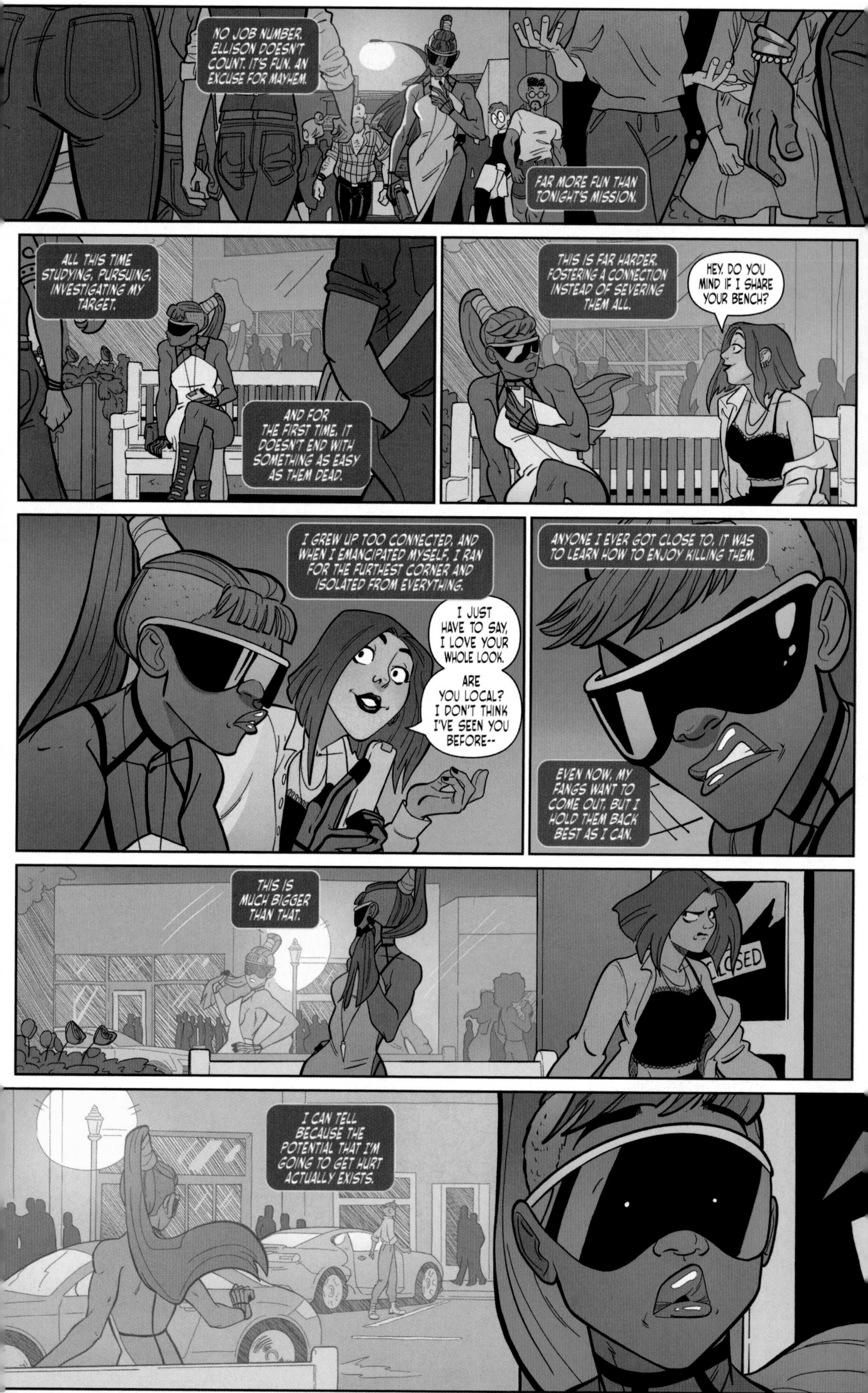
NO JOB NUMBER. ELLISON DOESN'T COUNT. IT'S FUN. AN EXCUSE FOR MAYHEM.
FAR MORE FUN THAN TONIGHT'S MISSION.
ALL THIS TIME STUDYING, PURSUING, INVESTIGATING MY TARGET.
AND FOR THE FIRST TIME, IT DOESN'T END WITH SOMETHING AS EASY AS THEM DEAD.
THIS IS FAR HARDER. FOSTERING A CONNECTION INSTEAD OF SEVERING THEM ALL.
HEY. DO YOU MIND IF I SHARE YOUR BENCH?
I GREW UP TOO CONNECTED, AND WHEN I EMANCIPATED MYSELF, I RAN FOR THE FURTHEST CORNER AND ISOLATED FROM EVERYTHING.
I JUST HAVE TO SAY, I LOVE YOUR WHOLE LOOK.
ARE YOU LOCAL? I DON'T THINK I'VE SEEN YOU BEFORE--
ANYONE I EVER GOT CLOSE TO, IT WAS TO LEARN HOW TO ENJOY KILLING THEM.
EVEN NOW, MY FANGS WANT TO COME OUT, BUT I HOLD THEM BACK BEST AS I CAN.
THIS IS MUCH BIGGER THAN THAT.
LOSED
I CAN TELL BECAUSE THE POTENTIAL THAT I'M GOING TO GET HURT ACTUALLY EXISTS.

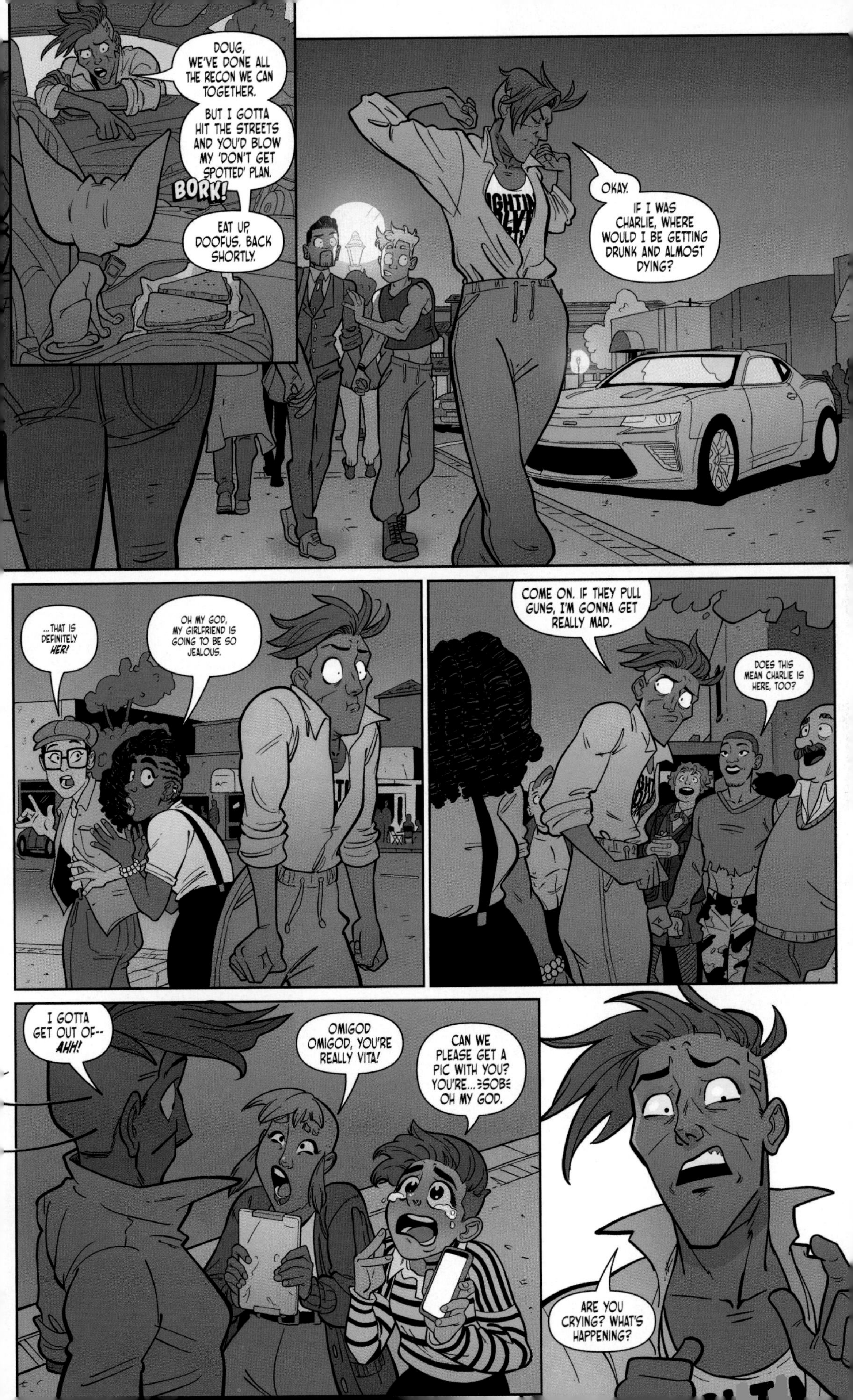
DOUG, WE'VE DONE ALL THE RECON WE CAN TOGETHER.
BUT I GOTTA HIT THE STREETS AND YOU'D BLOW MY 'DON'T GET SPOTTED' PLAN.
BORK!
EAT UP, DOOFUS. BACK SHORTLY.
OKAY.
IF I WAS CHARLIE, WHERE WOULD I BE GETTING DRUNK AND ALMOST DYING?
...THAT IS DEFINITELY HER!
OH MY GOD, MY GIRLFRIEND IS GOING TO BE SO JEALOUS.
COME ON. IF THEY PULL GUNS, I'M GONNA GET REALLY MAD.
DOES THIS MEAN CHARLIE IS HERE, TOO?
I GOTTA GET OUT OF-- AHH!
OMIGOD OMIGOD, YOU'RE REALLY VITA!
CAN WE PLEASE GET A PIC WITH YOU? YOU'RE... ≠SOB≠ OH MY GOD.
ARE YOU CRYING? WHAT'S HAPPENING?

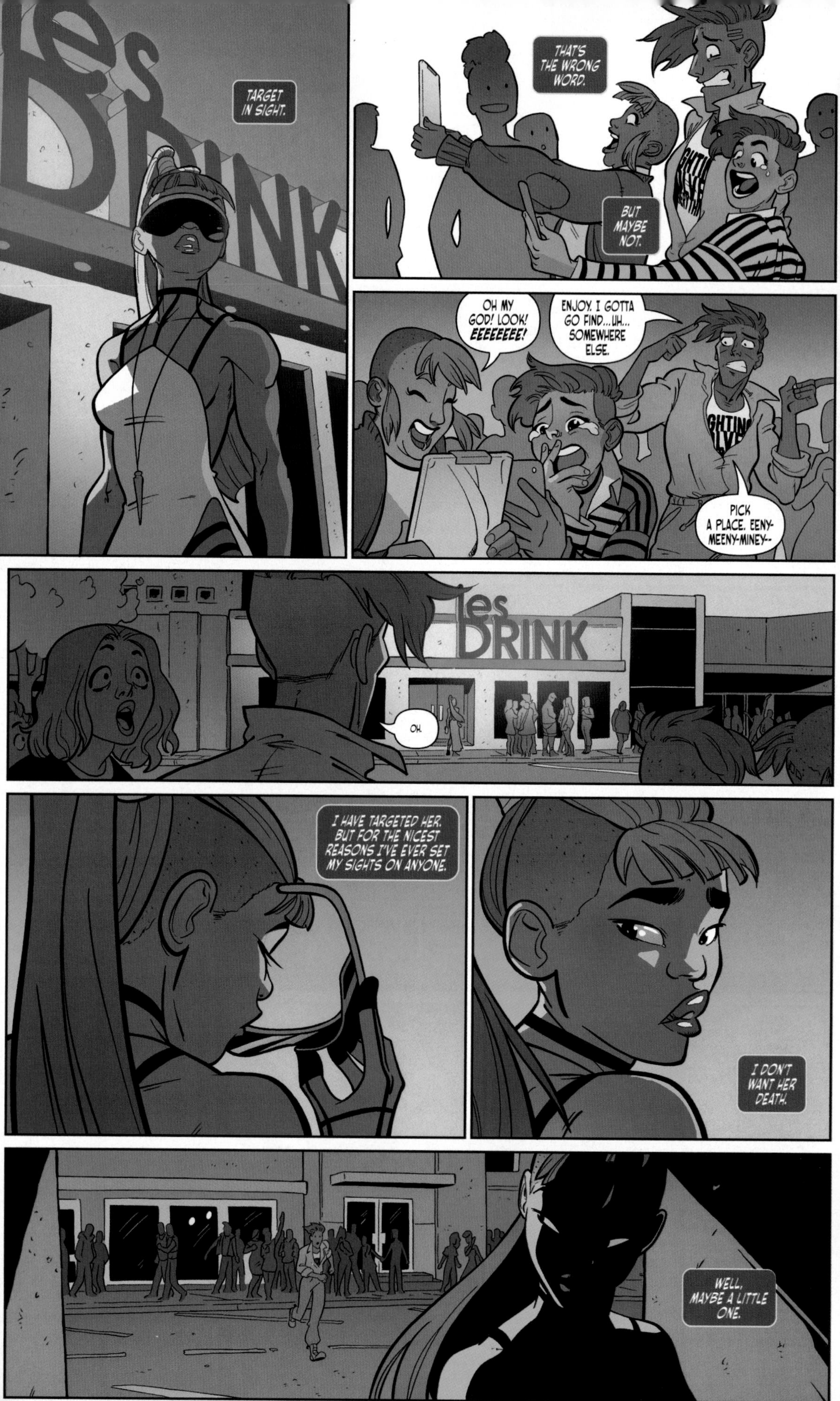
TARGET IN SIGHT.
THAT'S THE WRONG WORD.
BUT MAYBE NOT.
OH MY GOD! LOOK! EEEEEEEE!
ENJOY. I GOTTA GO FIND...UH... SOMEWHERE ELSE.
PICK A PLACE. EENY-MEENY-MINEY--
LES DRINK
OH.
I HAVE TARGETED HER. BUT FOR THE NICEST REASONS I'VE EVER SET MY SIGHTS ON ANYONE.
I DON'T WANT HER DEATH.
WELL, MAYBE A LITTLE ONE.

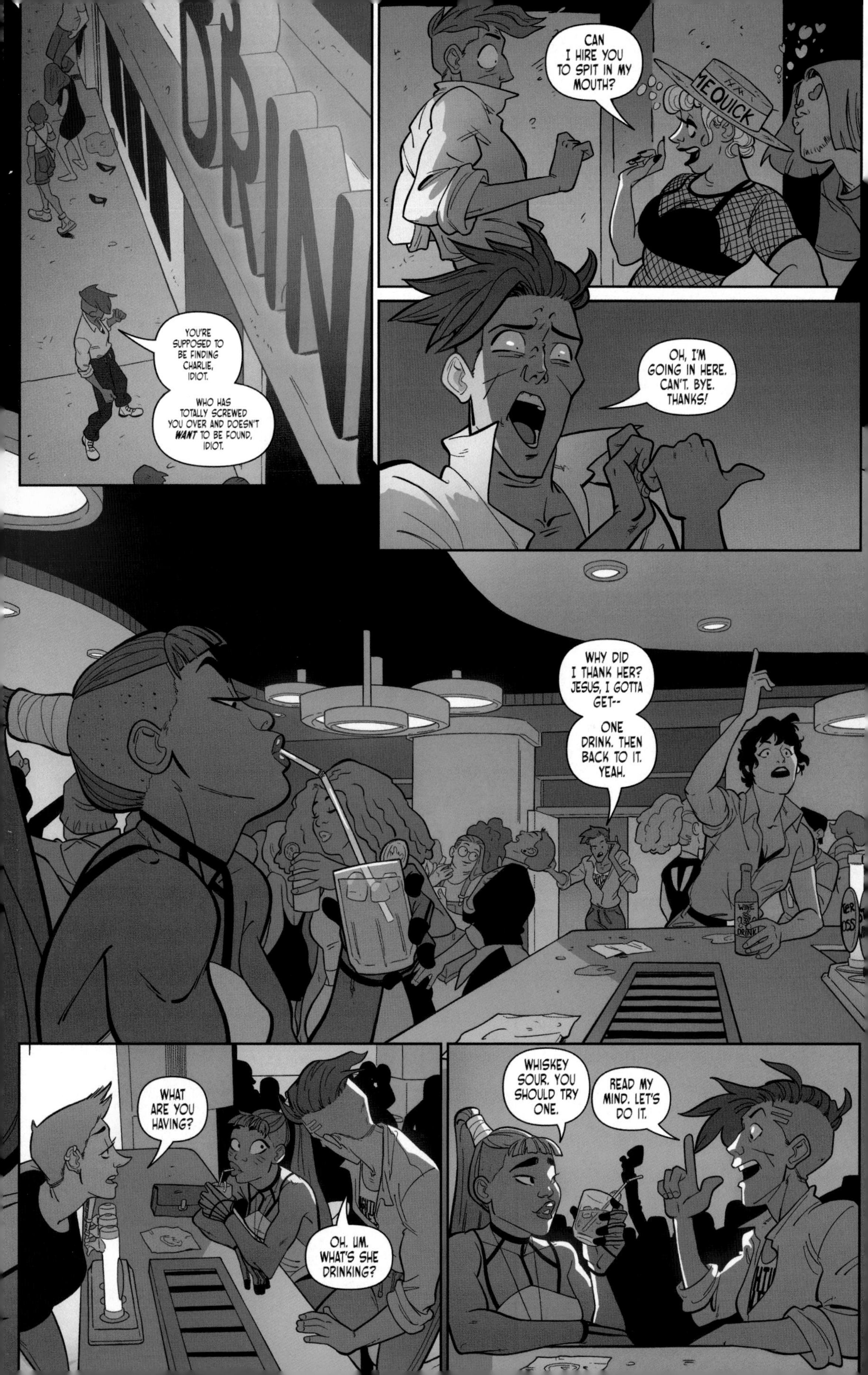
YOU'RE SUPPOSED TO BE FINDING CHARLIE, IDIOT.
WHO HAS TOTALLY SCREWED YOU OVER AND DOESN'T WANT TO BE FOUND, IDIOT.
CAN I HIRE YOU TO SPIT IN MY MOUTH?
ME QUICK
OH, I'M GOING IN HERE. CAN'T. BYE. THANKS!
WHY DID I THANK HER? JESUS, I GOTTA GET--
ONE DRINK. THEN BACK TO IT. YEAH.
WHAT ARE YOU HAVING?
OH. UM. WHAT'S SHE DRINKING?
WHISKEY SOUR. YOU SHOULD TRY ONE.
READ MY MIND. LET'S DO IT.

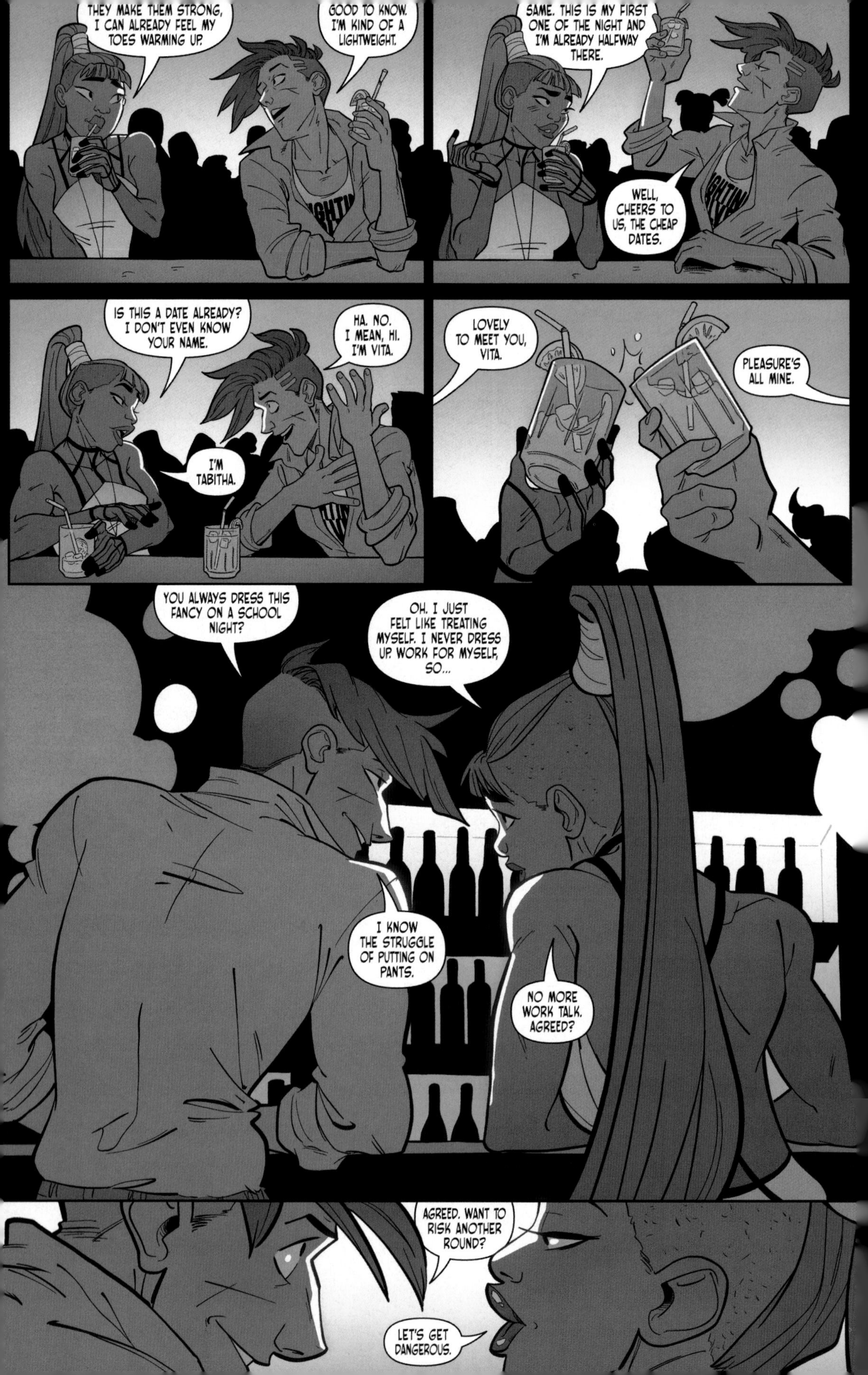
THEY MAKE THEM STRONG, I CAN ALREADY FEEL MY TOES WARMING UP.
GOOD TO KNOW. I'M KIND OF A LIGHTWEIGHT.
SAME. THIS IS MY FIRST ONE OF THE NIGHT AND I'M ALREADY HALFWAY THERE.
WELL, CHEERS TO US, THE CHEAP DATES.
IS THIS A DATE ALREADY? I DON'T EVEN KNOW YOUR NAME.
HA. NO. I MEAN, HI. I'M VITA.
I'M TABITHA.
LOVELY TO MEET YOU, VITA.
PLEASURE'S ALL MINE.
YOU ALWAYS DRESS THIS FANCY ON A SCHOOL NIGHT?
OH. I JUST FELT LIKE TREATING MYSELF. I NEVER DRESS UP. WORK FOR MYSELF, SO...
I KNOW THE STRUGGLE OF PUTTING ON PANTS.
NO MORE WORK TALK. AGREED?
AGREED. WANT TO RISK ANOTHER ROUND?
LET'S GET DANGEROUS.

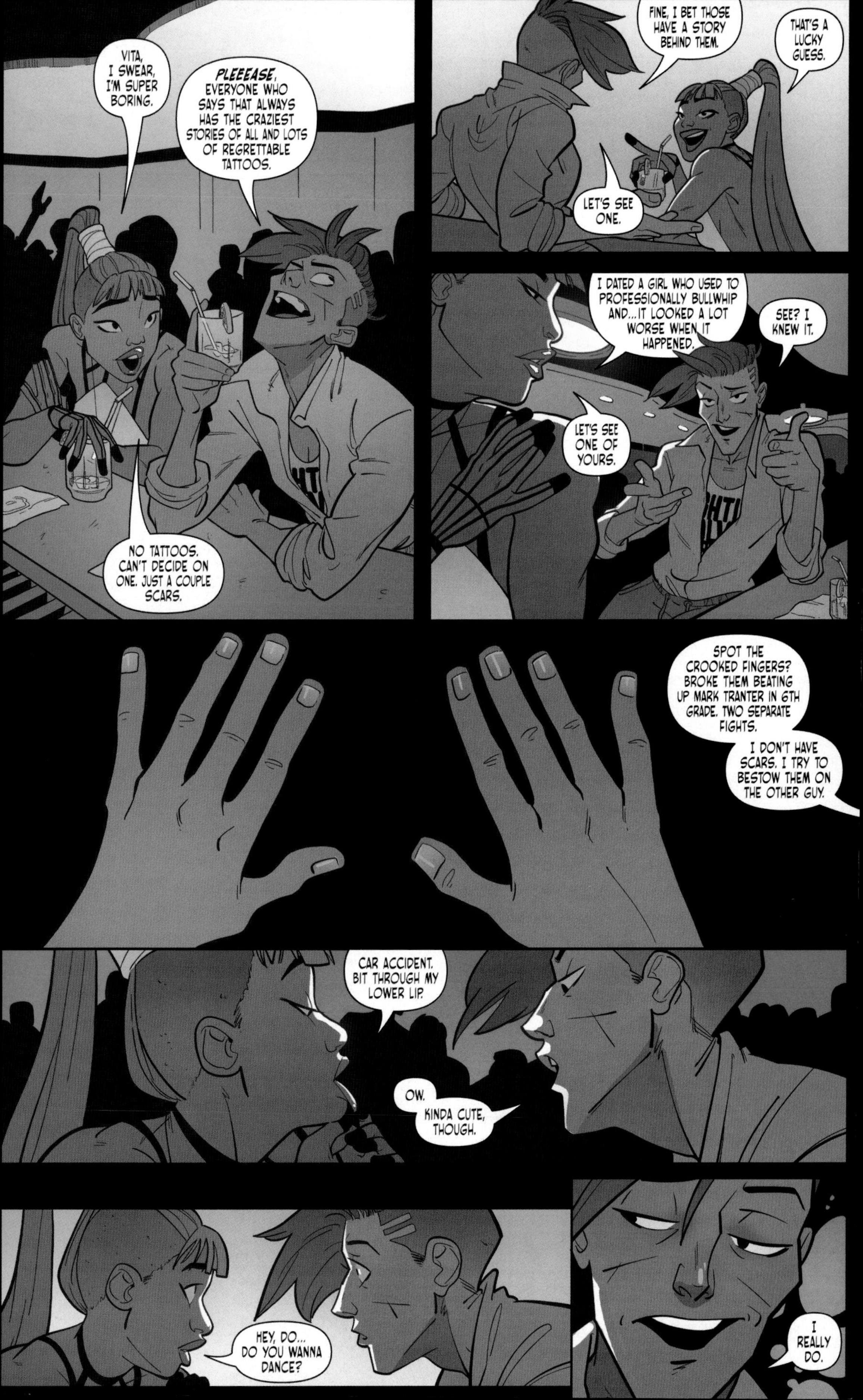

VITA, I SWEAR, I'M SUPER BORING.
PLEEEASE, EVERYONE WHO SAYS THAT ALWAYS HAS THE CRAZIEST STORIES OF ALL AND LOTS OF REGRETTABLE TATTOOS.
NO TATTOOS. CAN'T DECIDE ON ONE. JUST A COUPLE SCARS.
FINE, I BET THOSE HAVE A STORY BEHIND THEM.
THAT'S A LUCKY GUESS.
LET'S SEE ONE.
I DATED A GIRL WHO USED TO PROFESSIONALLY BULLWHIP AND...IT LOOKED A LOT WORSE WHEN IT HAPPENED.
SEE? I KNEW IT.
LET'S SEE ONE OF YOURS.
SPOT THE CROOKED FINGERS? BROKE THEM BEATING UP MARK TRANTER IN 6TH GRADE. TWO SEPARATE FIGHTS.
I DON'T HAVE SCARS. I TRY TO BESTOW THEM ON THE OTHER GUY.
CAR ACCIDENT. BIT THROUGH MY LOWER LIP.
OW.
KINDA CUTE, THOUGH.
HEY, DO... DO YOU WANNA DANCE?
I REALLY DO.

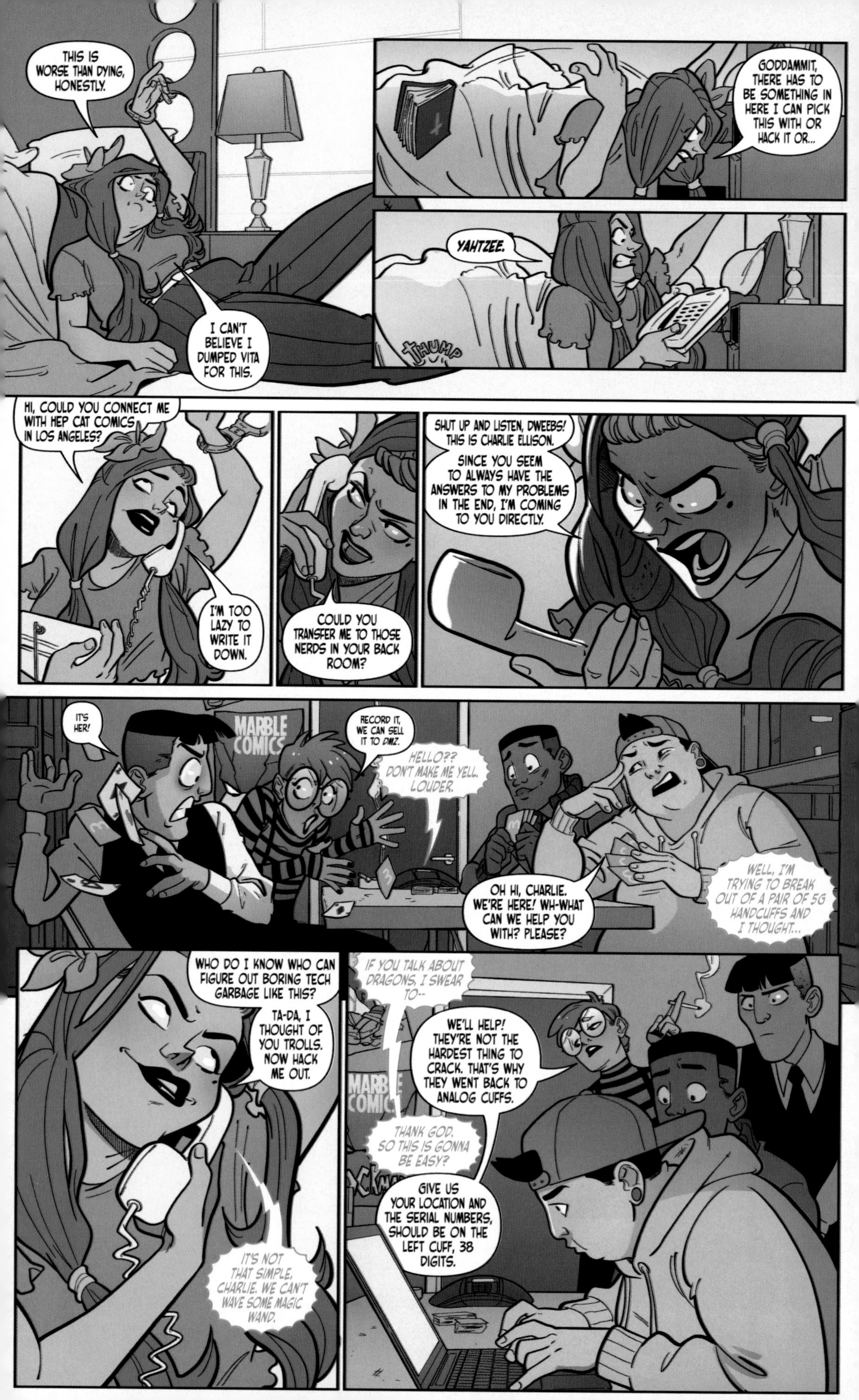
THIS IS WORSE THAN DYING, HONESTLY.
I CAN'T BELIEVE I DUMPED VITA FOR THIS.
GODDAMMIT, THERE HAS TO BE SOMETHING IN HERE I CAN PICK THIS WITH OR HACK IT OR...
YAHTZEE.
THUMP
HI, COULD YOU CONNECT ME WITH HEP CAT COMICS IN LOS ANGELES?
I'M TOO LAZY TO WRITE IT DOWN.
COULD YOU TRANSFER ME TO THOSE NERDS IN YOUR BACK ROOM?
SHUT UP AND LISTEN, DWEEBS! THIS IS CHARLIE ELLISON.
SINCE YOU SEEM TO ALWAYS HAVE THE ANSWERS TO MY PROBLEMS IN THE END, I'M COMING TO YOU DIRECTLY.
IT'S HER!
MARBLE COMICS
RECORD IT, WE CAN SELL IT TO DMZ.
HELLO?? DON'T MAKE ME YELL. LOUDER.
OH HI, CHARLIE. WE'RE HERE! WH-WHAT CAN WE HELP YOU WITH? PLEASE?
WELL, I'M TRYING TO BREAK OUT OF A PAIR OF 5G HANDCUFFS AND I THOUGHT...
WHO DO I KNOW WHO CAN FIGURE OUT BORING TECH GARBAGE LIKE THIS?
TA-DA, I THOUGHT OF YOU TROLLS. NOW HACK ME OUT.
IT'S NOT THAT SIMPLE, CHARLIE. WE CAN'T WAVE SOME MAGIC WAND.
IF YOU TALK ABOUT DRAGONS, I SWEAR TO--
WE'LL HELP! THEY'RE NOT THE HARDEST THING TO CRACK. THAT'S WHY THEY WENT BACK TO ANALOG CUFFS.
THANK GOD. SO THIS IS GONNA BE EASY?
GIVE US YOUR LOCATION AND THE SERIAL NUMBERS, SHOULD BE ON THE LEFT CUFF, 38 DIGITS.

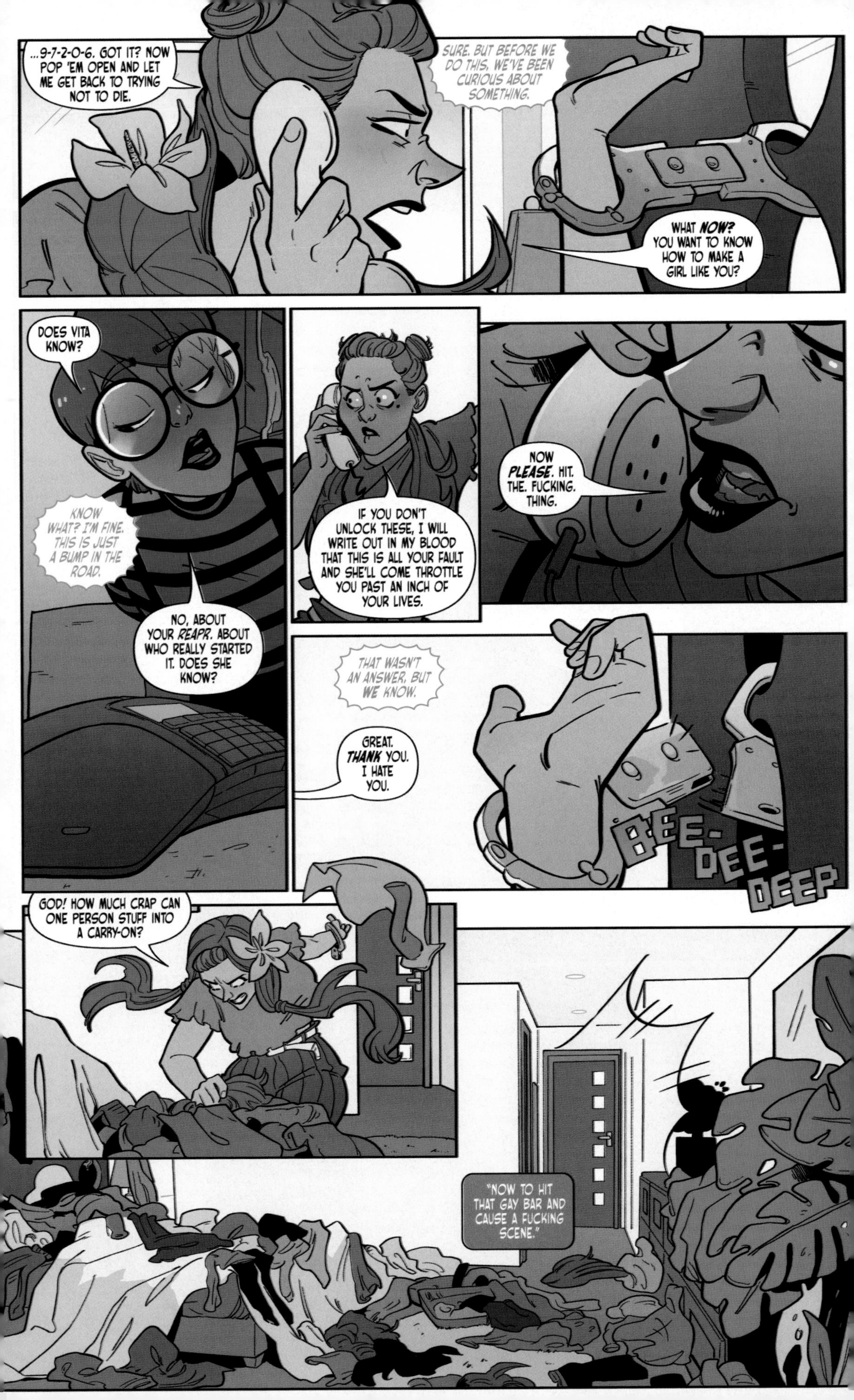
...9-7-2-0-6. GOT IT? NOW POP 'EM OPEN AND LET ME GET BACK TO TRYING NOT TO DIE.
SURE. BUT BEFORE WE DO THIS, WE'VE BEEN CURIOUS ABOUT SOMETHING.
WHAT NOW? YOU WANT TO KNOW HOW TO MAKE A GIRL LIKE YOU?
DOES VITA KNOW?
KNOW WHAT? I'M FINE. THIS IS JUST A BUMP IN THE ROAD.
NO, ABOUT YOUR REAPR. ABOUT WHO REALLY STARTED IT. DOES SHE KNOW?
IF YOU DON'T UNLOCK THESE, I WILL WRITE OUT IN MY BLOOD THAT THIS IS ALL YOUR FAULT AND SHE'LL COME THROTTLE YOU PAST AN INCH OF YOUR LIVES.
NOW PLEASE. HIT. THE. FUCKING. THING.
THAT WASN'T AN ANSWER, BUT WE KNOW.
GREAT. THANK YOU. I HATE YOU.
BEE-DEE-DEEP
GOD! HOW MUCH CRAP CAN ONE PERSON STUFF INTO A CARRY-ON?
"NOW TO HIT THAT GAY BAR AND CAUSE A FUCKING SCENE."

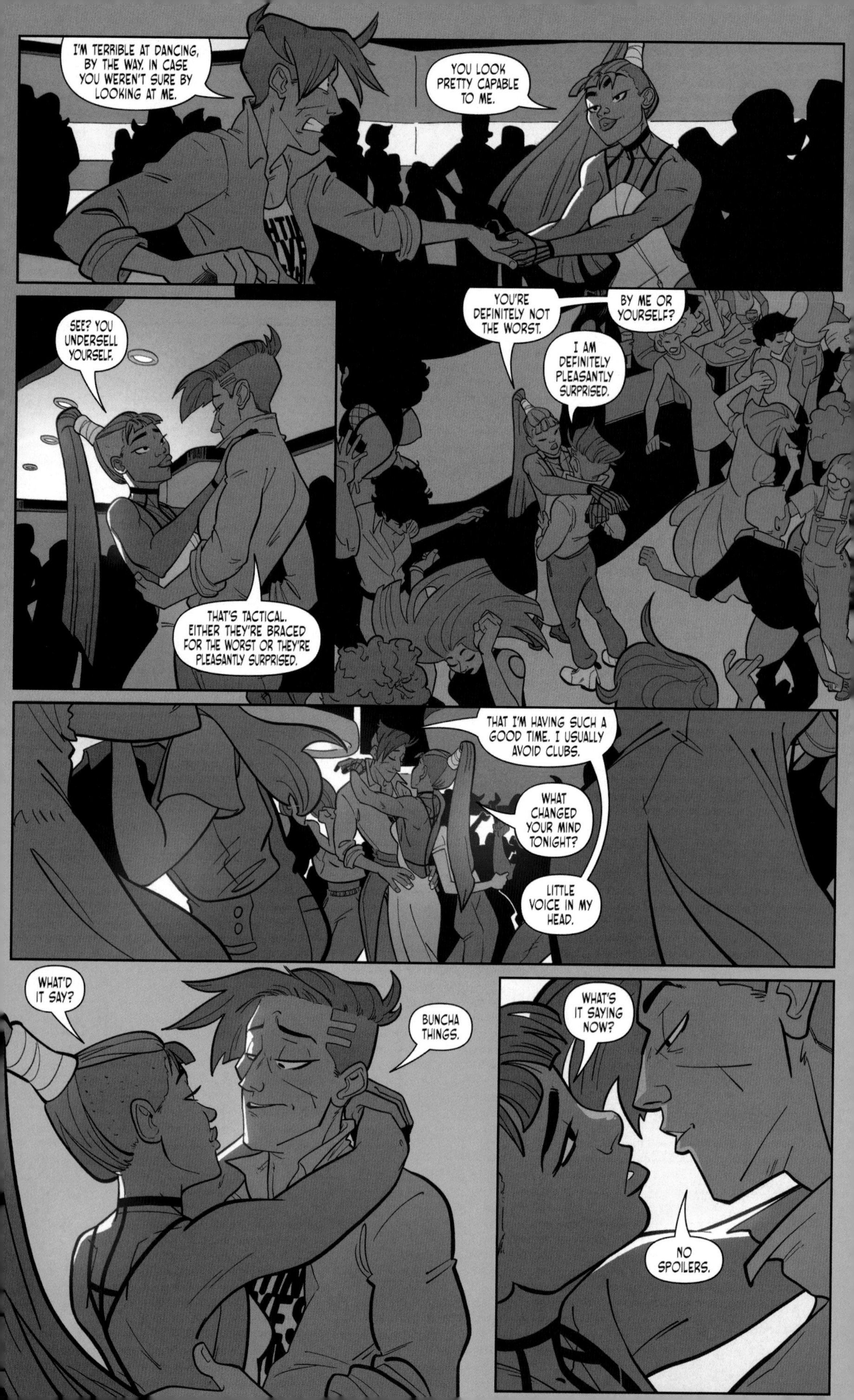
I'M TERRIBLE AT DANCING, BY THE WAY. IN CASE YOU WEREN'T SURE BY LOOKING AT ME.
YOU LOOK PRETTY CAPABLE TO ME.
SEE? YOU UNDERSELL YOURSELF.
THAT'S TACTICAL. EITHER THEY'RE BRACED FOR THE WORST OR THEY'RE PLEASANTLY SURPRISED.
YOU'RE DEFINITELY NOT THE WORST.
BY ME OR YOURSELF?
I AM DEFINITELY PLEASANTLY SURPRISED.
THAT I'M HAVING SUCH A GOOD TIME. I USUALLY AVOID CLUBS.
WHAT CHANGED YOUR MIND TONIGHT?
LITTLE VOICE IN MY HEAD.
WHAT'D IT SAY?
BUNCHA THINGS.
WHAT'S IT SAYING NOW?
NO SPOILERS.

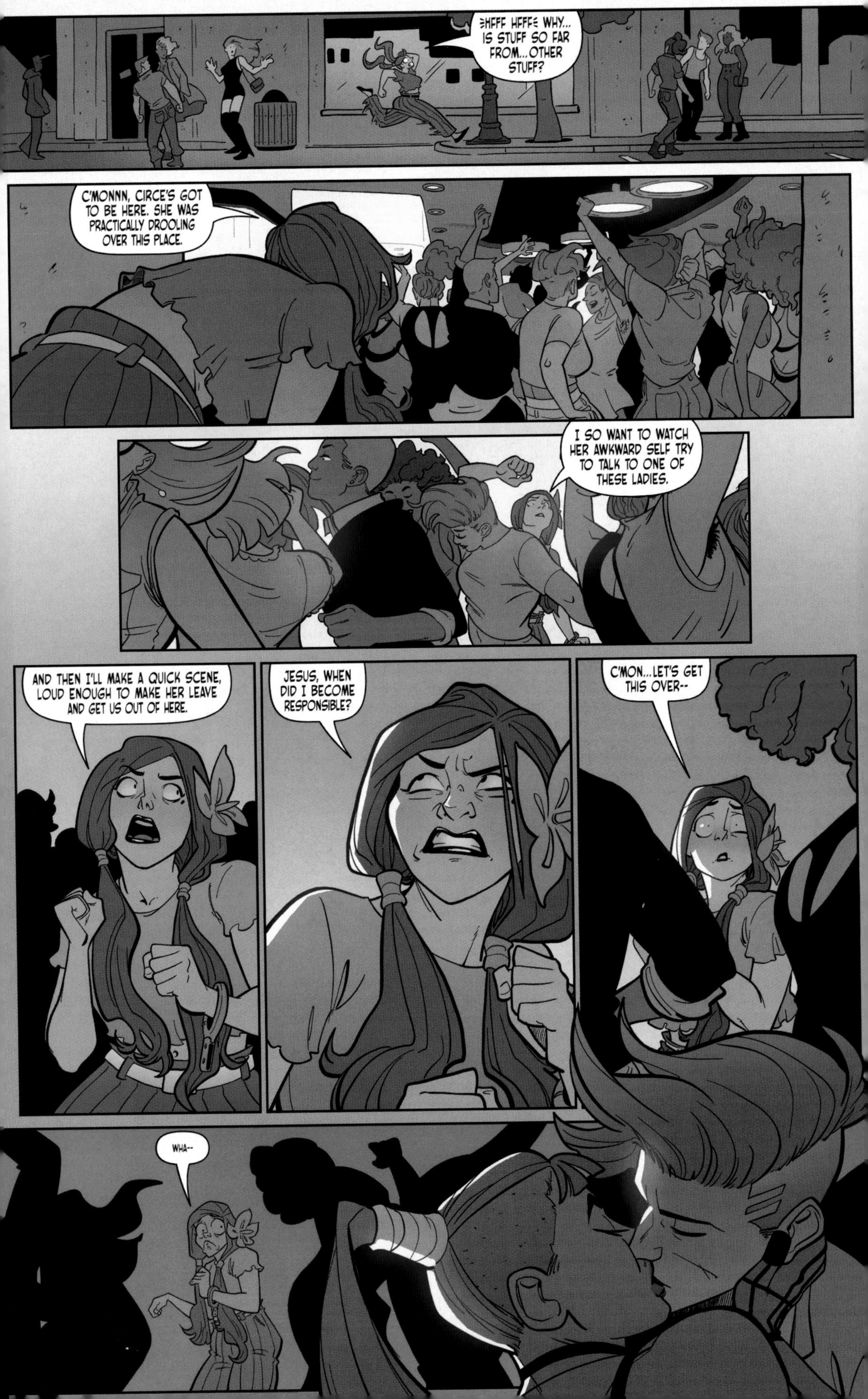
≡HFFF HFFF≡ WHY... IS STUFF SO FAR FROM...OTHER STUFF?
C'MONNN, CIRCE'S GOT TO BE HERE. SHE WAS PRACTICALLY DROOLING OVER THIS PLACE.
I SO WANT TO WATCH HER AWKWARD SELF TRY TO TALK TO ONE OF THESE LADIES.
AND THEN I'LL MAKE A QUICK SCENE, LOUD ENOUGH TO MAKE HER LEAVE AND GET US OUT OF HERE.
JESUS, WHEN DID I BECOME RESPONSIBLE?
C'MON...LET'S GET THIS OVER--
WHA--

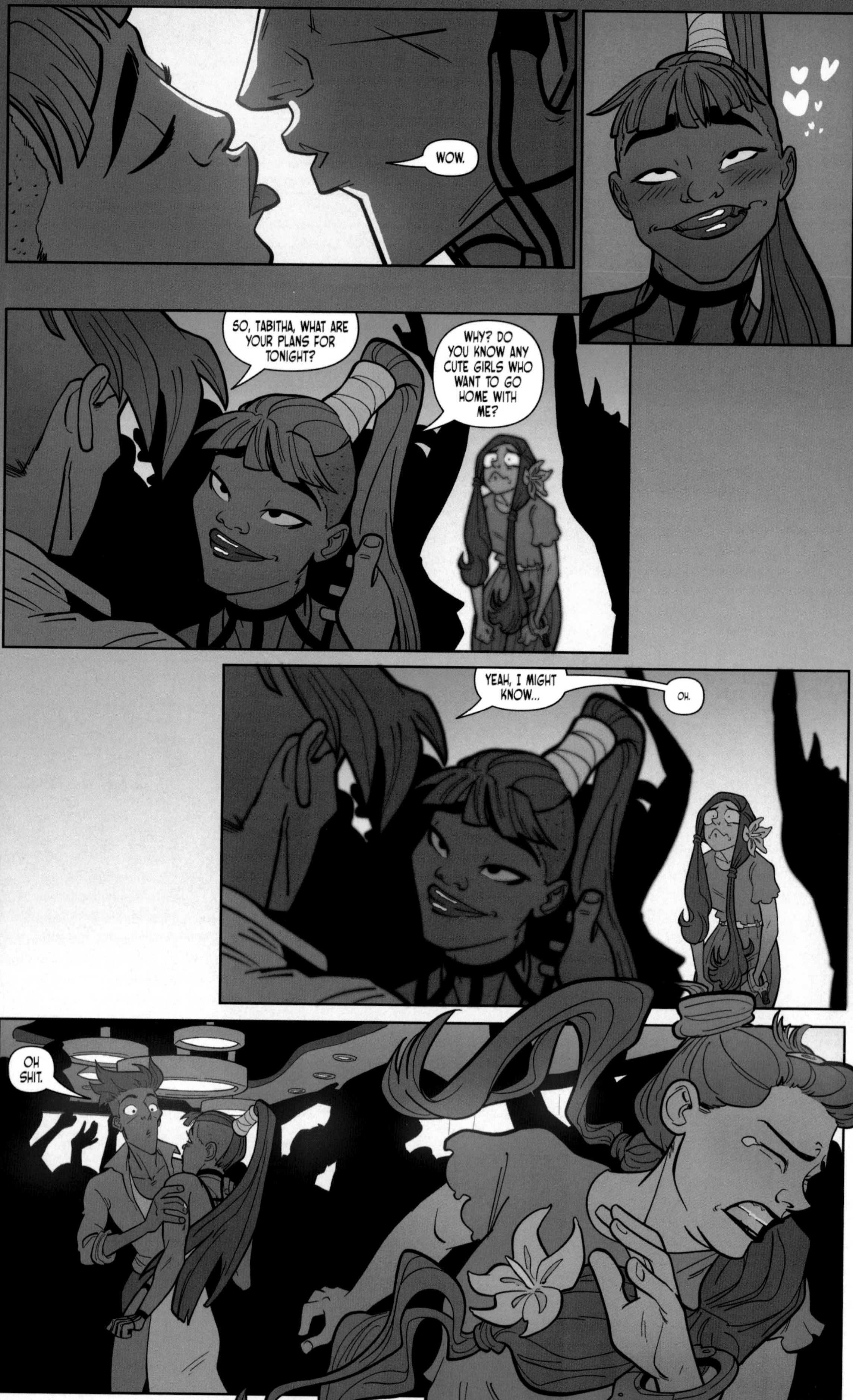
WOW.
SO, TABITHA, WHAT ARE YOUR PLANS FOR TONIGHT?
WHY? DO YOU KNOW ANY CUTE GIRLS WHO WANT TO GO HOME WITH ME?
YEAH, I MIGHT KNOW...
OH.
OH SHIT.

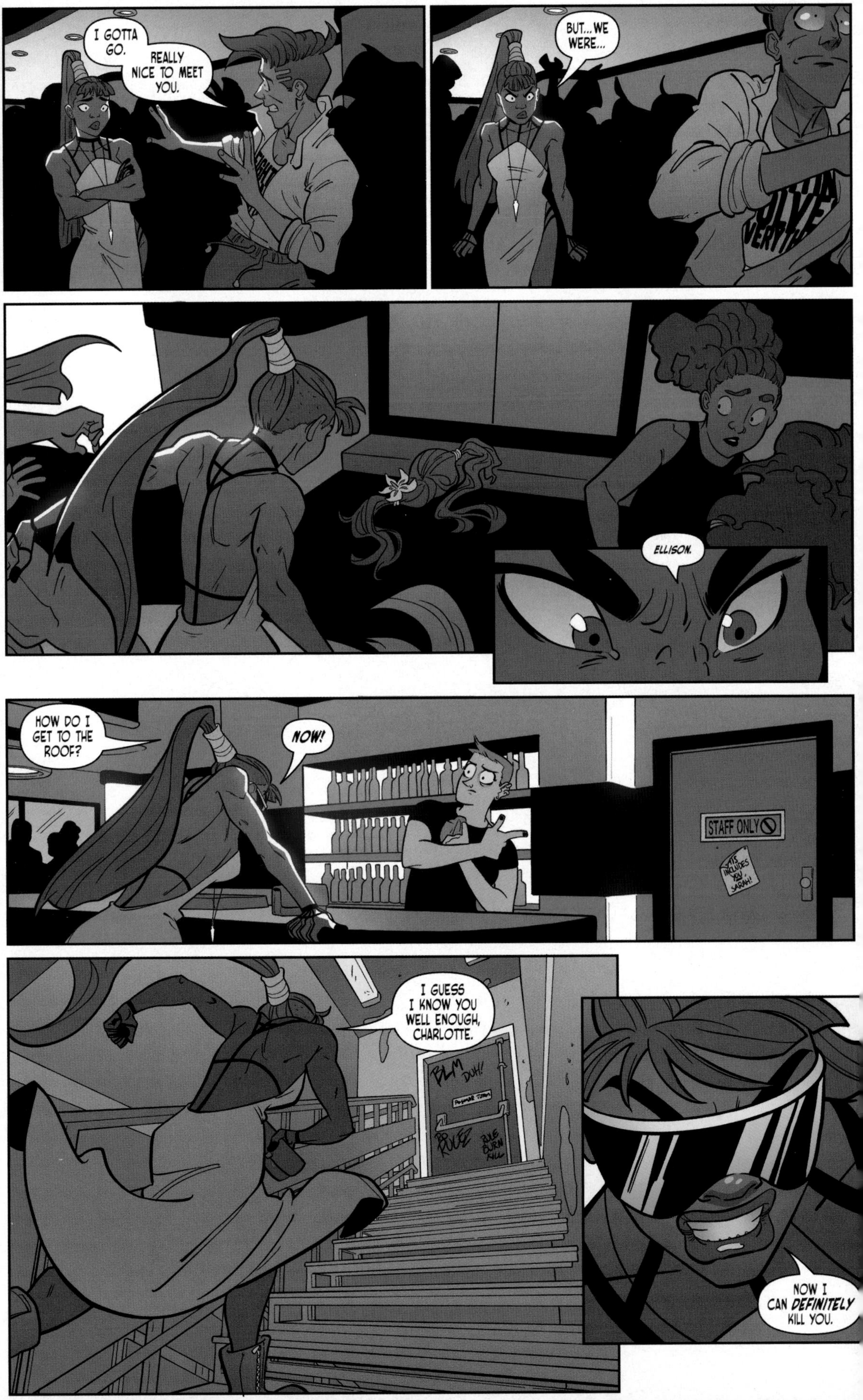
I GOTTA GO.
REALLY NICE TO MEET YOU.
BUT...WE WERE...
ELLISON.
HOW DO I GET TO THE ROOF?
NOW!
STAFF ONLY
I GUESS I KNOW YOU WELL ENOUGH, CHARLOTTE.
NOW I CAN DEFINITELY KILL YOU.

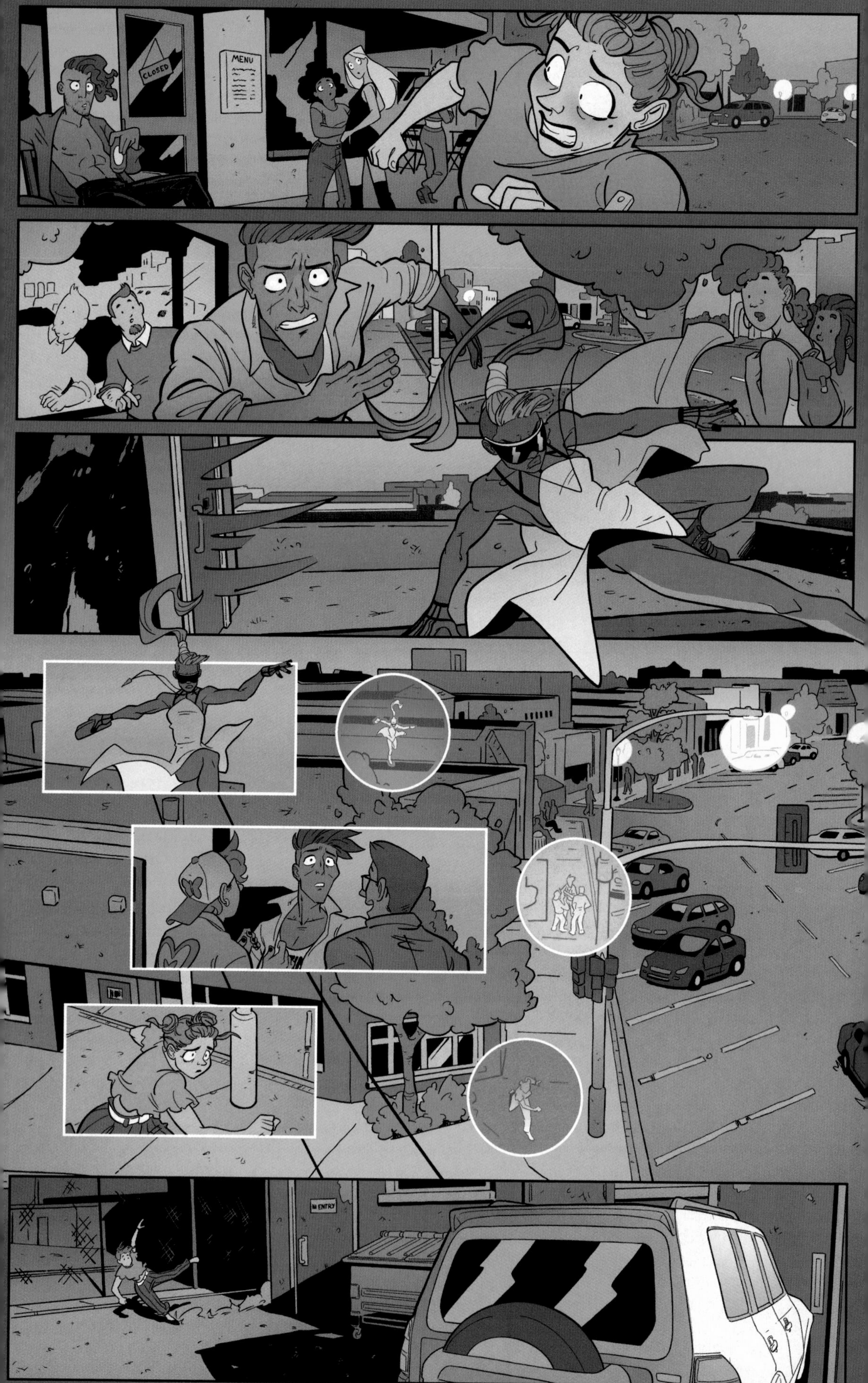
CLOSED
MENU
ENTRY

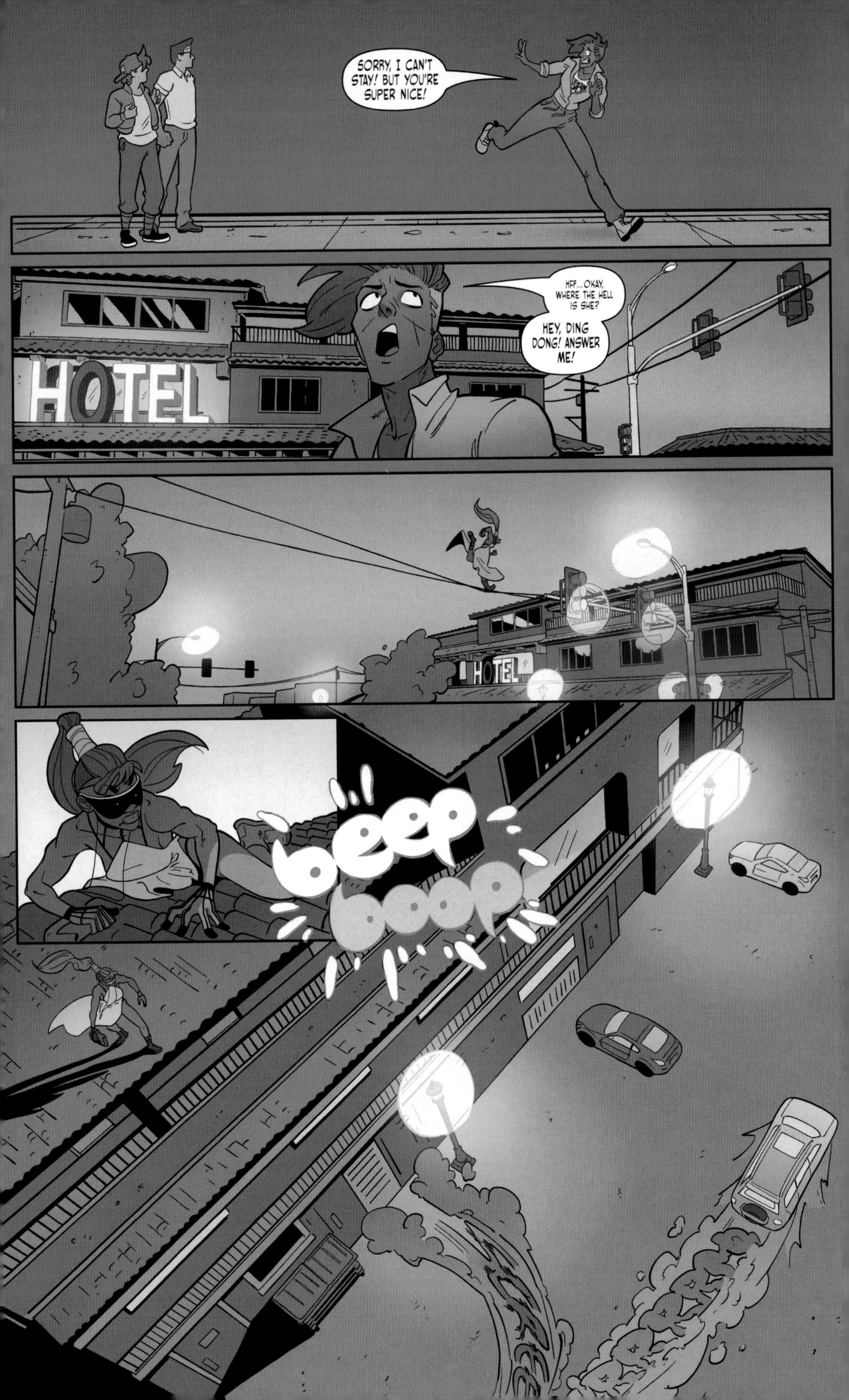
SORRY, I CAN'T STAY! BUT YOU'RE SUPER NICE!
HFF...OKAY, WHERE THE HELL IS SHE?
HEY, DING DONG! ANSWER ME!
HOTEL
HOTEL
BEEP
BOOP

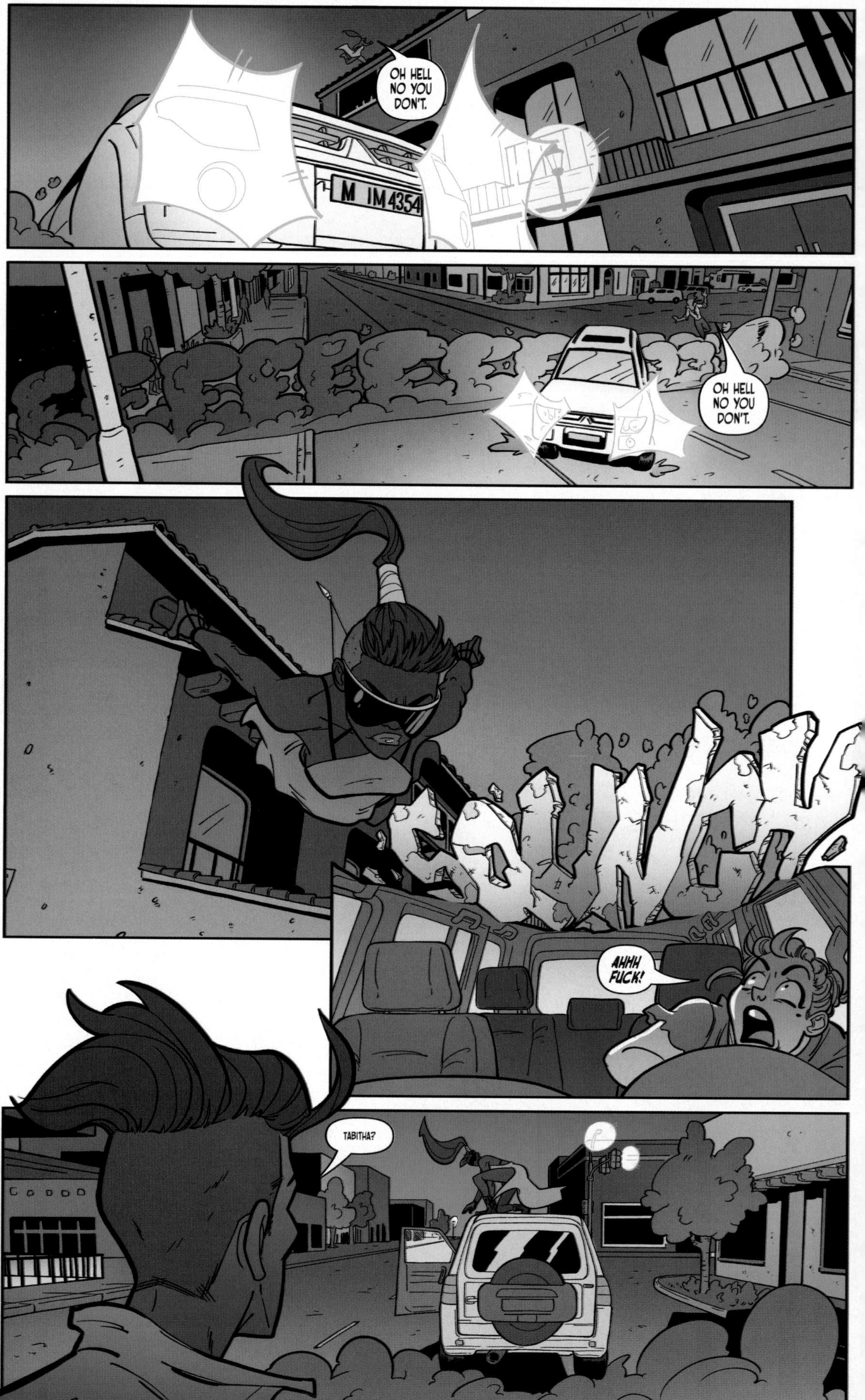
OH HELL NO YOU DON'T.
M IM4354
OH HELL NO YOU DON'T.
AHHH FUCK!
TABITHA?

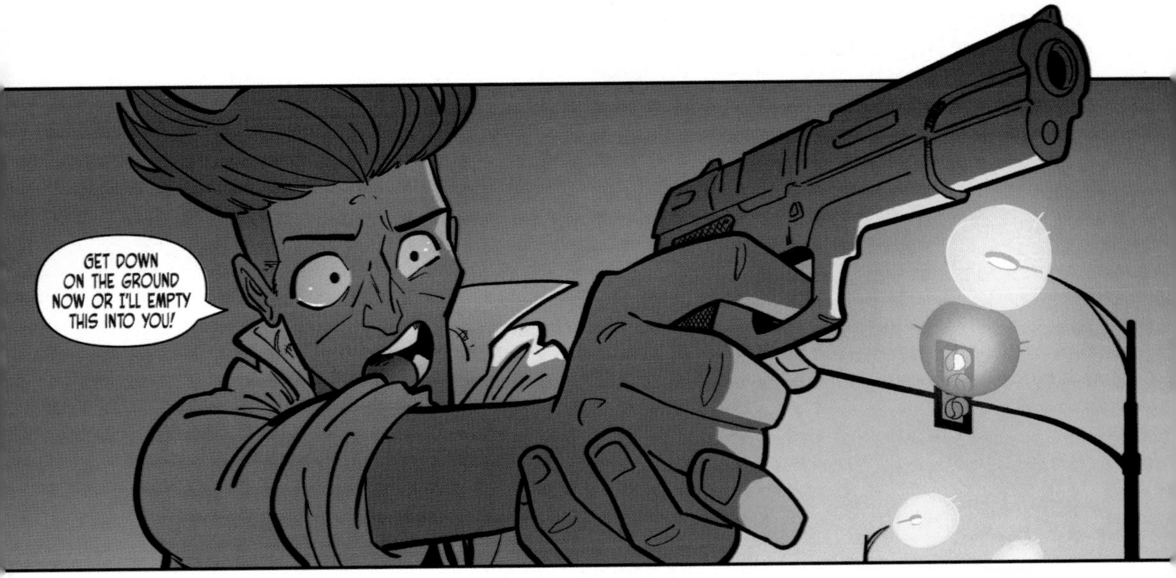
GET DOWN ON THE GROUND NOW OR I'LL EMPTY THIS INTO YOU!

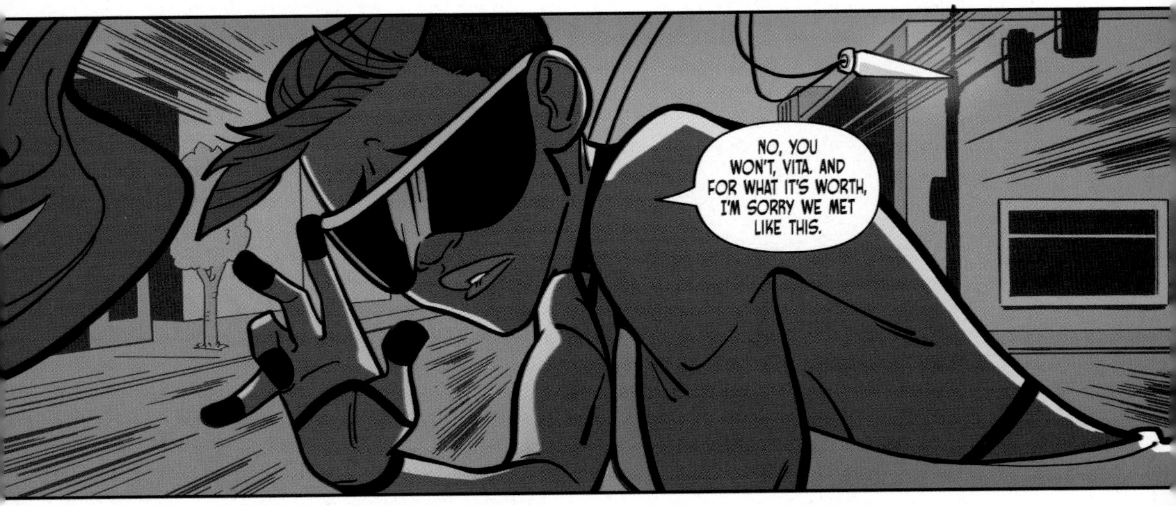
NO, YOU WON'T, VITA. AND FOR WHAT IT'S WORTH, I'M SORRY WE MET LIKE THIS.

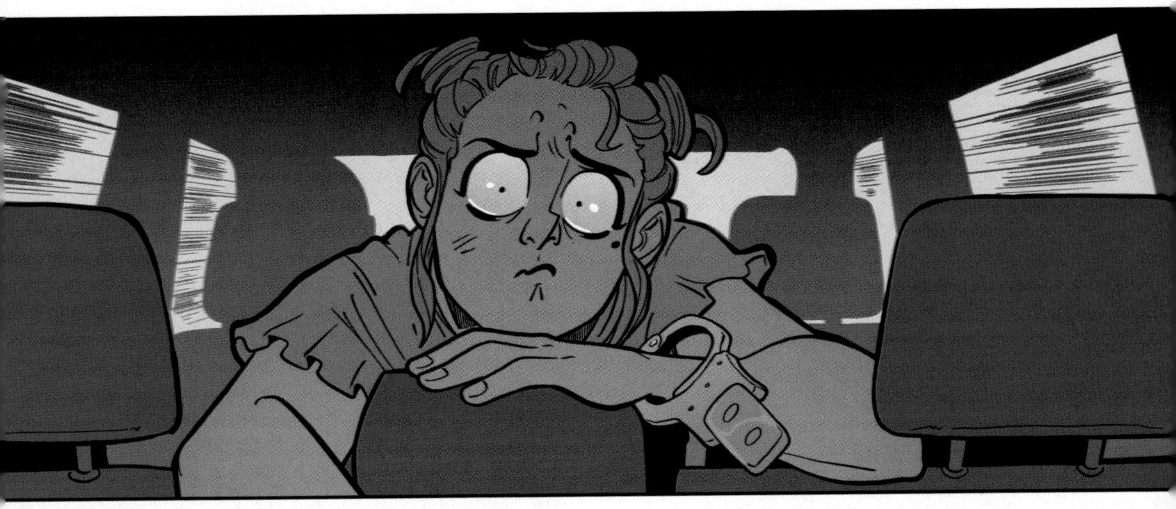

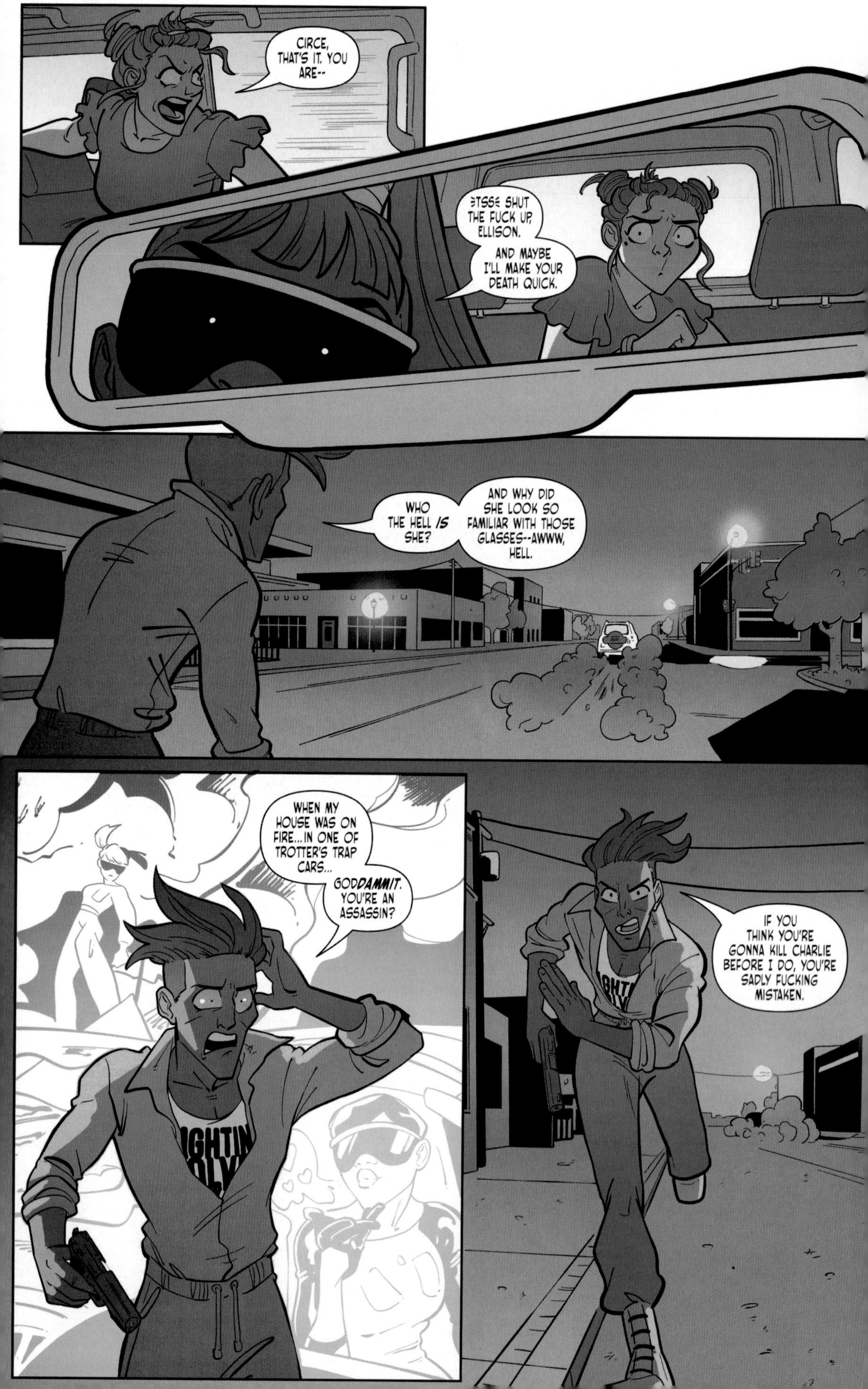
CIRCE, THAT'S IT. YOU ARE--
ƎTSSƐ SHUT THE FUCK UP, ELLISON.
AND MAYBE I'LL MAKE YOUR DEATH QUICK.
WHO THE HELL *IS* SHE?
AND WHY DID SHE LOOK SO FAMILIAR WITH THOSE GLASSES--AWWW, HELL.
WHEN MY HOUSE WAS ON FIRE... IN ONE OF TROTTER'S TRAP CARS...
GOD***DAMMIT***. YOU'RE AN ASSASSIN?
IF YOU THINK YOU'RE GONNA KILL CHARLIE BEFORE I DO, YOU'RE SADLY FUCKING MISTAKEN.

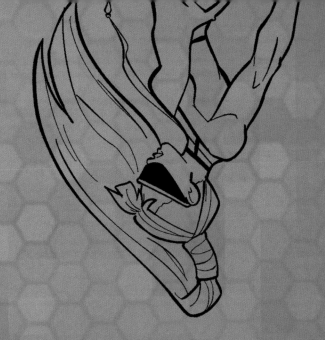

CHAPTER FIFTEEN

UNFORGIVING GIRL

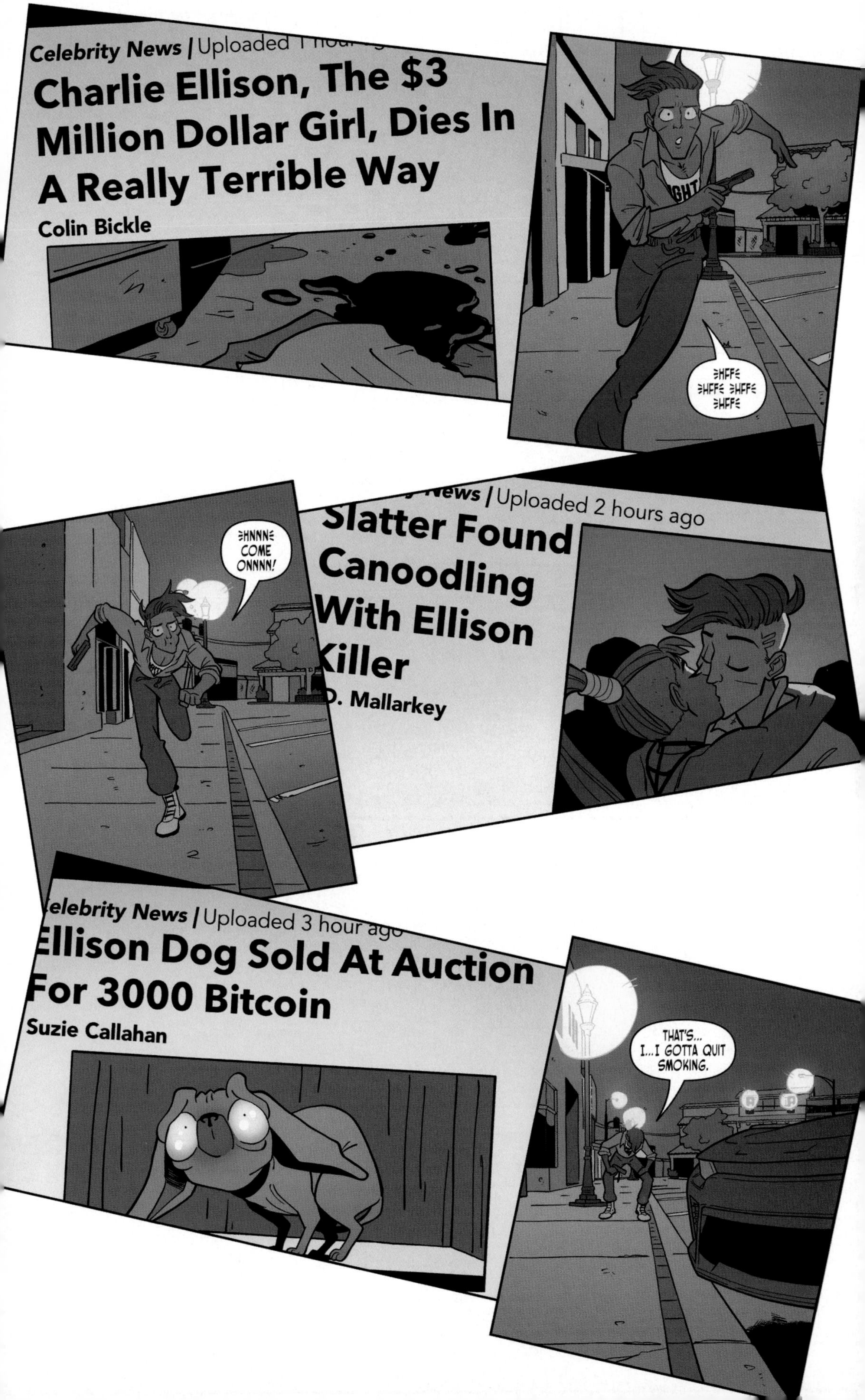
Celebrity News | Uploaded
Charlie Ellison, The $3 Million Dollar Girl, Dies In A Really Terrible Way
Colin Bickle
HFF HFF HFF HFF
HNNN COME ONNNN!
News | Uploaded 2 hours ago
Slatter Found Canoodling With Ellison Killer
D. Mallarkey
elebrity News | Uploaded 3 hour ago
llison Dog Sold At Auction For 3000 Bitcoin
Suzie Callahan
THAT'S... I...I GOTTA QUIT SMOKING.

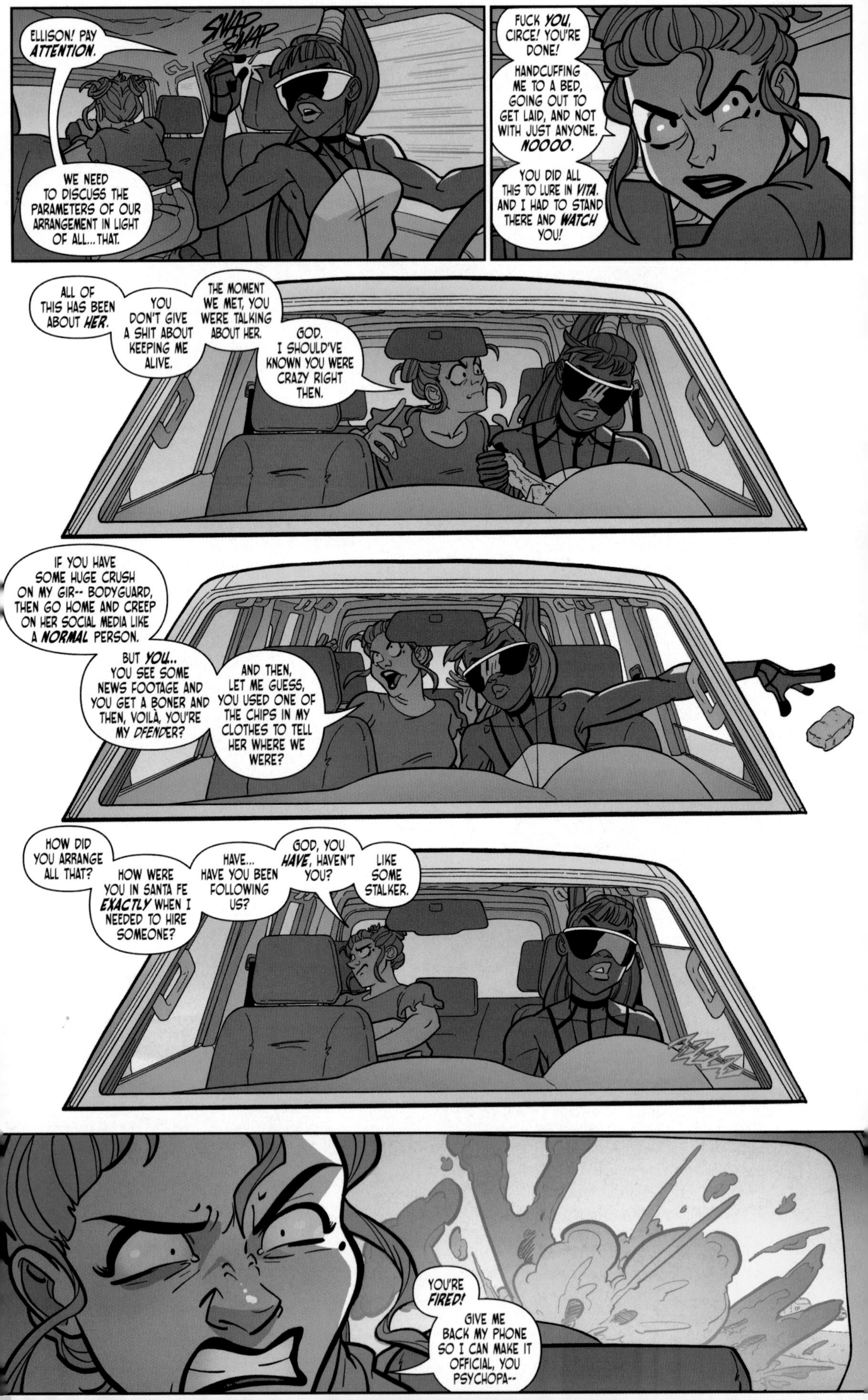
SNAP SNAP
ELLISON! PAY ATTENTION.
WE NEED TO DISCUSS THE PARAMETERS OF OUR ARRANGEMENT IN LIGHT OF ALL...THAT.
FUCK YOU, CIRCE! YOU'RE DONE!
HANDCUFFING ME TO A BED, GOING OUT TO GET LAID, AND NOT WITH JUST ANYONE. NOOOO.
YOU DID ALL THIS TO LURE IN VITA. AND I HAD TO STAND THERE AND WATCH YOU!
ALL OF THIS HAS BEEN ABOUT HER.
YOU DON'T GIVE A SHIT ABOUT KEEPING ME ALIVE.
THE MOMENT WE MET, YOU WERE TALKING ABOUT HER.
GOD. I SHOULD'VE KNOWN YOU WERE CRAZY RIGHT THEN.
IF YOU HAVE SOME HUGE CRUSH ON MY GIR-- BODYGUARD, THEN GO HOME AND CREEP ON HER SOCIAL MEDIA LIKE A NORMAL PERSON.
BUT YOU.. YOU SEE SOME NEWS FOOTAGE AND YOU GET A BONER AND THEN, VOILÀ, YOU'RE MY DFENDER?
AND THEN, LET ME GUESS, YOU USED ONE OF THE CHIPS IN MY CLOTHES TO TELL HER WHERE WE WERE?
HOW DID YOU ARRANGE ALL THAT?
HOW WERE YOU IN SANTA FE EXACTLY WHEN I NEEDED TO HIRE SOMEONE?
HAVE... HAVE YOU BEEN FOLLOWING US?
GOD, YOU HAVE, HAVEN'T YOU?
LIKE SOME STALKER.
YOU'RE FIRED!
GIVE ME BACK MY PHONE SO I CAN MAKE IT OFFICIAL, YOU PSYCHOPA--

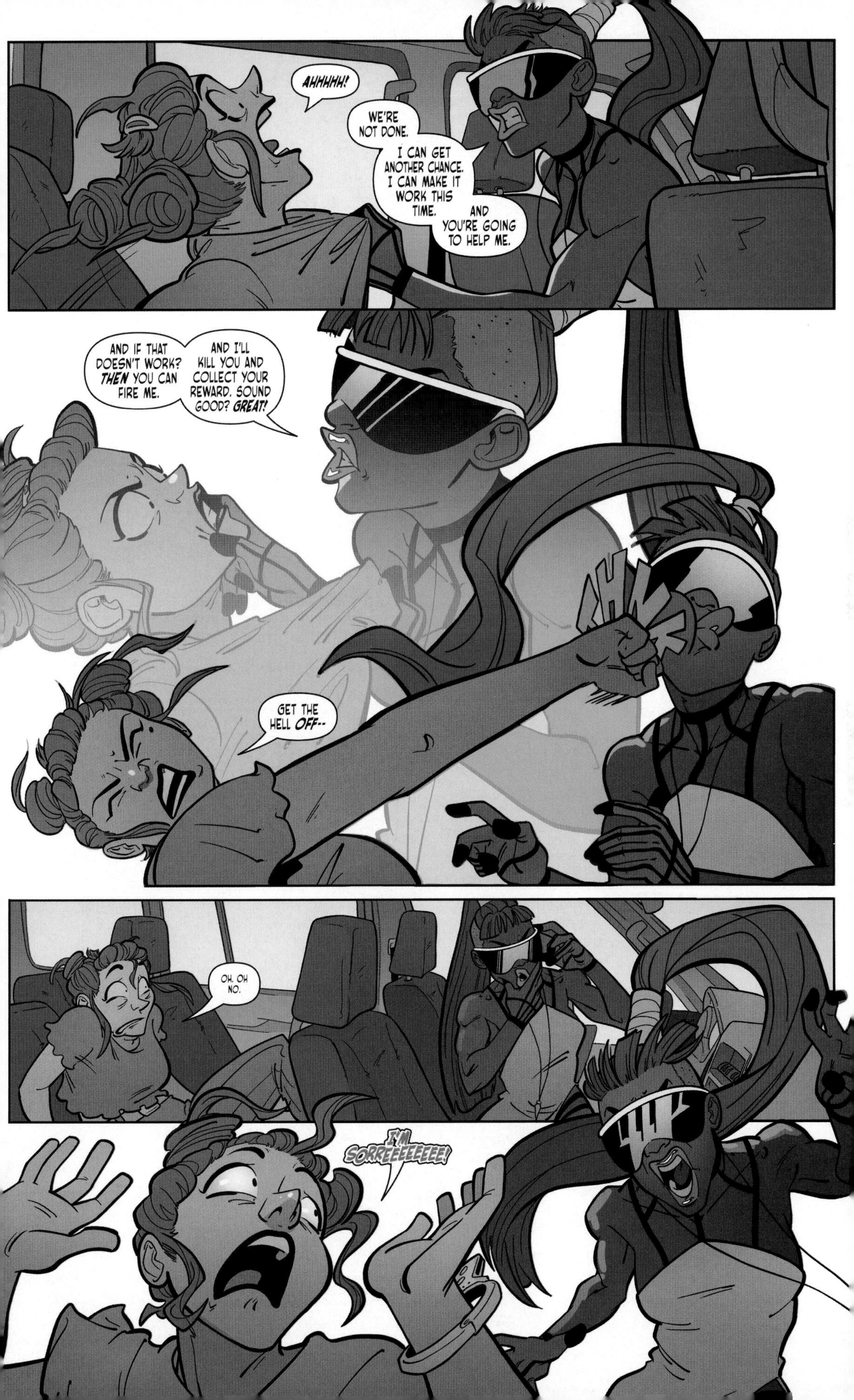
AHHHHH!
WE'RE NOT DONE.
I CAN GET ANOTHER CHANCE. I CAN MAKE IT WORK THIS TIME.
AND YOU'RE GOING TO HELP ME.
AND IF THAT DOESN'T WORK? THEN YOU CAN FIRE ME.
AND I'LL KILL YOU AND COLLECT YOUR REWARD. SOUND GOOD? GREAT!
GET THE HELL OFF--
OH. OH NO.
I'M SORREEEEEEEE!

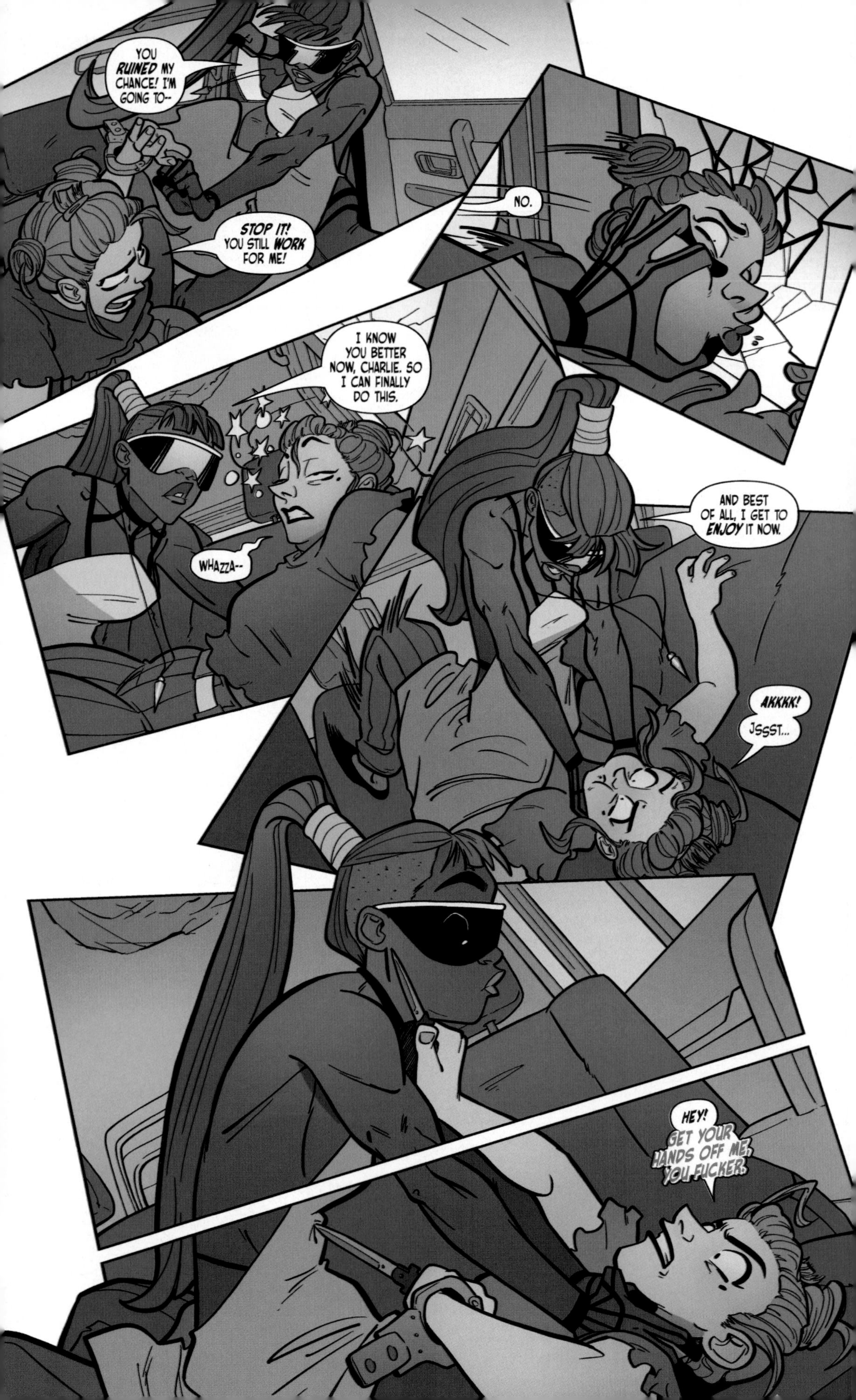
YOU RUINED MY CHANCE! I'M GOING TO--
STOP IT! YOU STILL WORK FOR ME!
NO.
I KNOW YOU BETTER NOW, CHARLIE. SO I CAN FINALLY DO THIS.
WHAZZA--
AND BEST OF ALL, I GET TO ENJOY IT NOW.
AKKKK!
JSSST...
HEY! GET YOUR HANDS OFF ME, YOU FUCKER.

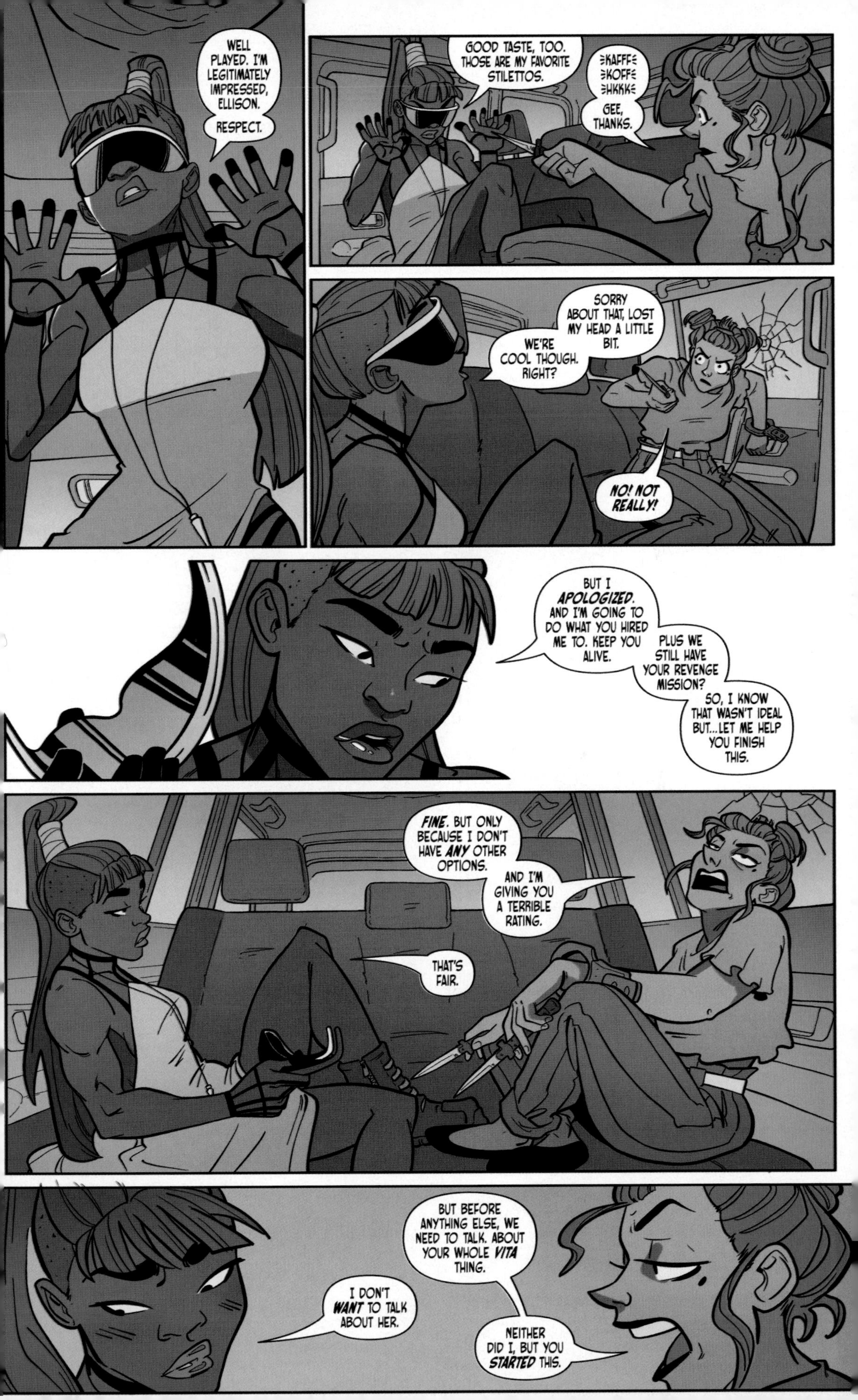
WELL PLAYED. I'M LEGITIMATELY IMPRESSED, ELLISON.
RESPECT.
GOOD TASTE, TOO. THOSE ARE MY FAVORITE STILETTOS.
KAFF KOFF HKKK
GEE, THANKS.
SORRY ABOUT THAT, LOST MY HEAD A LITTLE BIT.
WE'RE COOL THOUGH. RIGHT?
NO! NOT REALLY!
BUT I APOLOGIZED. AND I'M GOING TO DO WHAT YOU HIRED ME TO. KEEP YOU ALIVE.
PLUS WE STILL HAVE YOUR REVENGE MISSION?
SO, I KNOW THAT WASN'T IDEAL BUT...LET ME HELP YOU FINISH THIS.
FINE. BUT ONLY BECAUSE I DON'T HAVE ANY OTHER OPTIONS.
AND I'M GIVING YOU A TERRIBLE RATING.
THAT'S FAIR.
BUT BEFORE ANYTHING ELSE, WE NEED TO TALK. ABOUT YOUR WHOLE VITA THING.
I DON'T WANT TO TALK ABOUT HER.
NEITHER DID I, BUT YOU STARTED THIS.

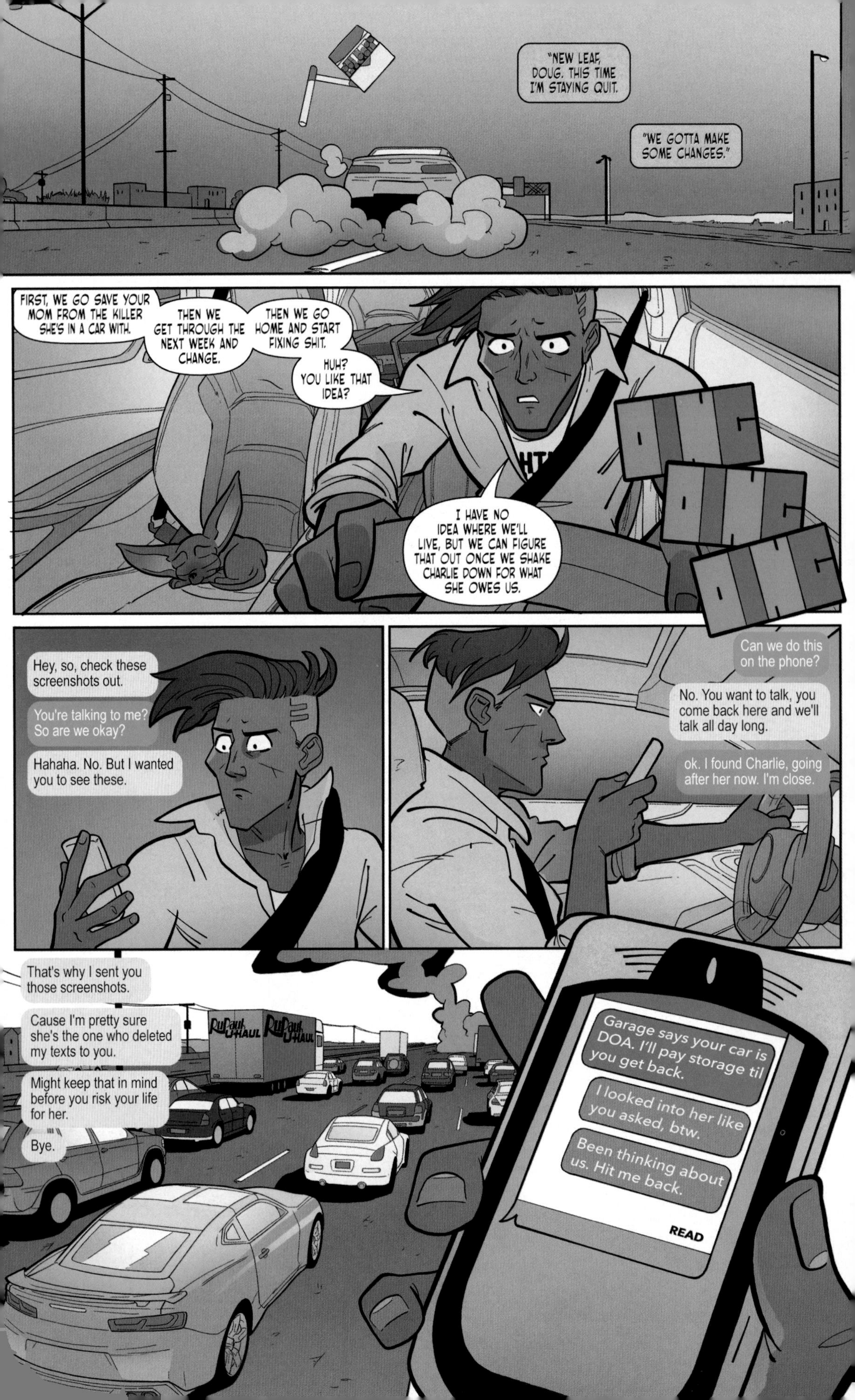

"NEW LEAF, DOUG. THIS TIME I'M STAYING QUIT.
"WE GOTTA MAKE SOME CHANGES."
FIRST, WE GO SAVE YOUR MOM FROM THE KILLER SHE'S IN A CAR WITH.
THEN WE GET THROUGH THE NEXT WEEK AND CHANGE.
THEN WE GO HOME AND START FIXING SHIT.
HUH? YOU LIKE THAT IDEA?
I HAVE NO IDEA WHERE WE'LL LIVE, BUT WE CAN FIGURE THAT OUT ONCE WE SHAKE CHARLIE DOWN FOR WHAT SHE OWES US.
DING
DING
DING
Hey, so, check these screenshots out.
You're talking to me? So are we okay?
Hahaha. No. But I wanted you to see these.
Can we do this on the phone?
No. You want to talk, you come back here and we'll talk all day long.
ok. I found Charlie, going after her now. I'm close.
That's why I sent you those screenshots.
Cause I'm pretty sure she's the one who deleted my texts to you.
Might keep that in mind before you risk your life for her.
Bye.
RuPaul U-HAUL
Garage says your car is DOA. I'll pay storage til you get back.
I looked into her like you asked, btw.
Been thinking about us. Hit me back.
READ

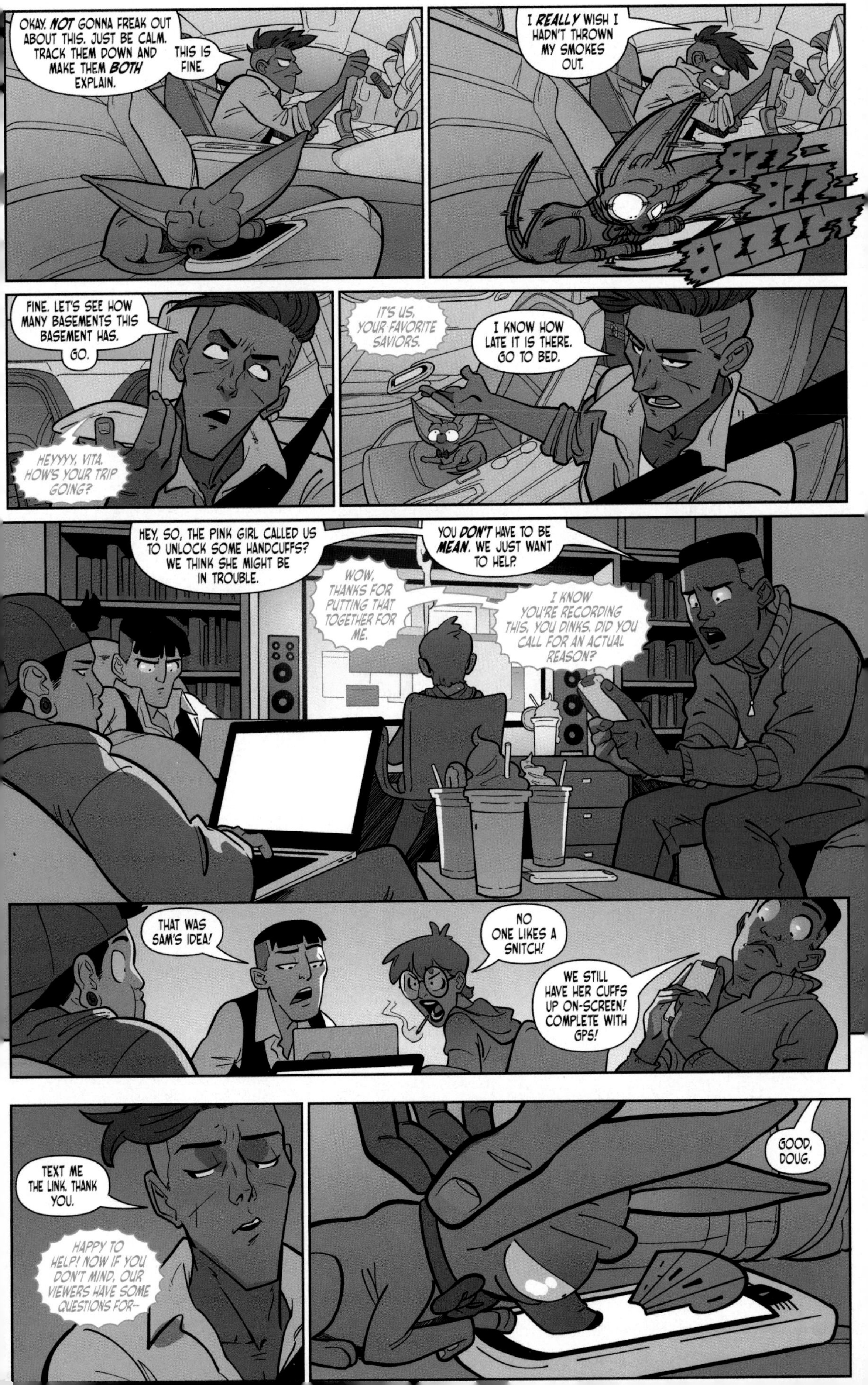
OKAY. NOT GONNA FREAK OUT ABOUT THIS. JUST BE CALM. TRACK THEM DOWN AND MAKE THEM BOTH EXPLAIN.
THIS IS FINE.
I REALLY WISH I HADN'T THROWN MY SMOKES OUT.
BZZ- BZZ- BZZZZZT
FINE. LET'S SEE HOW MANY BASEMENTS THIS BASEMENT HAS.
GO.
HEYYYY, VITA. HOW'S YOUR TRIP GOING?
IT'S US, YOUR FAVORITE SAVIORS.
I KNOW HOW LATE IT IS THERE. GO TO BED.
HEY, SO, THE PINK GIRL CALLED US TO UNLOCK SOME HANDCUFFS? WE THINK SHE MIGHT BE IN TROUBLE.
YOU DON'T HAVE TO BE MEAN. WE JUST WANT TO HELP.
WOW, THANKS FOR PUTTING THAT TOGETHER FOR ME.
I KNOW YOU'RE RECORDING THIS, YOU DINKS. DID YOU CALL FOR AN ACTUAL REASON?
THAT WAS SAM'S IDEA!
NO ONE LIKES A SNITCH!
WE STILL HAVE HER CUFFS UP ON-SCREEN! COMPLETE WITH GPS!
TEXT ME THE LINK. THANK YOU.
HAPPY TO HELP! NOW IF YOU DON'T MIND, OUR VIEWERS HAVE SOME QUESTIONS FOR--
GOOD, DOUG.

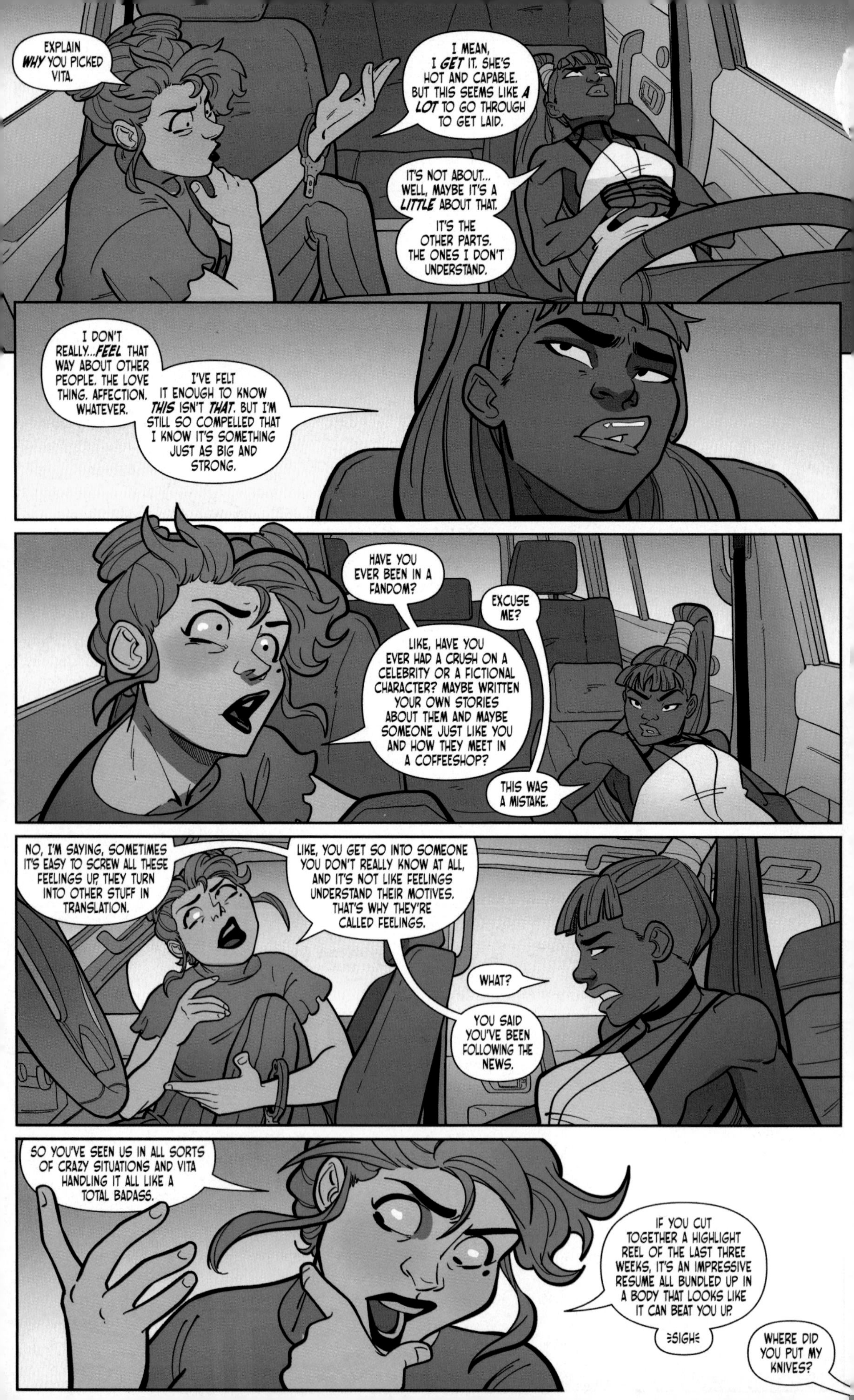
EXPLAIN WHY YOU PICKED VITA.
I MEAN, I GET IT. SHE'S HOT AND CAPABLE. BUT THIS SEEMS LIKE A LOT TO GO THROUGH TO GET LAID.
IT'S NOT ABOUT... WELL, MAYBE IT'S A LITTLE ABOUT THAT.
IT'S THE OTHER PARTS. THE ONES I DON'T UNDERSTAND.
I DON'T REALLY...FEEL THAT WAY ABOUT OTHER PEOPLE. THE LOVE THING. AFFECTION. WHATEVER.
I'VE FELT IT ENOUGH TO KNOW THIS ISN'T THAT. BUT I'M STILL SO COMPELLED THAT I KNOW IT'S SOMETHING JUST AS BIG AND STRONG.
HAVE YOU EVER BEEN IN A FANDOM?
EXCUSE ME?
LIKE, HAVE YOU EVER HAD A CRUSH ON A CELEBRITY OR A FICTIONAL CHARACTER? MAYBE WRITTEN YOUR OWN STORIES ABOUT THEM AND MAYBE SOMEONE JUST LIKE YOU AND HOW THEY MEET IN A COFFEESHOP?
THIS WAS A MISTAKE.
NO, I'M SAYING, SOMETIMES IT'S EASY TO SCREW ALL THESE FEELINGS UP. THEY TURN INTO OTHER STUFF IN TRANSLATION.
LIKE, YOU GET SO INTO SOMEONE YOU DON'T REALLY KNOW AT ALL, AND IT'S NOT LIKE FEELINGS UNDERSTAND THEIR MOTIVES. THAT'S WHY THEY'RE CALLED FEELINGS.
WHAT?
YOU SAID YOU'VE BEEN FOLLOWING THE NEWS.
SO YOU'VE SEEN US IN ALL SORTS OF CRAZY SITUATIONS AND VITA HANDLING IT ALL LIKE A TOTAL BADASS.
IF YOU CUT TOGETHER A HIGHLIGHT REEL OF THE LAST THREE WEEKS, IT'S AN IMPRESSIVE RESUME ALL BUNDLED UP IN A BODY THAT LOOKS LIKE IT CAN BEAT YOU UP.
ƎSIGHƐ
WHERE DID YOU PUT MY KNIVES?

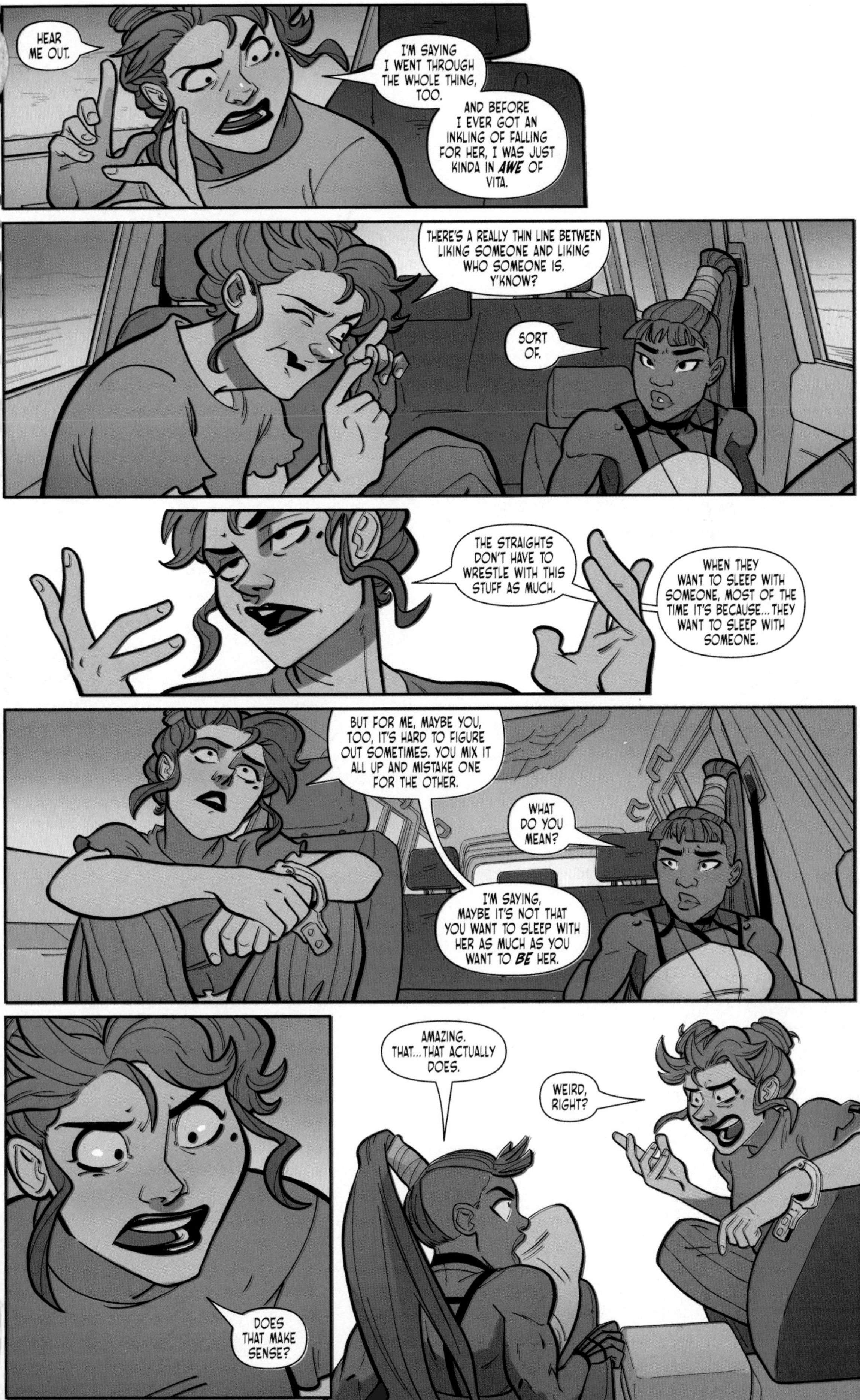
HEAR ME OUT.
I'M SAYING I WENT THROUGH THE WHOLE THING, TOO.
AND BEFORE I EVER GOT AN INKLING OF FALLING FOR HER, I WAS JUST KINDA IN *AWE* OF VITA.
THERE'S A REALLY THIN LINE BETWEEN LIKING SOMEONE AND LIKING WHO SOMEONE IS. Y'KNOW?
SORT OF.
THE STRAIGHTS DON'T HAVE TO WRESTLE WITH THIS STUFF AS MUCH.
WHEN THEY WANT TO SLEEP WITH SOMEONE, MOST OF THE TIME IT'S BECAUSE... THEY WANT TO SLEEP WITH SOMEONE.
BUT FOR ME, MAYBE YOU, TOO, IT'S HARD TO FIGURE OUT SOMETIMES. YOU MIX IT ALL UP AND MISTAKE ONE FOR THE OTHER.
WHAT DO YOU MEAN?
I'M SAYING, MAYBE IT'S NOT THAT YOU WANT TO SLEEP WITH HER AS MUCH AS YOU WANT TO *BE* HER.
DOES THAT MAKE SENSE?
AMAZING. THAT... THAT ACTUALLY DOES.
WEIRD, RIGHT?

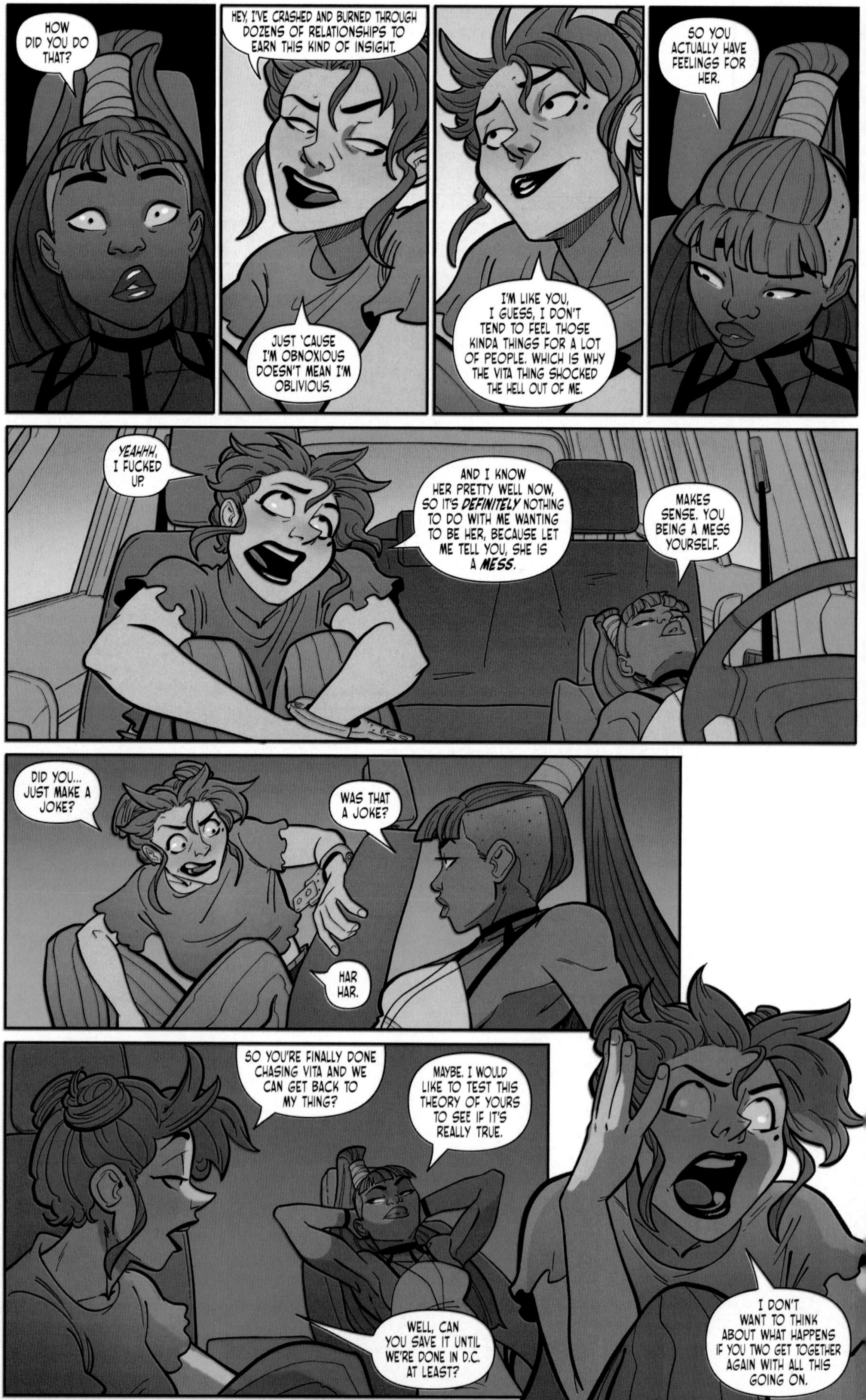
HOW DID YOU DO THAT?
HEY, I'VE CRASHED AND BURNED THROUGH DOZENS OF RELATIONSHIPS TO EARN THIS KIND OF INSIGHT.
JUST 'CAUSE I'M OBNOXIOUS DOESN'T MEAN I'M OBLIVIOUS.
I'M LIKE YOU, I GUESS, I DON'T TEND TO FEEL THOSE KINDA THINGS FOR A LOT OF PEOPLE. WHICH IS WHY THE VITA THING SHOCKED THE HELL OUT OF ME.
SO YOU ACTUALLY HAVE FEELINGS FOR HER.
YEAHHH, I FUCKED UP.
AND I KNOW HER PRETTY WELL NOW, SO IT'S DEFINITELY NOTHING TO DO WITH ME WANTING TO BE HER, BECAUSE LET ME TELL YOU, SHE IS A MESS.
MAKES SENSE. YOU BEING A MESS YOURSELF.
DID YOU... JUST MAKE A JOKE?
WAS THAT A JOKE?
HAR HAR.
SO YOU'RE FINALLY DONE CHASING VITA AND WE CAN GET BACK TO MY THING?
MAYBE. I WOULD LIKE TO TEST THIS THEORY OF YOURS TO SEE IF IT'S REALLY TRUE.
WELL, CAN YOU SAVE IT UNTIL WE'RE DONE IN D.C. AT LEAST?
I DON'T WANT TO THINK ABOUT WHAT HAPPENS IF YOU TWO GET TOGETHER AGAIN WITH ALL THIS GOING ON.

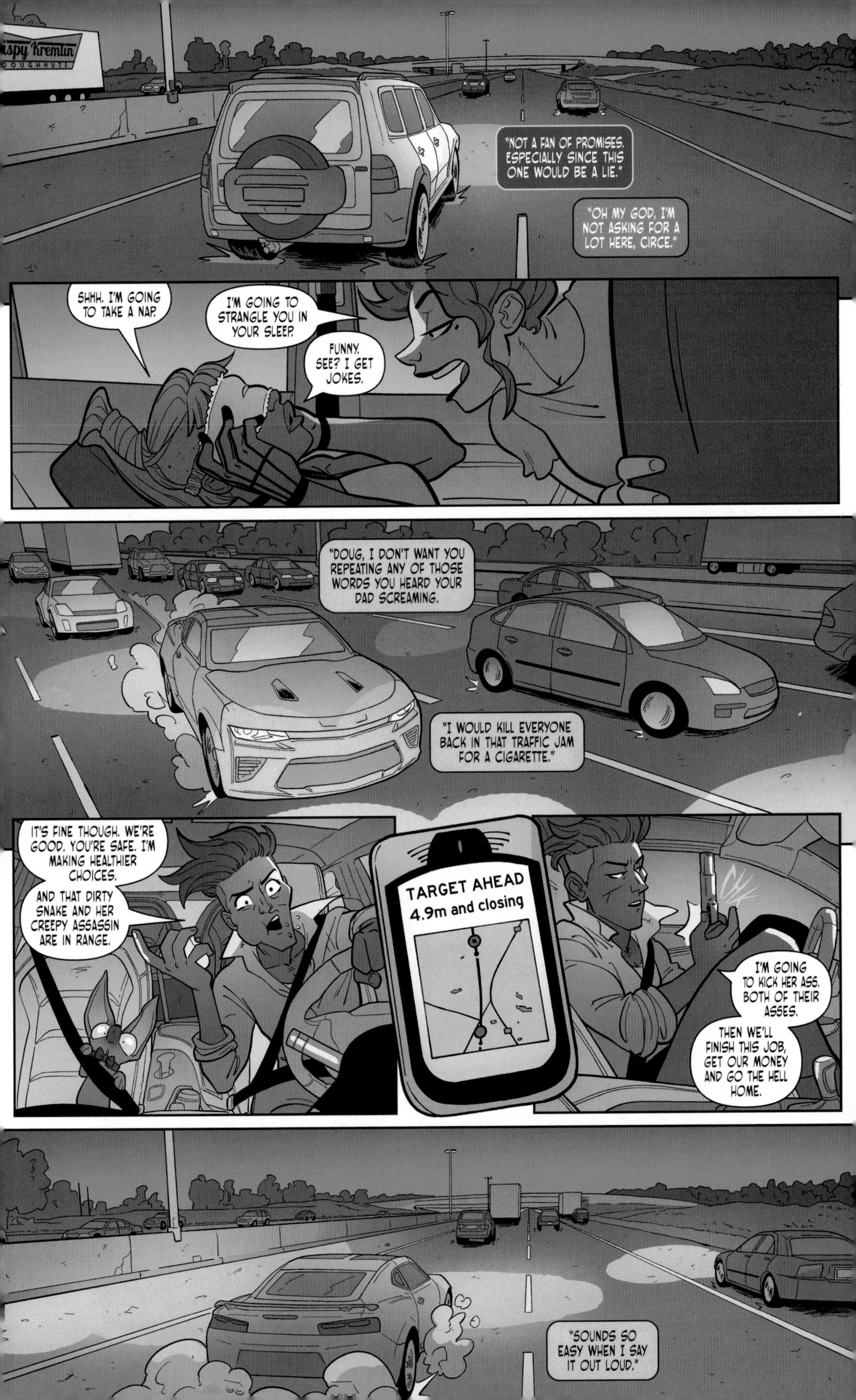

Krispy Kremlin DOUGHNUTS
"NOT A FAN OF PROMISES. ESPECIALLY SINCE THIS ONE WOULD BE A LIE."
"OH MY GOD, I'M NOT ASKING FOR A LOT HERE, CIRCE."
SHHH. I'M GOING TO TAKE A NAP.
I'M GOING TO STRANGLE YOU IN YOUR SLEEP.
FUNNY. SEE? I GET JOKES.
"DOUG, I DON'T WANT YOU REPEATING ANY OF THOSE WORDS YOU HEARD YOUR DAD SCREAMING.
"I WOULD KILL EVERYONE BACK IN THAT TRAFFIC JAM FOR A CIGARETTE."
IT'S FINE THOUGH. WE'RE GOOD. YOU'RE SAFE. I'M MAKING HEALTHIER CHOICES.
AND THAT DIRTY SNAKE AND HER CREEPY ASSASSIN ARE IN RANGE.
TARGET AHEAD
4.9m and closing
I'M GOING TO KICK HER ASS. BOTH OF THEIR ASSES.
THEN WE'LL FINISH THIS JOB, GET OUR MONEY AND GO THE HELL HOME.
"SOUNDS SO EASY WHEN I SAY IT OUT LOUD."

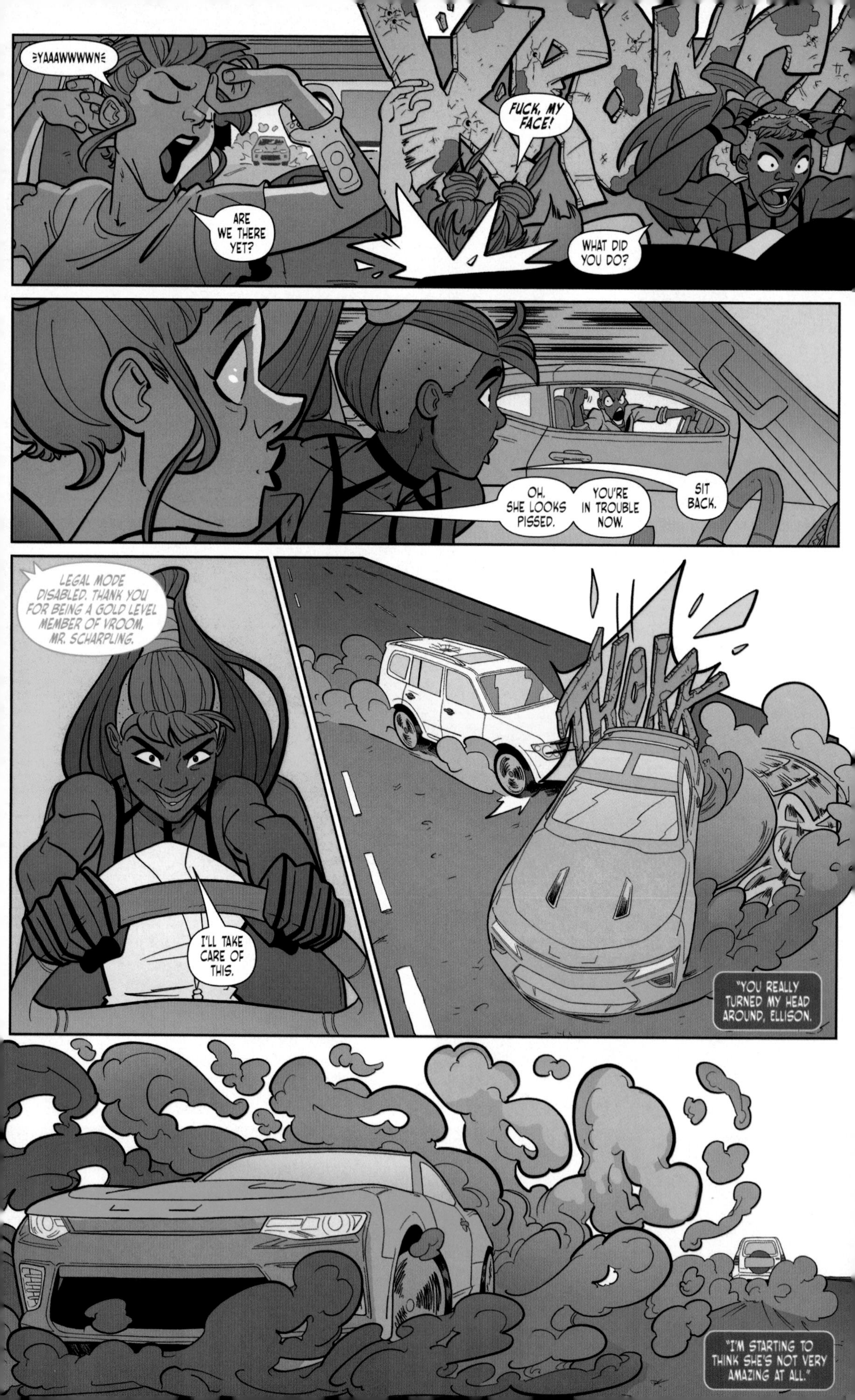
YAAAWWWWN
ARE WE THERE YET?
FUCK, MY FACE!
WHAT DID YOU DO?
OH. SHE LOOKS PISSED.
YOU'RE IN TROUBLE NOW.
SIT BACK.
LEGAL MODE DISABLED. THANK YOU FOR BEING A GOLD LEVEL MEMBER OF VROOM, MR. SCHARPLING.
I'LL TAKE CARE OF THIS.
THOK
"YOU REALLY TURNED MY HEAD AROUND, ELLISON.
"I'M STARTING TO THINK SHE'S NOT VERY AMAZING AT ALL."

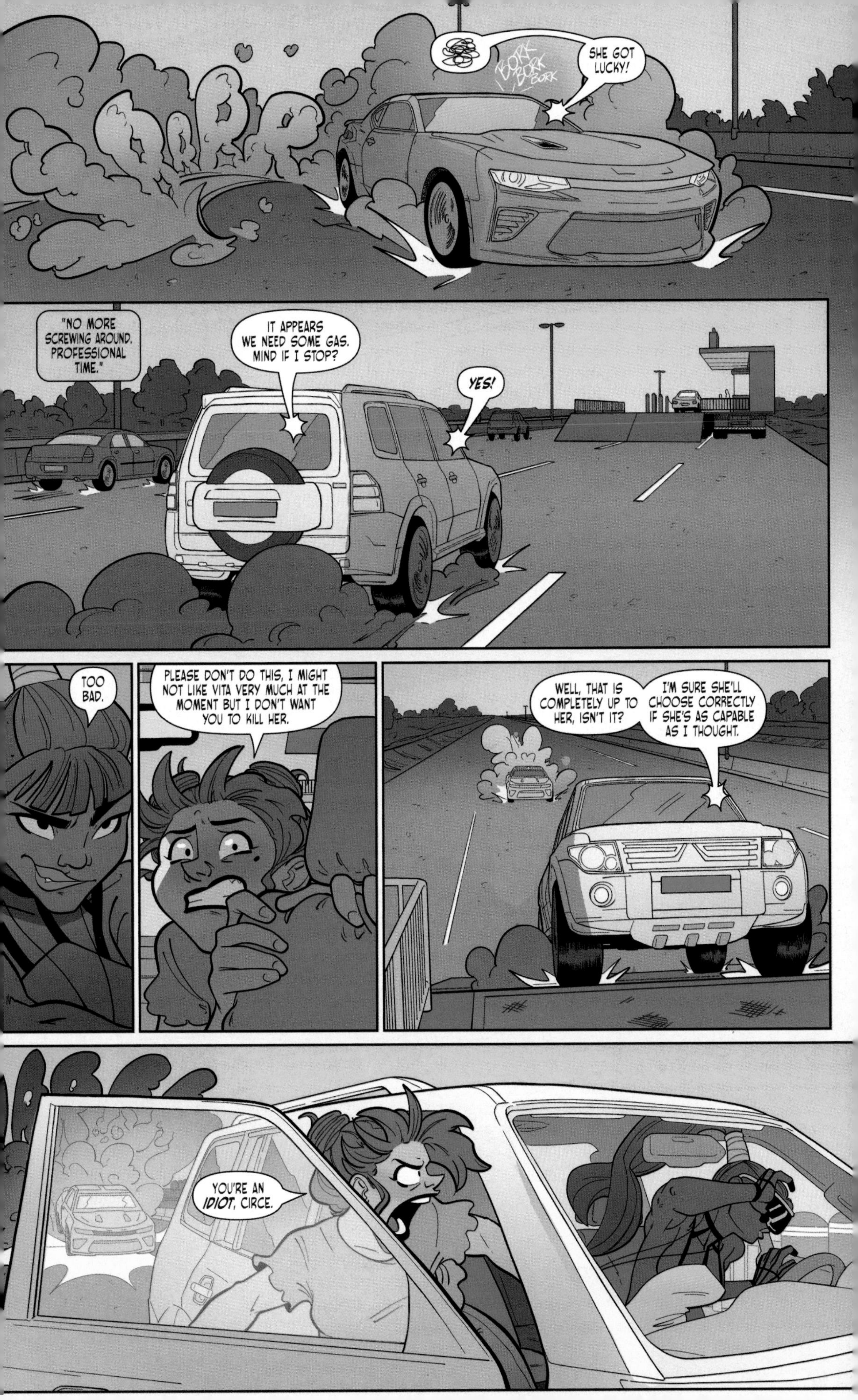
BORK BORK BORK
SHE GOT LUCKY!
"NO MORE SCREWING AROUND. PROFESSIONAL TIME."
IT APPEARS WE NEED SOME GAS. MIND IF I STOP?
YES!
TOO BAD.
PLEASE DON'T DO THIS, I MIGHT NOT LIKE VITA VERY MUCH AT THE MOMENT BUT I DON'T WANT YOU TO KILL HER.
WELL, THAT IS COMPLETELY UP TO HER, ISN'T IT?
I'M SURE SHE'LL CHOOSE CORRECTLY IF SHE'S AS CAPABLE AS I THOUGHT.
YOU'RE AN *IDIOT*, CIRCE.

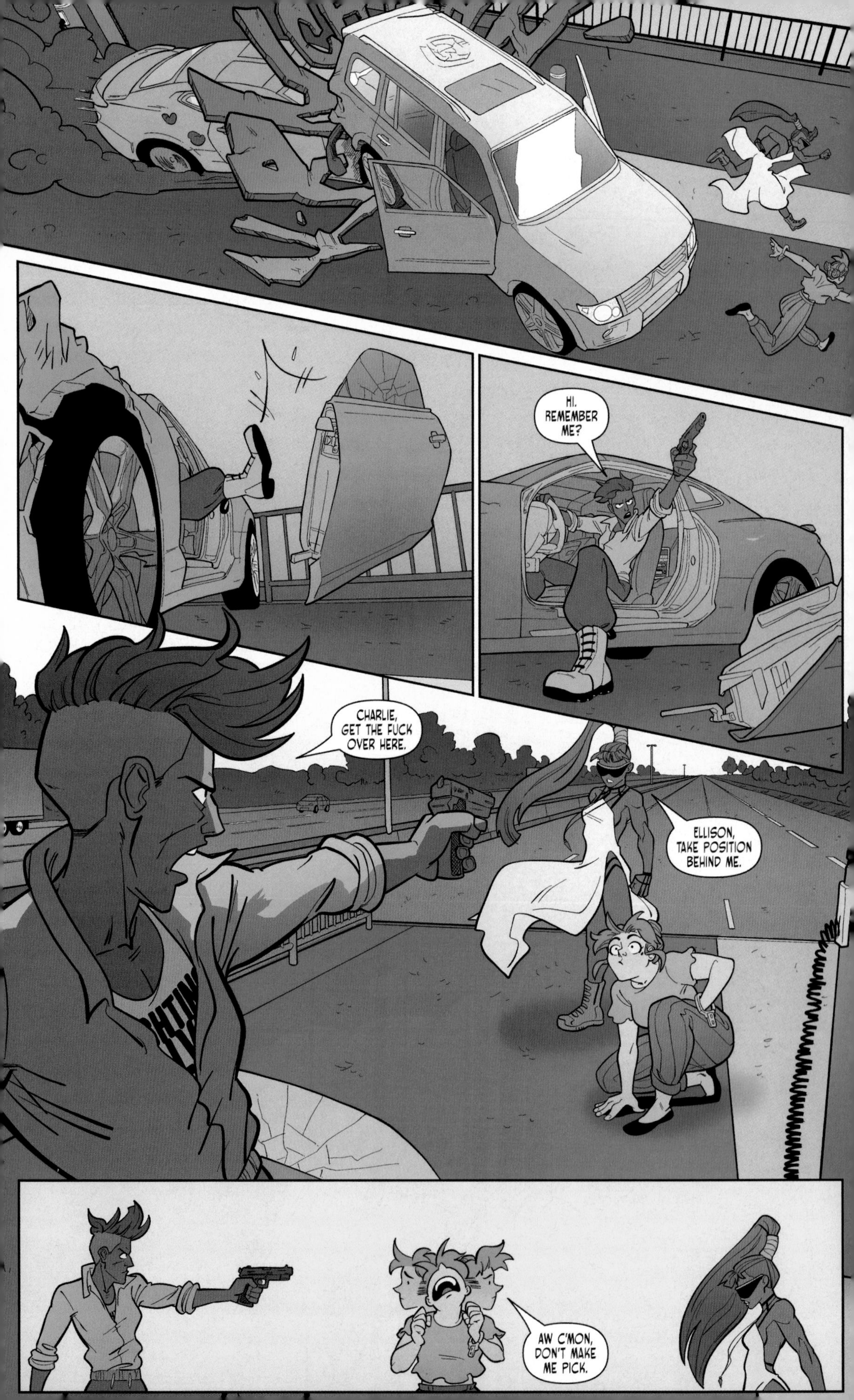
HI. REMEMBER ME?
CHARLIE, GET THE FUCK OVER HERE.
ELLISON, TAKE POSITION BEHIND ME.
AW C'MON, DON'T MAKE ME PICK.

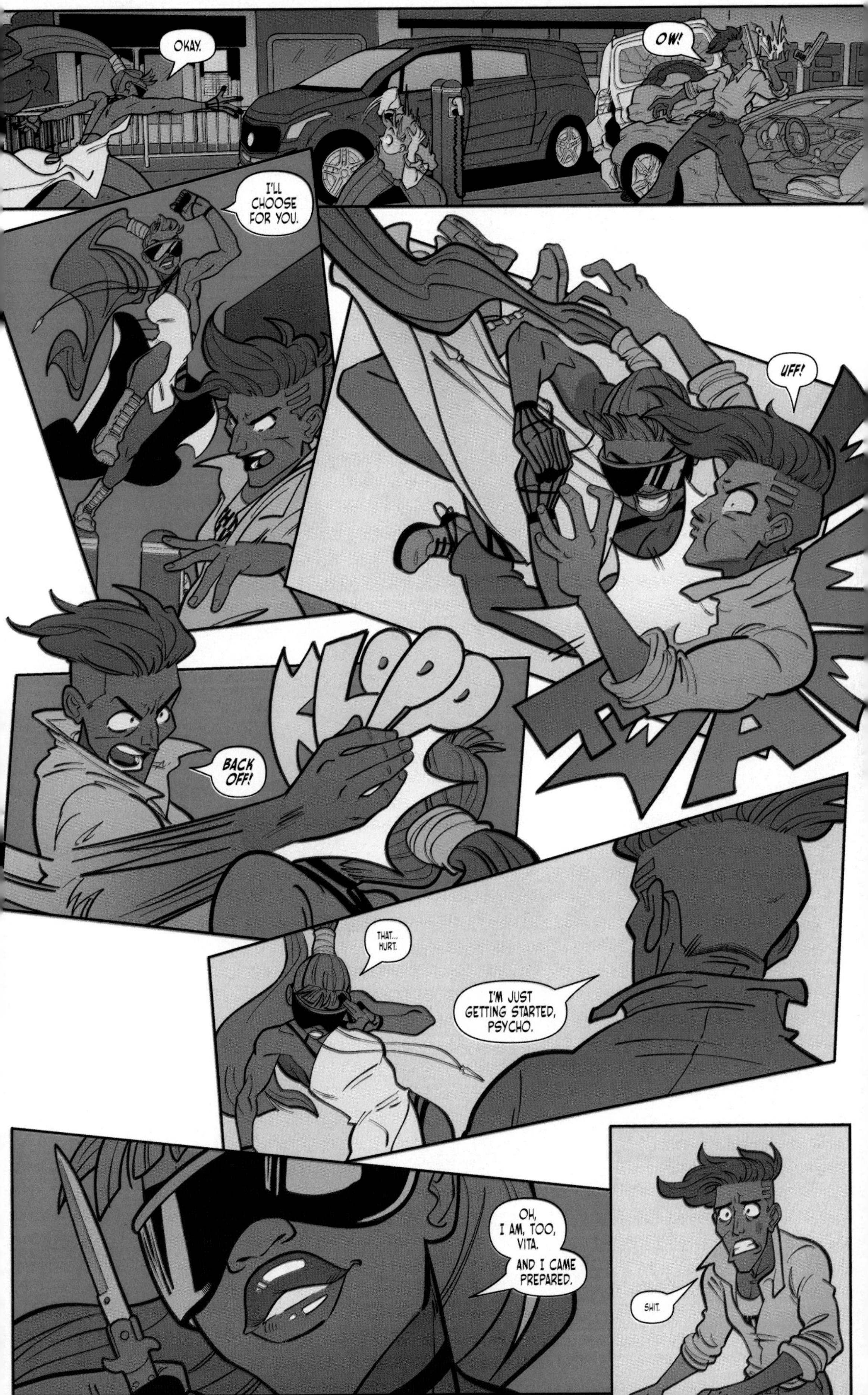
OKAY.
OW!
I'LL CHOOSE FOR YOU.
UFF!
BACK OFF!
THAT... HURT.
I'M JUST GETTING STARTED, PSYCHO.
OH, I AM, TOO, VITA.
AND I CAME PREPARED.
SHIT.

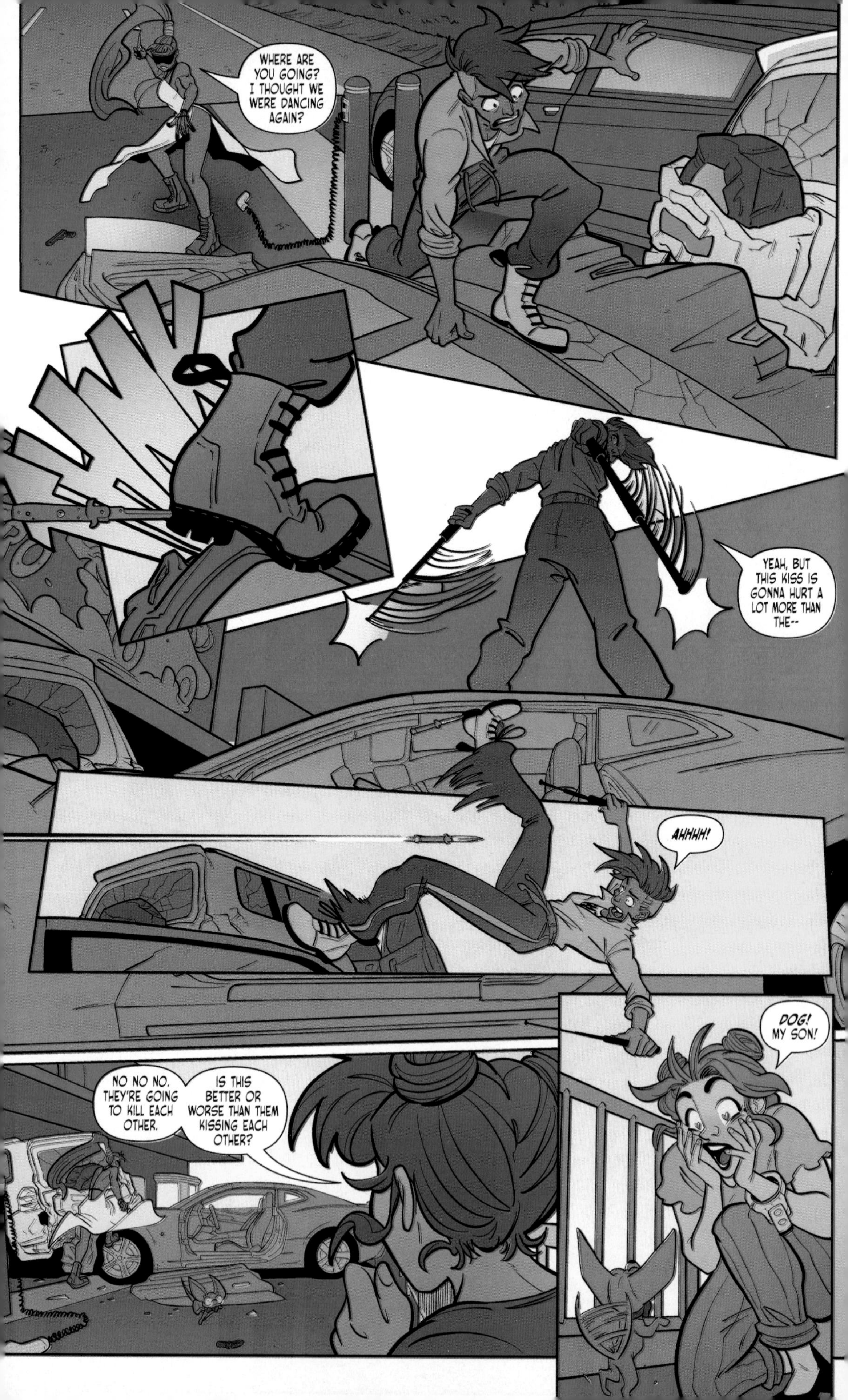
WHERE ARE YOU GOING? I THOUGHT WE WERE DANCING AGAIN?
YEAH, BUT THIS KISS IS GONNA HURT A LOT MORE THAN THE--
AHHHH!
DOG! MY SON!
NO NO NO. THEY'RE GOING TO KILL EACH OTHER.
IS THIS BETTER OR WORSE THAN THEM KISSING EACH OTHER?

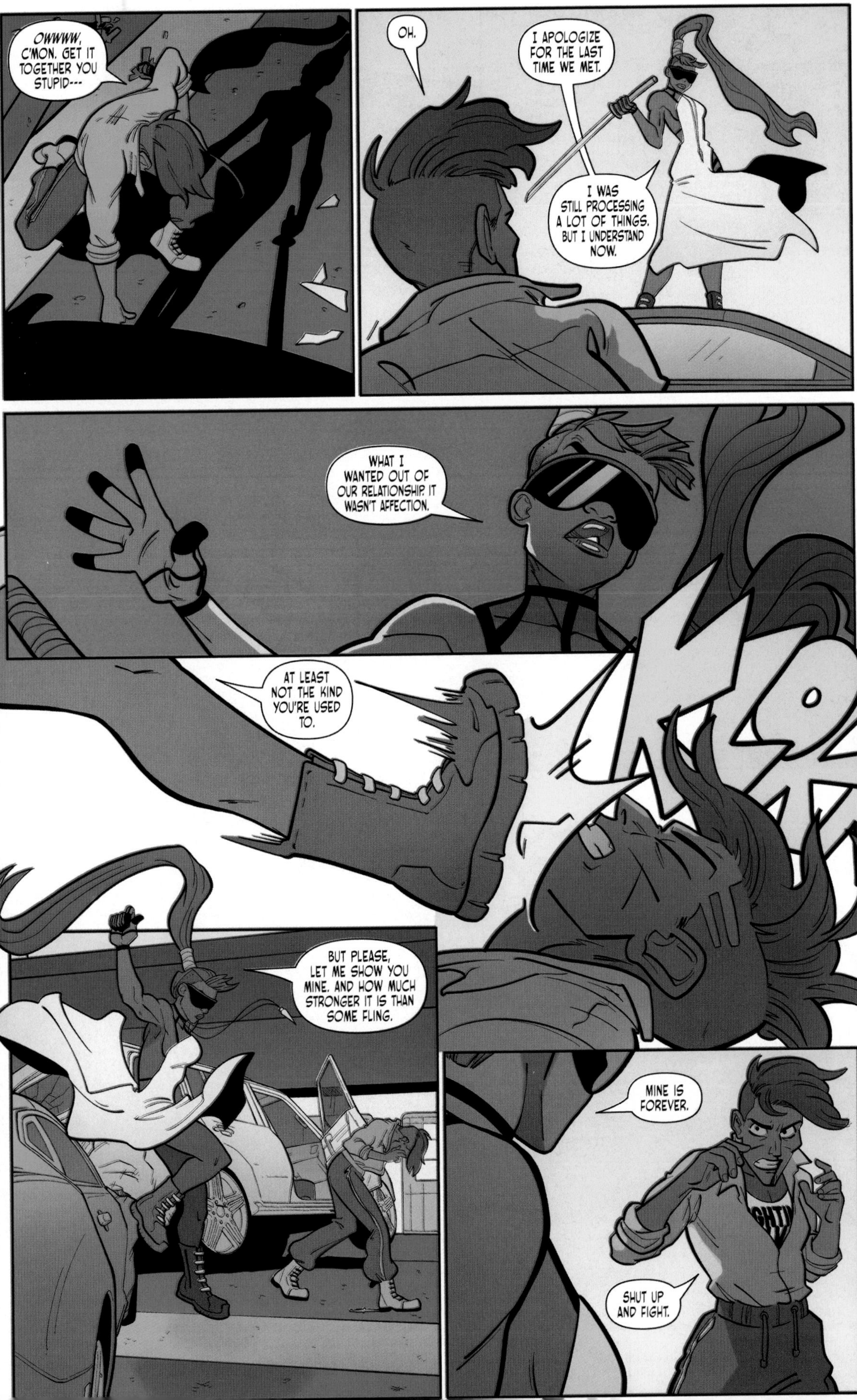
OWWWW, C'MON. GET IT TOGETHER YOU STUPID---
OH.
I APOLOGIZE FOR THE LAST TIME WE MET.
I WAS STILL PROCESSING A LOT OF THINGS. BUT I UNDERSTAND NOW.
WHAT I WANTED OUT OF OUR RELATIONSHIP. IT WASN'T AFFECTION.
AT LEAST NOT THE KIND YOU'RE USED TO.
BUT PLEASE, LET ME SHOW YOU MINE. AND HOW MUCH STRONGER IT IS THAN SOME FLING.
MINE IS FOREVER.
SHUT UP AND FIGHT.

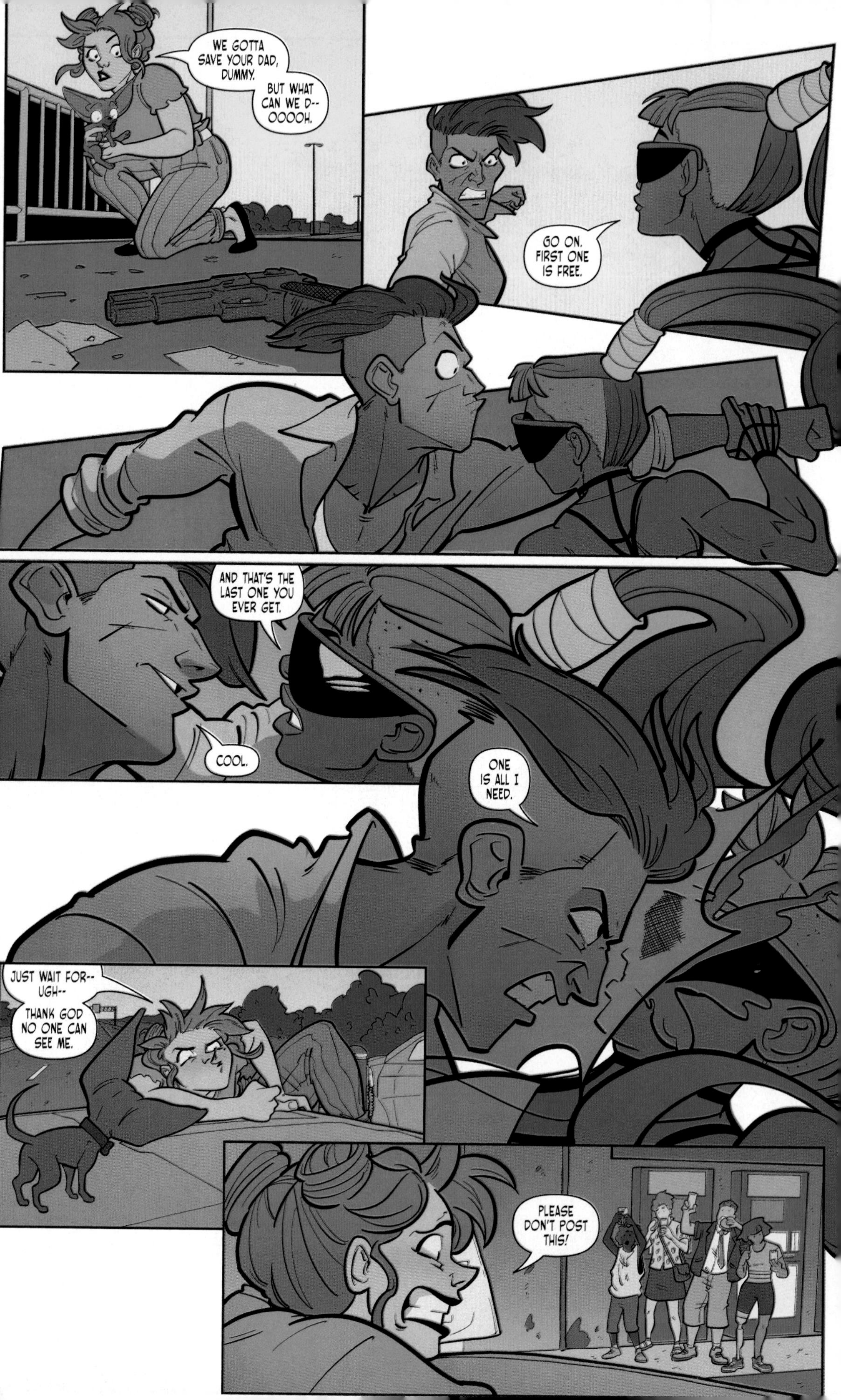
WE GOTTA SAVE YOUR DAD, DUMMY.
BUT WHAT CAN WE D-- OOOOH.
GO ON. FIRST ONE IS FREE.
AND THAT'S THE LAST ONE YOU EVER GET.
COOL.
ONE IS ALL I NEED.
JUST WAIT FOR-- UGH--
THANK GOD NO ONE CAN SEE ME.
PLEASE DON'T POST THIS!

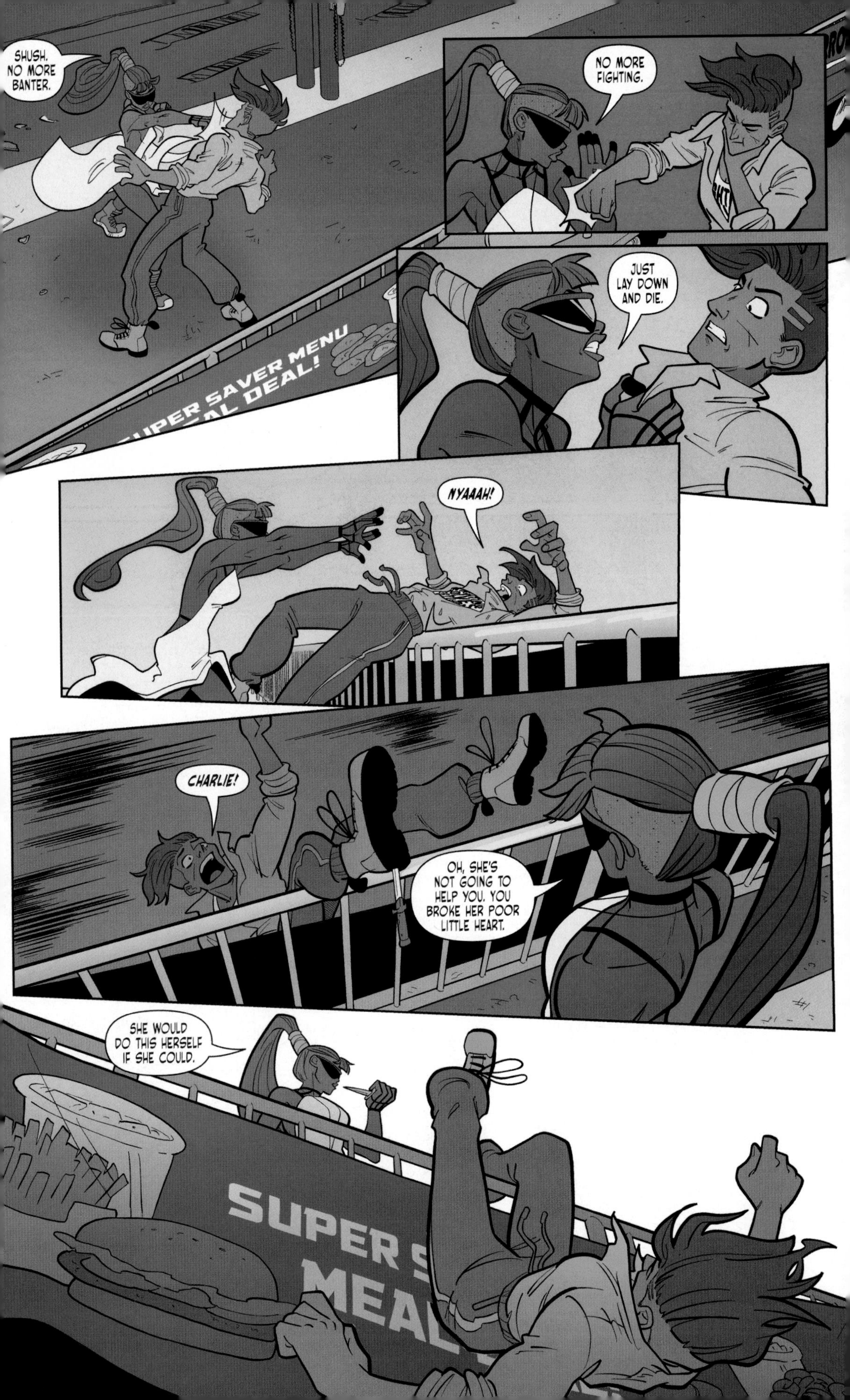
SHUSH. NO MORE BANTER.
NO MORE FIGHTING.
JUST LAY DOWN AND DIE.
SUPER SAVER MENU
AL DEAL!
NYAAAH!
CHARLIE!
OH, SHE'S NOT GOING TO HELP YOU. YOU BROKE HER POOR LITTLE HEART.
SHE WOULD DO THIS HERSELF IF SHE COULD.
SUPER S
MEAL

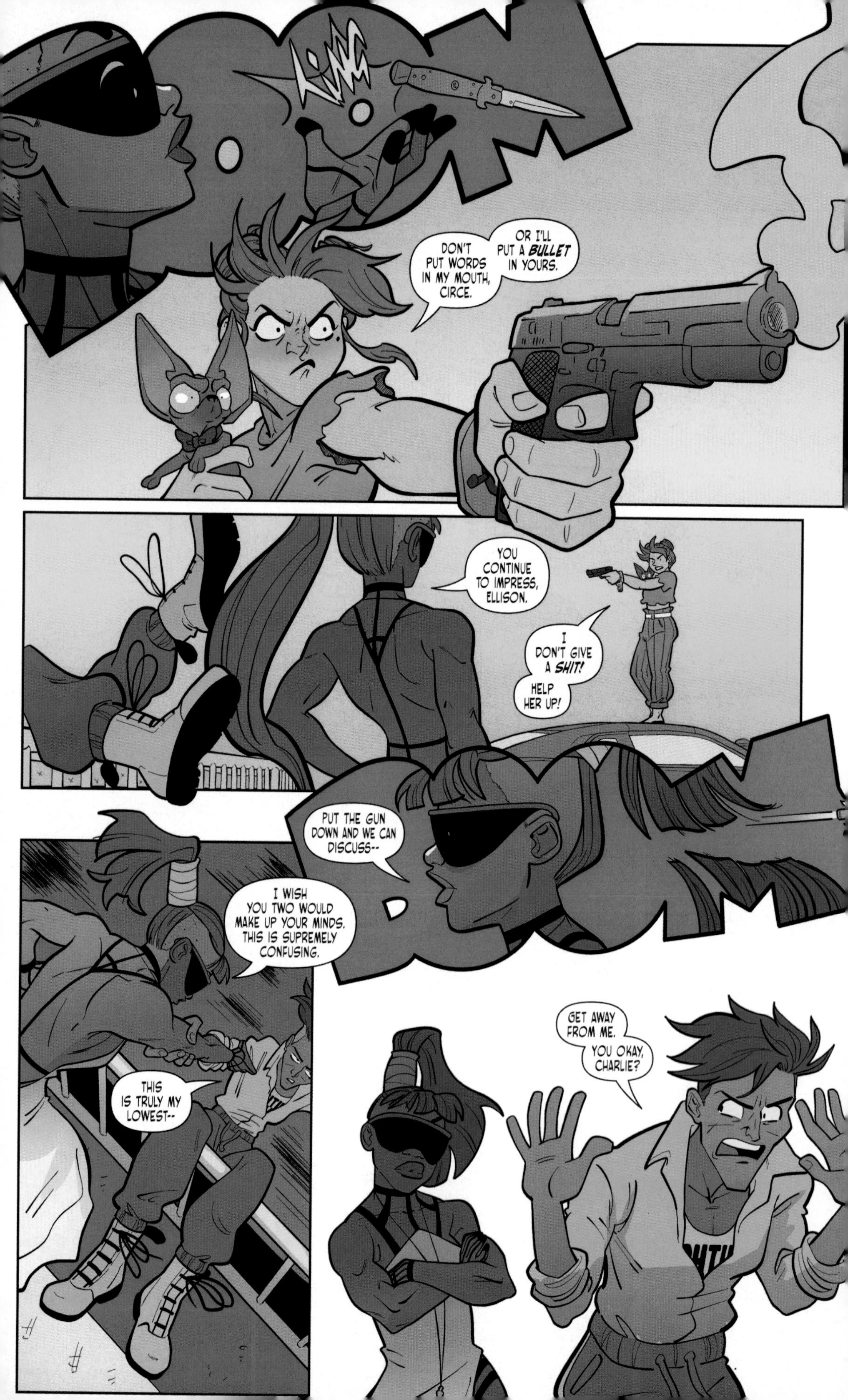
KING
DON'T PUT WORDS IN MY MOUTH, CIRCE.
OR I'LL PUT A BULLET IN YOURS.
YOU CONTINUE TO IMPRESS, ELLISON.
I DON'T GIVE A SHIT!
HELP HER UP!
PUT THE GUN DOWN AND WE CAN DISCUSS--
I WISH YOU TWO WOULD MAKE UP YOUR MINDS. THIS IS SUPREMELY CONFUSING.
THIS IS TRULY MY LOWEST--
GET AWAY FROM ME.
YOU OKAY, CHARLIE?

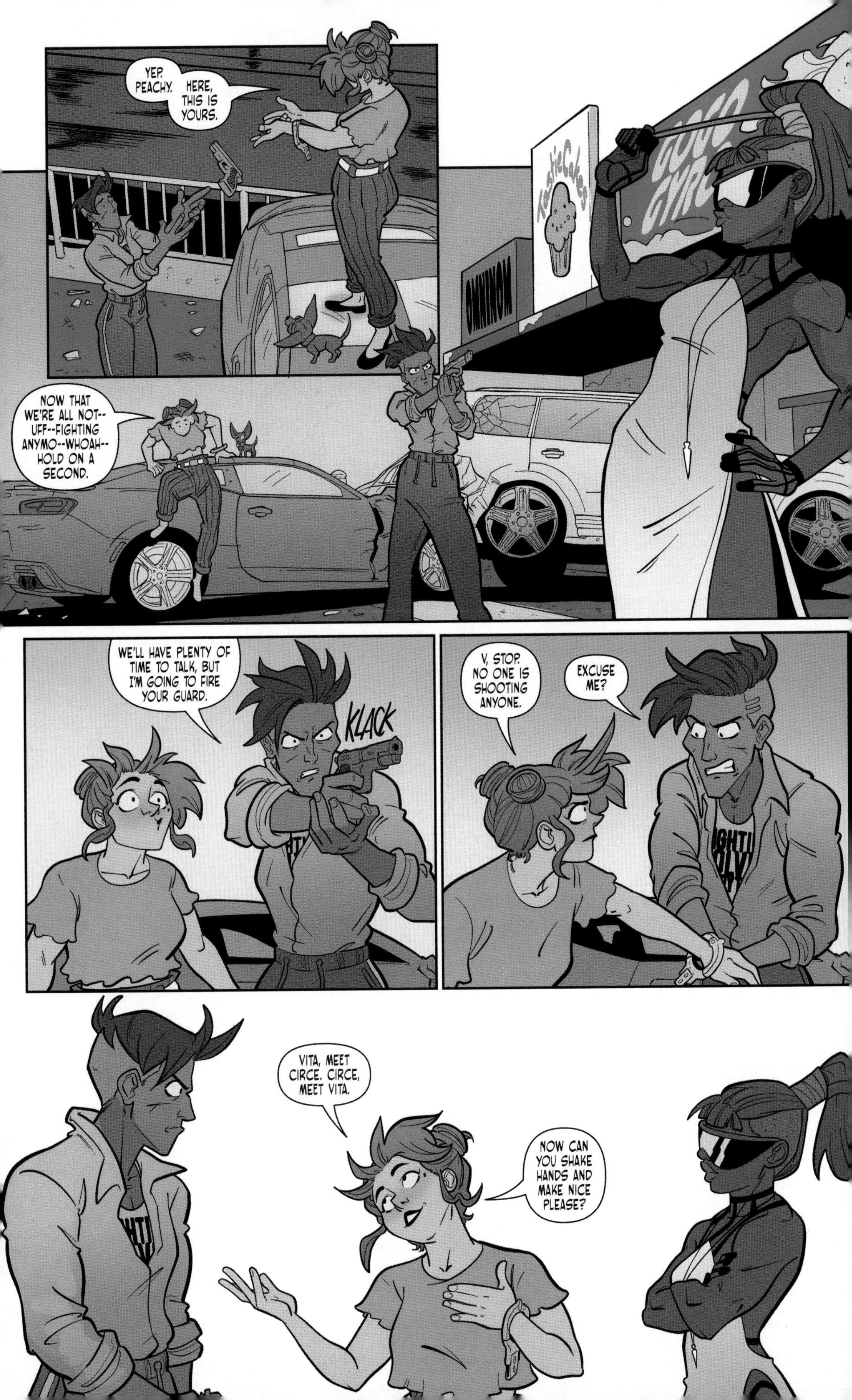
YEP. PEACHY.
HERE, THIS IS YOURS.
TastieCakes
OMNINOM
NOW THAT WE'RE ALL NOT--UFF--FIGHTING ANYMO--WHOAH--HOLD ON A SECOND.
WE'LL HAVE PLENTY OF TIME TO TALK, BUT I'M GOING TO FIRE YOUR GUARD.
KLACK
V, STOP. NO ONE IS SHOOTING ANYONE.
EXCUSE ME?
VITA, MEET CIRCE. CIRCE, MEET VITA.
NOW CAN YOU SHAKE HANDS AND MAKE NICE PLEASE?

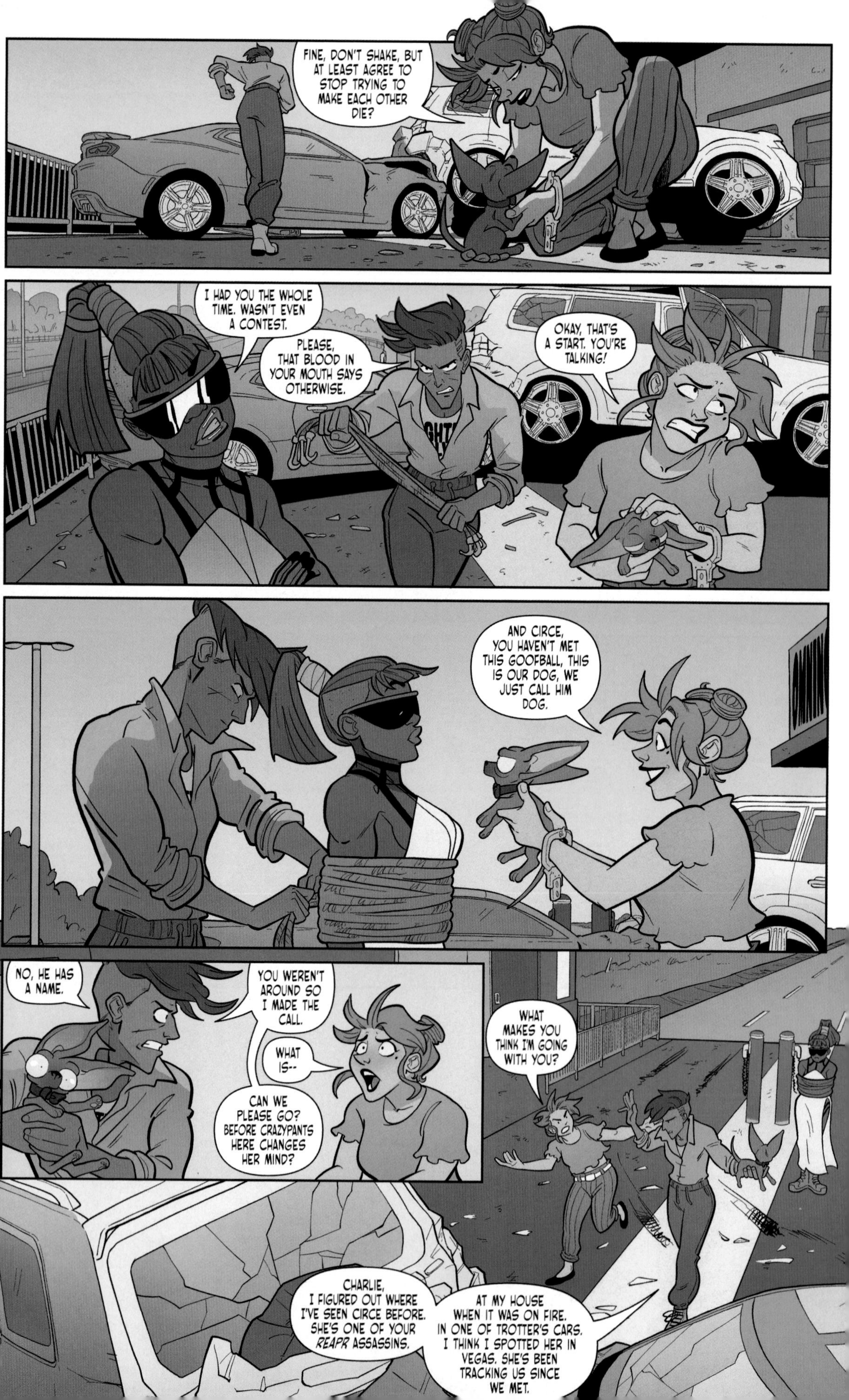
FINE, DON'T SHAKE, BUT AT LEAST AGREE TO STOP TRYING TO MAKE EACH OTHER DIE?
I HAD YOU THE WHOLE TIME. WASN'T EVEN A CONTEST.
PLEASE, THAT BLOOD IN YOUR MOUTH SAYS OTHERWISE.
OKAY, THAT'S A START. YOU'RE TALKING!
AND CIRCE, YOU HAVEN'T MET THIS GOOFBALL, THIS IS OUR DOG, WE JUST CALL HIM DOG.
NO, HE HAS A NAME.
YOU WEREN'T AROUND SO I MADE THE CALL.
WHAT IS--
CAN WE PLEASE GO? BEFORE CRAZYPANTS HERE CHANGES HER MIND?
WHAT MAKES YOU THINK I'M GOING WITH YOU?
CHARLIE, I FIGURED OUT WHERE I'VE SEEN CIRCE BEFORE. SHE'S ONE OF YOUR *REAPR* ASSASSINS.
AT MY HOUSE WHEN IT WAS ON FIRE. IN ONE OF TROTTER'S CARS. I THINK I SPOTTED HER IN VEGAS. SHE'S BEEN TRACKING US SINCE WE MET.

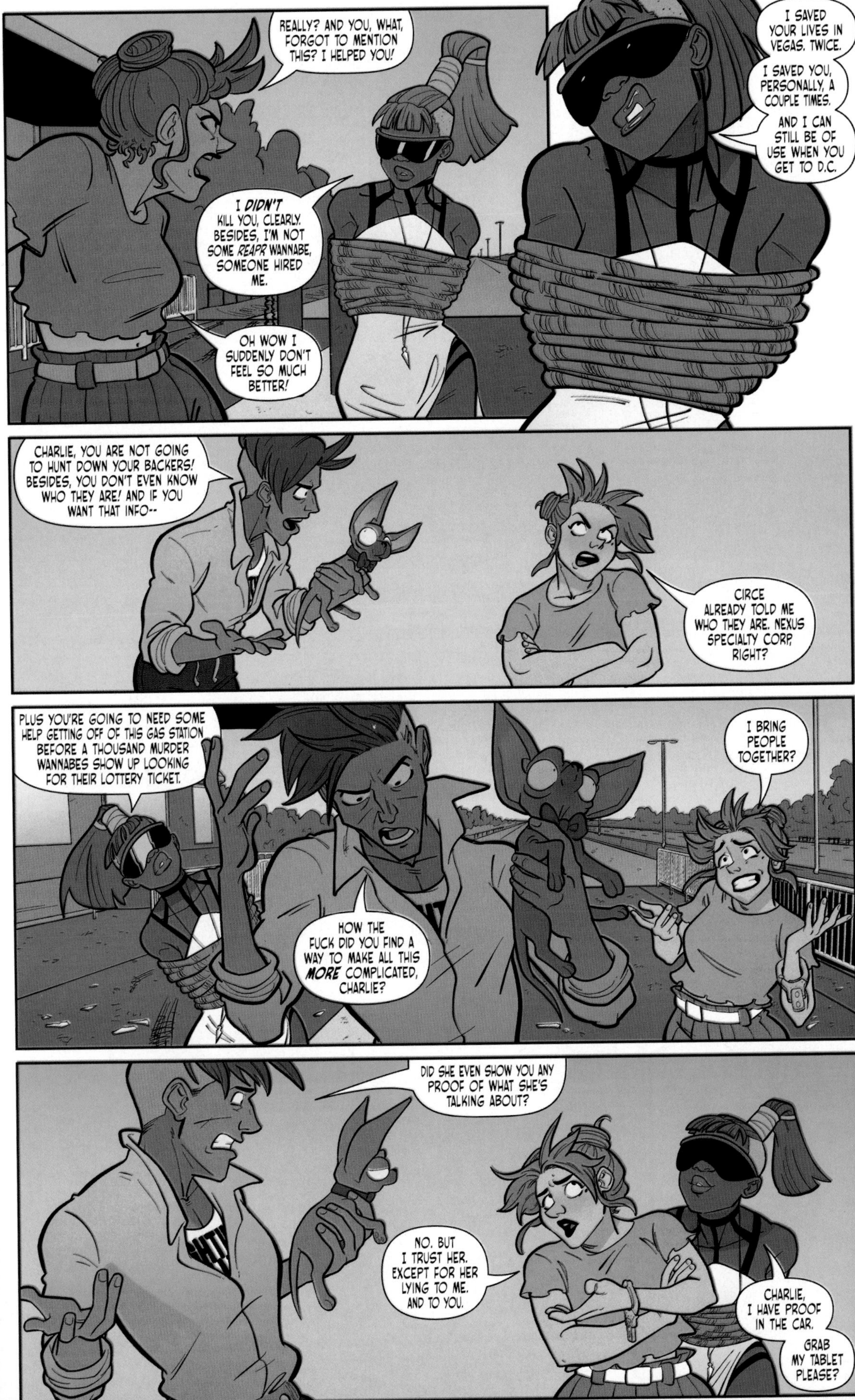
REALLY? AND YOU, WHAT, FORGOT TO MENTION THIS? I HELPED YOU!
I DIDN'T KILL YOU, CLEARLY. BESIDES, I'M NOT SOME REAPR WANNABE, SOMEONE HIRED ME.
OH WOW I SUDDENLY DON'T FEEL SO MUCH BETTER!
I SAVED YOUR LIVES IN VEGAS. TWICE.
I SAVED YOU, PERSONALLY, A COUPLE TIMES.
AND I CAN STILL BE OF USE WHEN YOU GET TO D.C.
CHARLIE, YOU ARE NOT GOING TO HUNT DOWN YOUR BACKERS! BESIDES, YOU DON'T EVEN KNOW WHO THEY ARE! AND IF YOU WANT THAT INFO--
CIRCE ALREADY TOLD ME WHO THEY ARE. NEXUS SPECIALTY CORP, RIGHT?
PLUS YOU'RE GOING TO NEED SOME HELP GETTING OFF OF THIS GAS STATION BEFORE A THOUSAND MURDER WANNABES SHOW UP LOOKING FOR THEIR LOTTERY TICKET.
HOW THE FUCK DID YOU FIND A WAY TO MAKE ALL THIS MORE COMPLICATED, CHARLIE?
I BRING PEOPLE TOGETHER?
DID SHE EVEN SHOW YOU ANY PROOF OF WHAT SHE'S TALKING ABOUT?
NO. BUT I TRUST HER. EXCEPT FOR HER LYING TO ME. AND TO YOU.
CHARLIE, I HAVE PROOF IN THE CAR.
GRAB MY TABLET PLEASE?

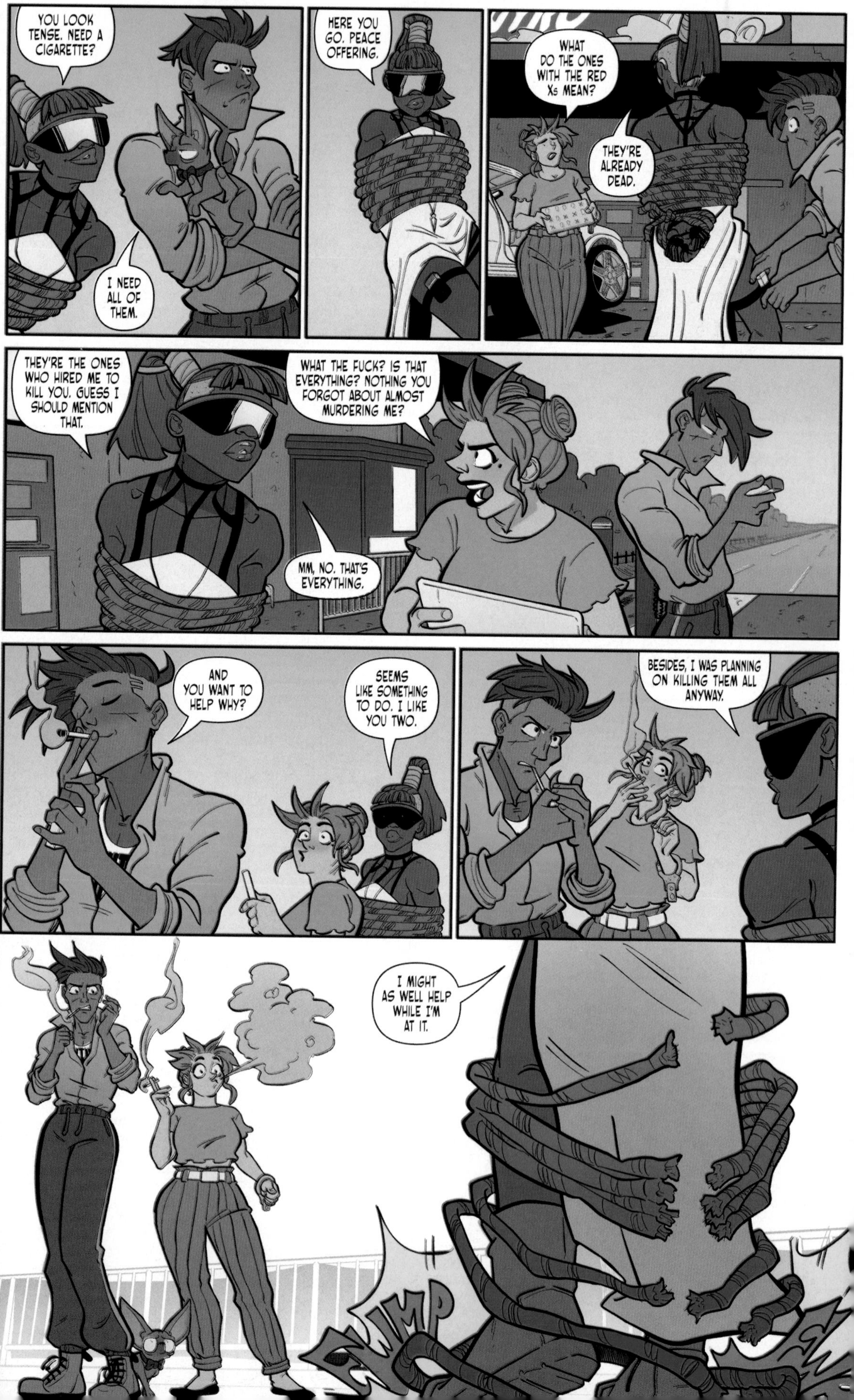
YOU LOOK TENSE. NEED A CIGARETTE?
I NEED ALL OF THEM.
HERE YOU GO. PEACE OFFERING.
WHAT DO THE ONES WITH THE RED Xs MEAN?
THEY'RE ALREADY DEAD.
THEY'RE THE ONES WHO HIRED ME TO KILL YOU. GUESS I SHOULD MENTION THAT.
WHAT THE FUCK? IS THAT EVERYTHING? NOTHING YOU FORGOT ABOUT ALMOST MURDERING ME?
MM, NO. THAT'S EVERYTHING.
AND YOU WANT TO HELP WHY?
SEEMS LIKE SOMETHING TO DO. I LIKE YOU TWO.
BESIDES, I WAS PLANNING ON KILLING THEM ALL ANYWAY.
I MIGHT AS WELL HELP WHILE I'M AT IT.
THUMP

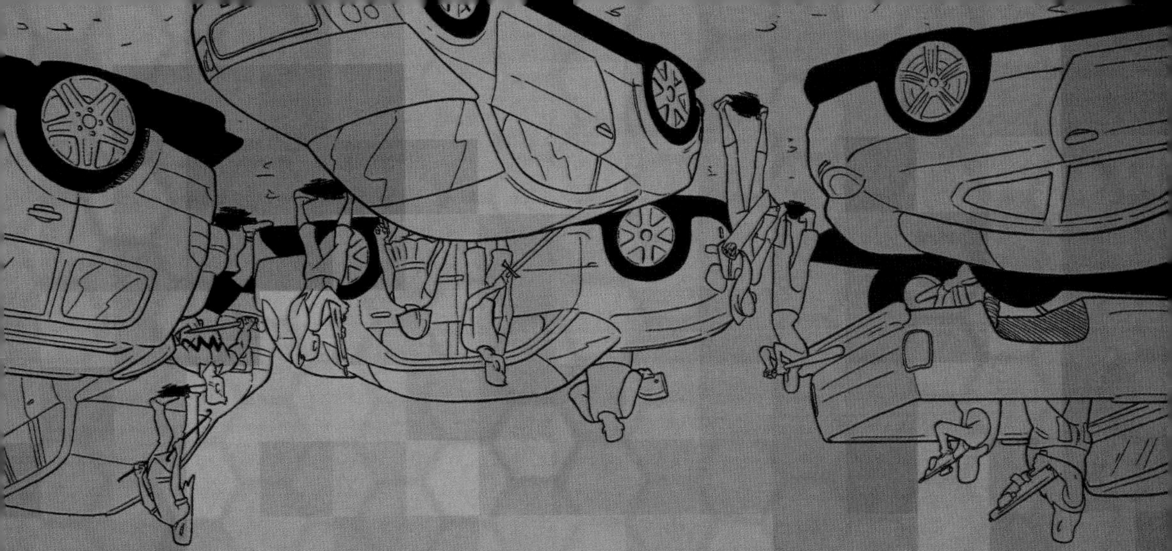

CHAPTER SIXTEEN

THE FEAR

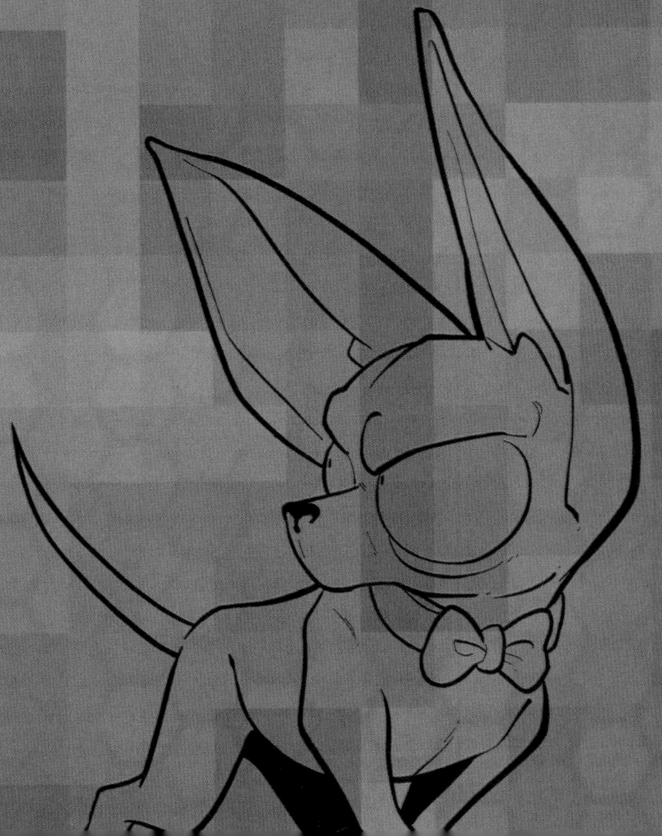

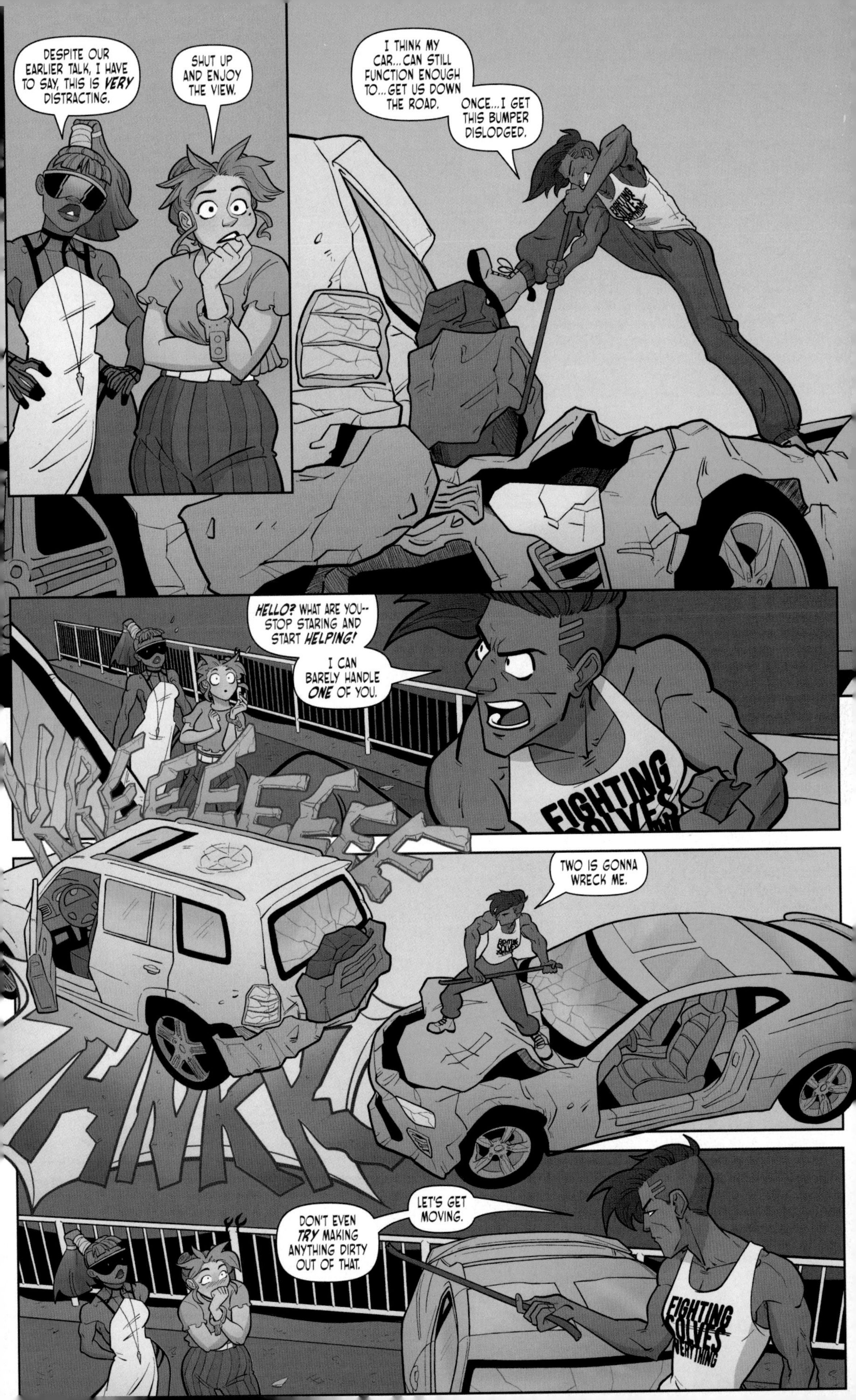
DESPITE OUR EARLIER TALK, I HAVE TO SAY, THIS IS VERY DISTRACTING.
SHUT UP AND ENJOY THE VIEW.
I THINK MY CAR... CAN STILL FUNCTION ENOUGH TO... GET US DOWN THE ROAD.
ONCE... I GET THIS BUMPER DISLODGED.
FIGHTING SOLVES EVERYTHING
HELLO? WHAT ARE YOU-- STOP STARING AND START HELPING!
I CAN BARELY HANDLE ONE OF YOU.
FIGHTING SOLVES
SKREEEEE
TWO IS GONNA WRECK ME.
LET'S GET MOVING.
DON'T EVEN TRY MAKING ANYTHING DIRTY OUT OF THAT.
FIGHTING SOLVES EVERYTHING

LITTLE PROBLEM WITH THAT, V.

OF COURSE. WHY DID I EVEN TURN *AROUND?*

WELL, LONG AS WE KEEP MOV--

DON'T SAY IT!

NOSE PUNCH DE-BRODERAN

ATTENTION: THIS MOBILE FUEL STATION WILL BE STOPPING FOR THE NEXT FOURTEEN MINUTES.

SHIT.

GOD, IT'S LIKE NO ONE TAUGHT YOU ABOUT JINXES.

CHURROPALOOZA

OMNINOM SNACKS GALORE!

LITERALLY BREAD

CHURROPALOOZA

STUFF FAC

I WAS STARTING TO ENJOY NOT SHOOTING REGULAR PEOPLE.

LET ME HANDLE THEM. *PLEASE?* I WANT TO SHOW YOU WHAT I CAN BRING TO THE TEAM.

NO WAY I'M GIVING YOU A WEAPON.

I DON'T NEED ONE. I'M CARRYING A DOZEN KNIVES. *PLUS,* NO PAPERWORK FOR YOU.

KLKKLAK

FIGHTIN

FIGHTING

GO HAVE FUN.

OH, I WILL.

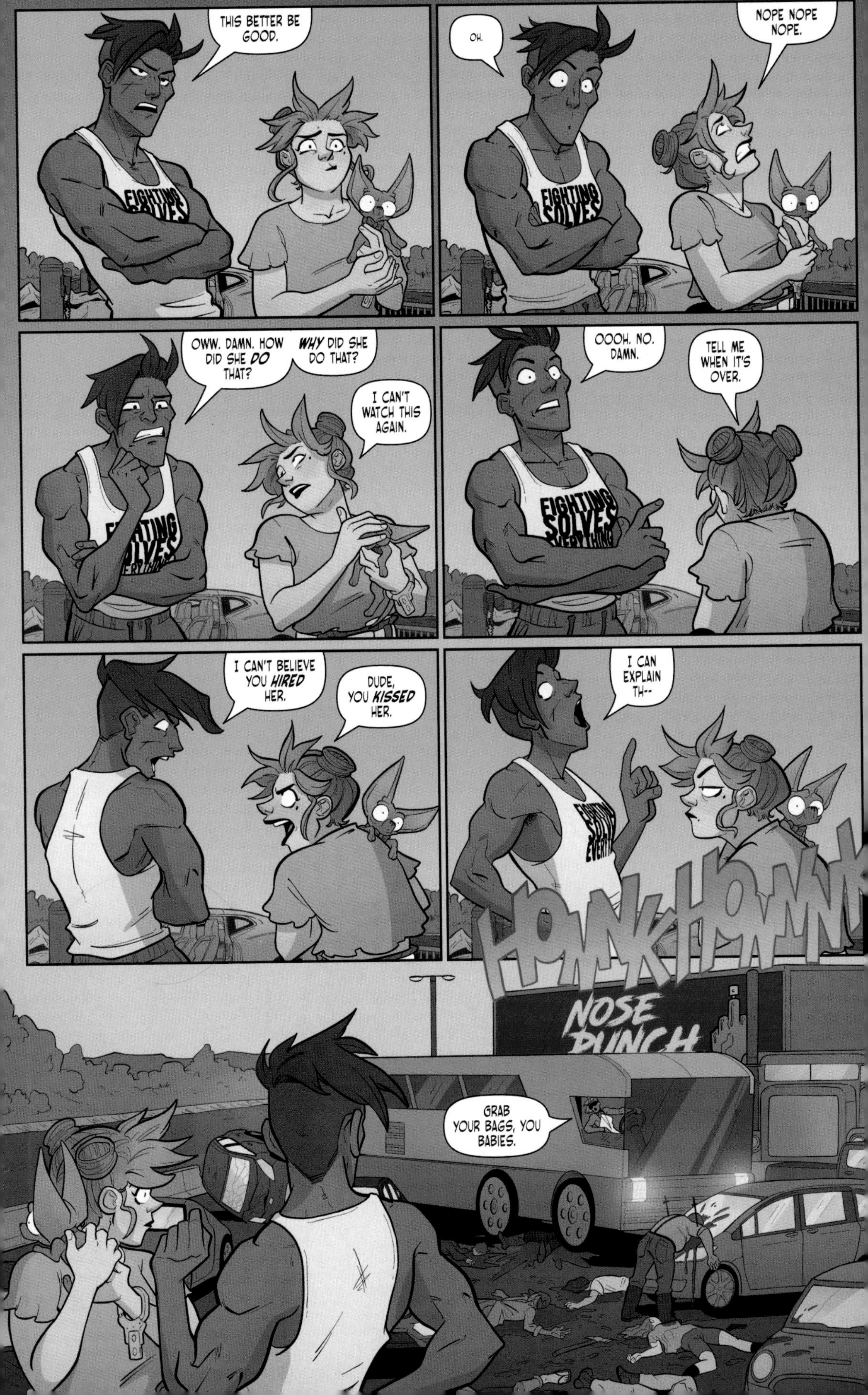
THIS BETTER BE GOOD.
FIGHTING SOLVES
OH.
NOPE NOPE NOPE.
FIGHTING SOLVES
OWW. DAMN. HOW DID SHE DO THAT?
WHY DID SHE DO THAT?
I CAN'T WATCH THIS AGAIN.
FIGHTING SOLVES
OOOH. NO. DAMN.
TELL ME WHEN IT'S OVER.
FIGHTING SOLVES EVERYTHING
I CAN'T BELIEVE YOU HIRED HER.
DUDE, YOU KISSED HER.
I CAN EXPLAIN TH--
HONK HONNNK
NOSE PUNCH
GRAB YOUR BAGS, YOU BABIES.

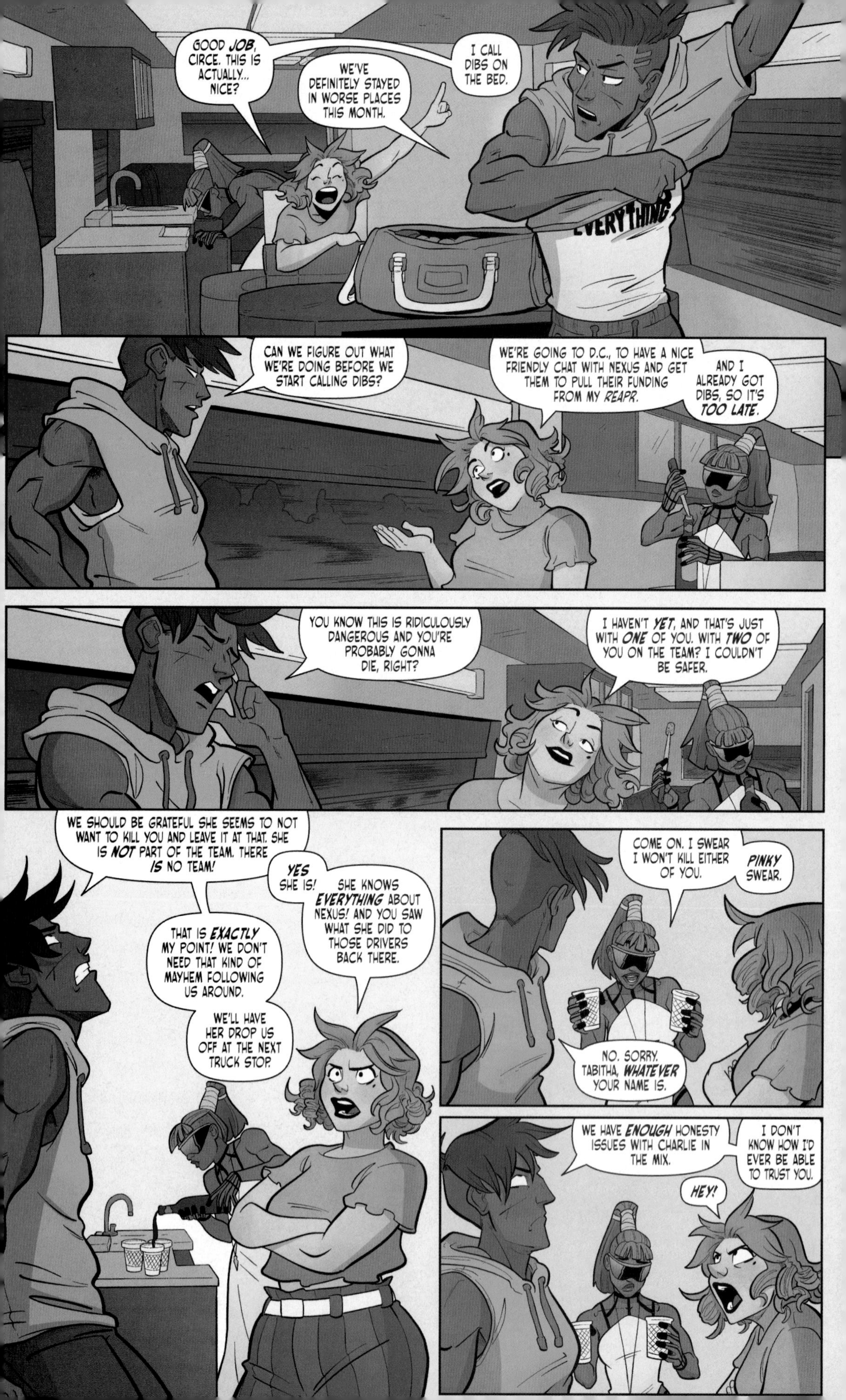

GOOD JOB, CIRCE. THIS IS ACTUALLY... NICE?
WE'VE DEFINITELY STAYED IN WORSE PLACES THIS MONTH.
I CALL DIBS ON THE BED.
EVERYTHING
CAN WE FIGURE OUT WHAT WE'RE DOING BEFORE WE START CALLING DIBS?
WE'RE GOING TO D.C., TO HAVE A NICE FRIENDLY CHAT WITH NEXUS AND GET THEM TO PULL THEIR FUNDING FROM MY REAPR.
AND I ALREADY GOT DIBS, SO IT'S TOO LATE.
YOU KNOW THIS IS RIDICULOUSLY DANGEROUS AND YOU'RE PROBABLY GONNA DIE, RIGHT?
I HAVEN'T YET, AND THAT'S JUST WITH ONE OF YOU. WITH TWO OF YOU ON THE TEAM? I COULDN'T BE SAFER.
WE SHOULD BE GRATEFUL SHE SEEMS TO NOT WANT TO KILL YOU AND LEAVE IT AT THAT. SHE IS NOT PART OF THE TEAM. THERE IS NO TEAM!
YES SHE IS!
SHE KNOWS EVERYTHING ABOUT NEXUS! AND YOU SAW WHAT SHE DID TO THOSE DRIVERS BACK THERE.
THAT IS EXACTLY MY POINT! WE DON'T NEED THAT KIND OF MAYHEM FOLLOWING US AROUND.
WE'LL HAVE HER DROP US OFF AT THE NEXT TRUCK STOP.
COME ON. I SWEAR I WON'T KILL EITHER OF YOU.
PINKY SWEAR.
NO. SORRY. TABITHA, WHATEVER YOUR NAME IS.
WE HAVE ENOUGH HONESTY ISSUES WITH CHARLIE IN THE MIX.
I DON'T KNOW HOW I'D EVER BE ABLE TO TRUST YOU.
HEY!

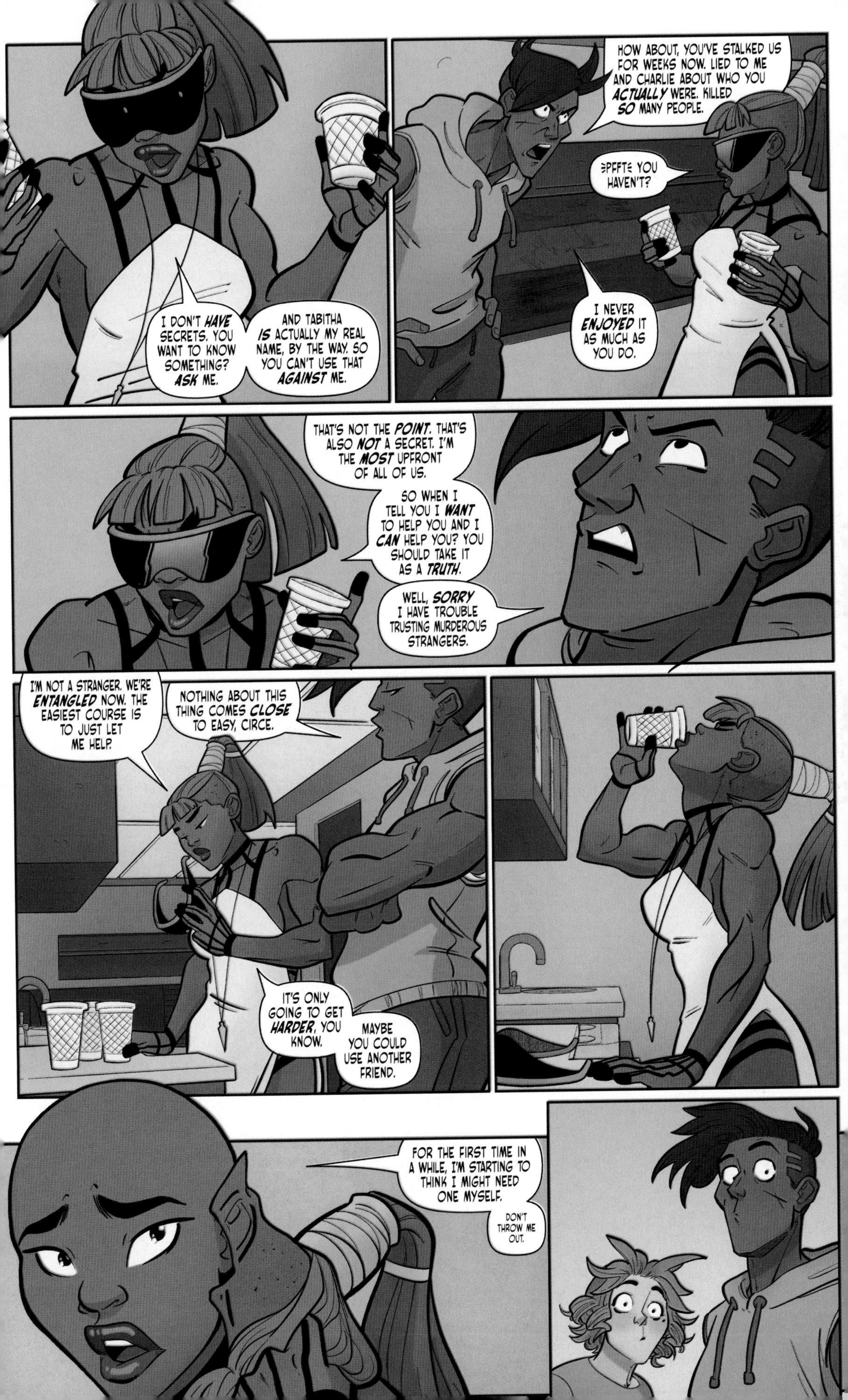
I DON'T HAVE SECRETS. YOU WANT TO KNOW SOMETHING? ASK ME.
AND TABITHA IS ACTUALLY MY REAL NAME, BY THE WAY. SO YOU CAN'T USE THAT AGAINST ME.
HOW ABOUT, YOU'VE STALKED US FOR WEEKS NOW. LIED TO ME AND CHARLIE ABOUT WHO YOU ACTUALLY WERE. KILLED SO MANY PEOPLE.
PFFT YOU HAVEN'T?
I NEVER ENJOYED IT AS MUCH AS YOU DO.
THAT'S NOT THE POINT. THAT'S ALSO NOT A SECRET. I'M THE MOST UPFRONT OF ALL OF US.
SO WHEN I TELL YOU I WANT TO HELP YOU AND I CAN HELP YOU? YOU SHOULD TAKE IT AS A TRUTH.
WELL, SORRY I HAVE TROUBLE TRUSTING MURDEROUS STRANGERS.
I'M NOT A STRANGER. WE'RE ENTANGLED NOW. THE EASIEST COURSE IS TO JUST LET ME HELP.
NOTHING ABOUT THIS THING COMES CLOSE TO EASY, CIRCE.
IT'S ONLY GOING TO GET HARDER, YOU KNOW.
MAYBE YOU COULD USE ANOTHER FRIEND.
FOR THE FIRST TIME IN A WHILE, I'M STARTING TO THINK I MIGHT NEED ONE MYSELF.
DON'T THROW ME OUT.

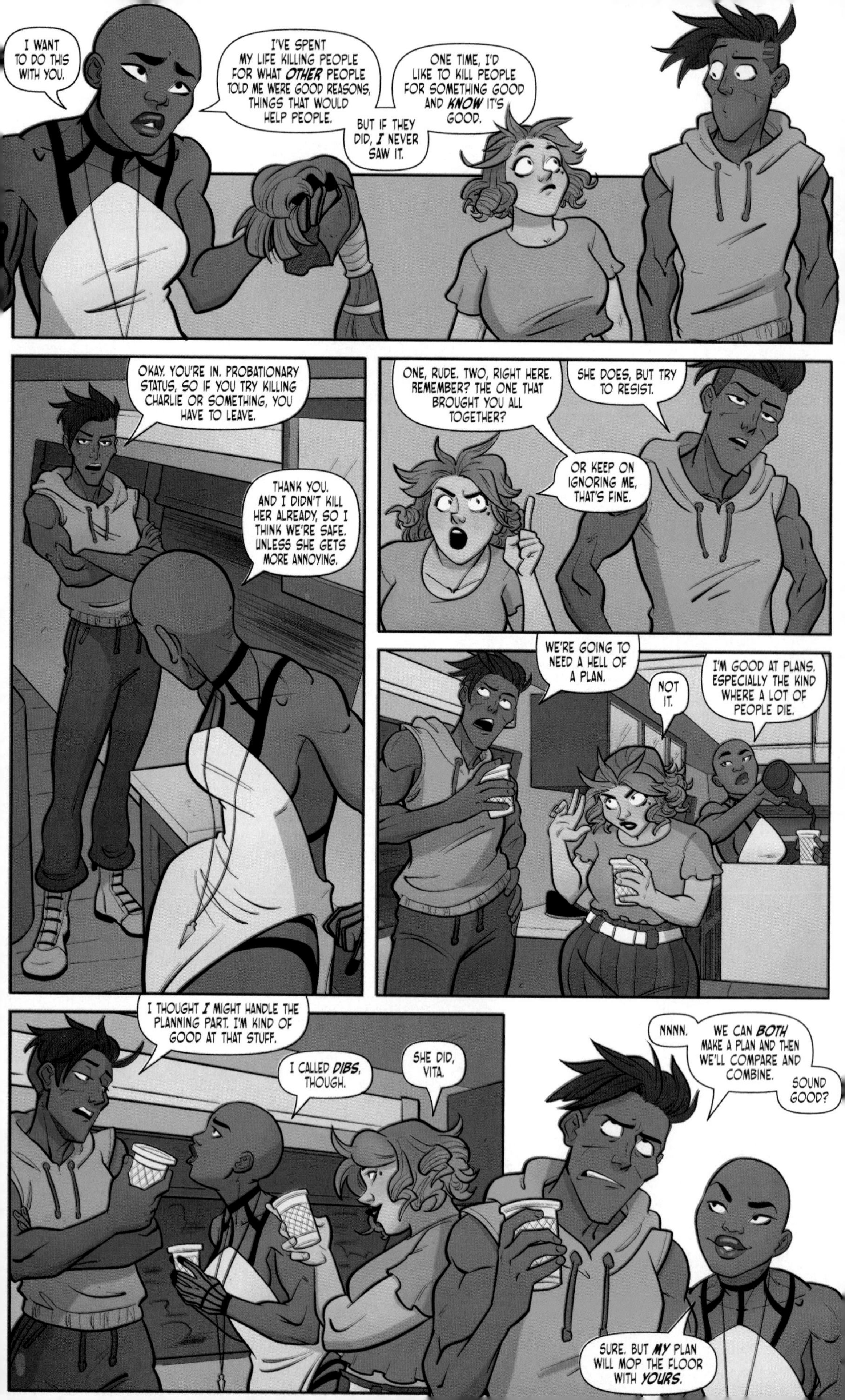

I WANT TO DO THIS WITH YOU.
I'VE SPENT MY LIFE KILLING PEOPLE FOR WHAT OTHER PEOPLE TOLD ME WERE GOOD REASONS, THINGS THAT WOULD HELP PEOPLE.
BUT IF THEY DID, I NEVER SAW IT.
ONE TIME, I'D LIKE TO KILL PEOPLE FOR SOMETHING GOOD AND KNOW IT'S GOOD.
OKAY. YOU'RE IN. PROBATIONARY STATUS, SO IF YOU TRY KILLING CHARLIE OR SOMETHING, YOU HAVE TO LEAVE.
THANK YOU. AND I DIDN'T KILL HER ALREADY, SO I THINK WE'RE SAFE. UNLESS SHE GETS MORE ANNOYING.
ONE, RUDE. TWO, RIGHT HERE. REMEMBER? THE ONE THAT BROUGHT YOU ALL TOGETHER?
SHE DOES, BUT TRY TO RESIST.
OR KEEP ON IGNORING ME, THAT'S FINE.
WE'RE GOING TO NEED A HELL OF A PLAN.
NOT IT.
I'M GOOD AT PLANS. ESPECIALLY THE KIND WHERE A LOT OF PEOPLE DIE.
I THOUGHT I MIGHT HANDLE THE PLANNING PART. I'M KIND OF GOOD AT THAT STUFF.
I CALLED DIBS, THOUGH.
SHE DID, VITA.
NNNN.
WE CAN BOTH MAKE A PLAN AND THEN WE'LL COMPARE AND COMBINE.
SOUND GOOD?
SURE. BUT MY PLAN WILL MOP THE FLOOR WITH YOURS.

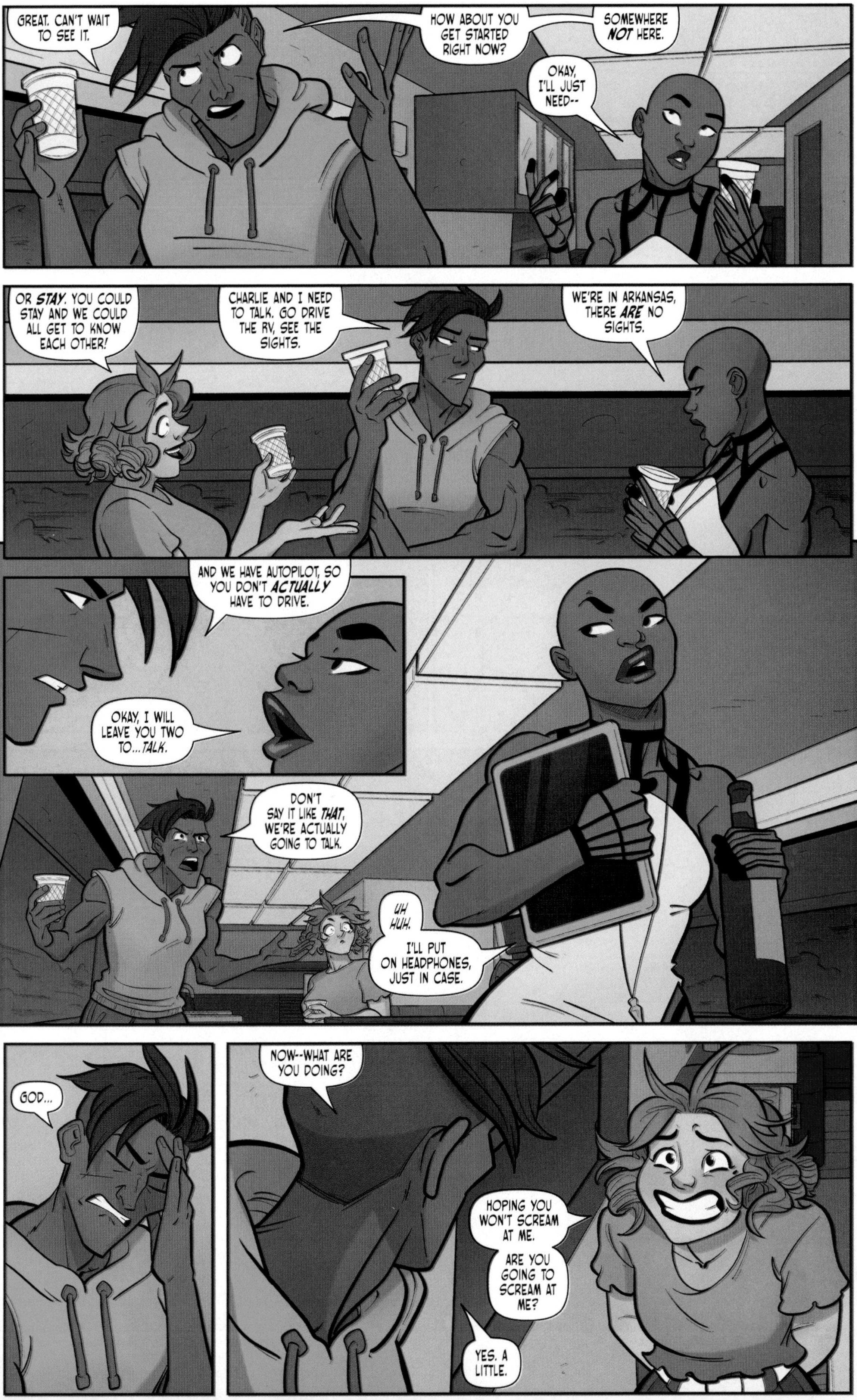
GREAT. CAN'T WAIT TO SEE IT.
HOW ABOUT YOU GET STARTED RIGHT NOW?
SOMEWHERE *NOT* HERE.
OKAY, I'LL JUST NEED--
OR *STAY*. YOU COULD STAY AND WE COULD ALL GET TO KNOW EACH OTHER!
CHARLIE AND I NEED TO TALK. GO DRIVE THE RV, SEE THE SIGHTS.
WE'RE IN ARKANSAS, THERE *ARE* NO SIGHTS.
AND WE HAVE AUTOPILOT, SO YOU DON'T *ACTUALLY* HAVE TO DRIVE.
OKAY, I WILL LEAVE YOU TWO TO...*TALK*.
DON'T SAY IT LIKE *THAT*, WE'RE ACTUALLY GOING TO TALK.
UH HUH.
I'LL PUT ON HEADPHONES, JUST IN CASE.
GOD...
NOW--WHAT ARE YOU DOING?
HOPING YOU WON'T SCREAM AT ME.
ARE YOU GOING TO SCREAM AT ME?
YES. A LITTLE.

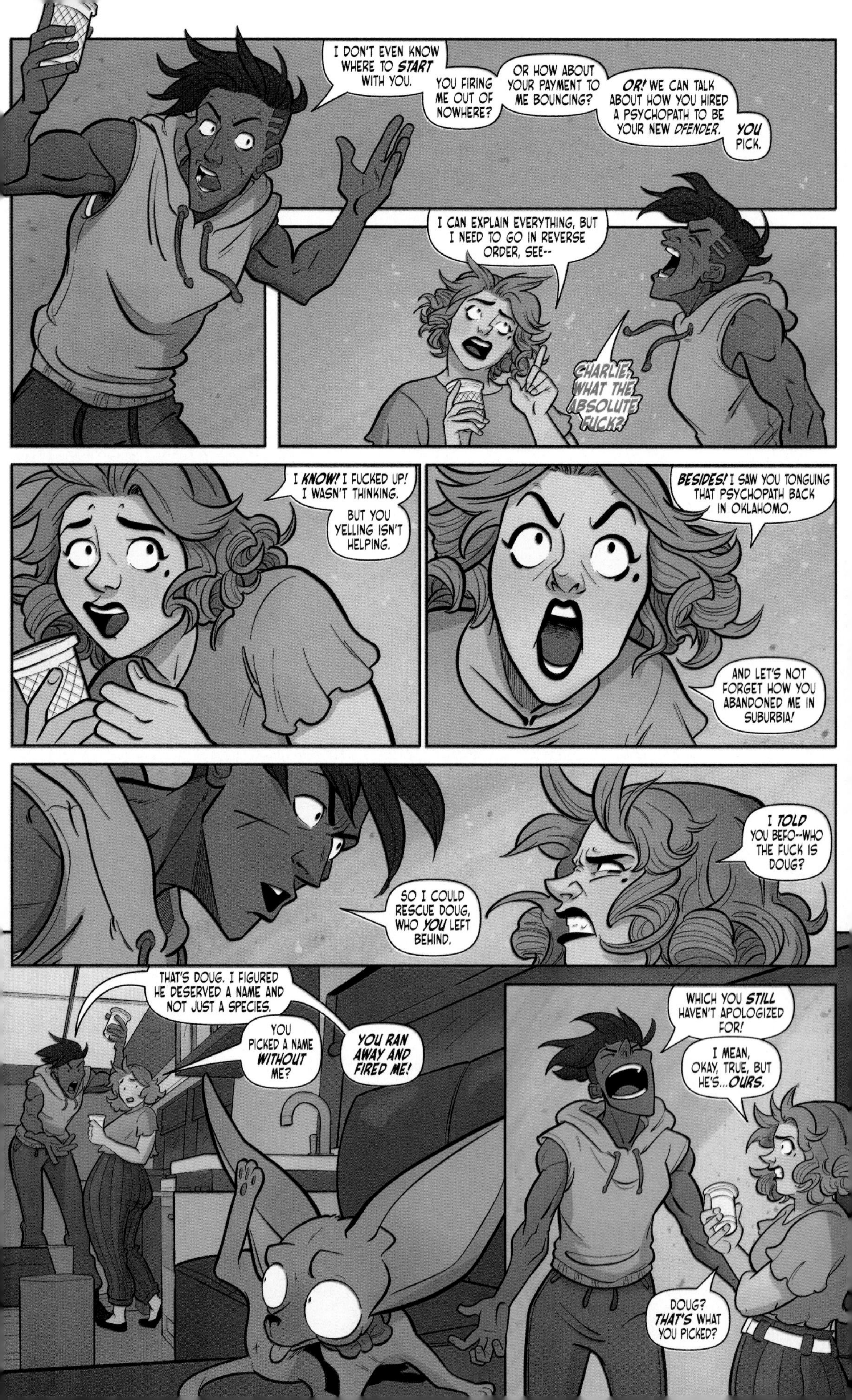

I DON'T EVEN KNOW WHERE TO START WITH YOU.
YOU FIRING ME OUT OF NOWHERE?
OR HOW ABOUT YOUR PAYMENT TO ME BOUNCING?
OR! WE CAN TALK ABOUT HOW YOU HIRED A PSYCHOPATH TO BE YOUR NEW DFENDER.
YOU PICK.
I CAN EXPLAIN EVERYTHING, BUT I NEED TO GO IN REVERSE ORDER, SEE--
CHARLIE, WHAT THE ABSOLUTE FUCK?
I KNOW! I FUCKED UP! I WASN'T THINKING.
BUT YOU YELLING ISN'T HELPING.
BESIDES! I SAW YOU TONGUING THAT PSYCHOPATH BACK IN OKLAHOMO.
AND LET'S NOT FORGET HOW YOU ABANDONED ME IN SUBURBIA!
SO I COULD RESCUE DOUG, WHO YOU LEFT BEHIND.
I TOLD YOU BEFO--WHO THE FUCK IS DOUG?
THAT'S DOUG. I FIGURED HE DESERVED A NAME AND NOT JUST A SPECIES.
YOU PICKED A NAME WITHOUT ME?
YOU RAN AWAY AND FIRED ME!
WHICH YOU STILL HAVEN'T APOLOGIZED FOR!
I MEAN, OKAY, TRUE, BUT HE'S...OURS.
DOUG? THAT'S WHAT YOU PICKED?

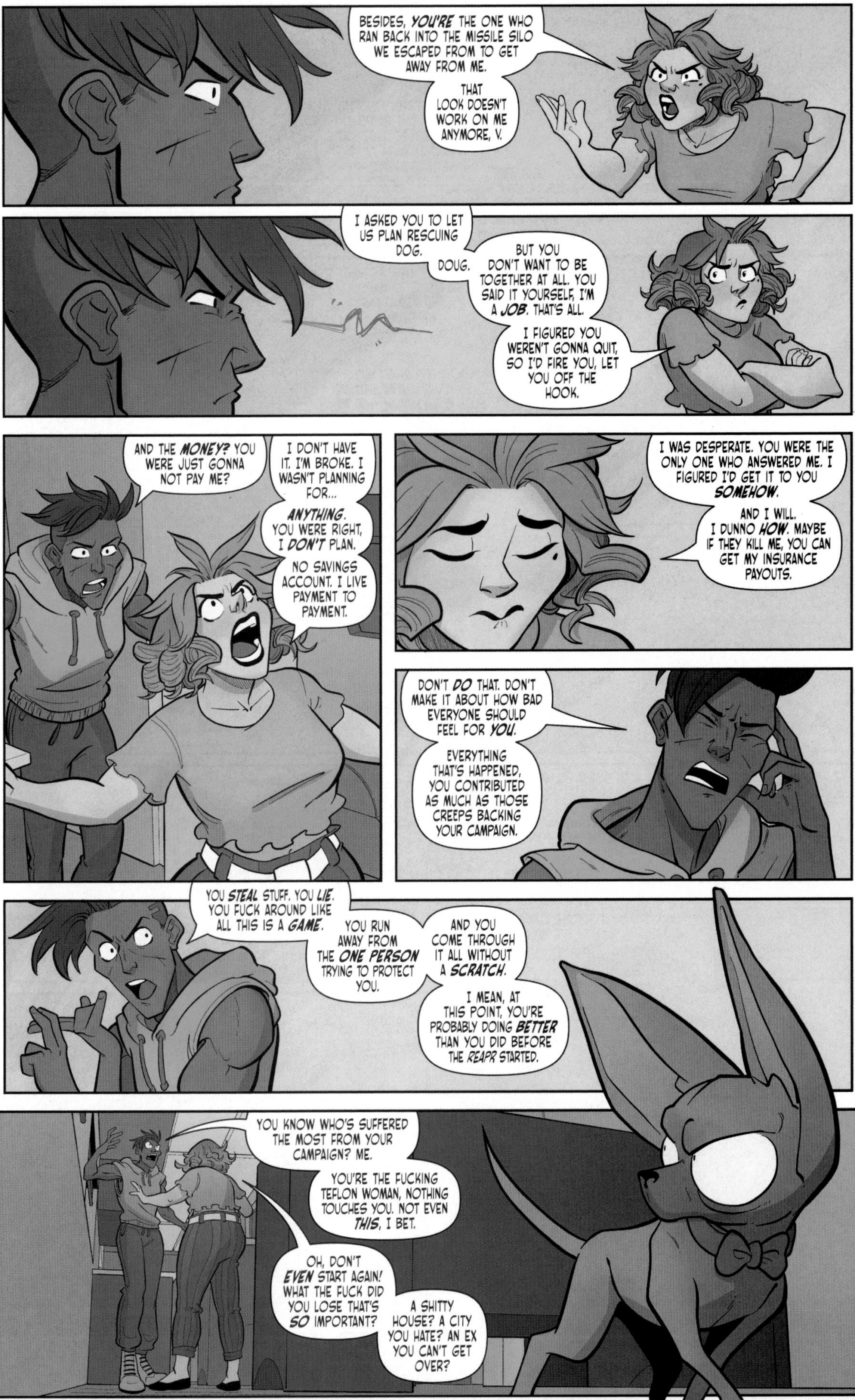
BESIDES, YOU'RE THE ONE WHO RAN BACK INTO THE MISSILE SILO WE ESCAPED FROM TO GET AWAY FROM ME.
THAT LOOK DOESN'T WORK ON ME ANYMORE, V.
I ASKED YOU TO LET US PLAN RESCUING DOG.
DOUG.
BUT YOU DON'T WANT TO BE TOGETHER AT ALL. YOU SAID IT YOURSELF, I'M A JOB. THAT'S ALL.
I FIGURED YOU WEREN'T GONNA QUIT, SO I'D FIRE YOU, LET YOU OFF THE HOOK.
AND THE MONEY? YOU WERE JUST GONNA NOT PAY ME?
I DON'T HAVE IT. I'M BROKE. I WASN'T PLANNING FOR...
ANYTHING. YOU WERE RIGHT, I DON'T PLAN.
NO SAVINGS ACCOUNT. I LIVE PAYMENT TO PAYMENT.
I WAS DESPERATE. YOU WERE THE ONLY ONE WHO ANSWERED ME. I FIGURED I'D GET IT TO YOU SOMEHOW.
AND I WILL. I DUNNO HOW. MAYBE IF THEY KILL ME, YOU CAN GET MY INSURANCE PAYOUTS.
DON'T DO THAT. DON'T MAKE IT ABOUT HOW BAD EVERYONE SHOULD FEEL FOR YOU.
EVERYTHING THAT'S HAPPENED, YOU CONTRIBUTED AS MUCH AS THOSE CREEPS BACKING YOUR CAMPAIGN.
YOU STEAL STUFF. YOU LIE. YOU FUCK AROUND LIKE ALL THIS IS A GAME.
YOU RUN AWAY FROM THE ONE PERSON TRYING TO PROTECT YOU.
AND YOU COME THROUGH IT ALL WITHOUT A SCRATCH.
I MEAN, AT THIS POINT, YOU'RE PROBABLY DOING BETTER THAN YOU DID BEFORE THE REAPR STARTED.
YOU KNOW WHO'S SUFFERED THE MOST FROM YOUR CAMPAIGN? ME.
YOU'RE THE FUCKING TEFLON WOMAN, NOTHING TOUCHES YOU. NOT EVEN THIS, I BET.
OH, DON'T EVEN START AGAIN! WHAT THE FUCK DID YOU LOSE THAT'S SO IMPORTANT?
A SHITTY HOUSE? A CITY YOU HATE? AN EX YOU CAN'T GET OVER?

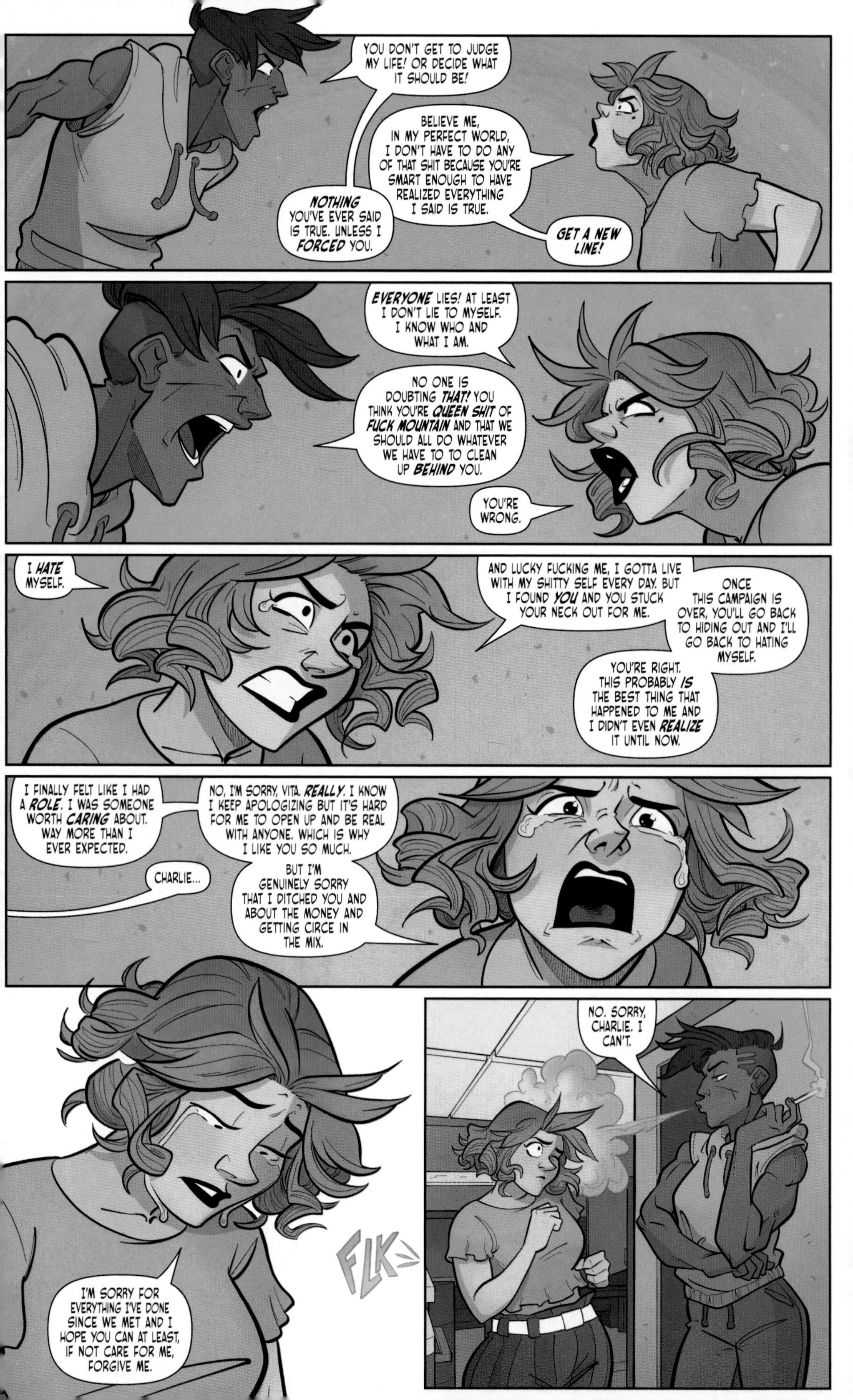

YOU DON'T GET TO JUDGE MY LIFE! OR DECIDE WHAT IT SHOULD BE!
BELIEVE ME, IN MY PERFECT WORLD, I DON'T HAVE TO DO ANY OF THAT SHIT BECAUSE YOU'RE SMART ENOUGH TO HAVE REALIZED EVERYTHING I SAID IS TRUE.
NOTHING YOU'VE EVER SAID IS TRUE. UNLESS I FORCED YOU.
GET A NEW LINE!
EVERYONE LIES! AT LEAST I DON'T LIE TO MYSELF. I KNOW WHO AND WHAT I AM.
NO ONE IS DOUBTING THAT! YOU THINK YOU'RE QUEEN SHIT OF FUCK MOUNTAIN AND THAT WE SHOULD ALL DO WHATEVER WE HAVE TO TO CLEAN UP BEHIND YOU.
YOU'RE WRONG.
I HATE MYSELF.
AND LUCKY FUCKING ME, I GOTTA LIVE WITH MY SHITTY SELF EVERY DAY. BUT I FOUND YOU AND YOU STUCK YOUR NECK OUT FOR ME.
ONCE THIS CAMPAIGN IS OVER, YOU'LL GO BACK TO HIDING OUT AND I'LL GO BACK TO HATING MYSELF.
YOU'RE RIGHT. THIS PROBABLY IS THE BEST THING THAT HAPPENED TO ME AND I DIDN'T EVEN REALIZE IT UNTIL NOW.
I FINALLY FELT LIKE I HAD A ROLE. I WAS SOMEONE WORTH CARING ABOUT. WAY MORE THAN I EVER EXPECTED.
CHARLIE...
NO, I'M SORRY, VITA. REALLY. I KNOW I KEEP APOLOGIZING BUT IT'S HARD FOR ME TO OPEN UP AND BE REAL WITH ANYONE. WHICH IS WHY I LIKE YOU SO MUCH.
BUT I'M GENUINELY SORRY THAT I DITCHED YOU AND ABOUT THE MONEY AND GETTING CIRCE IN THE MIX.
I'M SORRY FOR EVERYTHING I'VE DONE SINCE WE MET AND I HOPE YOU CAN AT LEAST, IF NOT CARE FOR ME, FORGIVE ME.
FLK
NO. SORRY, CHARLIE. I CAN'T.

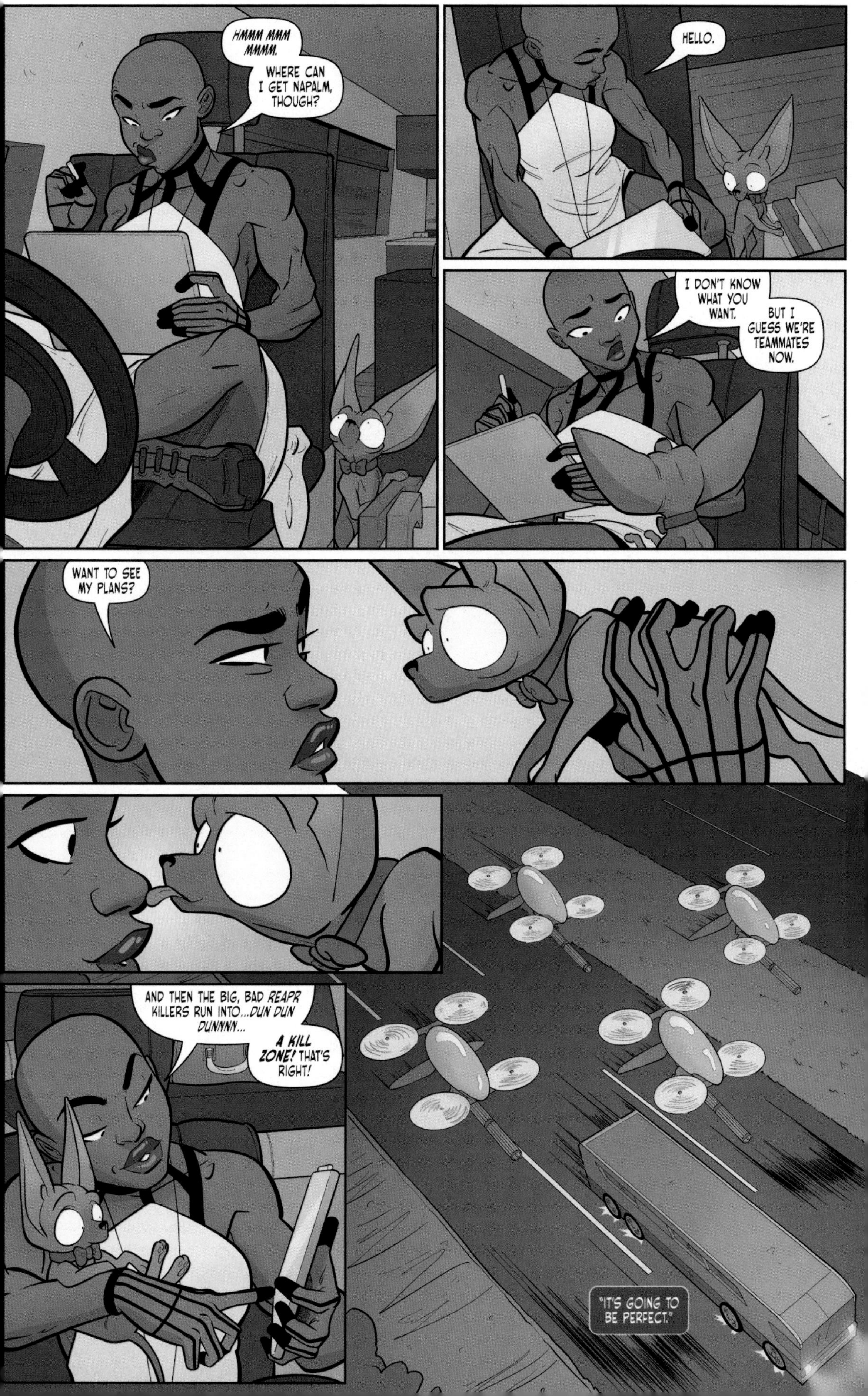
HMMM MMM MMMM.
WHERE CAN I GET NAPALM, THOUGH?
HELLO.
I DON'T KNOW WHAT YOU WANT.
BUT I GUESS WE'RE TEAMMATES NOW.
WANT TO SEE MY PLANS?
AND THEN THE BIG, BAD REAPR KILLERS RUN INTO...DUN DUN DUNNNN...
A KILL ZONE! THAT'S RIGHT!
"IT'S GOING TO BE PERFECT."

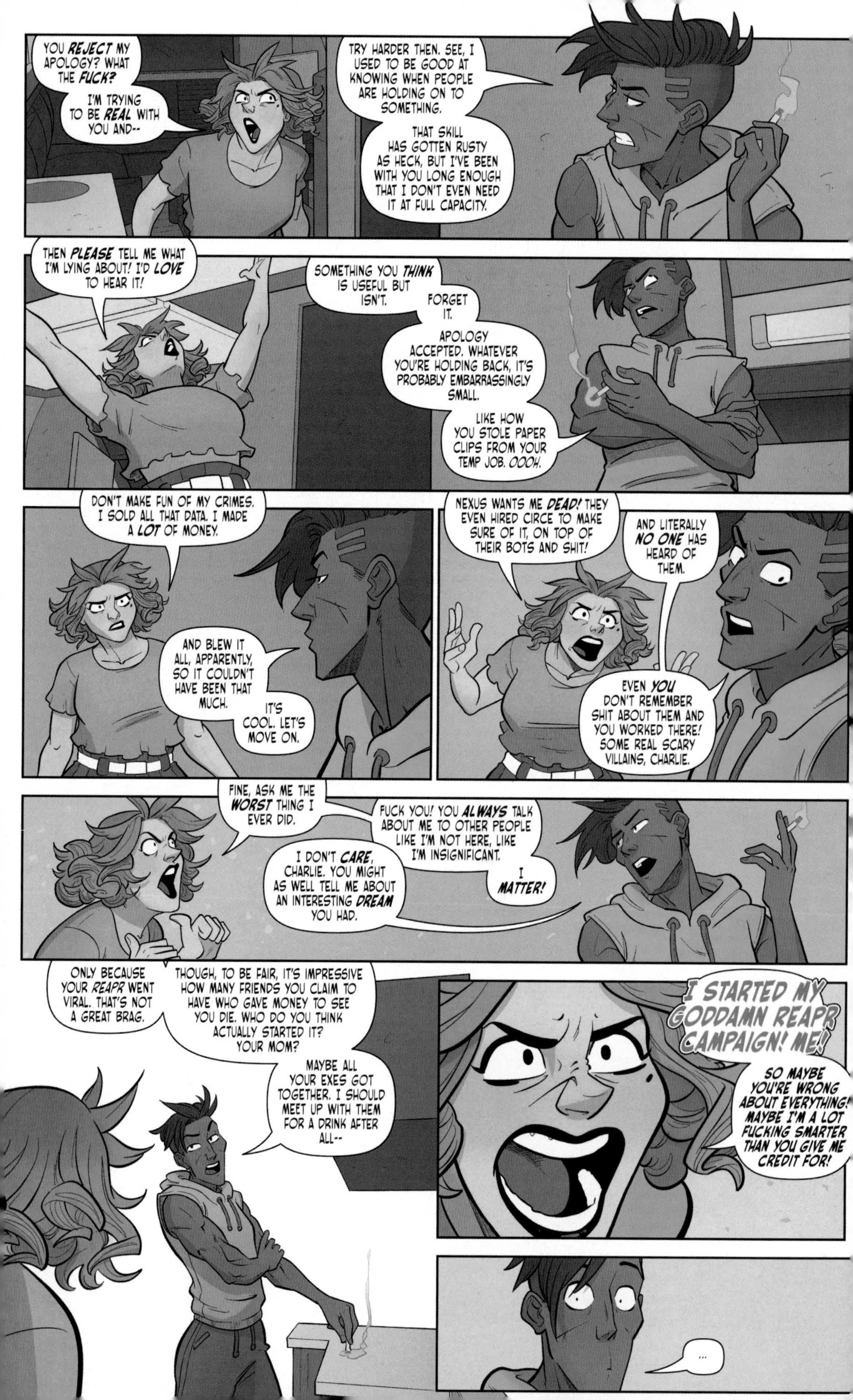
YOU REJECT MY APOLOGY? WHAT THE FUCK?
I'M TRYING TO BE REAL WITH YOU AND--
TRY HARDER THEN. SEE, I USED TO BE GOOD AT KNOWING WHEN PEOPLE ARE HOLDING ON TO SOMETHING.
THAT SKILL HAS GOTTEN RUSTY AS HECK, BUT I'VE BEEN WITH YOU LONG ENOUGH THAT I DON'T EVEN NEED IT AT FULL CAPACITY.
THEN PLEASE TELL ME WHAT I'M LYING ABOUT! I'D LOVE TO HEAR IT!
SOMETHING YOU THINK IS USEFUL BUT ISN'T.
FORGET IT.
APOLOGY ACCEPTED. WHATEVER YOU'RE HOLDING BACK, IT'S PROBABLY EMBARRASSINGLY SMALL.
LIKE HOW YOU STOLE PAPER CLIPS FROM YOUR TEMP JOB. OOOH.
DON'T MAKE FUN OF MY CRIMES. I SOLD ALL THAT DATA. I MADE A LOT OF MONEY.
AND BLEW IT ALL, APPARENTLY, SO IT COULDN'T HAVE BEEN THAT MUCH.
IT'S COOL. LET'S MOVE ON.
NEXUS WANTS ME DEAD! THEY EVEN HIRED CIRCE TO MAKE SURE OF IT, ON TOP OF THEIR BOTS AND SHIT!
AND LITERALLY NO ONE HAS HEARD OF THEM.
EVEN YOU DON'T REMEMBER SHIT ABOUT THEM AND YOU WORKED THERE! SOME REAL SCARY VILLAINS, CHARLIE.
FINE, ASK ME THE WORST THING I EVER DID.
FUCK YOU! YOU ALWAYS TALK ABOUT ME TO OTHER PEOPLE LIKE I'M NOT HERE, LIKE I'M INSIGNIFICANT.
I MATTER!
I DON'T CARE, CHARLIE. YOU MIGHT AS WELL TELL ME ABOUT AN INTERESTING DREAM YOU HAD.
ONLY BECAUSE YOUR REAPR WENT VIRAL. THAT'S NOT A GREAT BRAG.
THOUGH, TO BE FAIR, IT'S IMPRESSIVE HOW MANY FRIENDS YOU CLAIM TO HAVE WHO GAVE MONEY TO SEE YOU DIE. WHO DO YOU THINK ACTUALLY STARTED IT? YOUR MOM?
MAYBE ALL YOUR EXES GOT TOGETHER. I SHOULD MEET UP WITH THEM FOR A DRINK AFTER ALL--
I STARTED MY GODDAMN REAPR CAMPAIGN! ME!
SO MAYBE YOU'RE WRONG ABOUT EVERYTHING! MAYBE I'M A LOT FUCKING SMARTER THAN YOU GIVE ME CREDIT FOR!
...

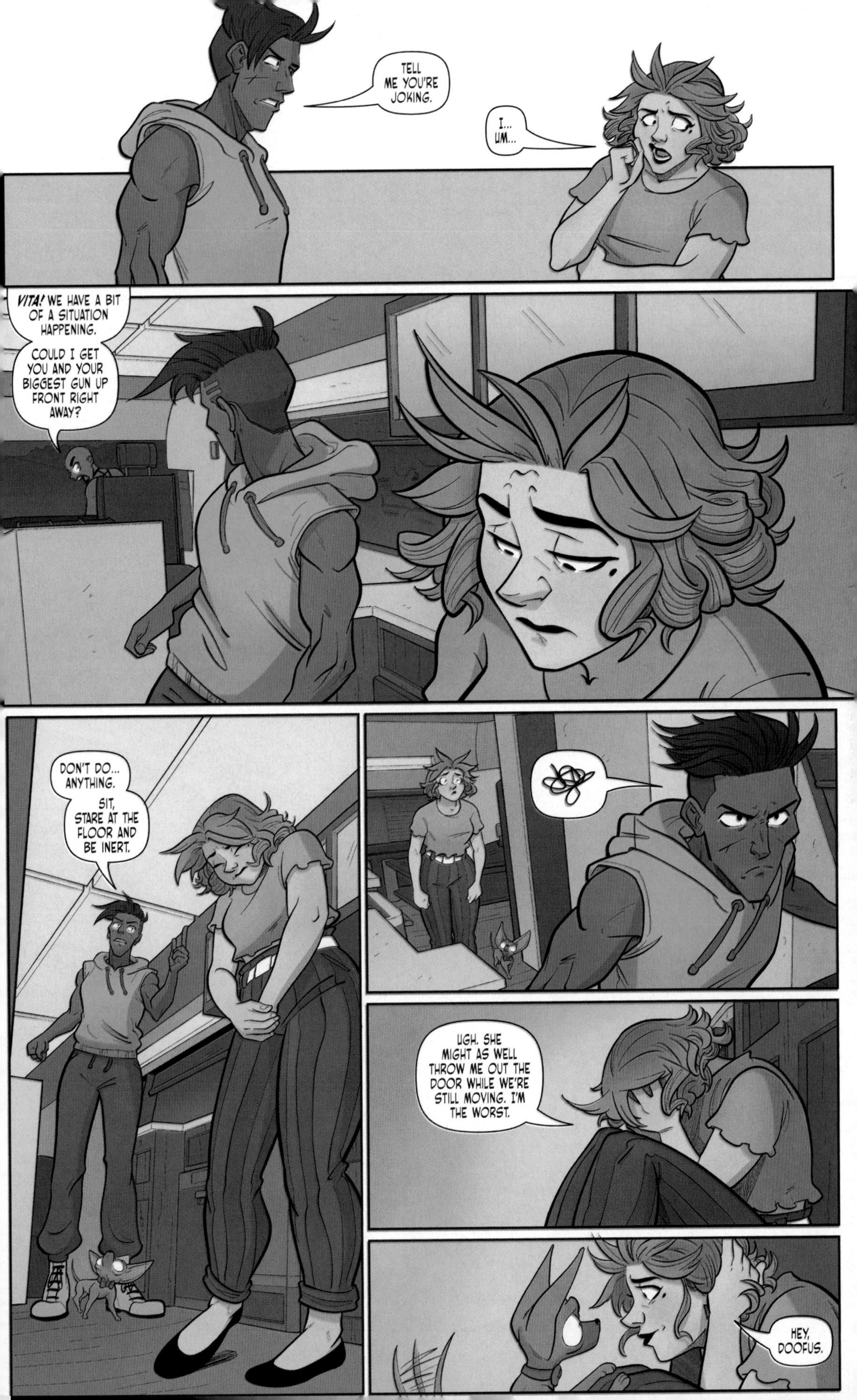
TELL ME YOU'RE JOKING.
I... UM...
VITA! WE HAVE A BIT OF A SITUATION HAPPENING.
COULD I GET YOU AND YOUR BIGGEST GUN UP FRONT RIGHT AWAY?
DON'T DO... ANYTHING.
SIT, STARE AT THE FLOOR AND BE INERT.
UGH. SHE MIGHT AS WELL THROW ME OUT THE DOOR WHILE WE'RE STILL MOVING. I'M THE WORST.
HEY, DOOFUS.

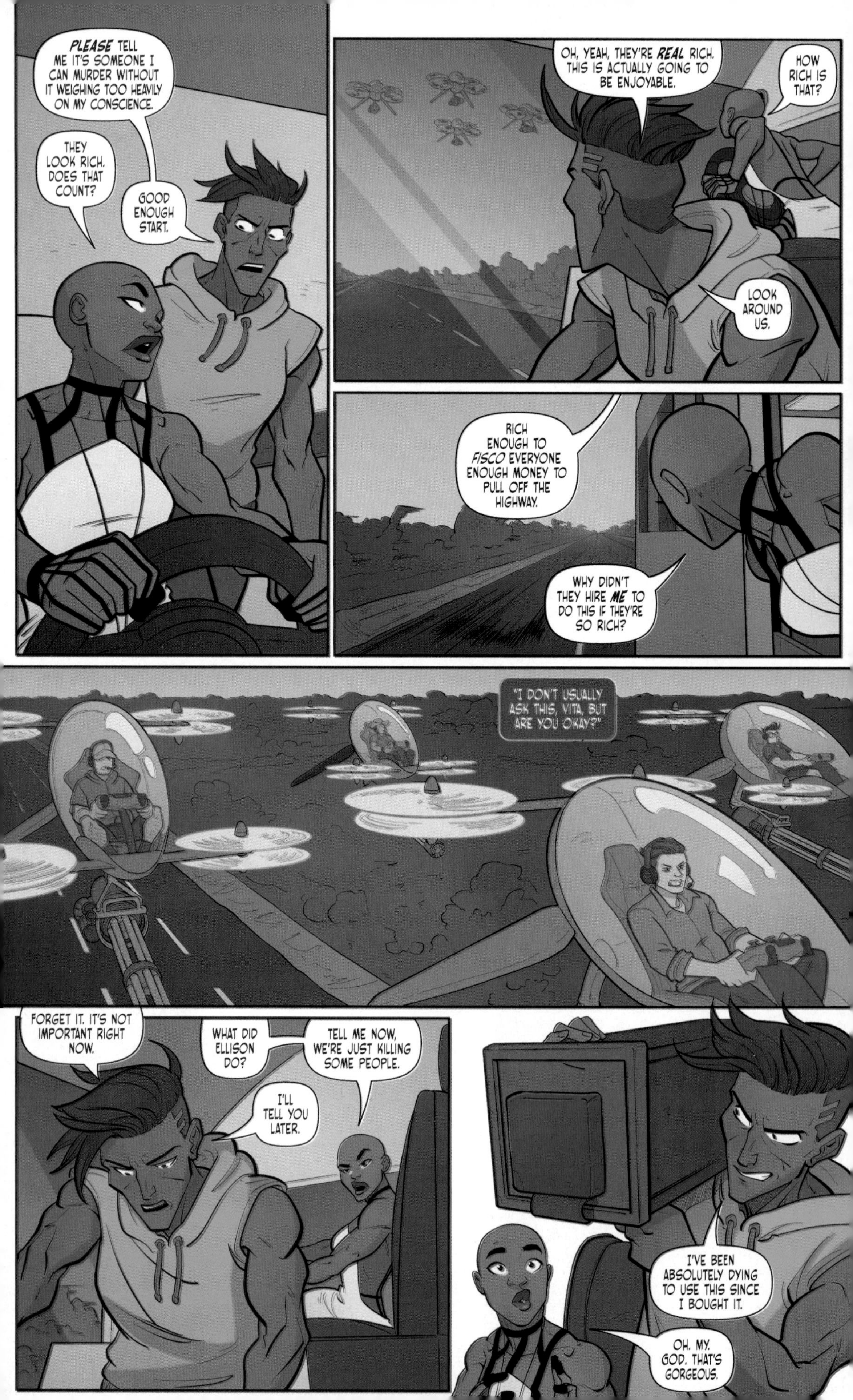
PLEASE TELL ME IT'S SOMEONE I CAN MURDER WITHOUT IT WEIGHING TOO HEAVILY ON MY CONSCIENCE.
THEY LOOK RICH. DOES THAT COUNT?
GOOD ENOUGH START.
OH, YEAH, THEY'RE REAL RICH. THIS IS ACTUALLY GOING TO BE ENJOYABLE.
HOW RICH IS THAT?
LOOK AROUND US.
RICH ENOUGH TO FISCO EVERYONE ENOUGH MONEY TO PULL OFF THE HIGHWAY.
WHY DIDN'T THEY HIRE ME TO DO THIS IF THEY'RE SO RICH?
"I DON'T USUALLY ASK THIS, VITA, BUT ARE YOU OKAY?"
FORGET IT. IT'S NOT IMPORTANT RIGHT NOW.
WHAT DID ELLISON DO?
TELL ME NOW, WE'RE JUST KILLING SOME PEOPLE.
I'LL TELL YOU LATER.
I'VE BEEN ABSOLUTELY DYING TO USE THIS SINCE I BOUGHT IT.
OH. MY. GOD. THAT'S GORGEOUS.

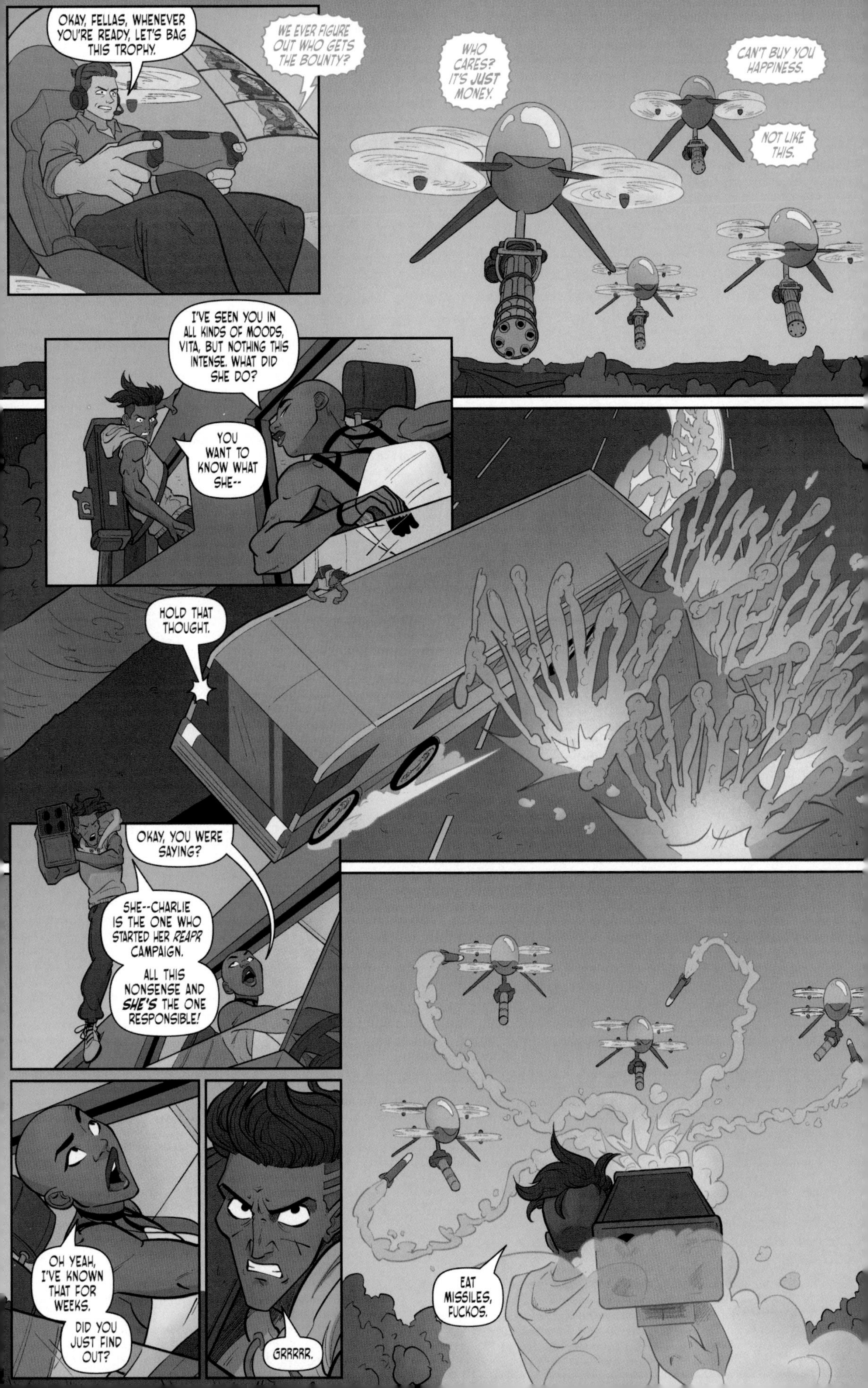
OKAY, FELLAS, WHENEVER YOU'RE READY, LET'S BAG THIS TROPHY.
WE EVER FIGURE OUT WHO GETS THE BOUNTY?
WHO CARES? IT'S JUST MONEY.
CAN'T BUY YOU HAPPINESS.
NOT LIKE THIS.
I'VE SEEN YOU IN ALL KINDS OF MOODS, VITA, BUT NOTHING THIS INTENSE. WHAT DID SHE DO?
YOU WANT TO KNOW WHAT SHE--
HOLD THAT THOUGHT.
OKAY, YOU WERE SAYING?
SHE--CHARLIE IS THE ONE WHO STARTED HER REAPR CAMPAIGN.
ALL THIS NONSENSE AND SHE'S THE ONE RESPONSIBLE!
OH YEAH, I'VE KNOWN THAT FOR WEEKS.
DID YOU JUST FIND OUT?
GRRRRR.
EAT MISSILES, FUCKOS.

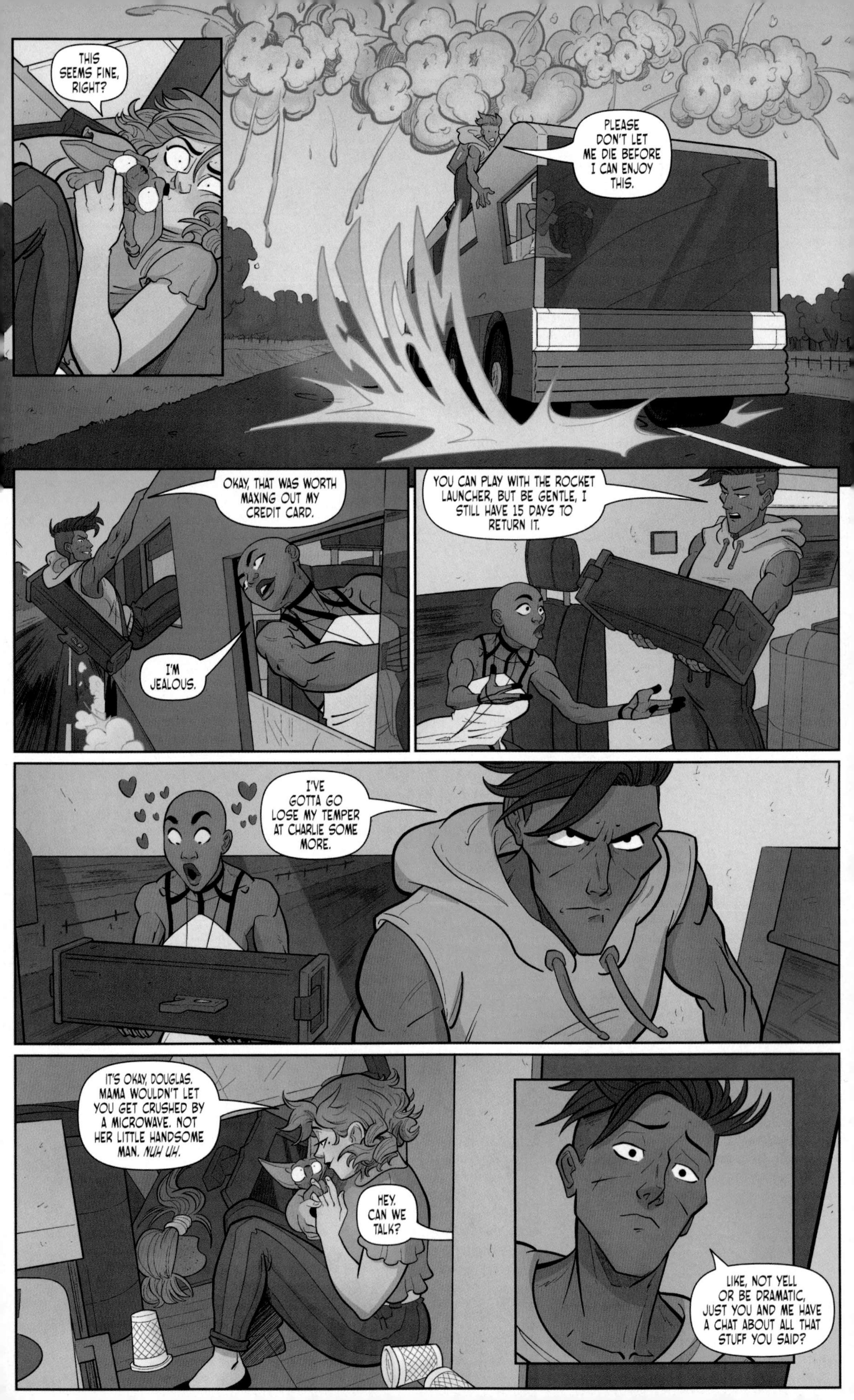
THIS SEEMS FINE, RIGHT?
PLEASE DON'T LET ME DIE BEFORE I CAN ENJOY THIS.
SLAM
OKAY, THAT WAS WORTH MAXING OUT MY CREDIT CARD.
I'M JEALOUS.
YOU CAN PLAY WITH THE ROCKET LAUNCHER, BUT BE GENTLE, I STILL HAVE 15 DAYS TO RETURN IT.
I'VE GOTTA GO LOSE MY TEMPER AT CHARLIE SOME MORE.
IT'S OKAY, DOUGLAS. MAMA WOULDN'T LET YOU GET CRUSHED BY A MICROWAVE. NOT HER LITTLE HANDSOME MAN. *NUH UH.*
HEY. CAN WE TALK?
LIKE, NOT YELL OR BE DRAMATIC, JUST YOU AND ME HAVE A CHAT ABOUT ALL THAT STUFF YOU SAID?

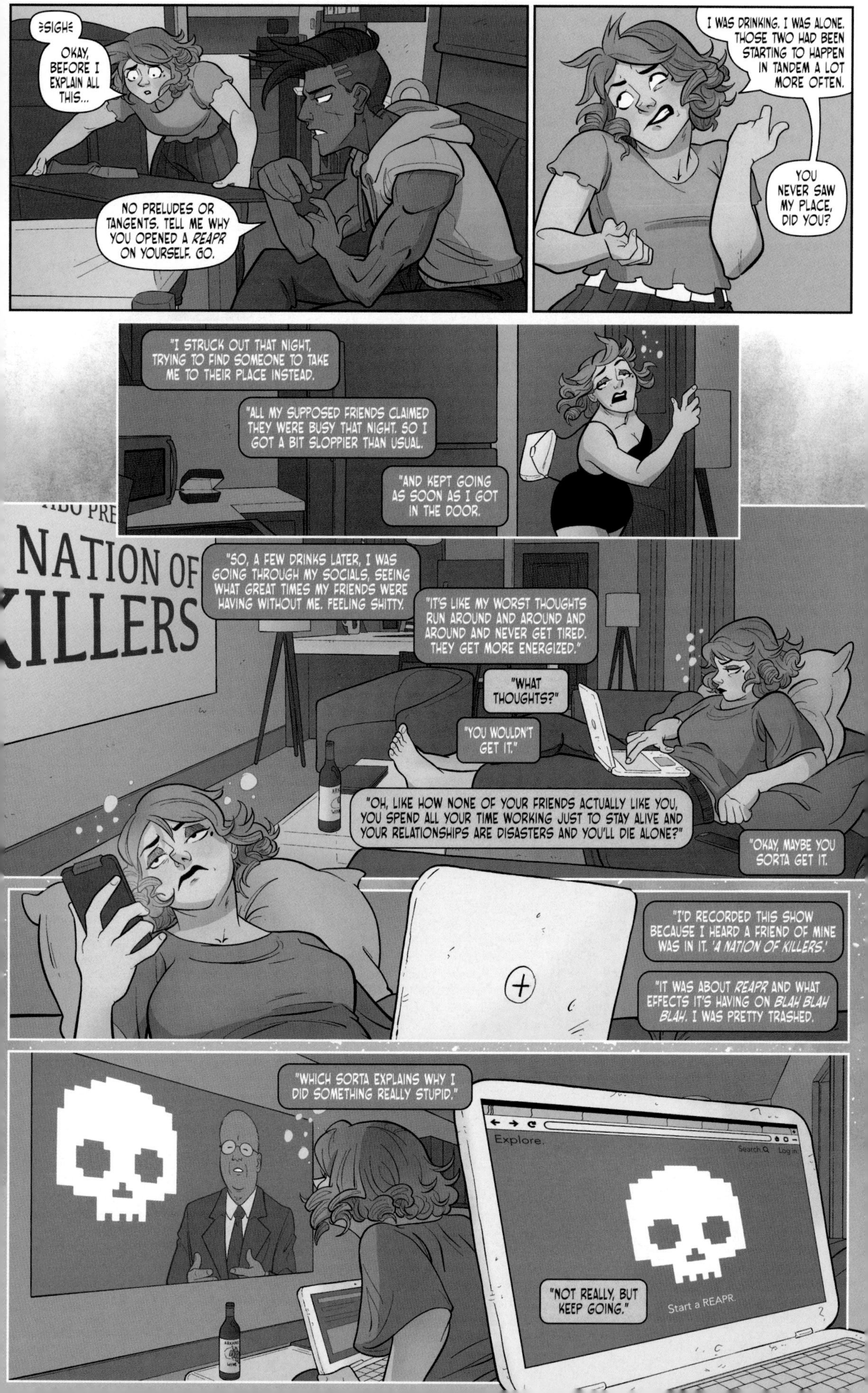
≡SIGH≡
OKAY, BEFORE I EXPLAIN ALL THIS...
NO PRELUDES OR TANGENTS. TELL ME WHY YOU OPENED A *REAPR* ON YOURSELF. GO.
I WAS DRINKING. I WAS ALONE. THOSE TWO HAD BEEN STARTING TO HAPPEN IN TANDEM A LOT MORE OFTEN.
YOU NEVER SAW MY PLACE, DID YOU?
"I STRUCK OUT THAT NIGHT, TRYING TO FIND SOMEONE TO TAKE ME TO THEIR PLACE INSTEAD.
"ALL MY SUPPOSED FRIENDS CLAIMED THEY WERE BUSY THAT NIGHT. SO I GOT A BIT SLOPPIER THAN USUAL.
"AND KEPT GOING AS SOON AS I GOT IN THE DOOR.
NATION OF
"SO, A FEW DRINKS LATER, I WAS GOING THROUGH MY SOCIALS, SEEING WHAT GREAT TIMES MY FRIENDS WERE HAVING WITHOUT ME. FEELING SHITTY.
"IT'S LIKE MY WORST THOUGHTS RUN AROUND AND AROUND AND AROUND AND NEVER GET TIRED. THEY GET MORE ENERGIZED."
"WHAT THOUGHTS?"
"YOU WOULDN'T GET IT."
"OH, LIKE HOW NONE OF YOUR FRIENDS ACTUALLY LIKE YOU, YOU SPEND ALL YOUR TIME WORKING JUST TO STAY ALIVE AND YOUR RELATIONSHIPS ARE DISASTERS AND YOU'LL DIE ALONE?"
"OKAY, MAYBE YOU SORTA GET IT.
"I'D RECORDED THIS SHOW BECAUSE I HEARD A FRIEND OF MINE WAS IN IT. *'A NATION OF KILLERS.'*
"IT WAS ABOUT *REAPR* AND WHAT EFFECTS IT'S HAVING ON *BLAH BLAH BLAH*. I WAS PRETTY TRASHED.
"WHICH SORTA EXPLAINS WHY I DID SOMETHING REALLY STUPID."
Explore.
Search
Log in
Start a REAPR.
"NOT REALLY, BUT KEEP GOING."

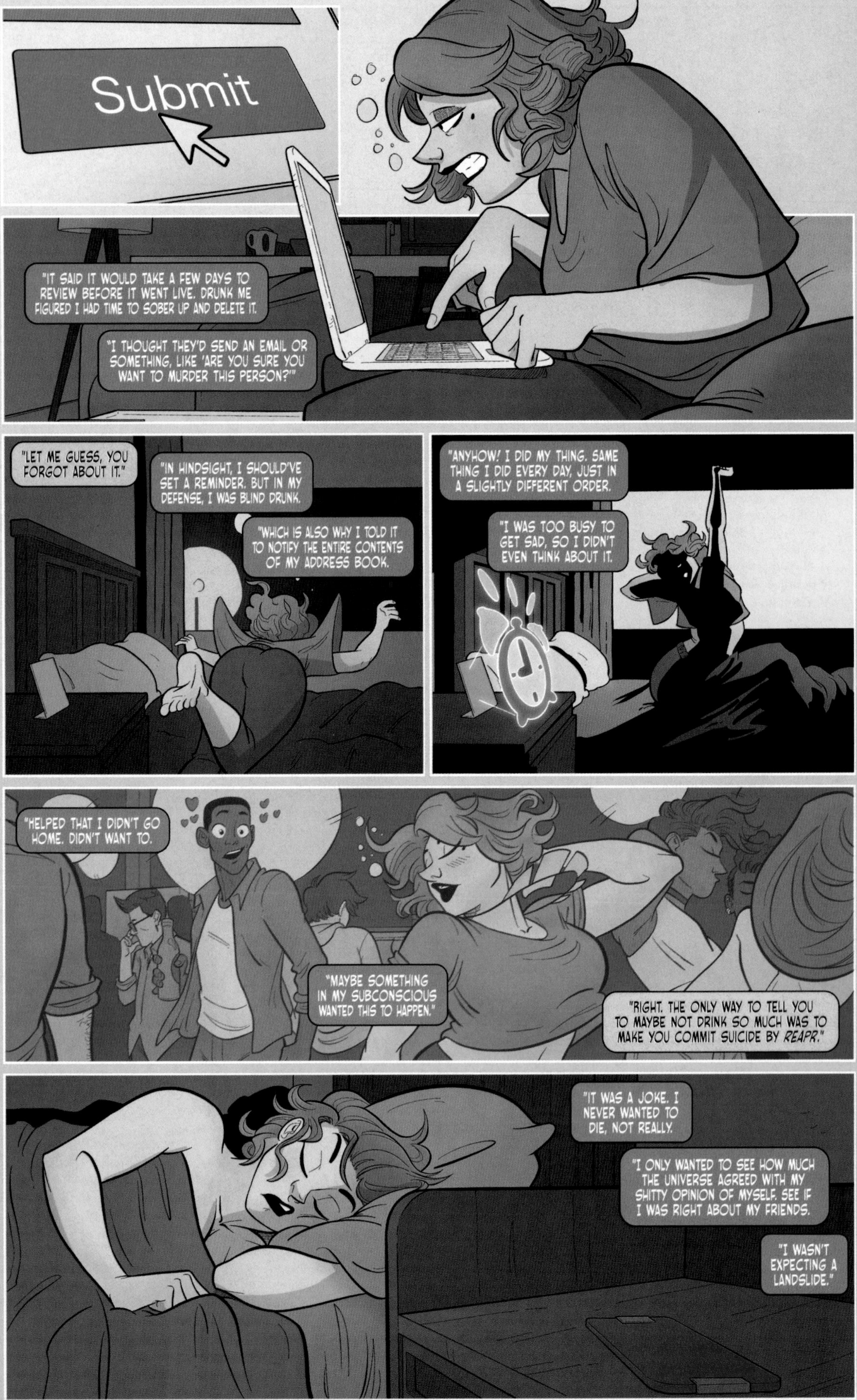

Submit
"IT SAID IT WOULD TAKE A FEW DAYS TO REVIEW BEFORE IT WENT LIVE. DRUNK ME FIGURED I HAD TIME TO SOBER UP AND DELETE IT.
"I THOUGHT THEY'D SEND AN EMAIL OR SOMETHING, LIKE 'ARE YOU SURE YOU WANT TO MURDER THIS PERSON?'"
"LET ME GUESS, YOU FORGOT ABOUT IT."
"IN HINDSIGHT, I SHOULD'VE SET A REMINDER. BUT IN MY DEFENSE, I WAS BLIND DRUNK.
"WHICH IS ALSO WHY I TOLD IT TO NOTIFY THE ENTIRE CONTENTS OF MY ADDRESS BOOK.
"ANYHOW! I DID MY THING. SAME THING I DID EVERY DAY, JUST IN A SLIGHTLY DIFFERENT ORDER.
"I WAS TOO BUSY TO GET SAD, SO I DIDN'T EVEN THINK ABOUT IT.
"HELPED THAT I DIDN'T GO HOME. DIDN'T WANT TO.
"MAYBE SOMETHING IN MY SUBCONSCIOUS WANTED THIS TO HAPPEN."
"RIGHT. THE ONLY WAY TO TELL YOU TO MAYBE NOT DRINK SO MUCH WAS TO MAKE YOU COMMIT SUICIDE BY *REAPR*."
"IT WAS A JOKE. I NEVER WANTED TO DIE, NOT REALLY.
"I ONLY WANTED TO SEE HOW MUCH THE UNIVERSE AGREED WITH MY SHITTY OPINION OF MYSELF. SEE IF I WAS RIGHT ABOUT MY FRIENDS.
"I WASN'T EXPECTING A LANDSLIDE."

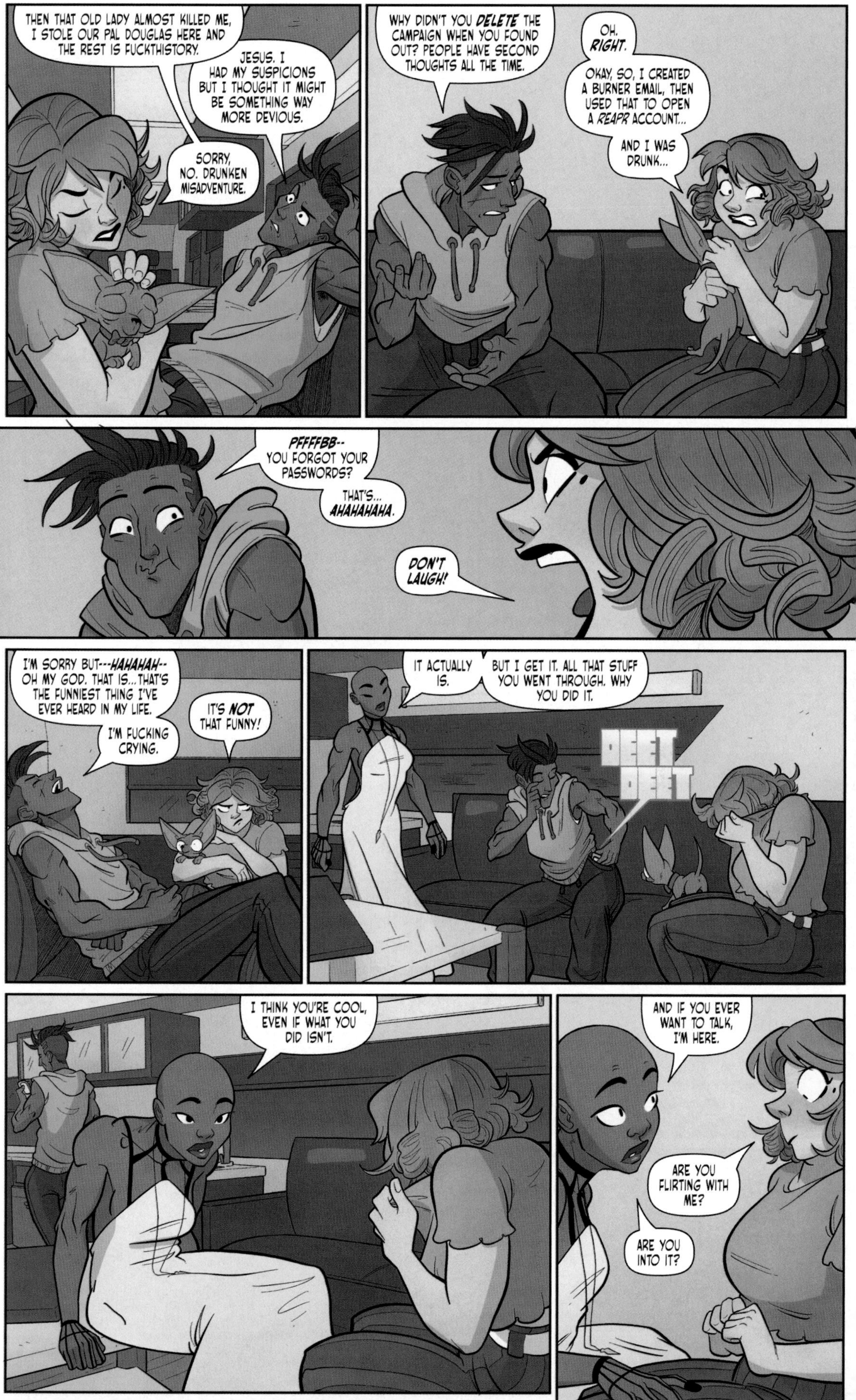
THEN THAT OLD LADY ALMOST KILLED ME, I STOLE OUR PAL DOUGLAS HERE AND THE REST IS FUCKTHISTORY.
JESUS. I HAD MY SUSPICIONS BUT I THOUGHT IT MIGHT BE SOMETHING WAY MORE DEVIOUS.
SORRY, NO. DRUNKEN MISADVENTURE.
WHY DIDN'T YOU DELETE THE CAMPAIGN WHEN YOU FOUND OUT? PEOPLE HAVE SECOND THOUGHTS ALL THE TIME.
OH. RIGHT.
OKAY, SO, I CREATED A BURNER EMAIL, THEN USED THAT TO OPEN A REAPR ACCOUNT...
AND I WAS DRUNK...
PFFFFBB-- YOU FORGOT YOUR PASSWORDS?
THAT'S... AHAHAHAHA.
DON'T LAUGH!
I'M SORRY BUT---HAHAHAH-- OH MY GOD. THAT IS...THAT'S THE FUNNIEST THING I'VE EVER HEARD IN MY LIFE.
I'M FUCKING CRYING.
IT'S NOT THAT FUNNY!
IT ACTUALLY IS.
BUT I GET IT. ALL THAT STUFF YOU WENT THROUGH. WHY YOU DID IT.
DEET DEET
I THINK YOU'RE COOL, EVEN IF WHAT YOU DID ISN'T.
AND IF YOU EVER WANT TO TALK, I'M HERE.
ARE YOU FLIRTING WITH ME?
ARE YOU INTO IT?

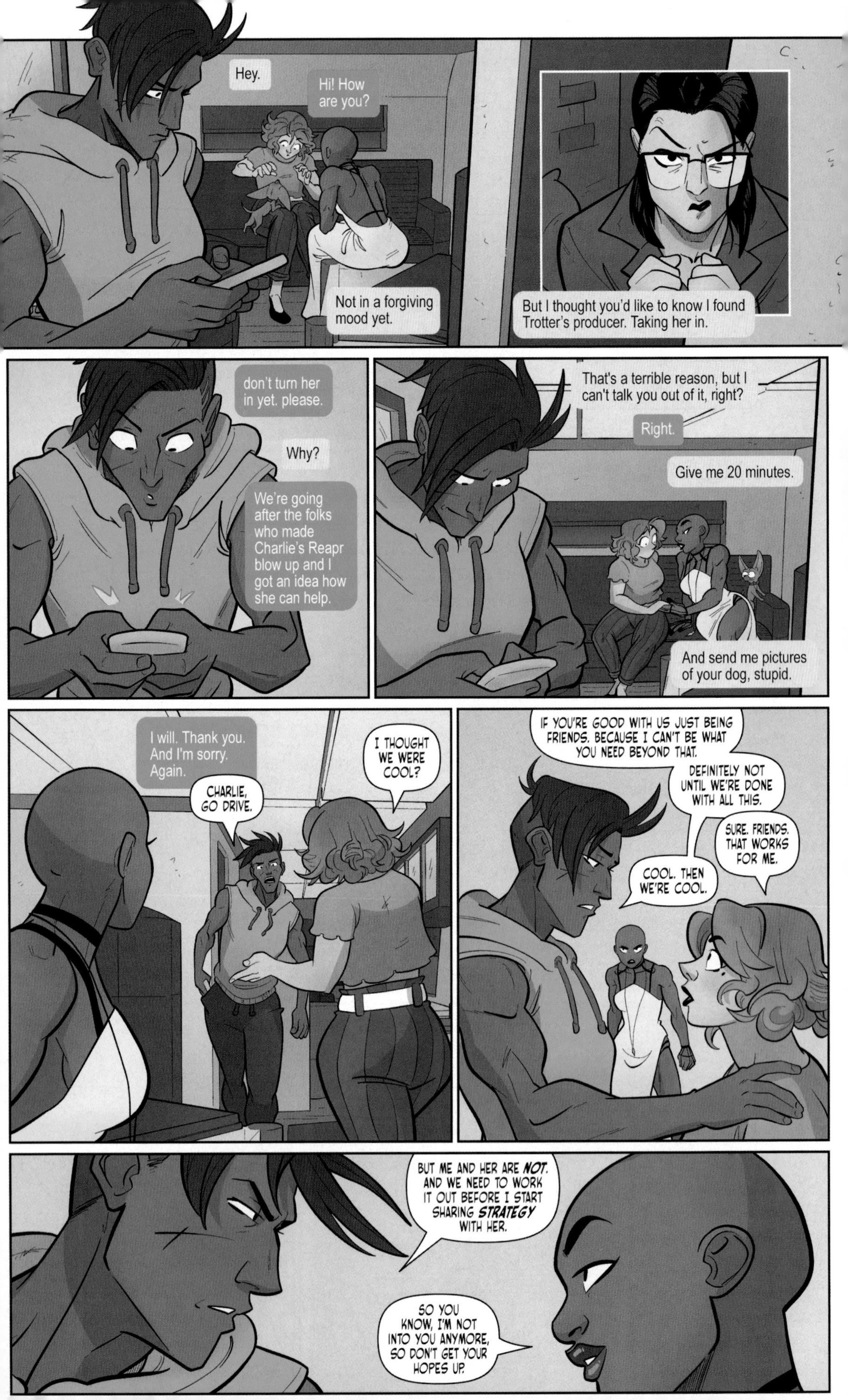

Hey.
Hi! How are you?
Not in a forgiving mood yet.
But I thought you'd like to know I found Trotter's producer. Taking her in.
don't turn her in yet. please.
Why?
We're going after the folks who made Charlie's Reapr blow up and I got an idea how she can help.
That's a terrible reason, but I can't talk you out of it, right?
Right.
Give me 20 minutes.
And send me pictures of your dog, stupid.
I will. Thank you. And I'm sorry. Again.
CHARLIE, GO DRIVE.
I THOUGHT WE WERE COOL?
IF YOU'RE GOOD WITH US JUST BEING FRIENDS. BECAUSE I CAN'T BE WHAT YOU NEED BEYOND THAT.
DEFINITELY NOT UNTIL WE'RE DONE WITH ALL THIS.
SURE. FRIENDS. THAT WORKS FOR ME.
COOL. THEN WE'RE COOL.
BUT ME AND HER ARE *NOT*. AND WE NEED TO WORK IT OUT BEFORE I START SHARING ***STRATEGY*** WITH HER.
SO YOU KNOW, I'M NOT INTO YOU ANYMORE, SO DON'T GET YOUR HOPES UP.

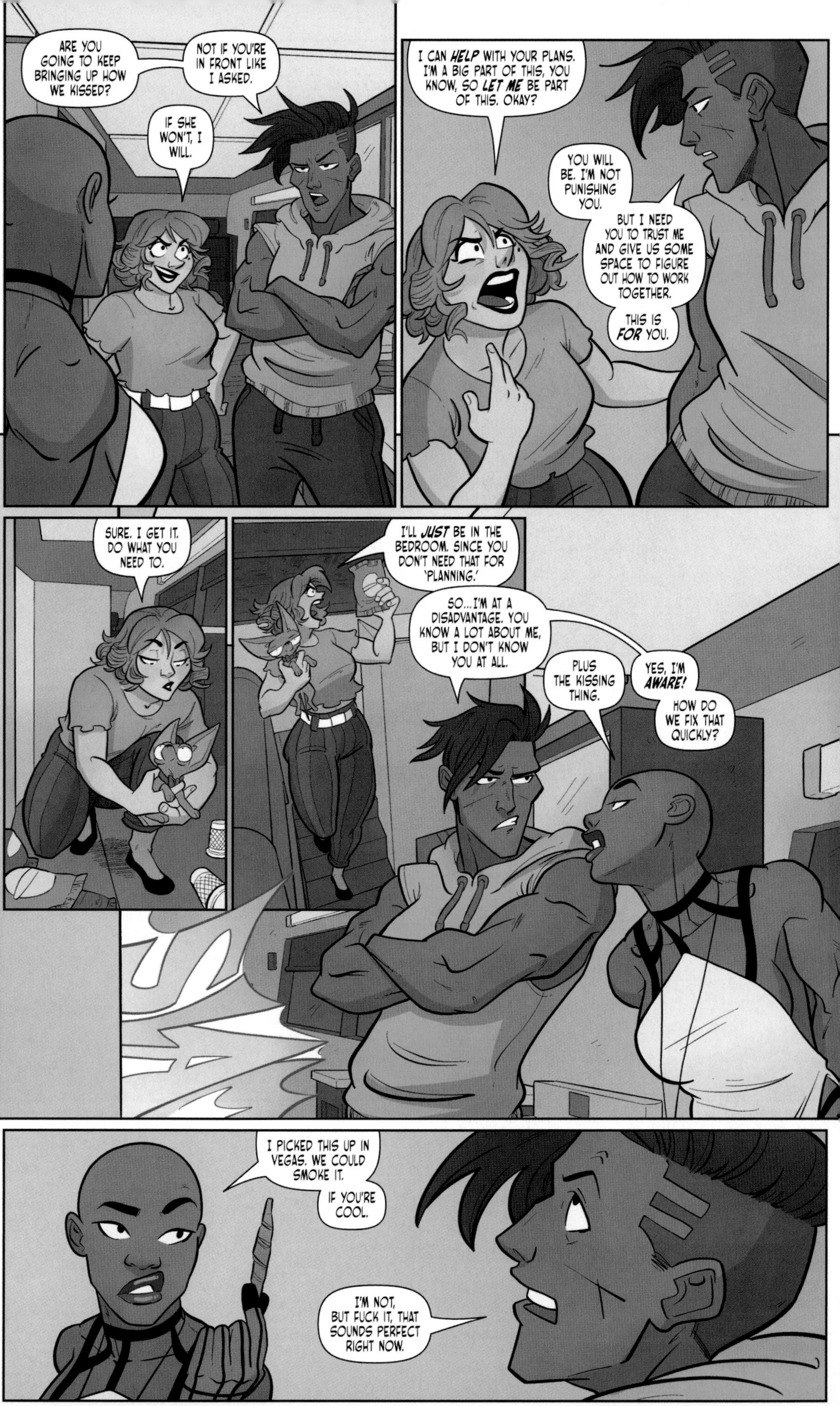
ARE YOU GOING TO KEEP BRINGING UP HOW WE KISSED?
NOT IF YOU'RE IN FRONT LIKE I ASKED.
IF SHE WON'T, I WILL.
I CAN HELP WITH YOUR PLANS. I'M A BIG PART OF THIS, YOU KNOW, SO LET ME BE PART OF THIS. OKAY?
YOU WILL BE. I'M NOT PUNISHING YOU.
BUT I NEED YOU TO TRUST ME AND GIVE US SOME SPACE TO FIGURE OUT HOW TO WORK TOGETHER.
THIS IS FOR YOU.
SURE. I GET IT. DO WHAT YOU NEED TO.
I'LL JUST BE IN THE BEDROOM. SINCE YOU DON'T NEED THAT FOR 'PLANNING.'
SO...I'M AT A DISADVANTAGE. YOU KNOW A LOT ABOUT ME, BUT I DON'T KNOW YOU AT ALL.
PLUS THE KISSING THING.
YES, I'M AWARE!
HOW DO WE FIX THAT QUICKLY?
I PICKED THIS UP IN VEGAS. WE COULD SMOKE IT.
IF YOU'RE COOL.
I'M NOT, BUT FUCK IT, THAT SOUNDS PERFECT RIGHT NOW.

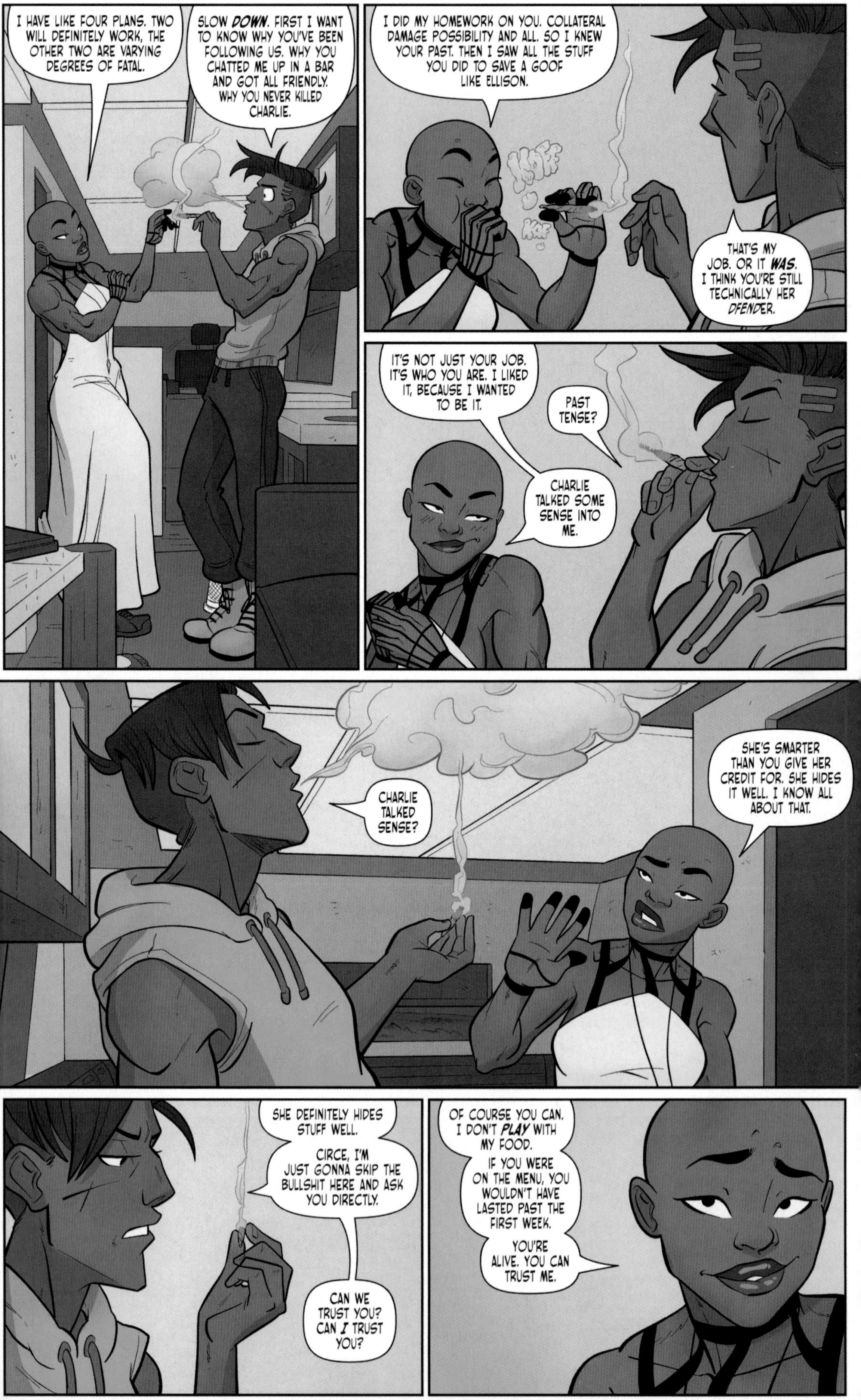
I HAVE LIKE FOUR PLANS. TWO WILL DEFINITELY WORK, THE OTHER TWO ARE VARYING DEGREES OF FATAL.
SLOW *DOWN*. FIRST I WANT TO KNOW WHY YOU'VE BEEN FOLLOWING US. WHY YOU CHATTED ME UP IN A BAR AND GOT ALL FRIENDLY. WHY YOU NEVER KILLED CHARLIE.
I DID MY HOMEWORK ON YOU. COLLATERAL DAMAGE POSSIBILITY AND ALL. SO I KNEW YOUR PAST. THEN I SAW ALL THE STUFF YOU DID TO SAVE A GOOF LIKE ELLISON.
KOFF
KOFF
THAT'S MY JOB. OR IT *WAS*. I THINK YOU'RE STILL TECHNICALLY HER *DFENDER*.
IT'S NOT JUST YOUR JOB. IT'S WHO YOU ARE. I LIKED IT, BECAUSE I WANTED TO BE IT.
PAST TENSE?
CHARLIE TALKED SOME SENSE INTO ME.
CHARLIE TALKED SENSE?
SHE'S SMARTER THAN YOU GIVE HER CREDIT FOR. SHE HIDES IT WELL. I KNOW ALL ABOUT THAT.
SHE DEFINITELY HIDES STUFF WELL.
CIRCE, I'M JUST GONNA SKIP THE BULLSHIT HERE AND ASK YOU DIRECTLY.
CAN WE TRUST YOU? CAN *I* TRUST YOU?
OF COURSE YOU CAN. I DON'T *PLAY* WITH MY FOOD.
IF YOU WERE ON THE MENU, YOU WOULDN'T HAVE LASTED PAST THE FIRST WEEK.
YOU'RE ALIVE. YOU CAN TRUST ME.

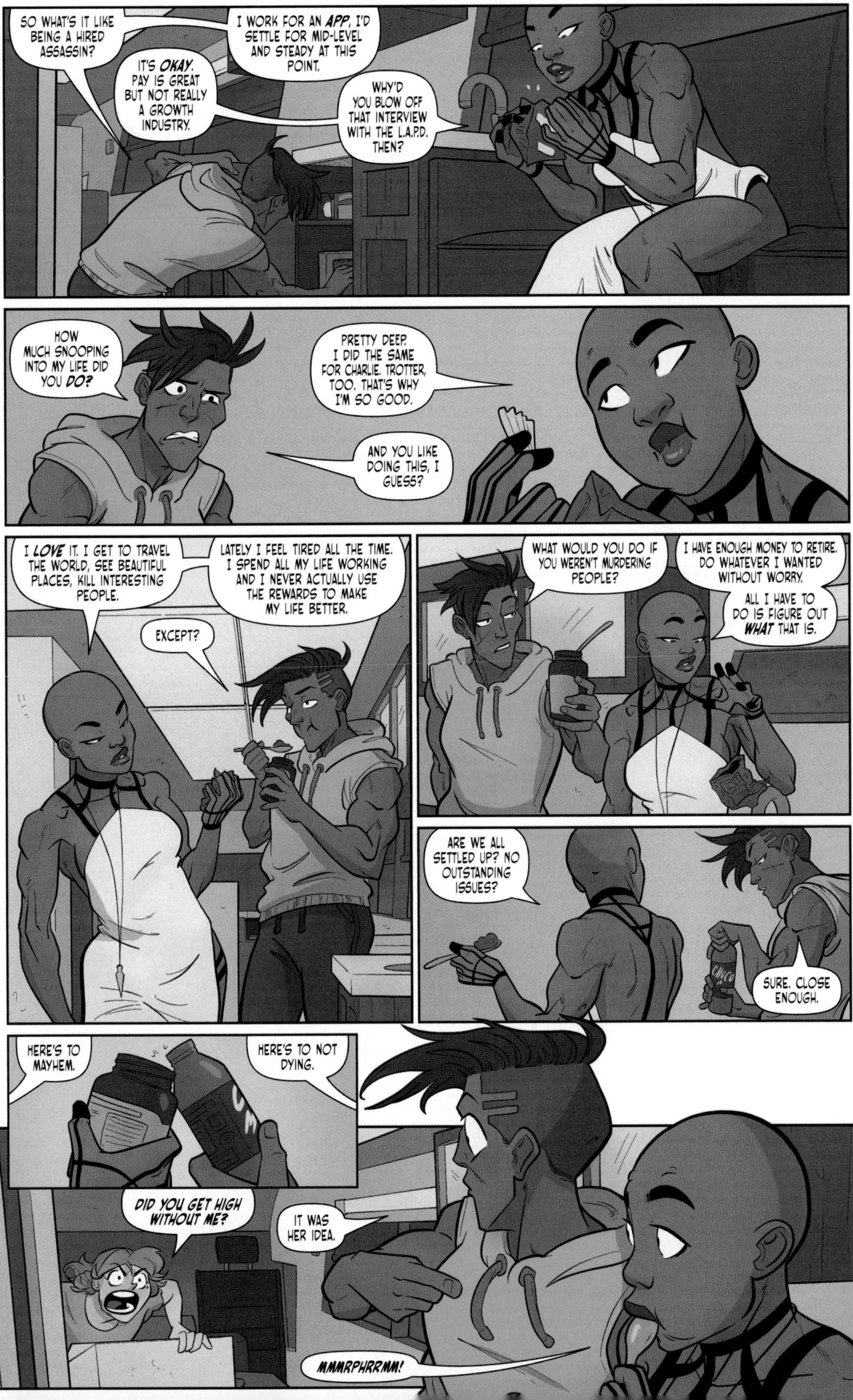
SO WHAT'S IT LIKE BEING A HIRED ASSASSIN?
I WORK FOR AN APP, I'D SETTLE FOR MID-LEVEL AND STEADY AT THIS POINT.
IT'S OKAY. PAY IS GREAT BUT NOT REALLY A GROWTH INDUSTRY.
WHY'D YOU BLOW OFF THAT INTERVIEW WITH THE L.A.P.D. THEN?
HOW MUCH SNOOPING INTO MY LIFE DID YOU DO?
PRETTY DEEP. I DID THE SAME FOR CHARLIE. TROTTER, TOO. THAT'S WHY I'M SO GOOD.
AND YOU LIKE DOING THIS, I GUESS?
I LOVE IT. I GET TO TRAVEL THE WORLD, SEE BEAUTIFUL PLACES, KILL INTERESTING PEOPLE.
LATELY I FEEL TIRED ALL THE TIME. I SPEND ALL MY LIFE WORKING AND I NEVER ACTUALLY USE THE REWARDS TO MAKE MY LIFE BETTER.
EXCEPT?
WHAT WOULD YOU DO IF YOU WEREN'T MURDERING PEOPLE?
I HAVE ENOUGH MONEY TO RETIRE. DO WHATEVER I WANTED WITHOUT WORRY.
ALL I HAVE TO DO IS FIGURE OUT WHAT THAT IS.
ARE WE ALL SETTLED UP? NO OUTSTANDING ISSUES?
SURE. CLOSE ENOUGH.
HERE'S TO MAYHEM.
HERE'S TO NOT DYING.
DID YOU GET HIGH WITHOUT ME?
IT WAS HER IDEA.
MMMRPHRRMM!

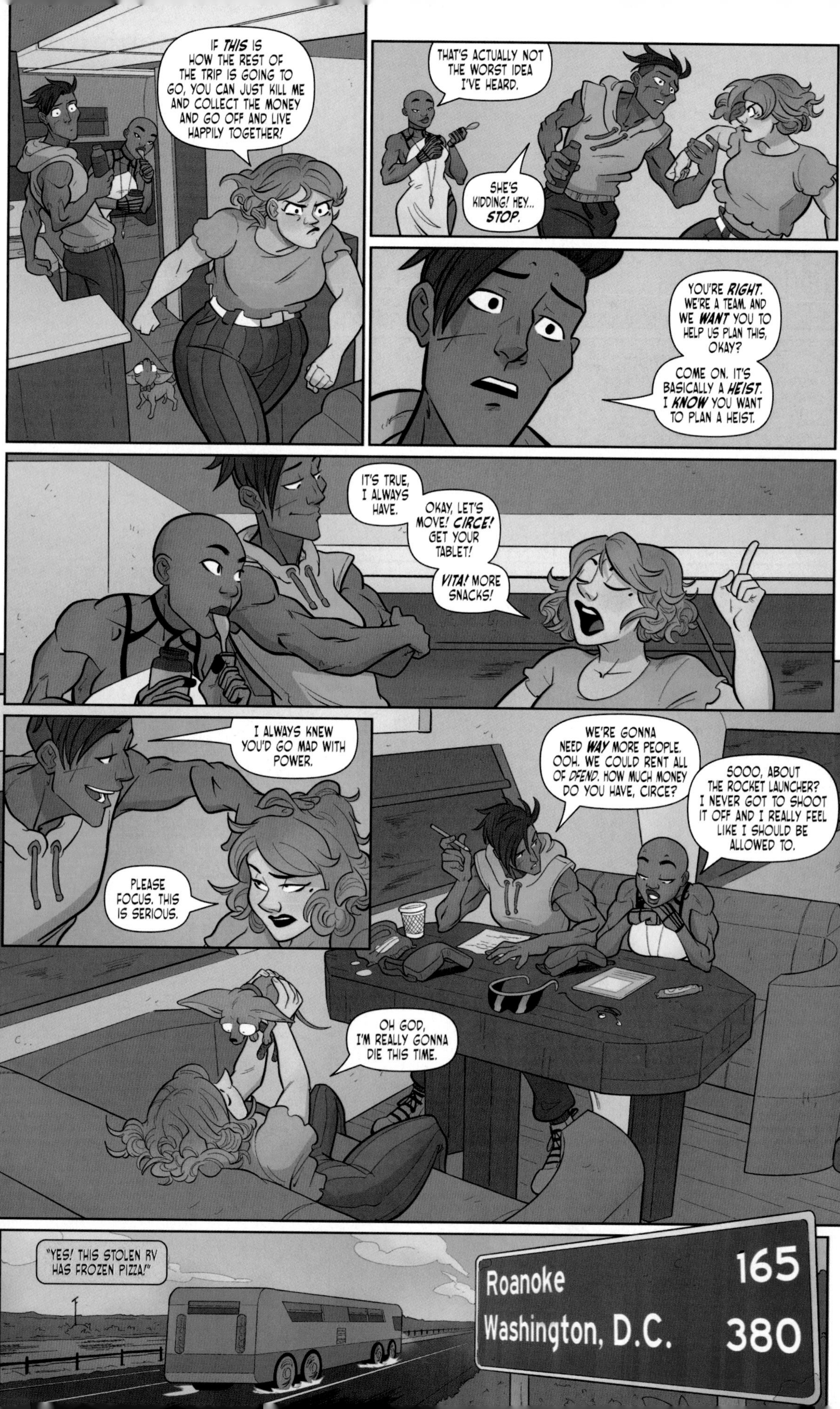
IF THIS IS HOW THE REST OF THE TRIP IS GOING TO GO, YOU CAN JUST KILL ME AND COLLECT THE MONEY AND GO OFF AND LIVE HAPPILY TOGETHER!
THAT'S ACTUALLY NOT THE WORST IDEA I'VE HEARD.
SHE'S KIDDING! HEY... STOP.
YOU'RE RIGHT. WE'RE A TEAM. AND WE WANT YOU TO HELP US PLAN THIS, OKAY?
COME ON. IT'S BASICALLY A HEIST. I KNOW YOU WANT TO PLAN A HEIST.
IT'S TRUE, I ALWAYS HAVE.
OKAY, LET'S MOVE! CIRCE! GET YOUR TABLET!
VITA! MORE SNACKS!
I ALWAYS KNEW YOU'D GO MAD WITH POWER.
PLEASE FOCUS. THIS IS SERIOUS.
WE'RE GONNA NEED WAY MORE PEOPLE. OOH. WE COULD RENT ALL OF DFEND. HOW MUCH MONEY DO YOU HAVE, CIRCE?
SOOO, ABOUT THE ROCKET LAUNCHER? I NEVER GOT TO SHOOT IT OFF AND I REALLY FEEL LIKE I SHOULD BE ALLOWED TO.
OH GOD, I'M REALLY GONNA DIE THIS TIME.
"YES! THIS STOLEN RV HAS FROZEN PIZZA!"
Roanoke 165
Washington, D.C. 380

CHAPTER SEVENTEEN

GET LOUD

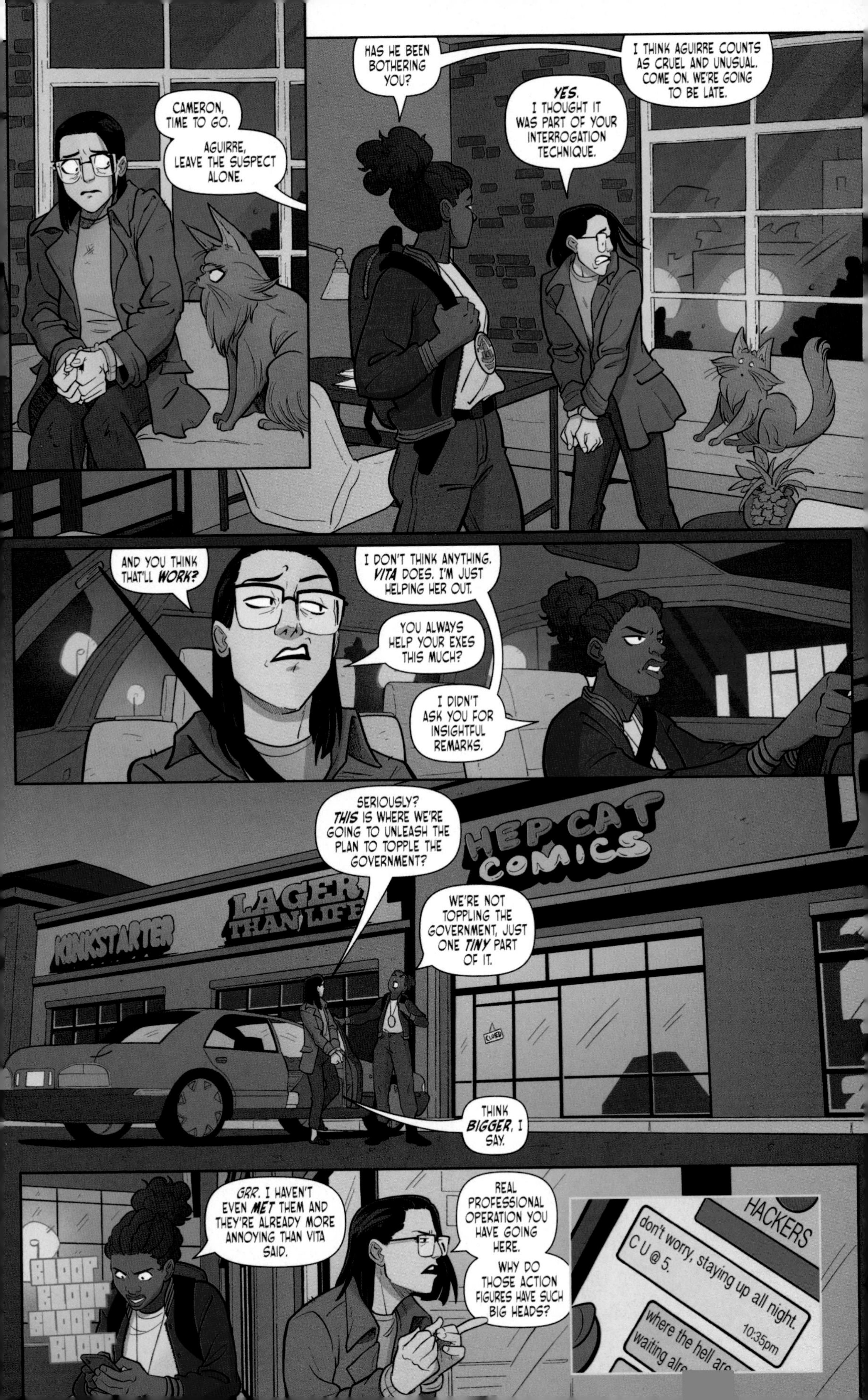

CAMERON, TIME TO GO.
AGUIRRE, LEAVE THE SUSPECT ALONE.
HAS HE BEEN BOTHERING YOU?
YES. I THOUGHT IT WAS PART OF YOUR INTERROGATION TECHNIQUE.
I THINK AGUIRRE COUNTS AS CRUEL AND UNUSUAL. COME ON. WE'RE GOING TO BE LATE.
AND YOU THINK THAT'LL WORK?
I DON'T THINK ANYTHING. VITA DOES. I'M JUST HELPING HER OUT.
YOU ALWAYS HELP YOUR EXES THIS MUCH?
I DIDN'T ASK YOU FOR INSIGHTFUL REMARKS.
SERIOUSLY? THIS IS WHERE WE'RE GOING TO UNLEASH THE PLAN TO TOPPLE THE GOVERNMENT?
HEP CAT COMICS
KINKSTARTER
LAGER THAN LIFE
WE'RE NOT TOPPLING THE GOVERNMENT, JUST ONE TINY PART OF IT.
CLOSED
THINK BIGGER, I SAY.
BLOOP BLOOP BLOOP BLOOP
GRR. I HAVEN'T EVEN MET THEM AND THEY'RE ALREADY MORE ANNOYING THAN VITA SAID.
REAL PROFESSIONAL OPERATION YOU HAVE GOING HERE.
WHY DO THOSE ACTION FIGURES HAVE SUCH BIG HEADS?
HACKERS
don't worry, staying up all night. C U @ 5.
10:35pm

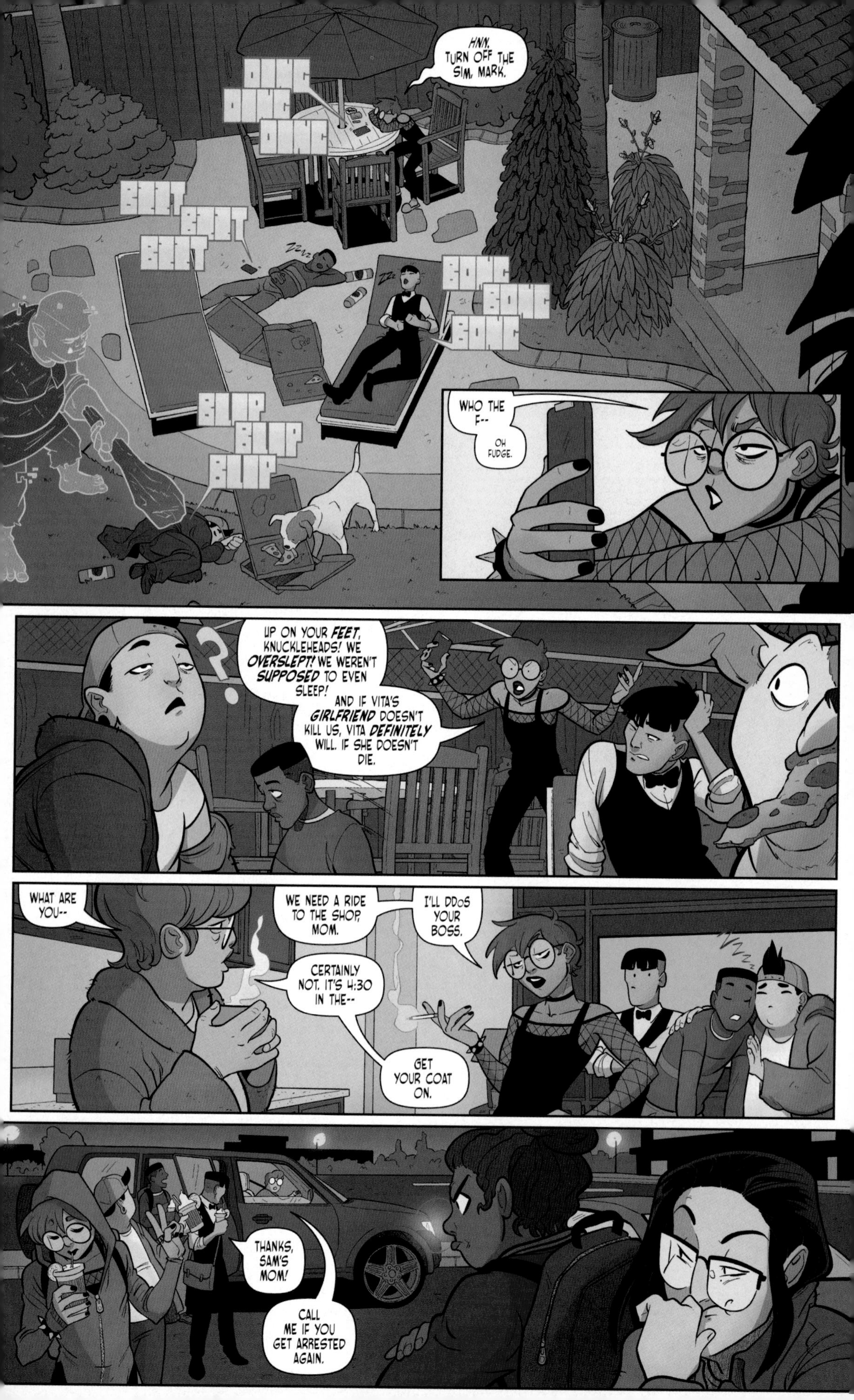

DING DING DING
HNN. TURN OFF THE SIM, MARK.
BZZT BZZT BZZT
BONG BONG BONG
BLIP BLIP BLIP
WHO THE F--
OH FUDGE.
UP ON YOUR FEET, KNUCKLEHEADS! WE OVERSLEPT! WE WEREN'T SUPPOSED TO EVEN SLEEP!
AND IF VITA'S GIRLFRIEND DOESN'T KILL US, VITA DEFINITELY WILL. IF SHE DOESN'T DIE.
WHAT ARE YOU--
WE NEED A RIDE TO THE SHOP, MOM.
CERTAINLY NOT. IT'S 4:30 IN THE--
I'LL DDoS YOUR BOSS.
GET YOUR COAT ON.
THANKS, SAM'S MOM!
CALL ME IF YOU GET ARRESTED AGAIN.

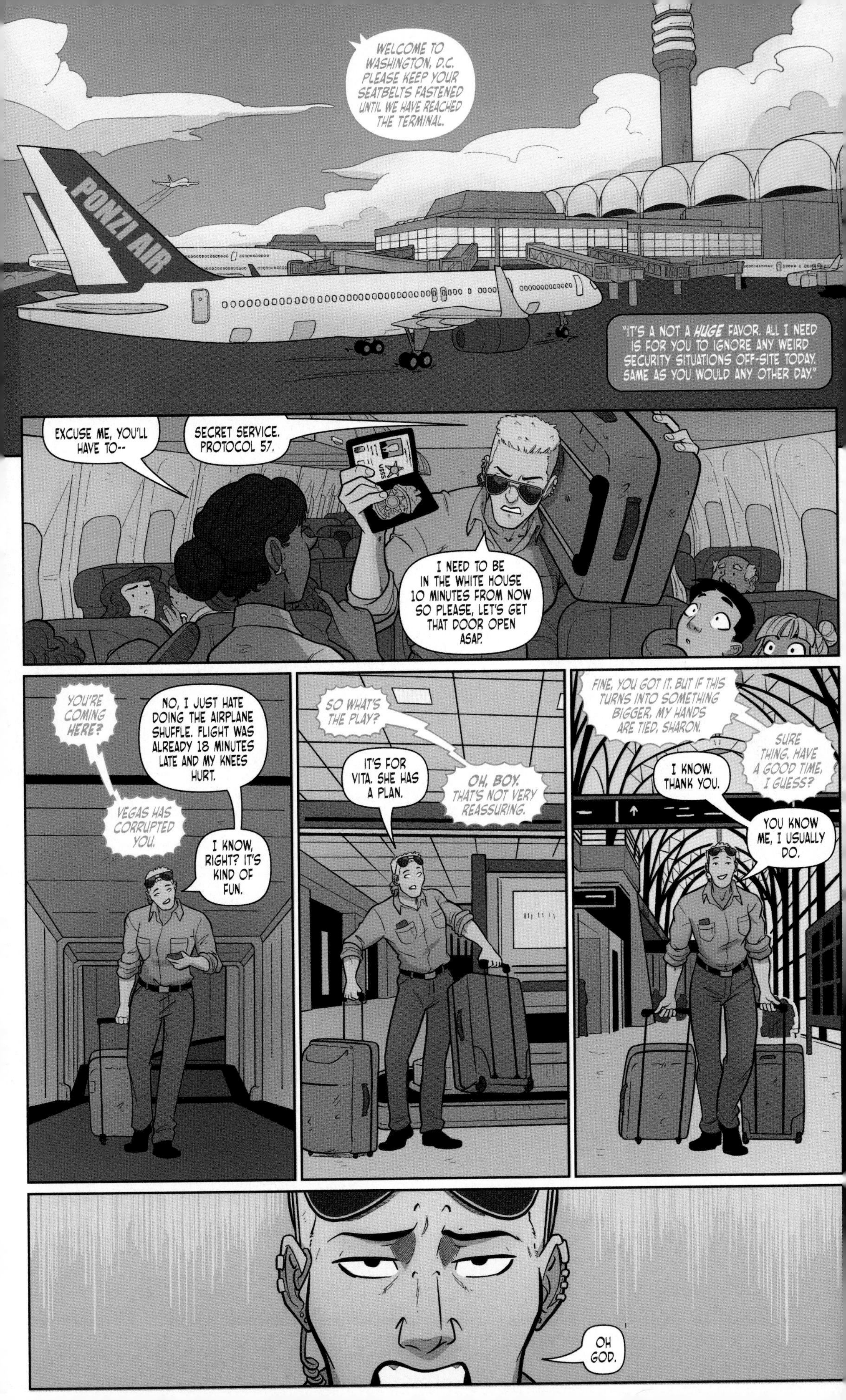
WELCOME TO WASHINGTON, D.C. PLEASE KEEP YOUR SEATBELTS FASTENED UNTIL WE HAVE REACHED THE TERMINAL.
PONZI AIR
"IT'S A NOT A HUGE FAVOR. ALL I NEED IS FOR YOU TO IGNORE ANY WEIRD SECURITY SITUATIONS OFF-SITE TODAY. SAME AS YOU WOULD ANY OTHER DAY."
EXCUSE ME, YOU'LL HAVE TO--
SECRET SERVICE. PROTOCOL 57.
I NEED TO BE IN THE WHITE HOUSE 10 MINUTES FROM NOW SO PLEASE, LET'S GET THAT DOOR OPEN ASAP.
YOU'RE COMING HERE?
NO, I JUST HATE DOING THE AIRPLANE SHUFFLE. FLIGHT WAS ALREADY 18 MINUTES LATE AND MY KNEES HURT.
VEGAS HAS CORRUPTED YOU.
I KNOW, RIGHT? IT'S KIND OF FUN.
SO WHAT'S THE PLAY?
IT'S FOR VITA. SHE HAS A PLAN.
OH, BOY. THAT'S NOT VERY REASSURING.
FINE, YOU GOT IT. BUT IF THIS TURNS INTO SOMETHING BIGGER, MY HANDS ARE TIED, SHARON.
I KNOW. THANK YOU.
SURE THING. HAVE A GOOD TIME, I GUESS?
YOU KNOW ME, I USUALLY DO.
OH GOD.

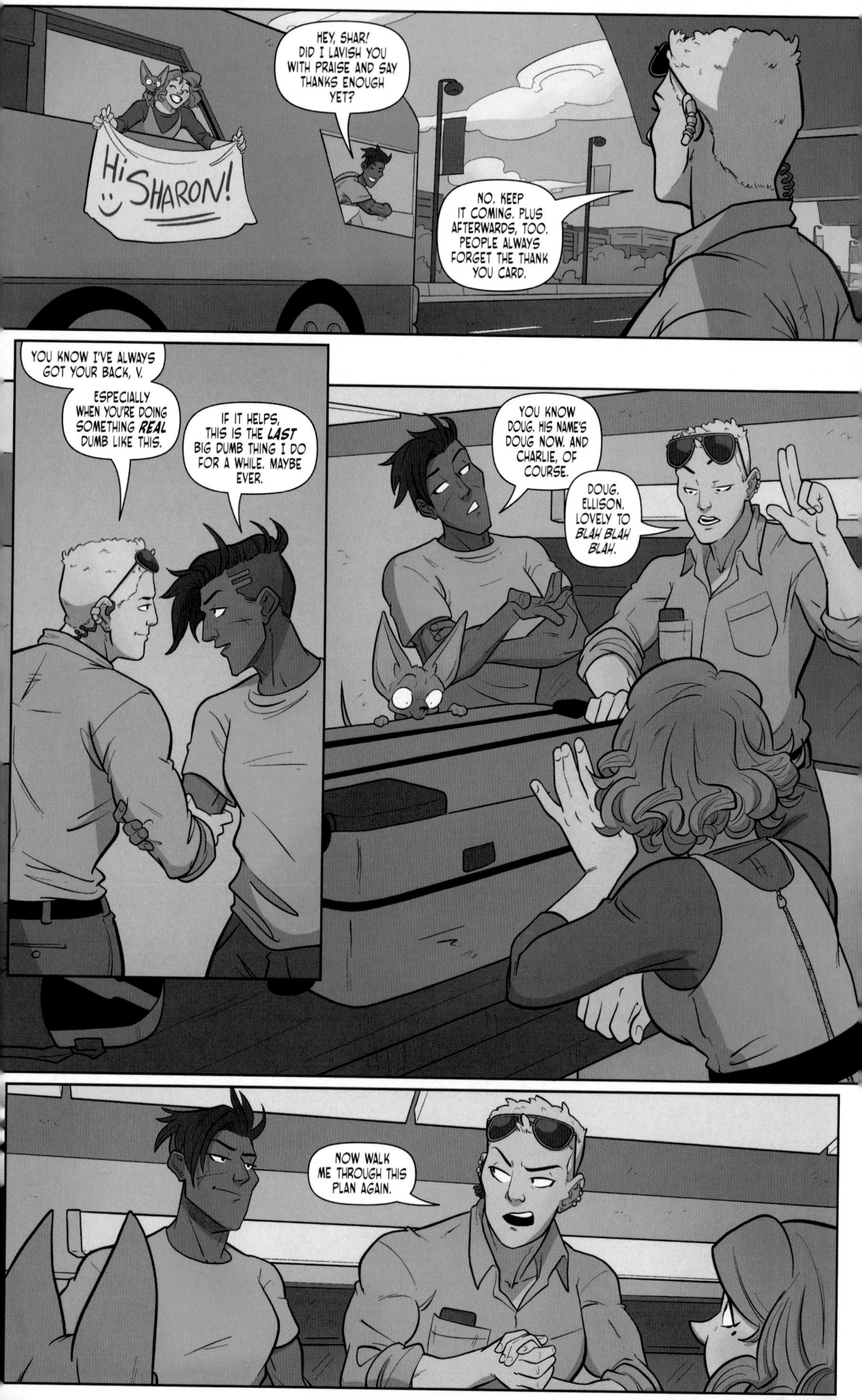
Hi SHARON!
HEY, SHAR! DID I LAVISH YOU WITH PRAISE AND SAY THANKS ENOUGH YET?
NO. KEEP IT COMING. PLUS AFTERWARDS, TOO. PEOPLE ALWAYS FORGET THE THANK YOU CARD.
YOU KNOW I'VE ALWAYS GOT YOUR BACK, V.
ESPECIALLY WHEN YOU'RE DOING SOMETHING REAL DUMB LIKE THIS.
IF IT HELPS, THIS IS THE LAST BIG DUMB THING I DO FOR A WHILE. MAYBE EVER.
YOU KNOW DOUG. HIS NAME'S DOUG NOW. AND CHARLIE, OF COURSE.
DOUG. ELLISON. LOVELY TO BLAH BLAH BLAH.
NOW WALK ME THROUGH THIS PLAN AGAIN.

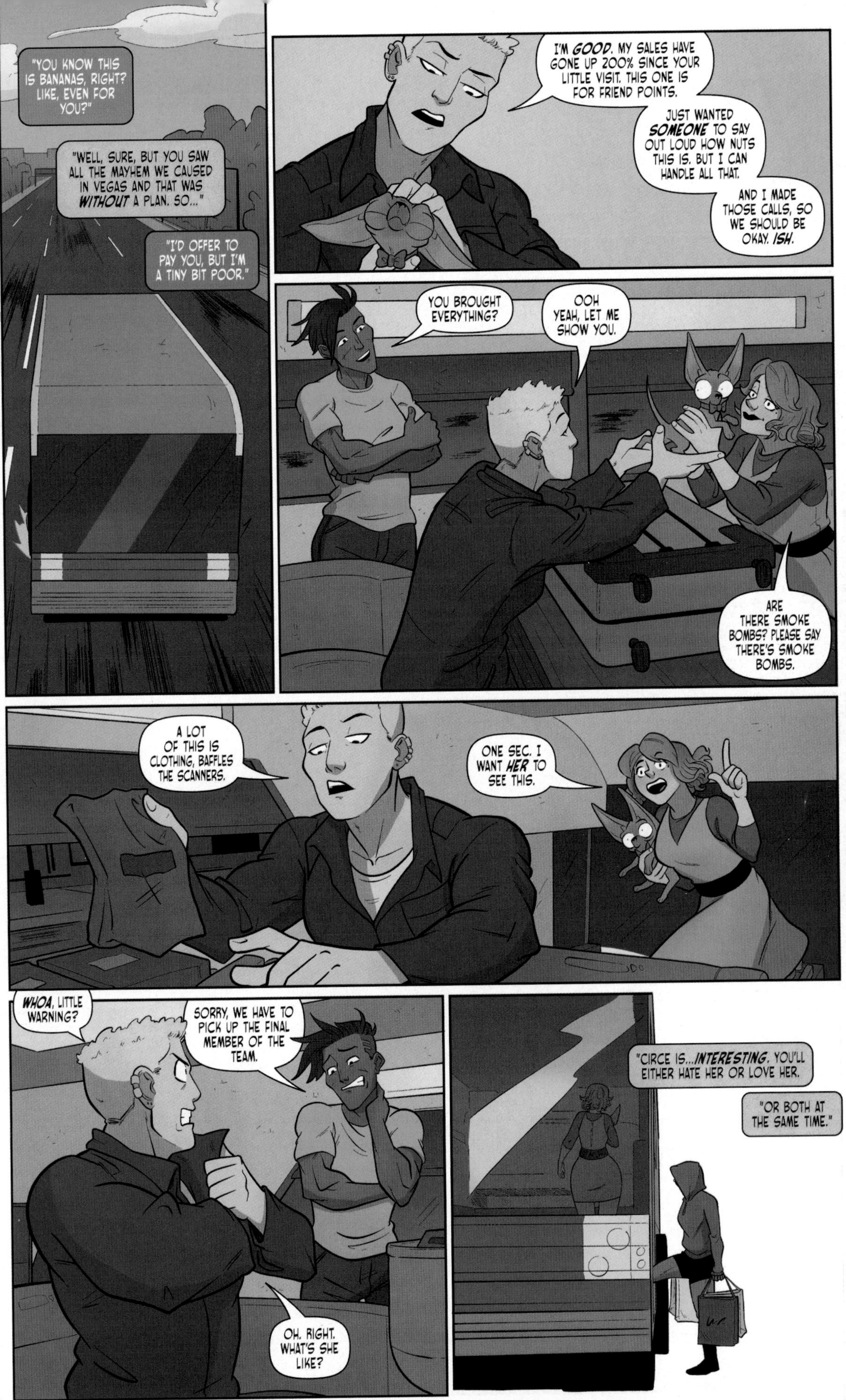
"YOU KNOW THIS IS BANANAS, RIGHT? LIKE, EVEN FOR YOU?"
"WELL, SURE, BUT YOU SAW ALL THE MAYHEM WE CAUSED IN VEGAS AND THAT WAS WITHOUT A PLAN. SO..."
"I'D OFFER TO PAY YOU, BUT I'M A TINY BIT POOR."
I'M GOOD. MY SALES HAVE GONE UP 200% SINCE YOUR LITTLE VISIT. THIS ONE IS FOR FRIEND POINTS.
JUST WANTED SOMEONE TO SAY OUT LOUD HOW NUTS THIS IS. BUT I CAN HANDLE ALL THAT.
AND I MADE THOSE CALLS, SO WE SHOULD BE OKAY. ISH.
YOU BROUGHT EVERYTHING?
OOH YEAH, LET ME SHOW YOU.
ARE THERE SMOKE BOMBS? PLEASE SAY THERE'S SMOKE BOMBS.
A LOT OF THIS IS CLOTHING, BAFFLES THE SCANNERS.
ONE SEC. I WANT HER TO SEE THIS.
WHOA, LITTLE WARNING?
SORRY, WE HAVE TO PICK UP THE FINAL MEMBER OF THE TEAM.
OH. RIGHT. WHAT'S SHE LIKE?
"CIRCE IS...INTERESTING. YOU'LL EITHER HATE HER OR LOVE HER.
"OR BOTH AT THE SAME TIME."

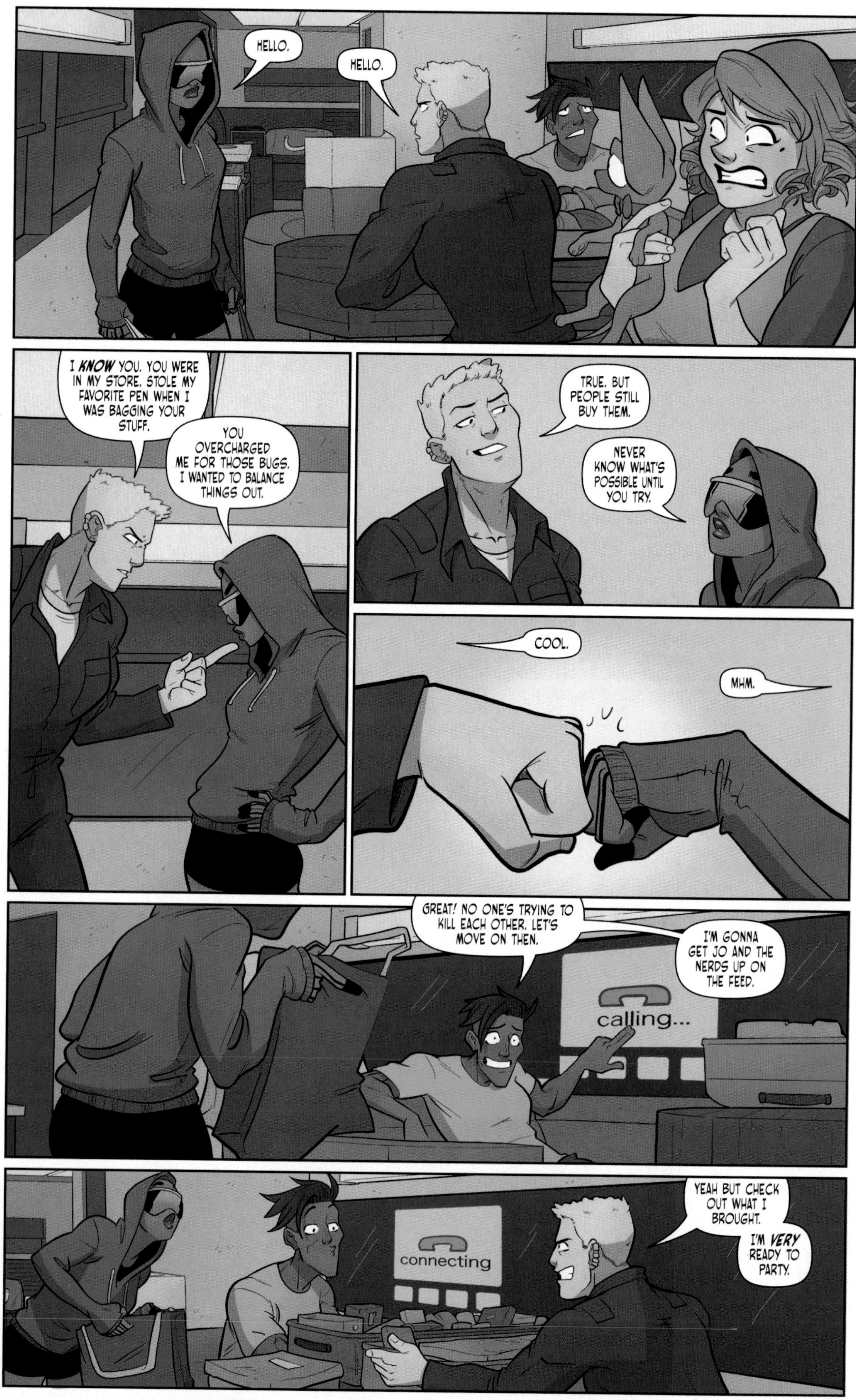
HELLO.
HELLO.
I KNOW YOU. YOU WERE IN MY STORE. STOLE MY FAVORITE PEN WHEN I WAS BAGGING YOUR STUFF.
YOU OVERCHARGED ME FOR THOSE BUGS. I WANTED TO BALANCE THINGS OUT.
TRUE. BUT PEOPLE STILL BUY THEM.
NEVER KNOW WHAT'S POSSIBLE UNTIL YOU TRY.
COOL.
MHM.
GREAT! NO ONE'S TRYING TO KILL EACH OTHER. LET'S MOVE ON THEN.
I'M GONNA GET JO AND THE NERDS UP ON THE FEED.
calling...
connecting
YEAH BUT CHECK OUT WHAT I BROUGHT.
I'M VERY READY TO PARTY.

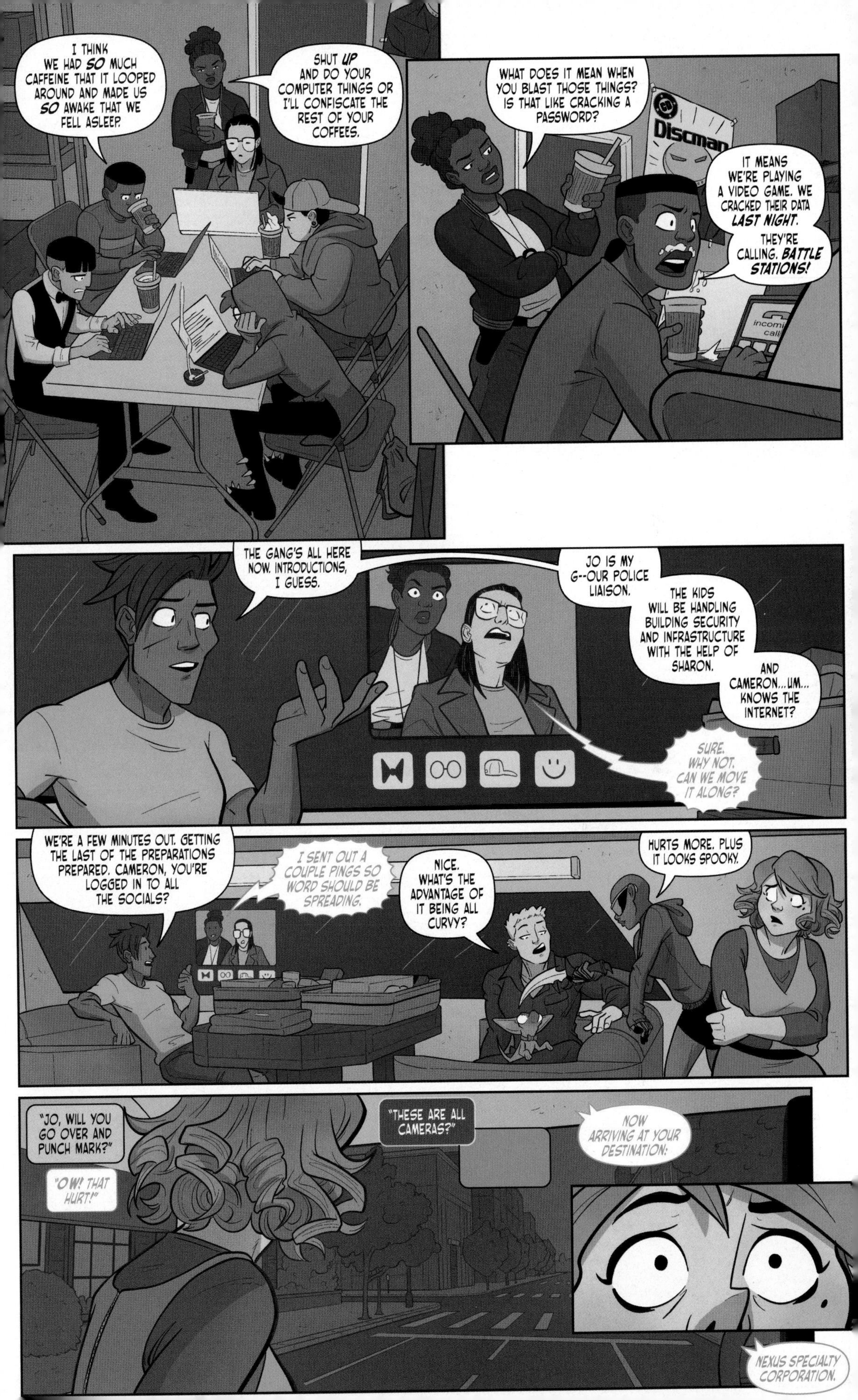
I THINK WE HAD SO MUCH CAFFEINE THAT IT LOOPED AROUND AND MADE US SO AWAKE THAT WE FELL ASLEEP.
SHUT UP AND DO YOUR COMPUTER THINGS OR I'LL CONFISCATE THE REST OF YOUR COFFEES.
WHAT DOES IT MEAN WHEN YOU BLAST THOSE THINGS? IS THAT LIKE CRACKING A PASSWORD?
Discman
IT MEANS WE'RE PLAYING A VIDEO GAME. WE CRACKED THEIR DATA LAST NIGHT.
THEY'RE CALLING. BATTLE STATIONS!
incoming call
THE GANG'S ALL HERE NOW. INTRODUCTIONS, I GUESS.
JO IS MY G--OUR POLICE LIAISON.
THE KIDS WILL BE HANDLING BUILDING SECURITY AND INFRASTRUCTURE WITH THE HELP OF SHARON.
AND CAMERON...UM... KNOWS THE INTERNET?
SURE. WHY NOT. CAN WE MOVE IT ALONG?
WE'RE A FEW MINUTES OUT. GETTING THE LAST OF THE PREPARATIONS PREPARED. CAMERON, YOU'RE LOGGED IN TO ALL THE SOCIALS?
I SENT OUT A COUPLE PINGS SO WORD SHOULD BE SPREADING.
NICE. WHAT'S THE ADVANTAGE OF IT BEING ALL CURVY?
HURTS MORE. PLUS IT LOOKS SPOOKY.
"JO, WILL YOU GO OVER AND PUNCH MARK?"
"OW! THAT HURT!"
"THESE ARE ALL CAMERAS?"
NOW ARRIVING AT YOUR DESTINATION:
NEXUS SPECIALTY CORPORATION.

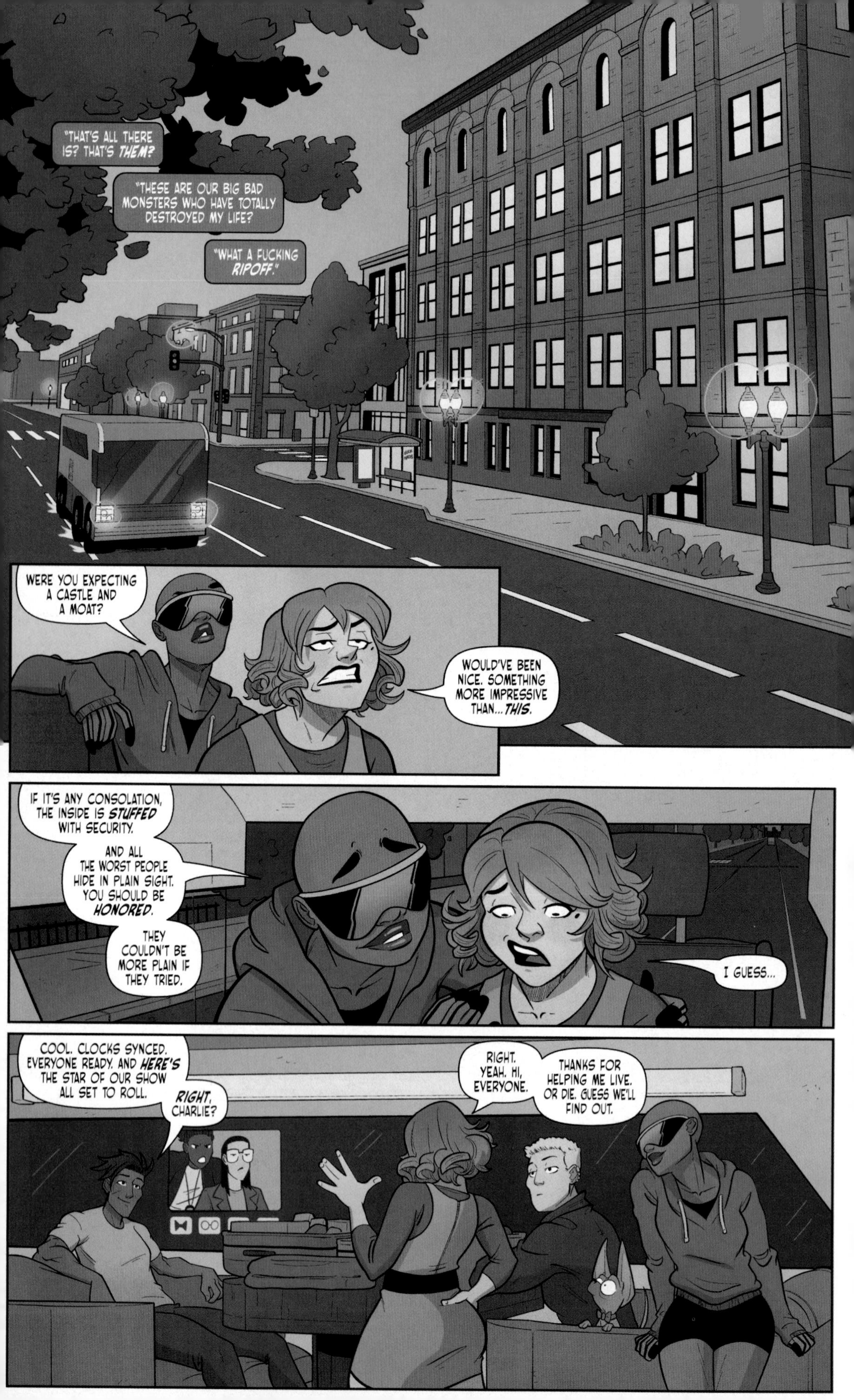
"THAT'S ALL THERE IS? THAT'S *THEM?*
"THESE ARE OUR BIG BAD MONSTERS WHO HAVE TOTALLY DESTROYED MY LIFE?
"WHAT A FUCKING *RIPOFF.*"
WERE YOU EXPECTING A CASTLE AND A MOAT?
WOULD'VE BEEN NICE. SOMETHING MORE IMPRESSIVE THAN... *THIS.*
IF IT'S ANY CONSOLATION, THE INSIDE IS *STUFFED* WITH SECURITY.
AND ALL THE WORST PEOPLE HIDE IN PLAIN SIGHT. YOU SHOULD BE *HONORED.*
THEY COULDN'T BE MORE PLAIN IF THEY TRIED.
I GUESS...
COOL. CLOCKS SYNCED. EVERYONE READY. AND *HERE'S* THE STAR OF OUR SHOW ALL SET TO ROLL.
RIGHT, CHARLIE?
RIGHT. YEAH. HI, EVERYONE.
THANKS FOR HELPING ME LIVE. OR DIE. GUESS WE'LL FIND OUT.

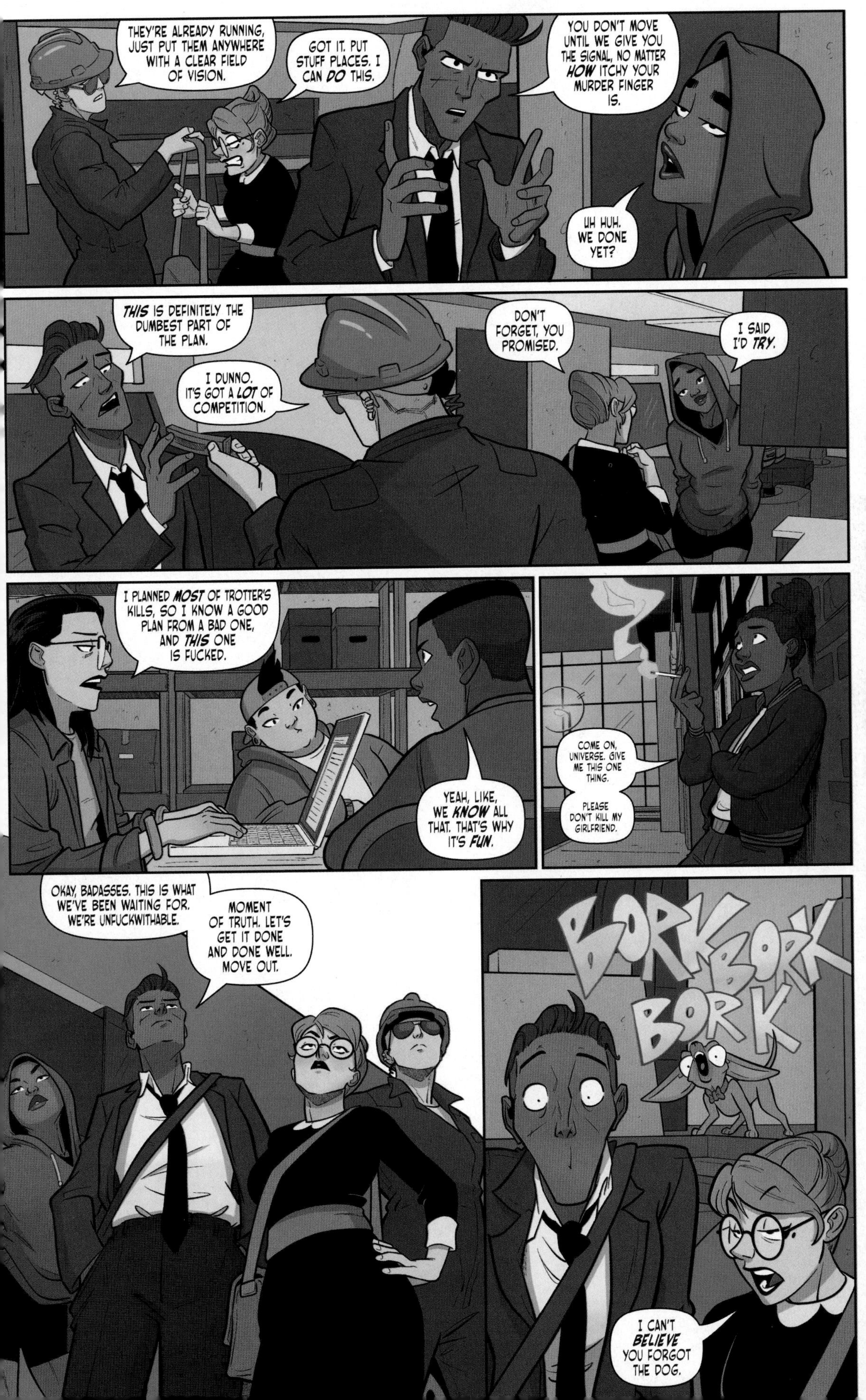
THEY'RE ALREADY RUNNING, JUST PUT THEM ANYWHERE WITH A CLEAR FIELD OF VISION.
GOT IT. PUT STUFF PLACES. I CAN DO THIS.
YOU DON'T MOVE UNTIL WE GIVE YOU THE SIGNAL, NO MATTER HOW ITCHY YOUR MURDER FINGER IS.
UH HUH. WE DONE YET?
THIS IS DEFINITELY THE DUMBEST PART OF THE PLAN.
I DUNNO. IT'S GOT A LOT OF COMPETITION.
DON'T FORGET, YOU PROMISED.
I SAID I'D TRY.
I PLANNED MOST OF TROTTER'S KILLS, SO I KNOW A GOOD PLAN FROM A BAD ONE, AND THIS ONE IS FUCKED.
YEAH, LIKE, WE KNOW ALL THAT. THAT'S WHY IT'S FUN.
COME ON, UNIVERSE. GIVE ME THIS ONE THING.
PLEASE DON'T KILL MY GIRLFRIEND.
OKAY, BADASSES. THIS IS WHAT WE'VE BEEN WAITING FOR. WE'RE UNFUCKWITHABLE.
MOMENT OF TRUTH. LET'S GET IT DONE AND DONE WELL. MOVE OUT.
BORK BORK BORK
I CAN'T BELIEVE YOU FORGOT THE DOG.

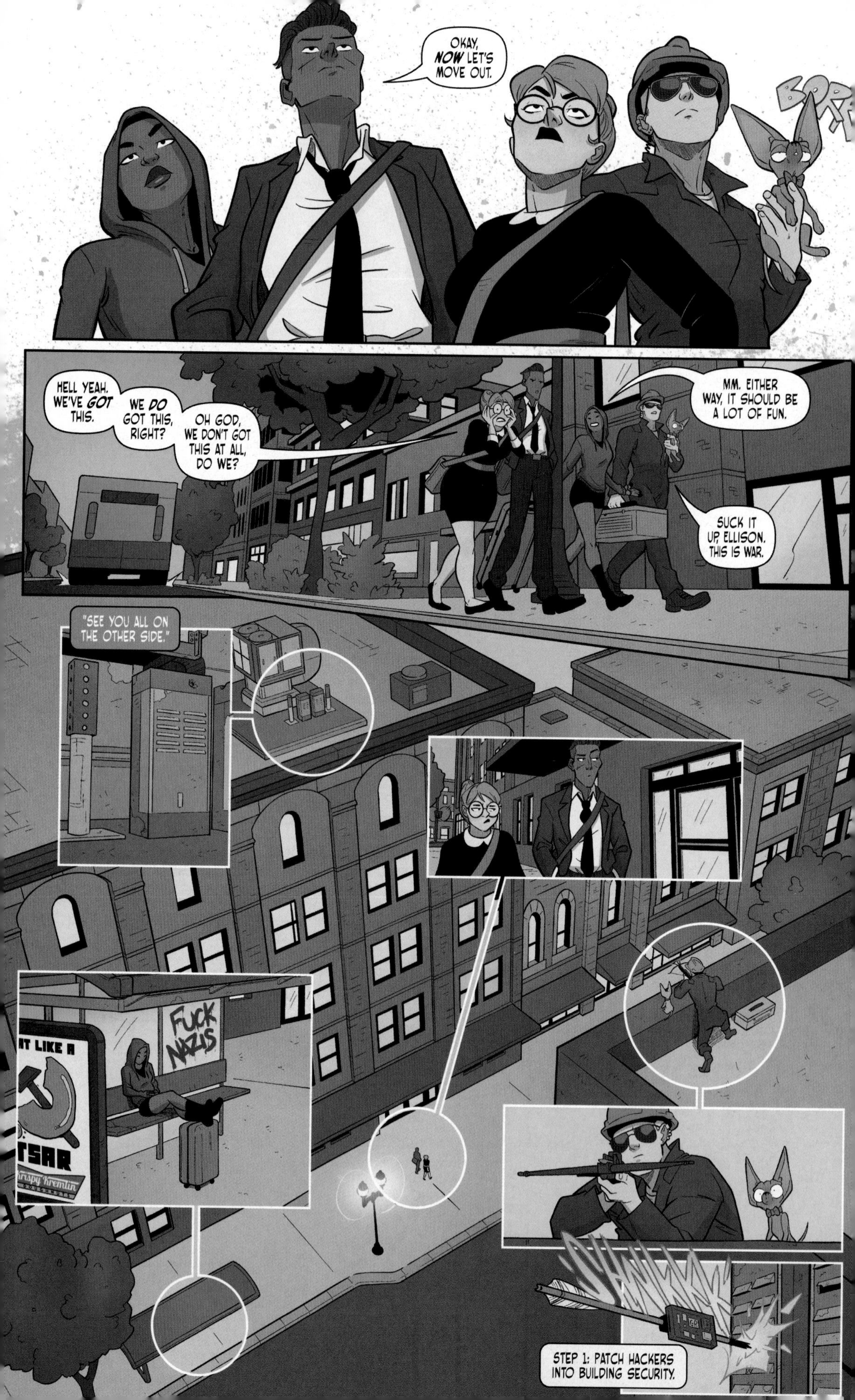
OKAY, NOW LET'S MOVE OUT.
HELL YEAH. WE'VE GOT THIS.
WE DO GOT THIS, RIGHT?
OH GOD, WE DON'T GOT THIS AT ALL, DO WE?
MM. EITHER WAY, IT SHOULD BE A LOT OF FUN.
SUCK IT UP, ELLISON. THIS IS WAR.
"SEE YOU ALL ON THE OTHER SIDE."
FUCK NAZIS
STEP 1: PATCH HACKERS INTO BUILDING SECURITY.

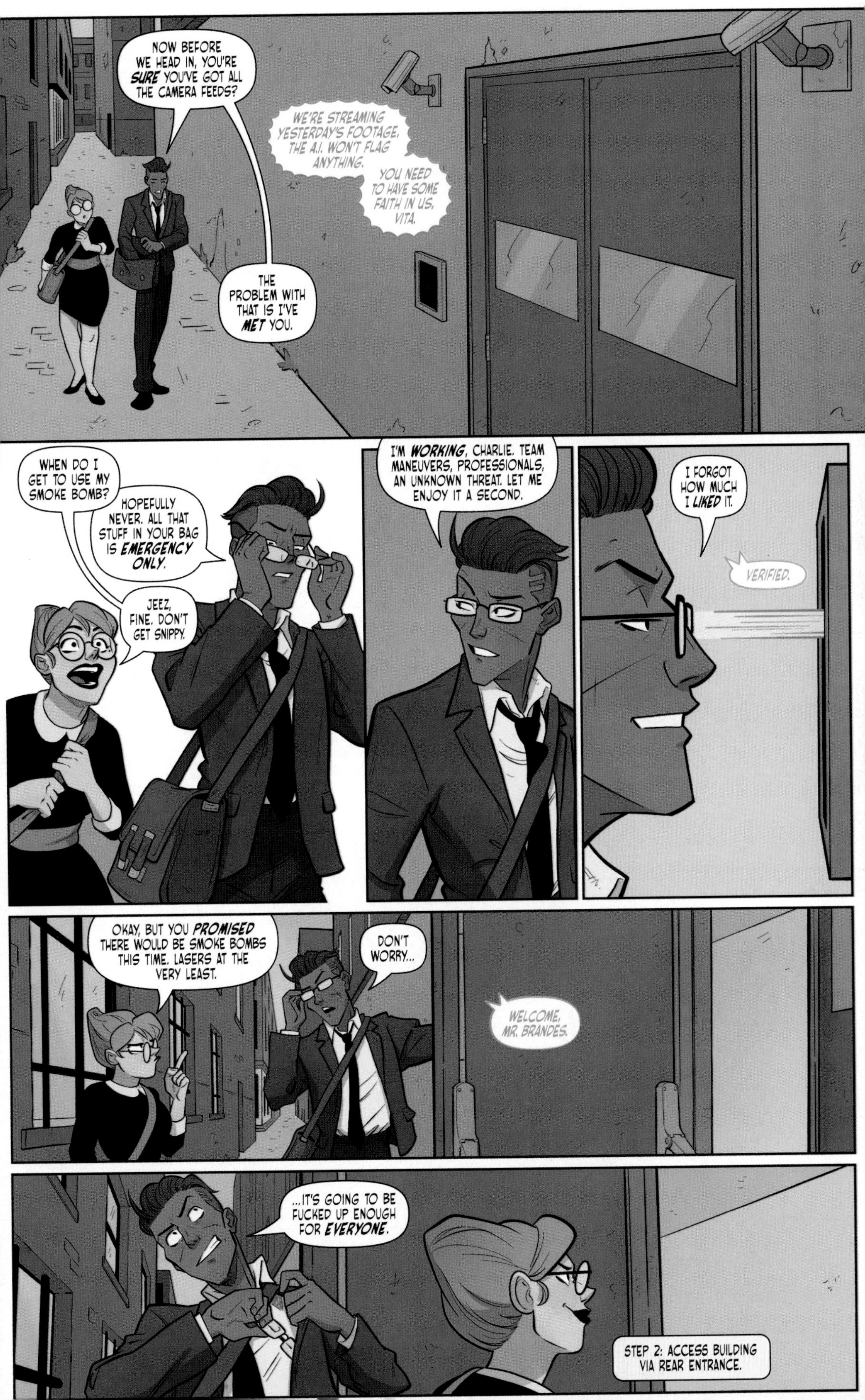
NOW BEFORE WE HEAD IN, YOU'RE SURE YOU'VE GOT ALL THE CAMERA FEEDS?
WE'RE STREAMING YESTERDAY'S FOOTAGE, THE A.I. WON'T FLAG ANYTHING.
YOU NEED TO HAVE SOME FAITH IN US, VITA.
THE PROBLEM WITH THAT IS I'VE MET YOU.
WHEN DO I GET TO USE MY SMOKE BOMB?
HOPEFULLY NEVER. ALL THAT STUFF IN YOUR BAG IS EMERGENCY ONLY.
JEEZ, FINE. DON'T GET SNIPPY.
I'M WORKING, CHARLIE. TEAM MANEUVERS, PROFESSIONALS, AN UNKNOWN THREAT. LET ME ENJOY IT A SECOND.
I FORGOT HOW MUCH I LIKED IT.
VERIFIED.
OKAY, BUT YOU PROMISED THERE WOULD BE SMOKE BOMBS THIS TIME. LASERS AT THE VERY LEAST.
DON'T WORRY...
WELCOME, MR. BRANDES.
...IT'S GOING TO BE FUCKED UP ENOUGH FOR EVERYONE.
STEP 2: ACCESS BUILDING VIA REAR ENTRANCE.

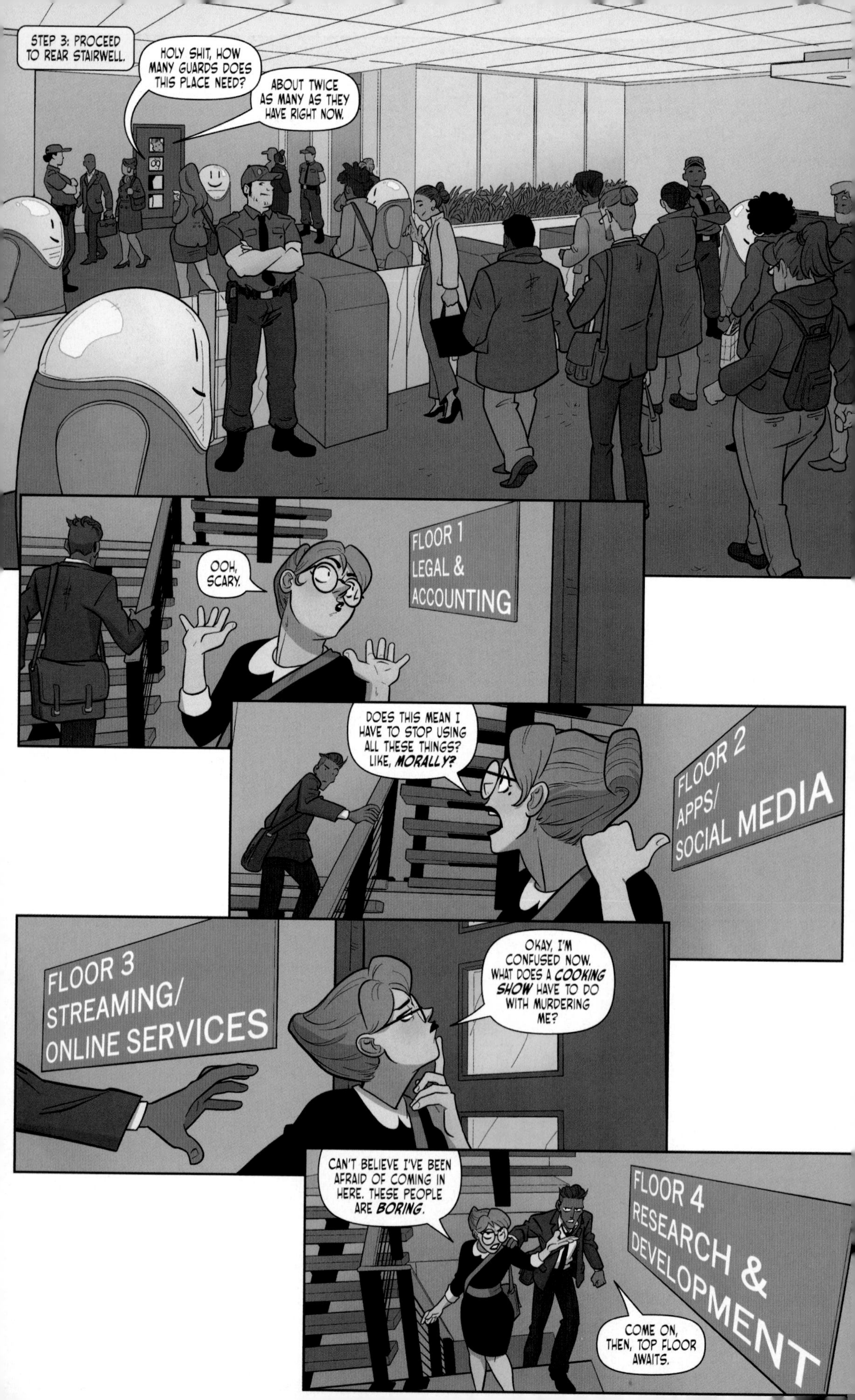
STEP 3: PROCEED TO REAR STAIRWELL.
HOLY SHIT, HOW MANY GUARDS DOES THIS PLACE NEED?
ABOUT TWICE AS MANY AS THEY HAVE RIGHT NOW.
FLOOR 1 LEGAL & ACCOUNTING
OOH, SCARY.
DOES THIS MEAN I HAVE TO STOP USING ALL THESE THINGS? LIKE, MORALLY?
FLOOR 2 APPS/ SOCIAL MEDIA
FLOOR 3 STREAMING/ ONLINE SERVICES
OKAY, I'M CONFUSED NOW. WHAT DOES A COOKING SHOW HAVE TO DO WITH MURDERING ME?
CAN'T BELIEVE I'VE BEEN AFRAID OF COMING IN HERE. THESE PEOPLE ARE BORING.
FLOOR 4 RESEARCH & DEVELOPMENT
COME ON, THEN, TOP FLOOR AWAITS.

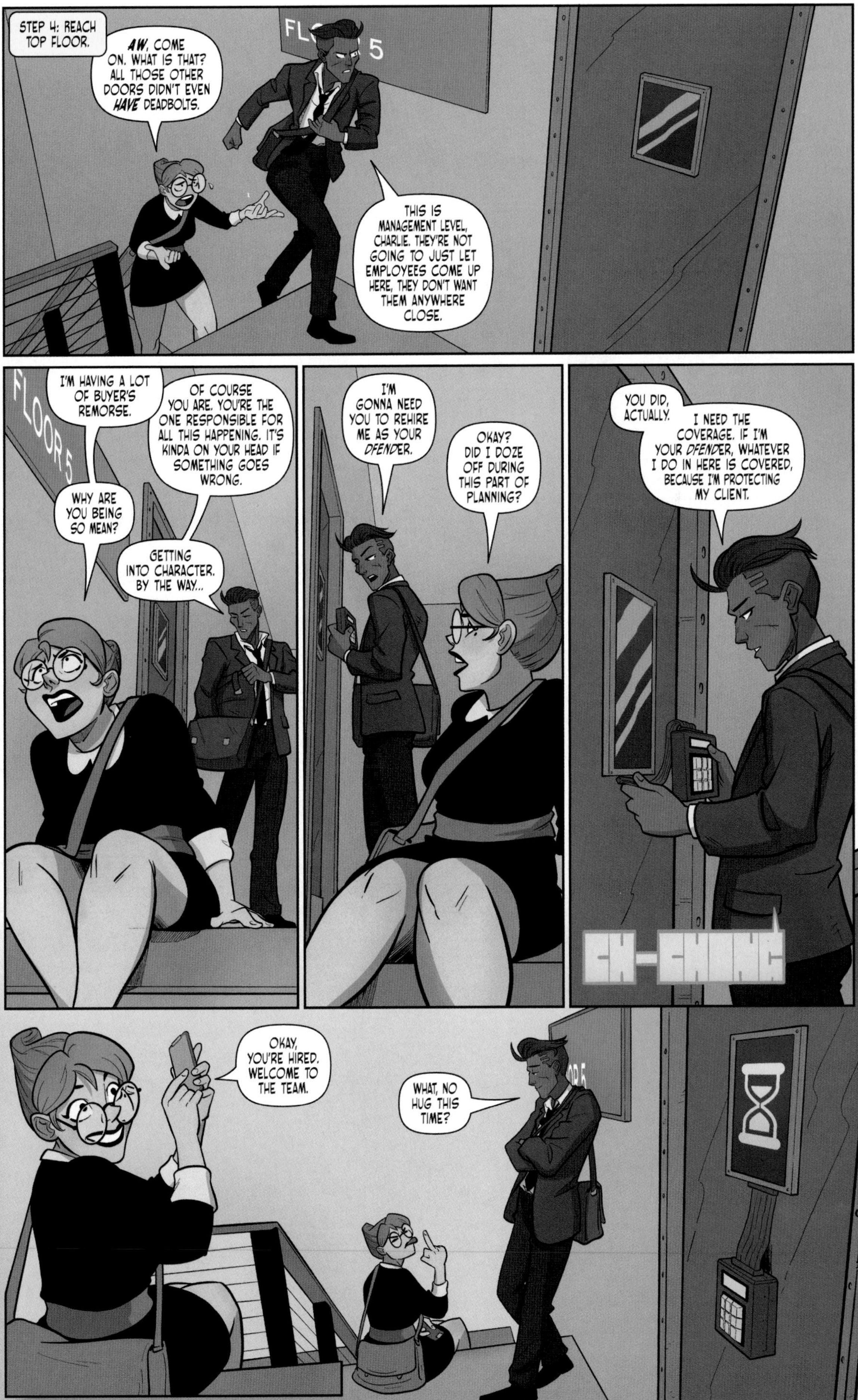

STEP 4: REACH TOP FLOOR.
FLOOR 5
AW, COME ON. WHAT IS THAT? ALL THOSE OTHER DOORS DIDN'T EVEN HAVE DEADBOLTS.
THIS IS MANAGEMENT LEVEL, CHARLIE. THEY'RE NOT GOING TO JUST LET EMPLOYEES COME UP HERE, THEY DON'T WANT THEM ANYWHERE CLOSE.
FLOOR 5
I'M HAVING A LOT OF BUYER'S REMORSE.
OF COURSE YOU ARE. YOU'RE THE ONE RESPONSIBLE FOR ALL THIS HAPPENING. IT'S KINDA ON YOUR HEAD IF SOMETHING GOES WRONG.
WHY ARE YOU BEING SO MEAN?
GETTING INTO CHARACTER. BY THE WAY...
I'M GONNA NEED YOU TO REHIRE ME AS YOUR DFENDER.
OKAY? DID I DOZE OFF DURING THIS PART OF PLANNING?
YOU DID, ACTUALLY.
I NEED THE COVERAGE. IF I'M YOUR DFENDER, WHATEVER I DO IN HERE IS COVERED, BECAUSE I'M PROTECTING MY CLIENT.
CH-CHUNG
OKAY, YOU'RE HIRED. WELCOME TO THE TEAM.
WHAT, NO HUG THIS TIME?

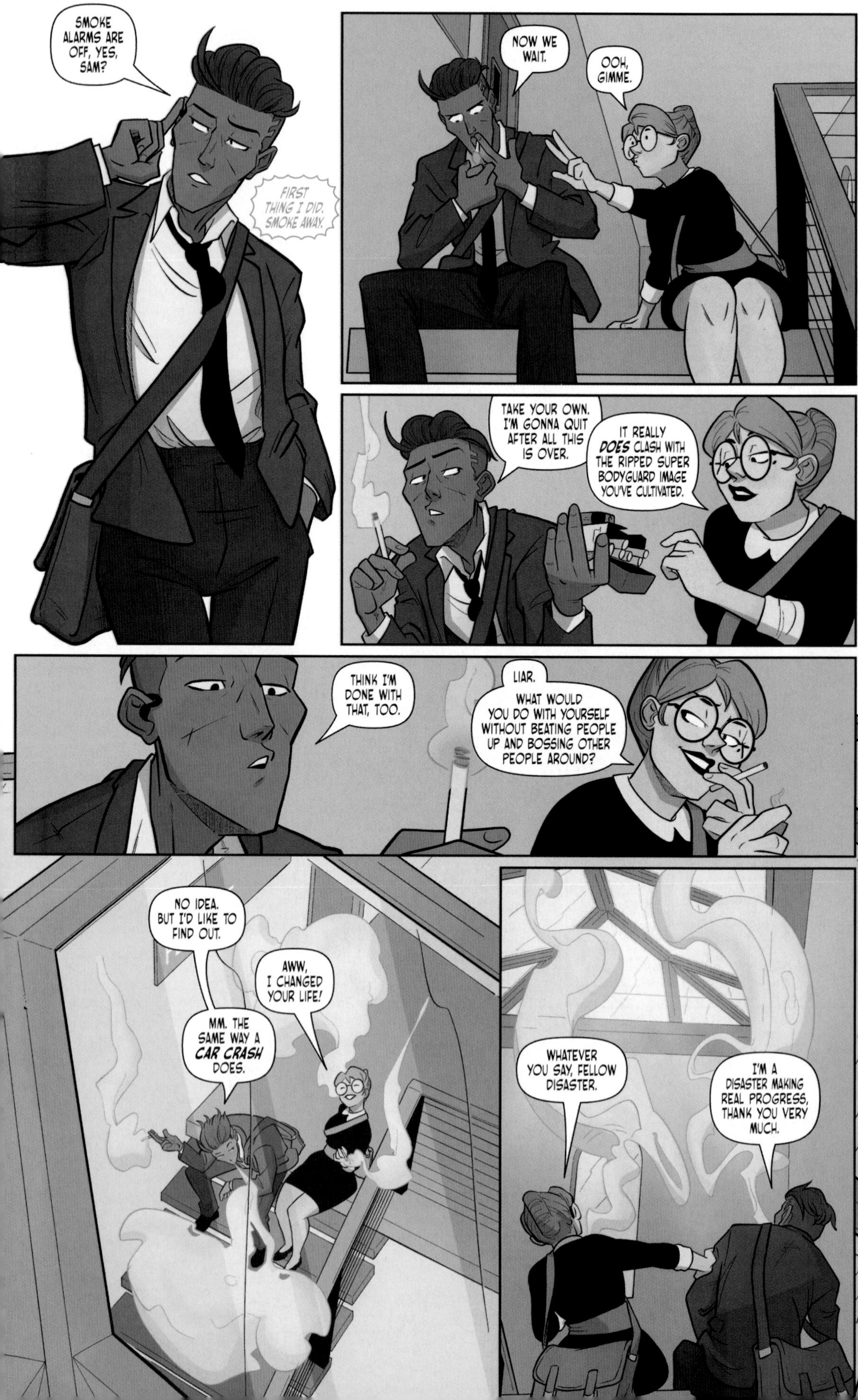
SMOKE ALARMS ARE OFF, YES, SAM?
FIRST THING I DID. SMOKE AWAY.
NOW WE WAIT.
OOH, GIMME.
TAKE YOUR OWN. I'M GONNA QUIT AFTER ALL THIS IS OVER.
IT REALLY DOES CLASH WITH THE RIPPED SUPER BODYGUARD IMAGE YOU'VE CULTIVATED.
THINK I'M DONE WITH THAT, TOO.
LIAR.
WHAT WOULD YOU DO WITH YOURSELF WITHOUT BEATING PEOPLE UP AND BOSSING OTHER PEOPLE AROUND?
NO IDEA. BUT I'D LIKE TO FIND OUT.
AWW, I CHANGED YOUR LIFE!
MM. THE SAME WAY A CAR CRASH DOES.
WHATEVER YOU SAY, FELLOW DISASTER.
I'M A DISASTER MAKING REAL PROGRESS, THANK YOU VERY MUCH.

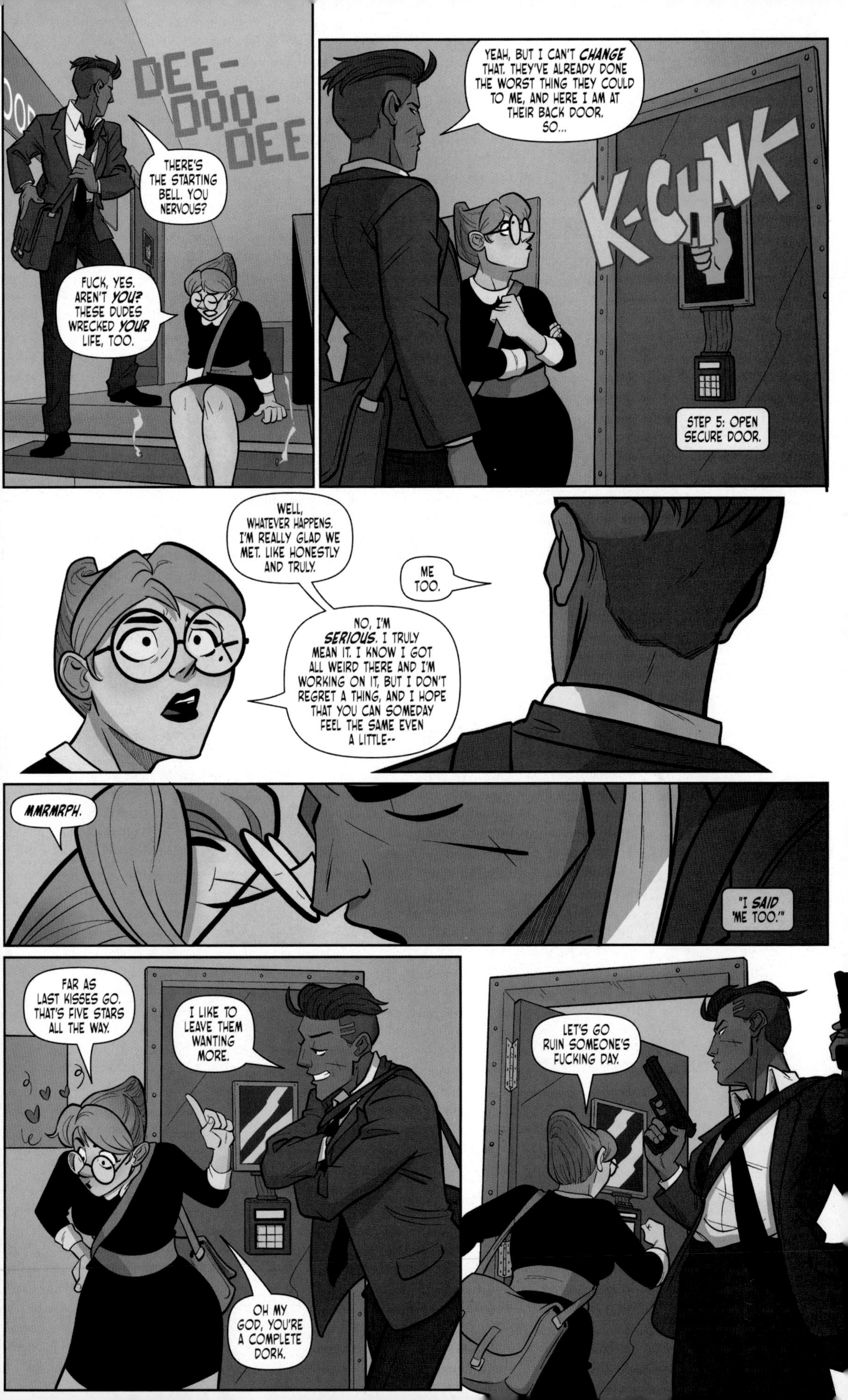
DEE-DOO-DEE
THERE'S THE STARTING BELL. YOU NERVOUS?
FUCK, YES. AREN'T YOU? THESE DUDES WRECKED YOUR LIFE, TOO.
YEAH, BUT I CAN'T CHANGE THAT. THEY'VE ALREADY DONE THE WORST THING THEY COULD TO ME, AND HERE I AM AT THEIR BACK DOOR. SO...
K-CHNK
STEP 5: OPEN SECURE DOOR.
WELL, WHATEVER HAPPENS. I'M REALLY GLAD WE MET. LIKE HONESTLY AND TRULY.
ME TOO.
NO, I'M SERIOUS. I TRULY MEAN IT. I KNOW I GOT ALL WEIRD THERE AND I'M WORKING ON IT, BUT I DON'T REGRET A THING, AND I HOPE THAT YOU CAN SOMEDAY FEEL THE SAME EVEN A LITTLE--
MMRMRPH.
"I SAID 'ME TOO.'"
FAR AS LAST KISSES GO. THAT'S FIVE STARS ALL THE WAY.
I LIKE TO LEAVE THEM WANTING MORE.
OH MY GOD, YOU'RE A COMPLETE DORK.
LET'S GO RUIN SOMEONE'S FUCKING DAY.

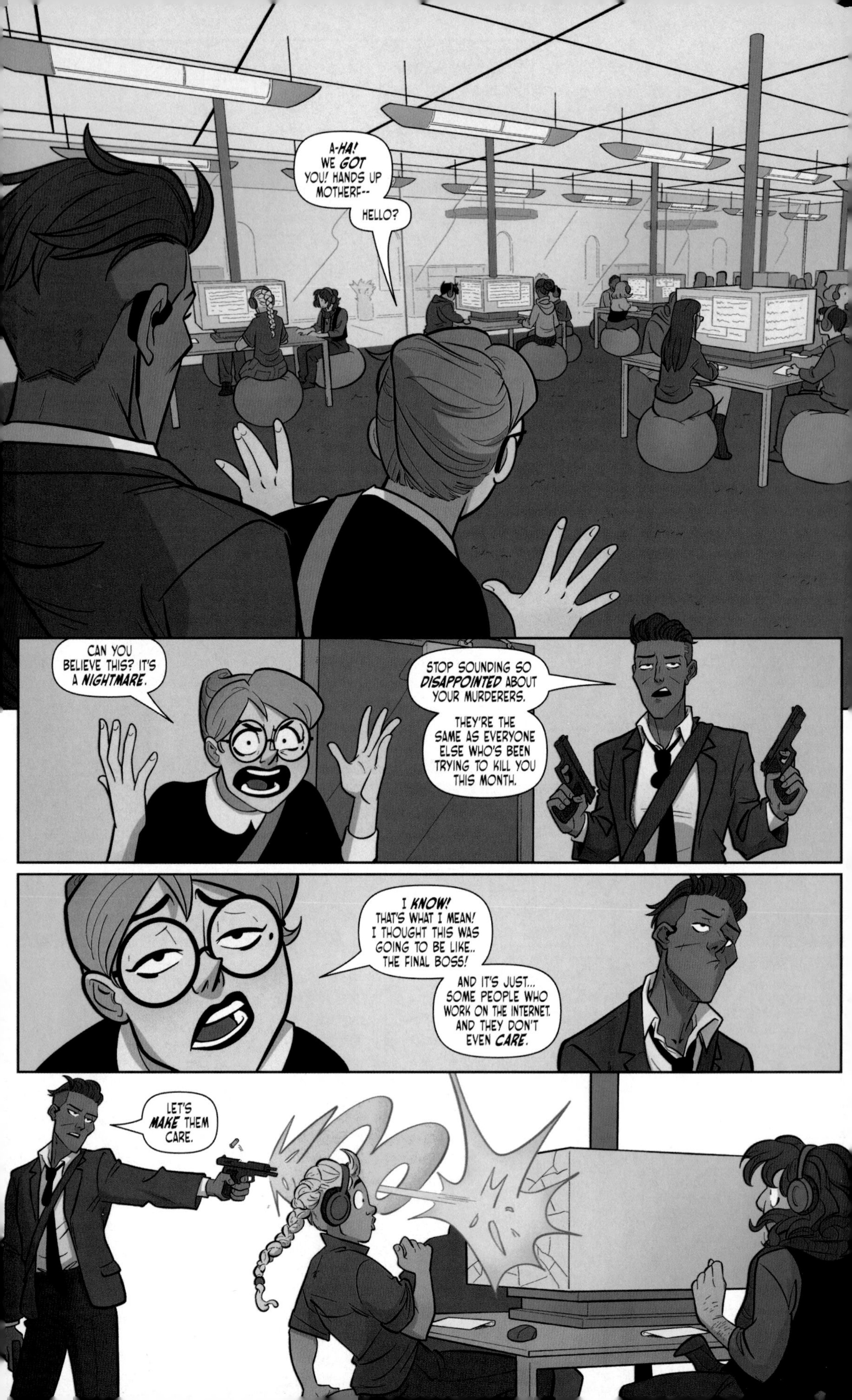
A-HA! WE GOT YOU! HANDS UP MOTHERF--
HELLO?
CAN YOU BELIEVE THIS? IT'S A NIGHTMARE.
STOP SOUNDING SO DISAPPOINTED ABOUT YOUR MURDERERS.
THEY'RE THE SAME AS EVERYONE ELSE WHO'S BEEN TRYING TO KILL YOU THIS MONTH.
I KNOW! THAT'S WHAT I MEAN! I THOUGHT THIS WAS GOING TO BE LIKE.. THE FINAL BOSS!
AND IT'S JUST... SOME PEOPLE WHO WORK ON THE INTERNET. AND THEY DON'T EVEN CARE.
LET'S MAKE THEM CARE.

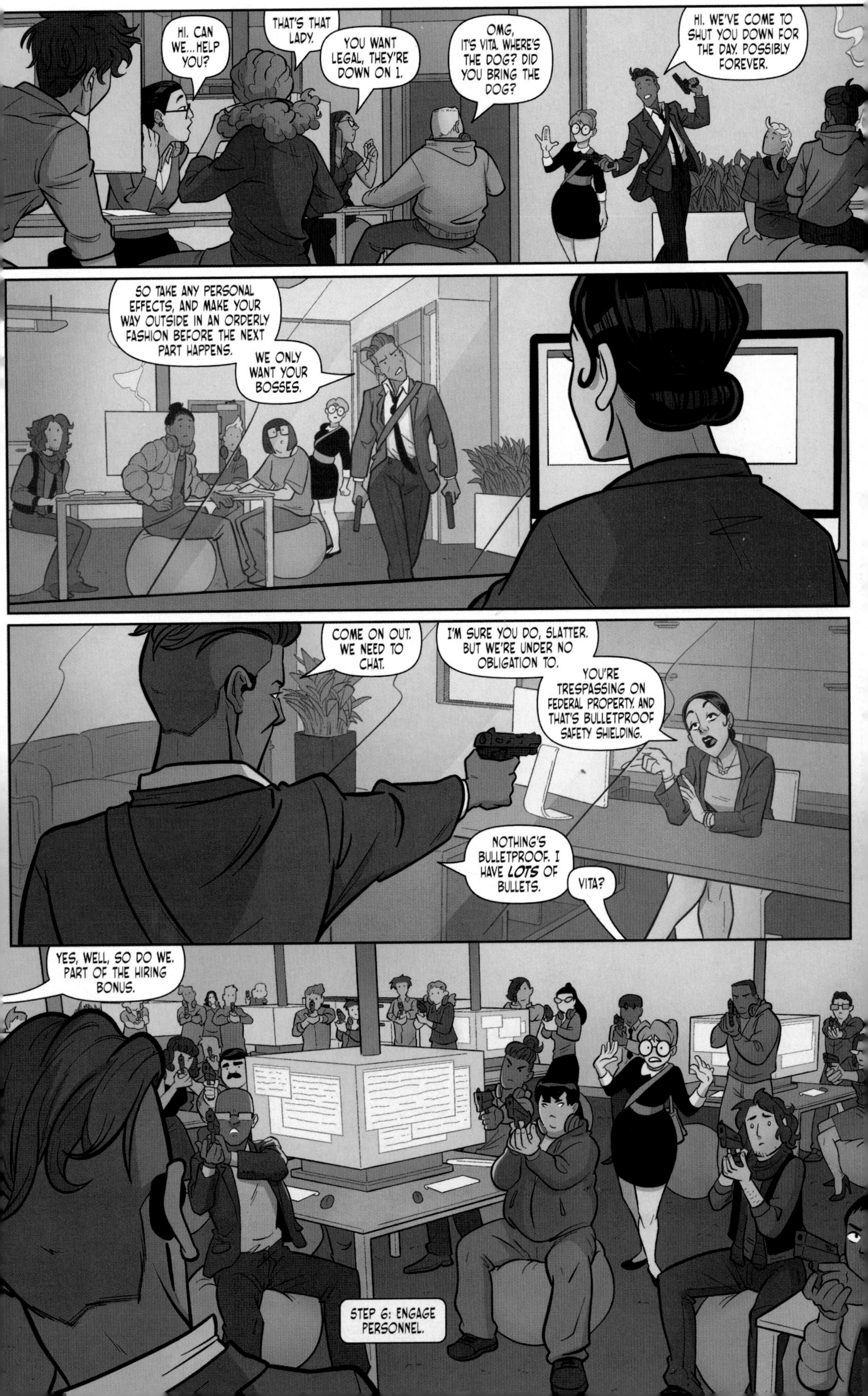
HI. CAN WE...HELP YOU?
THAT'S THAT LADY.
YOU WANT LEGAL, THEY'RE DOWN ON 1.
OMG, IT'S VITA. WHERE'S THE DOG? DID YOU BRING THE DOG?
HI. WE'VE COME TO SHUT YOU DOWN FOR THE DAY. POSSIBLY FOREVER.
SO TAKE ANY PERSONAL EFFECTS, AND MAKE YOUR WAY OUTSIDE IN AN ORDERLY FASHION BEFORE THE NEXT PART HAPPENS.
WE ONLY WANT YOUR BOSSES.
COME ON OUT. WE NEED TO CHAT.
I'M SURE YOU DO, SLATTER. BUT WE'RE UNDER NO OBLIGATION TO.
YOU'RE TRESPASSING ON FEDERAL PROPERTY. AND THAT'S BULLETPROOF SAFETY SHIELDING.
NOTHING'S BULLETPROOF. I HAVE *LOTS* OF BULLETS.
VITA?
YES, WELL, SO DO WE. PART OF THE HIRING BONUS.
STEP 6: ENGAGE PERSONNEL.

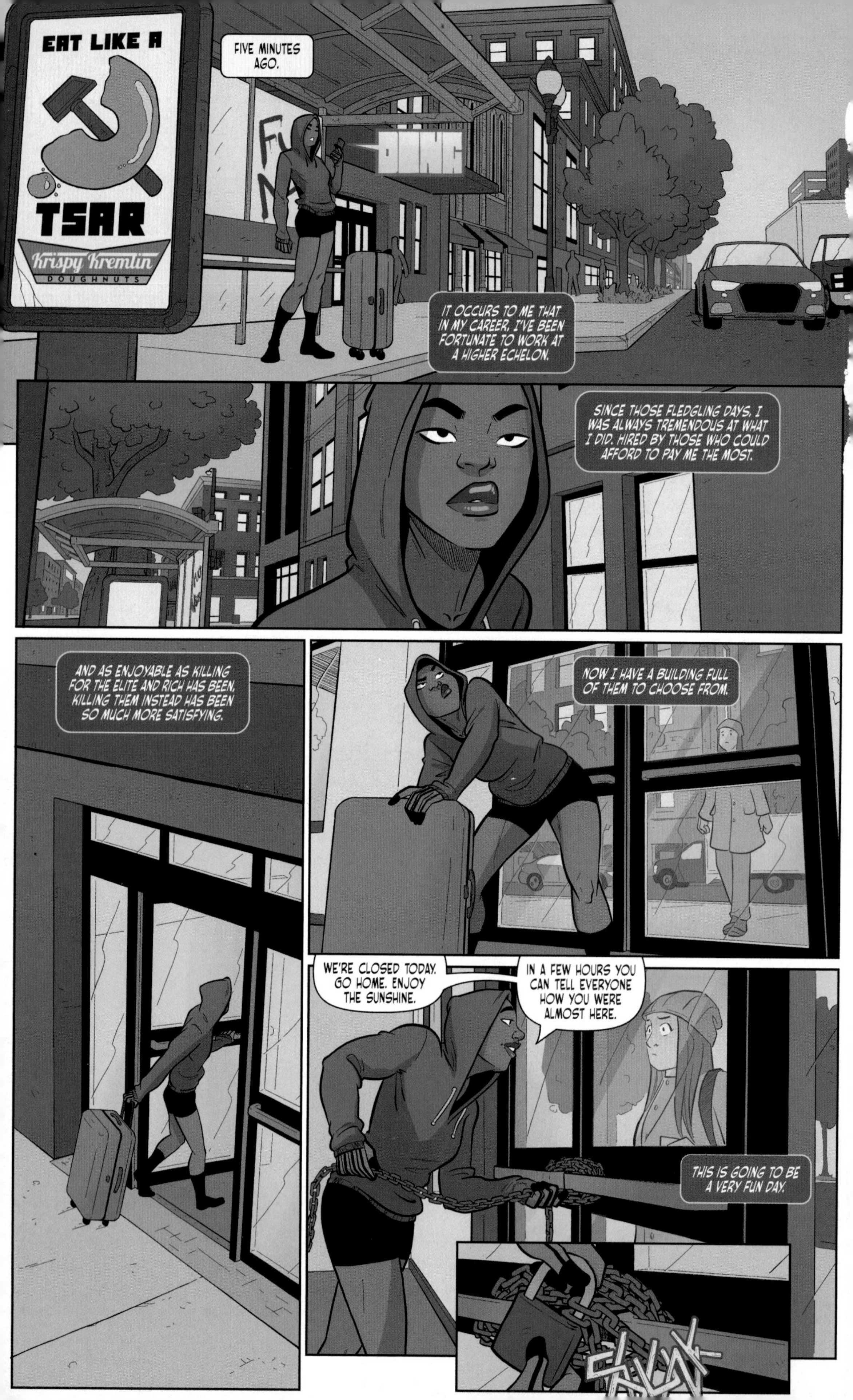
EAT LIKE A
TSAR
Krispy Kremlin
DOUGHNUTS
FIVE MINUTES AGO.
IT OCCURS TO ME THAT IN MY CAREER, I'VE BEEN FORTUNATE TO WORK AT A HIGHER ECHELON.
SINCE THOSE FLEDGLING DAYS, I WAS ALWAYS TREMENDOUS AT WHAT I DID. HIRED BY THOSE WHO COULD AFFORD TO PAY ME THE MOST.
AND AS ENJOYABLE AS KILLING FOR THE ELITE AND RICH HAS BEEN, KILLING THEM INSTEAD HAS BEEN SO MUCH MORE SATISFYING.
NOW I HAVE A BUILDING FULL OF THEM TO CHOOSE FROM.
WE'RE CLOSED TODAY. GO HOME. ENJOY THE SUNSHINE.
IN A FEW HOURS YOU CAN TELL EVERYONE HOW YOU WERE ALMOST HERE.
THIS IS GOING TO BE A VERY FUN DAY.

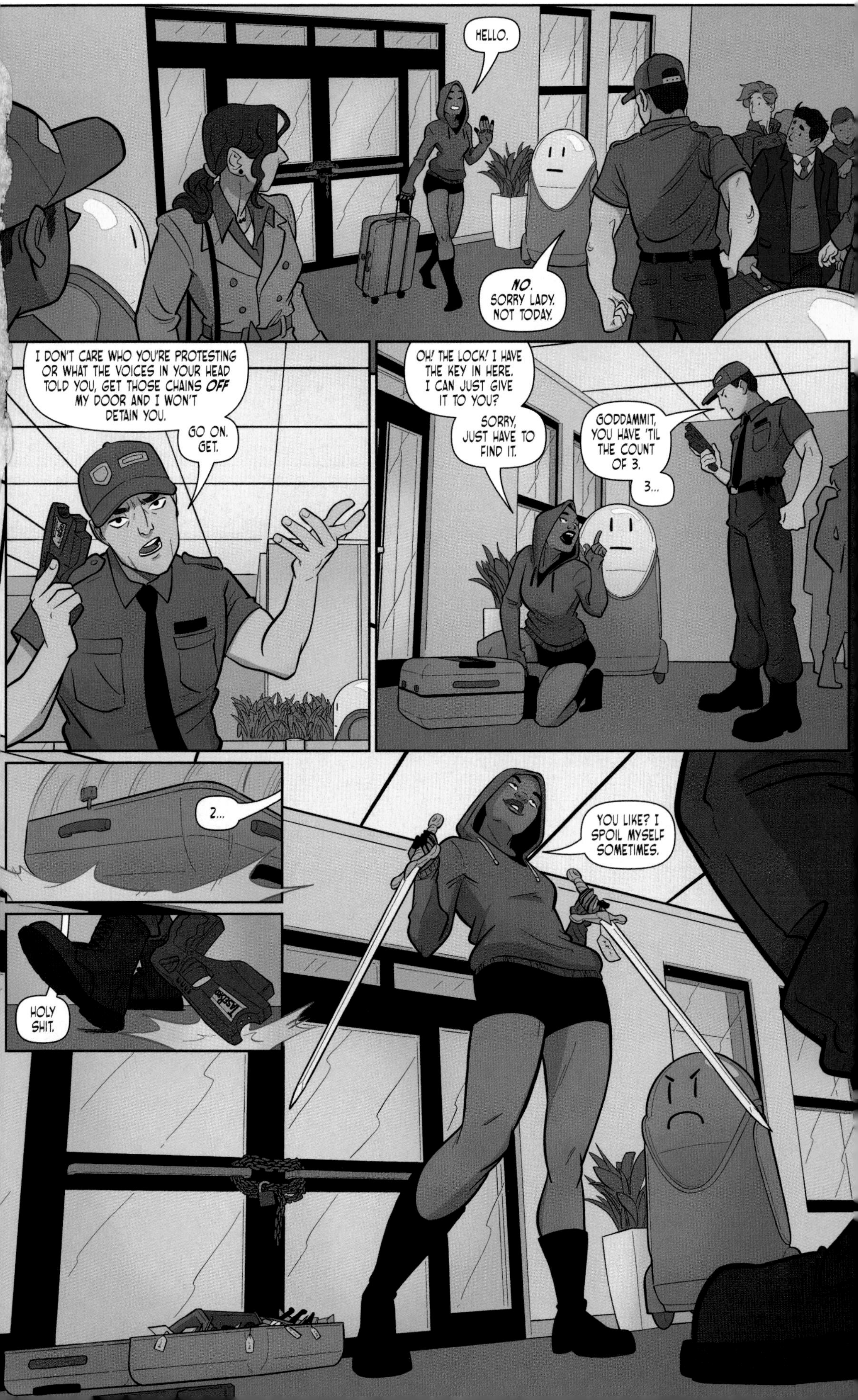
HELLO.
NO. SORRY LADY. NOT TODAY.
I DON'T CARE WHO YOU'RE PROTESTING OR WHAT THE VOICES IN YOUR HEAD TOLD YOU, GET THOSE CHAINS OFF MY DOOR AND I WON'T DETAIN YOU.
GO ON. GET.
OH! THE LOCK! I HAVE THE KEY IN HERE. I CAN JUST GIVE IT TO YOU?
SORRY, JUST HAVE TO FIND IT.
GODDAMMIT, YOU HAVE 'TIL THE COUNT OF 3.
3...
2...
HOLY SHIT.
YOU LIKE? I SPOIL MYSELF SOMETIMES.

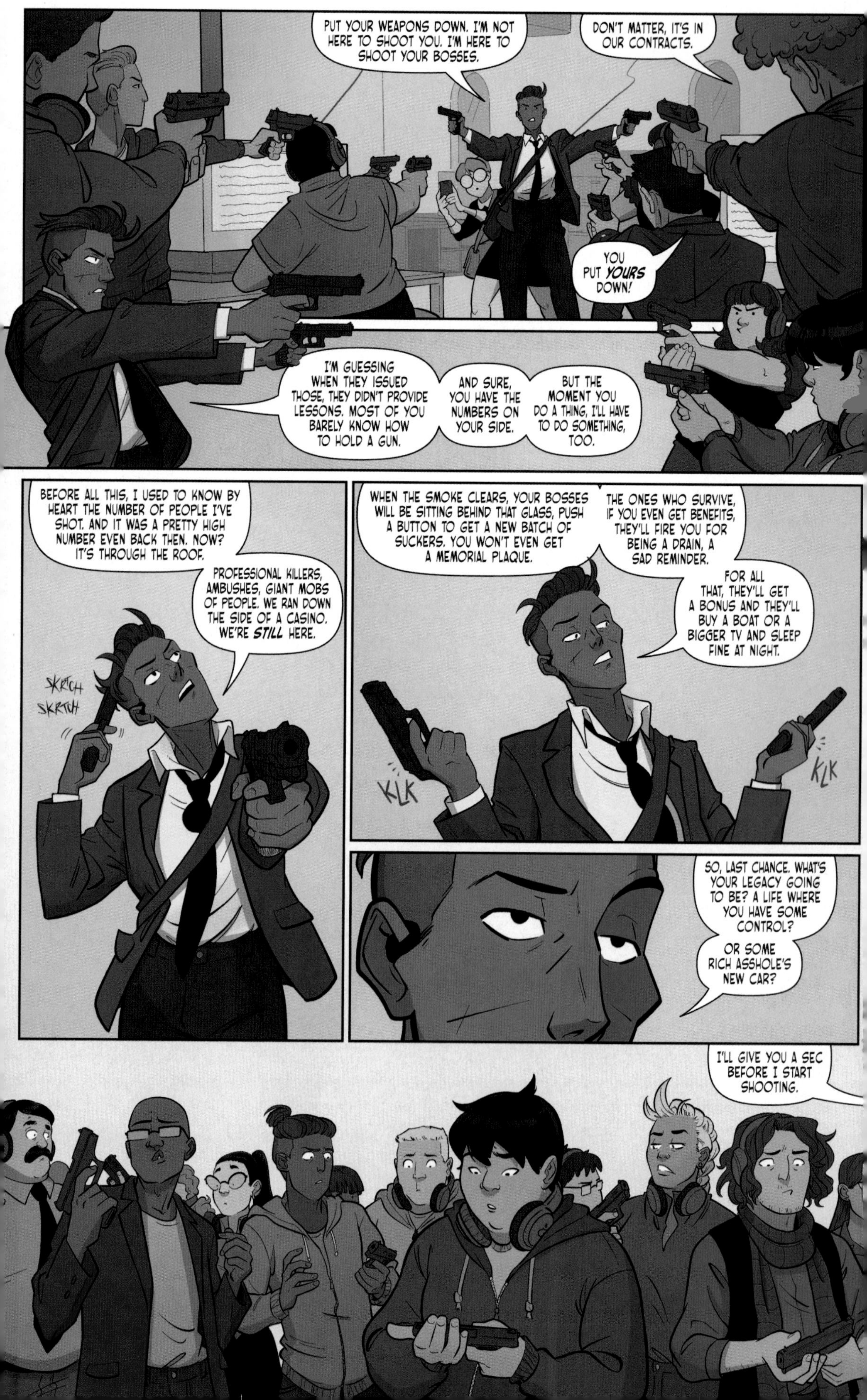
PUT YOUR WEAPONS DOWN. I'M NOT HERE TO SHOOT YOU. I'M HERE TO SHOOT YOUR BOSSES.
DON'T MATTER, IT'S IN OUR CONTRACTS.
YOU PUT *YOURS* DOWN!
I'M GUESSING WHEN THEY ISSUED THOSE, THEY DIDN'T PROVIDE LESSONS. MOST OF YOU BARELY KNOW HOW TO HOLD A GUN.
AND SURE, YOU HAVE THE NUMBERS ON YOUR SIDE.
BUT THE MOMENT YOU DO A THING, I'LL HAVE TO DO SOMETHING, TOO.
BEFORE ALL THIS, I USED TO KNOW BY HEART THE NUMBER OF PEOPLE I'VE SHOT. AND IT WAS A PRETTY HIGH NUMBER EVEN BACK THEN. NOW? IT'S THROUGH THE ROOF.
PROFESSIONAL KILLERS, AMBUSHES, GIANT MOBS OF PEOPLE. WE RAN DOWN THE SIDE OF A CASINO. WE'RE *STILL* HERE.
SKRTCH
SKRTCH
WHEN THE SMOKE CLEARS, YOUR BOSSES WILL BE SITTING BEHIND THAT GLASS, PUSH A BUTTON TO GET A NEW BATCH OF SUCKERS. YOU WON'T EVEN GET A MEMORIAL PLAQUE.
THE ONES WHO SURVIVE, IF YOU EVEN GET BENEFITS, THEY'LL FIRE YOU FOR BEING A DRAIN, A SAD REMINDER.
FOR ALL THAT, THEY'LL GET A BONUS AND THEY'LL BUY A BOAT OR A BIGGER TV AND SLEEP FINE AT NIGHT.
KLK
KLK
SO, LAST CHANCE. WHAT'S YOUR LEGACY GOING TO BE? A LIFE WHERE YOU HAVE SOME CONTROL?
OR SOME RICH ASSHOLE'S NEW CAR?
I'LL GIVE YOU A SEC BEFORE I START SHOOTING.

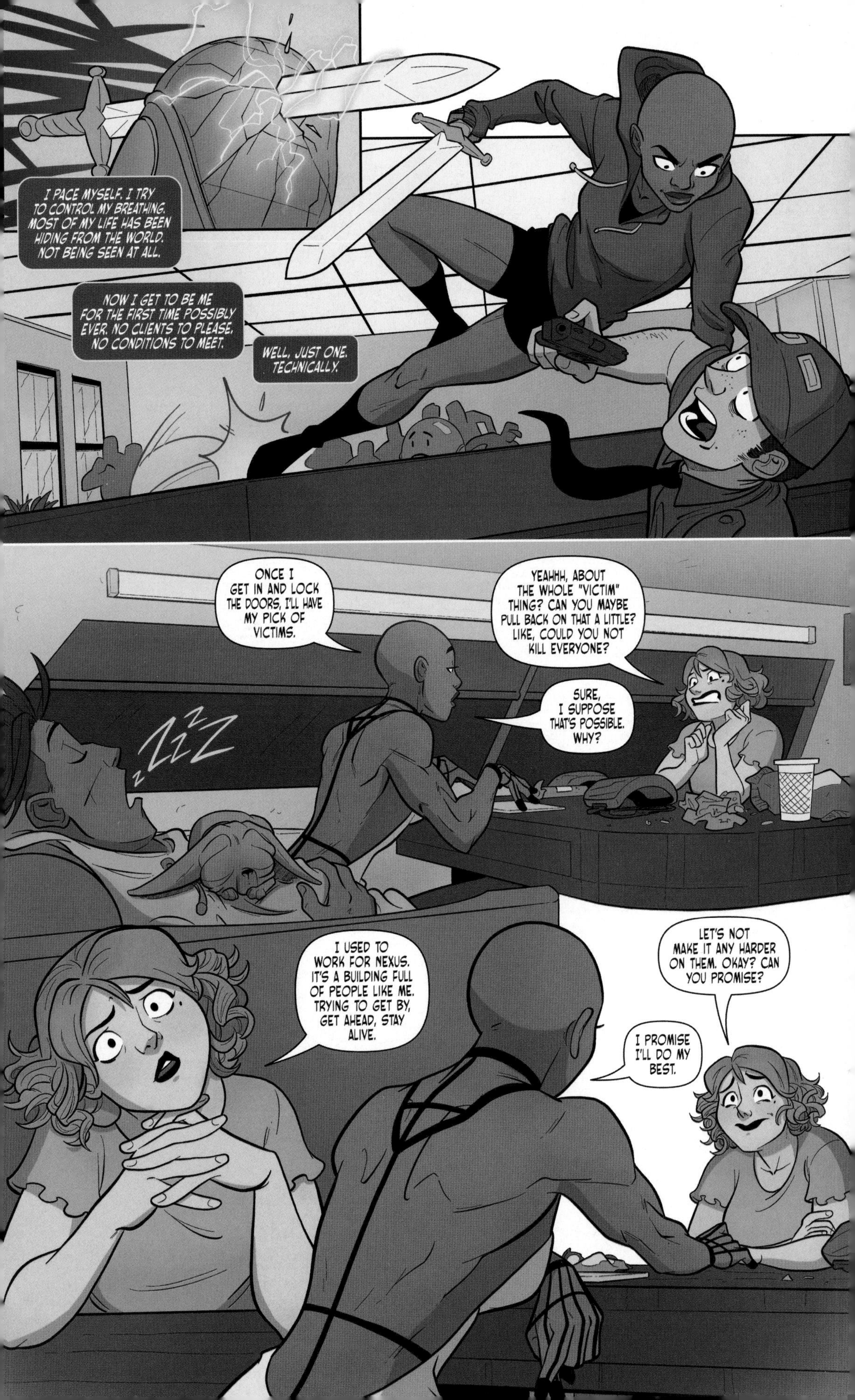
I PACE MYSELF. I TRY TO CONTROL MY BREATHING. MOST OF MY LIFE HAS BEEN HIDING FROM THE WORLD. NOT BEING SEEN AT ALL.
NOW I GET TO BE ME FOR THE FIRST TIME POSSIBLY EVER. NO CLIENTS TO PLEASE, NO CONDITIONS TO MEET.
WELL, JUST ONE. TECHNICALLY.
ONCE I GET IN AND LOCK THE DOORS, I'LL HAVE MY PICK OF VICTIMS.
YEAHHH, ABOUT THE WHOLE "VICTIM" THING? CAN YOU MAYBE PULL BACK ON THAT A LITTLE? LIKE, COULD YOU NOT KILL EVERYONE?
SURE, I SUPPOSE THAT'S POSSIBLE. WHY?
ZZZ
I USED TO WORK FOR NEXUS. IT'S A BUILDING FULL OF PEOPLE LIKE ME. TRYING TO GET BY, GET AHEAD, STAY ALIVE.
LET'S NOT MAKE IT ANY HARDER ON THEM. OKAY? CAN YOU PROMISE?
I PROMISE I'LL DO MY BEST.

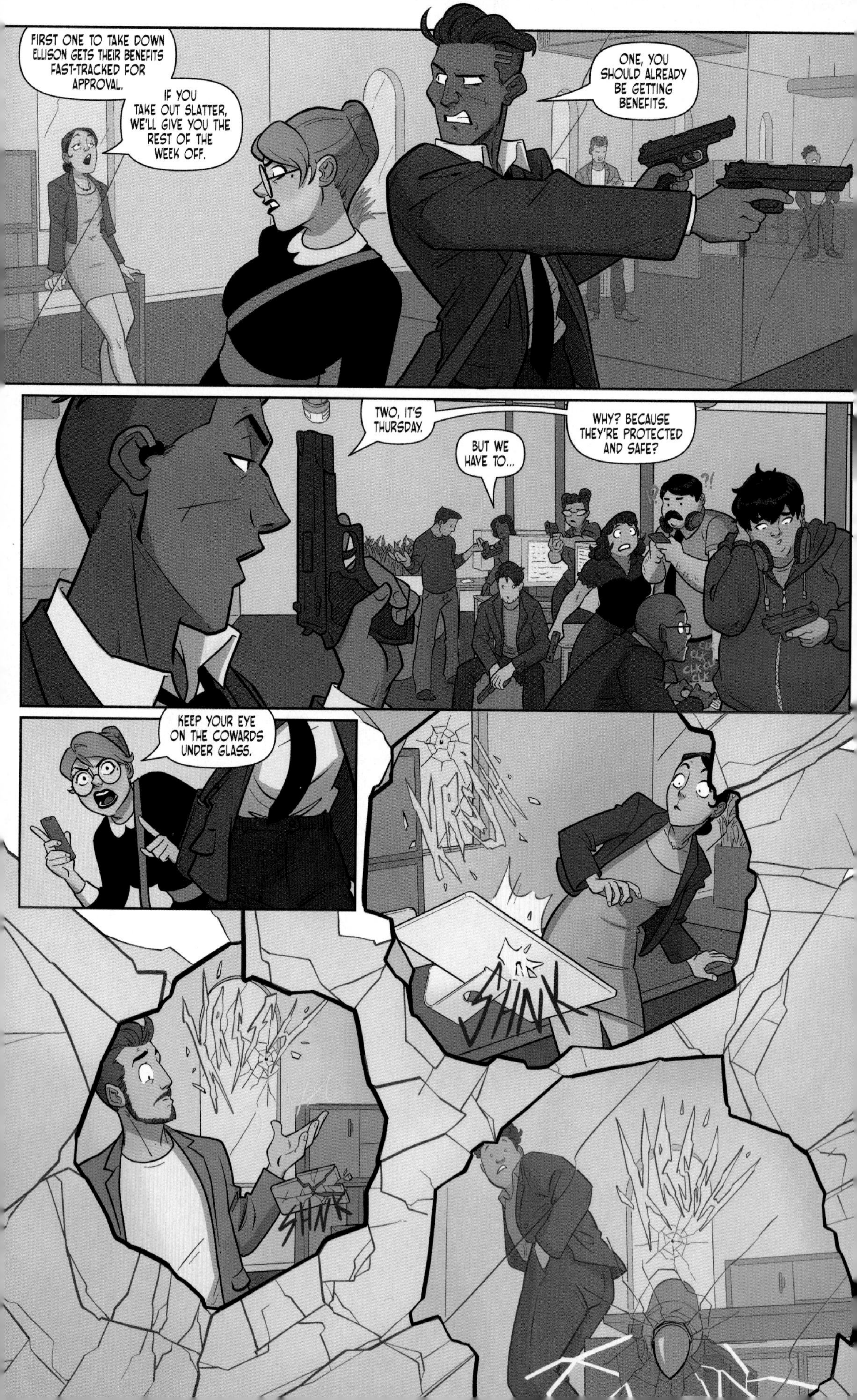
FIRST ONE TO TAKE DOWN ELLISON GETS THEIR BENEFITS FAST-TRACKED FOR APPROVAL.
IF YOU TAKE OUT SLATTER, WE'LL GIVE YOU THE REST OF THE WEEK OFF.
ONE, YOU SHOULD ALREADY BE GETTING BENEFITS.
TWO, IT'S THURSDAY.
BUT WE HAVE TO...
WHY? BECAUSE THEY'RE PROTECTED AND SAFE?
?!
CLK CLK CLK CLK CLK
KEEP YOUR EYE ON THE COWARDS UNDER GLASS.
SHNK
SHNK

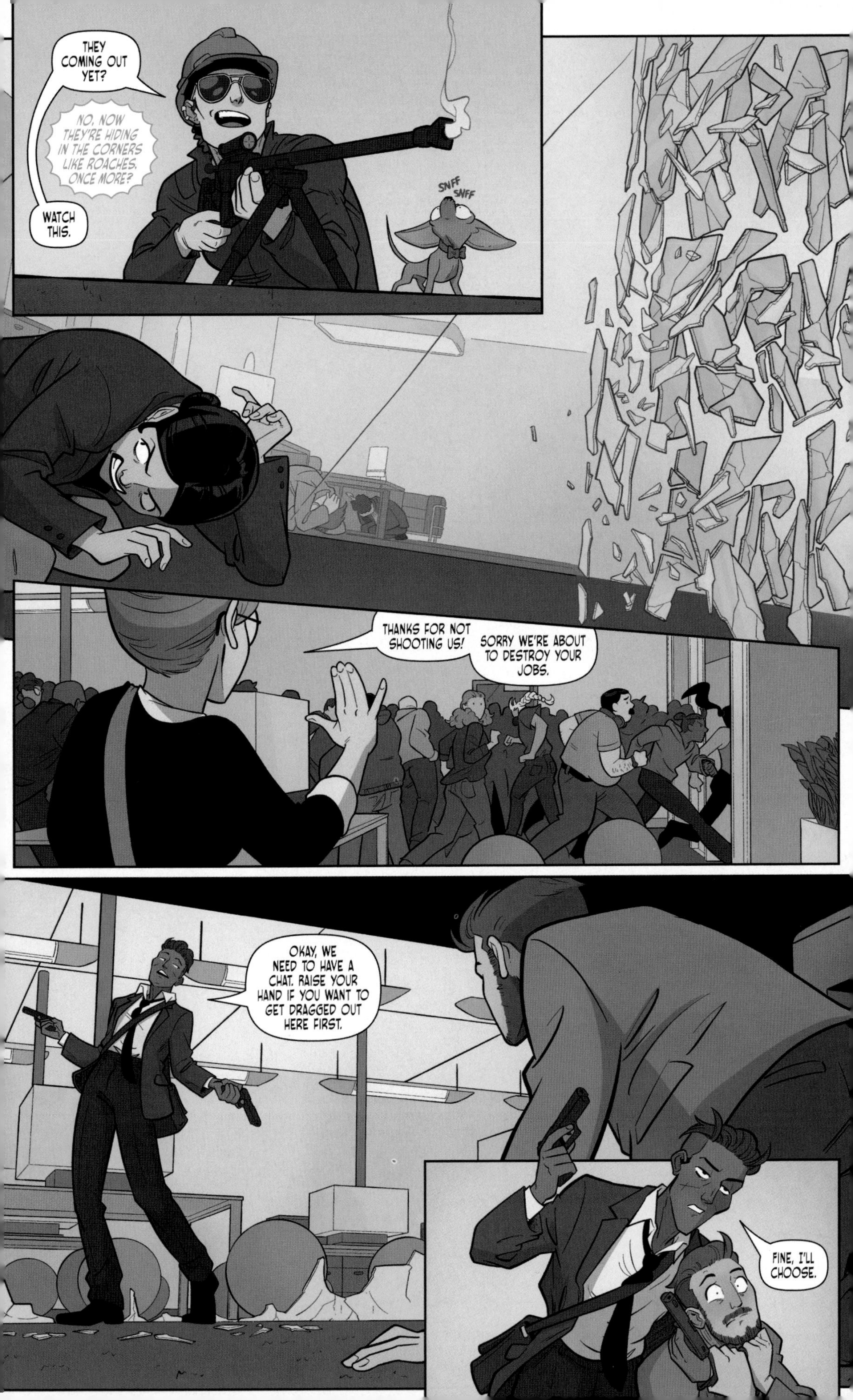
THEY COMING OUT YET?
NO, NOW THEY'RE HIDING IN THE CORNERS LIKE ROACHES. ONCE MORE?
WATCH THIS.
SNFF SNFF
THANKS FOR NOT SHOOTING US!
SORRY WE'RE ABOUT TO DESTROY YOUR JOBS.
OKAY, WE NEED TO HAVE A CHAT. RAISE YOUR HAND IF YOU WANT TO GET DRAGGED OUT HERE FIRST.
FINE, I'LL CHOOSE.

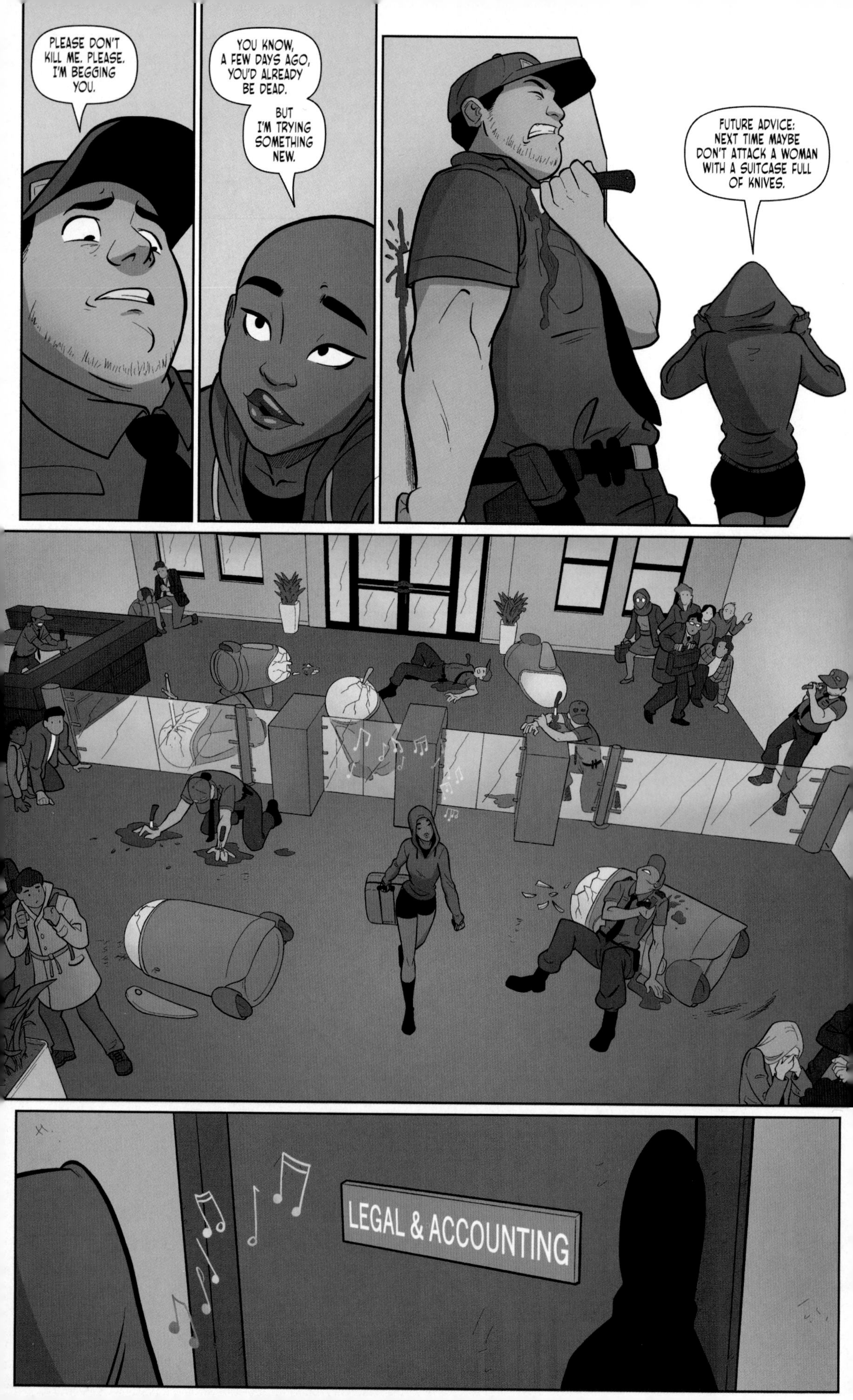
PLEASE DON'T KILL ME. PLEASE. I'M BEGGING YOU.
YOU KNOW, A FEW DAYS AGO, YOU'D ALREADY BE DEAD.
BUT I'M TRYING SOMETHING NEW.
FUTURE ADVICE: NEXT TIME MAYBE DON'T ATTACK A WOMAN WITH A SUITCASE FULL OF KNIVES.
LEGAL & ACCOUNTING

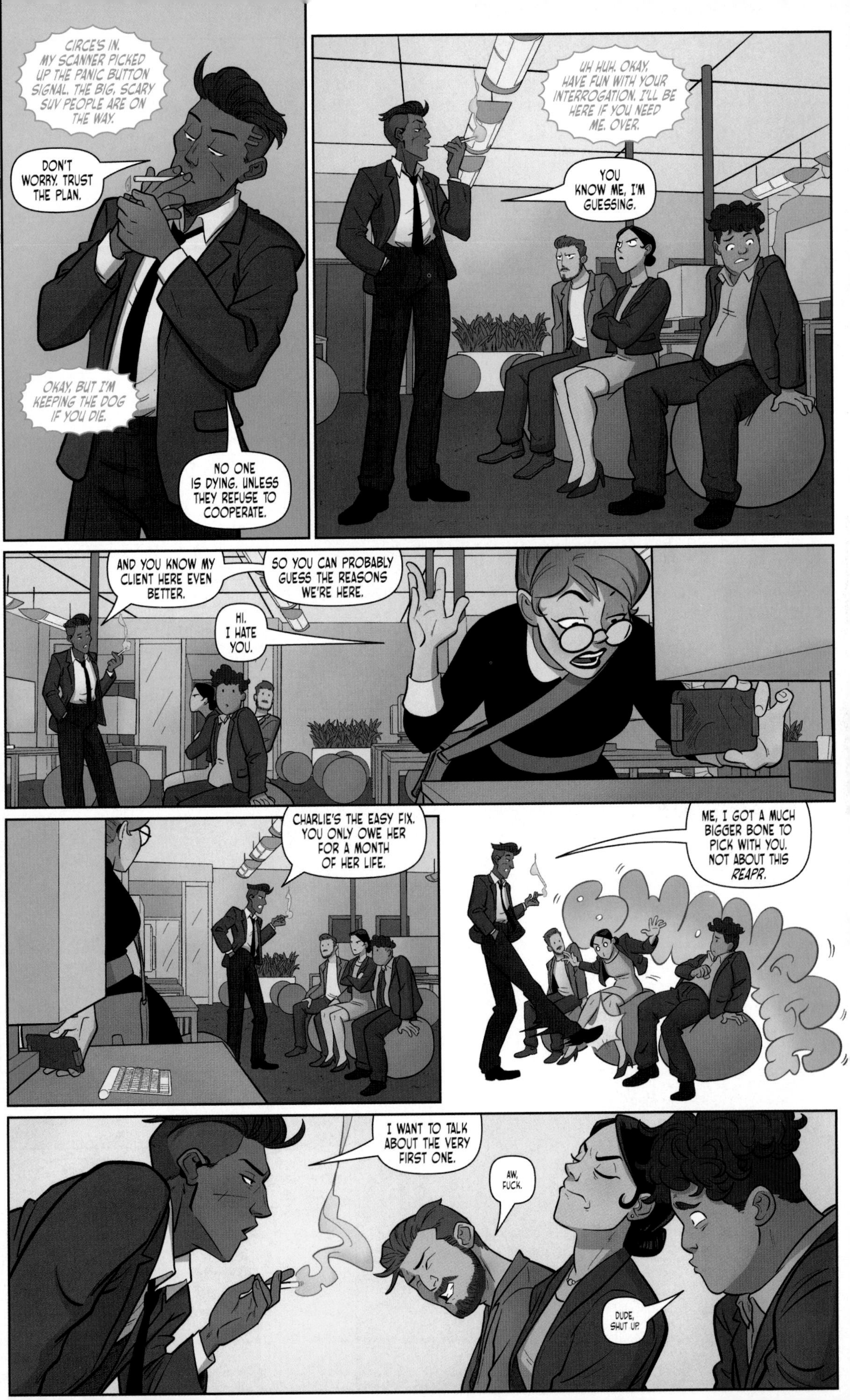
CIRCE'S IN. MY SCANNER PICKED UP THE PANIC BUTTON SIGNAL. THE BIG, SCARY SUV PEOPLE ARE ON THE WAY.
DON'T WORRY. TRUST THE PLAN.
OKAY, BUT I'M KEEPING THE DOG IF YOU DIE.
NO ONE IS DYING. UNLESS THEY REFUSE TO COOPERATE.
UH HUH. OKAY. HAVE FUN WITH YOUR INTERROGATION. I'LL BE HERE IF YOU NEED ME. OVER.
YOU KNOW ME, I'M GUESSING.
AND YOU KNOW MY CLIENT HERE EVEN BETTER.
SO YOU CAN PROBABLY GUESS THE REASONS WE'RE HERE.
HI. I HATE YOU.
CHARLIE'S THE EASY FIX. YOU ONLY OWE HER FOR A MONTH OF HER LIFE.
ME, I GOT A MUCH BIGGER BONE TO PICK WITH YOU. NOT ABOUT THIS *REAPR*.
I WANT TO TALK ABOUT THE VERY FIRST ONE.
AW, FUCK.
DUDE, SHUT UP.

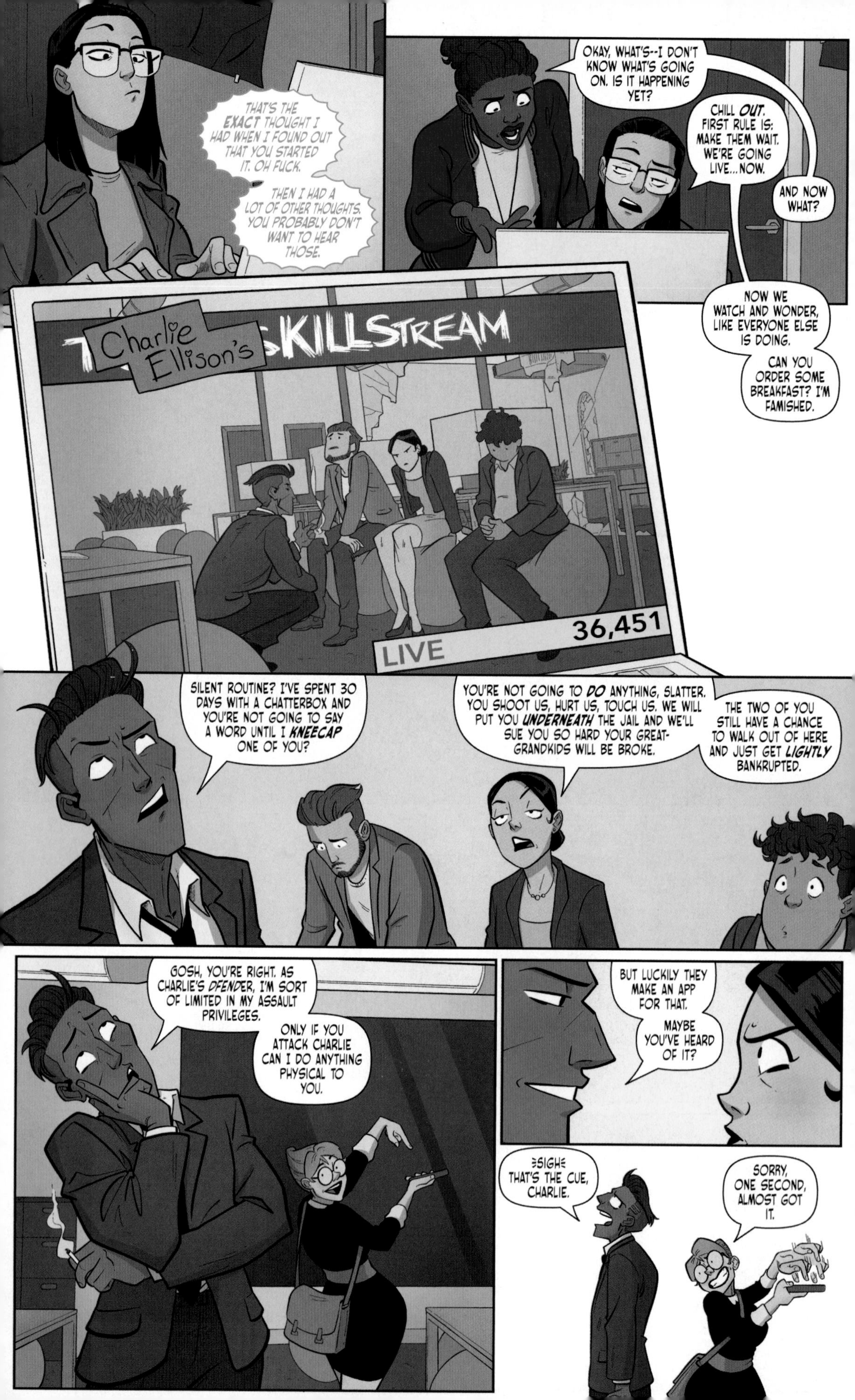
THAT'S THE EXACT THOUGHT I HAD WHEN I FOUND OUT THAT YOU STARTED IT. OH FUCK.
THEN I HAD A LOT OF OTHER THOUGHTS. YOU PROBABLY DON'T WANT TO HEAR THOSE.
OKAY, WHAT'S--I DON'T KNOW WHAT'S GOING ON. IS IT HAPPENING YET?
CHILL OUT. FIRST RULE IS: MAKE THEM WAIT. WE'RE GOING LIVE...NOW.
AND NOW WHAT?
NOW WE WATCH AND WONDER, LIKE EVERYONE ELSE IS DOING.
CAN YOU ORDER SOME BREAKFAST? I'M FAMISHED.
Charlie Ellison's SKILLSTREAM
36,451
LIVE
SILENT ROUTINE? I'VE SPENT 30 DAYS WITH A CHATTERBOX AND YOU'RE NOT GOING TO SAY A WORD UNTIL I KNEECAP ONE OF YOU?
YOU'RE NOT GOING TO DO ANYTHING, SLATTER. YOU SHOOT US, HURT US, TOUCH US. WE WILL PUT YOU UNDERNEATH THE JAIL AND WE'LL SUE YOU SO HARD YOUR GREAT-GRANDKIDS WILL BE BROKE.
THE TWO OF YOU STILL HAVE A CHANCE TO WALK OUT OF HERE AND JUST GET LIGHTLY BANKRUPTED.
GOSH, YOU'RE RIGHT. AS CHARLIE'S DFENDER, I'M SORT OF LIMITED IN MY ASSAULT PRIVILEGES.
ONLY IF YOU ATTACK CHARLIE CAN I DO ANYTHING PHYSICAL TO YOU.
BUT LUCKILY THEY MAKE AN APP FOR THAT.
MAYBE YOU'VE HEARD OF IT?
=SIGH= THAT'S THE CUE, CHARLIE.
SORRY, ONE SECOND, ALMOST GOT IT.

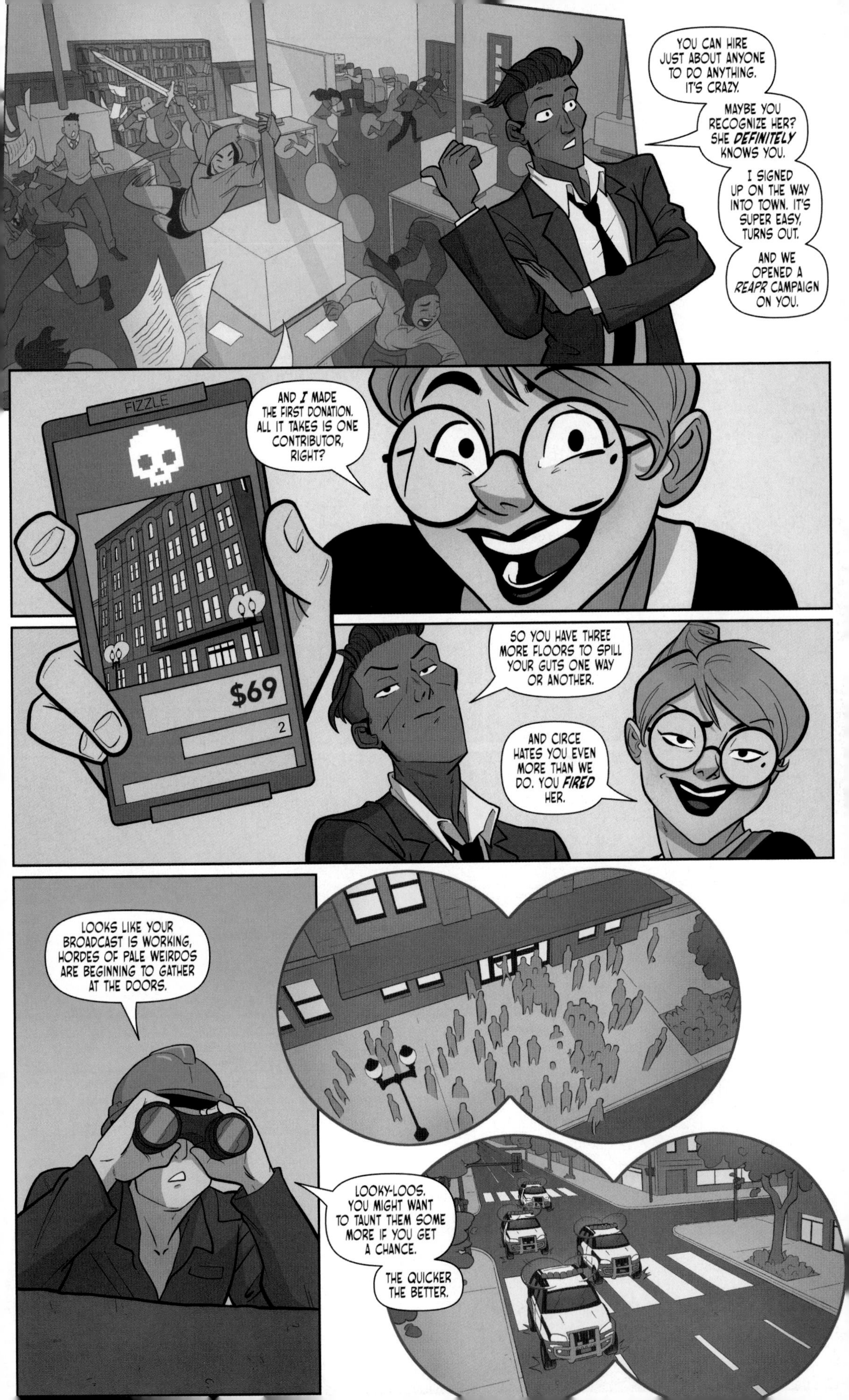
YOU CAN HIRE JUST ABOUT ANYONE TO DO ANYTHING. IT'S CRAZY.
MAYBE YOU RECOGNIZE HER? SHE DEFINITELY KNOWS YOU.
I SIGNED UP ON THE WAY INTO TOWN. IT'S SUPER EASY, TURNS OUT.
AND WE OPENED A REAPR CAMPAIGN ON YOU.
FIZZLE
AND I MADE THE FIRST DONATION. ALL IT TAKES IS ONE CONTRIBUTOR, RIGHT?
$69
2
SO YOU HAVE THREE MORE FLOORS TO SPILL YOUR GUTS ONE WAY OR ANOTHER.
AND CIRCE HATES YOU EVEN MORE THAN WE DO. YOU FIRED HER.
LOOKS LIKE YOUR BROADCAST IS WORKING, HORDES OF PALE WEIRDOS ARE BEGINNING TO GATHER AT THE DOORS.
LOOKY-LOOS. YOU MIGHT WANT TO TAUNT THEM SOME MORE IF YOU GET A CHANCE.
THE QUICKER THE BETTER.

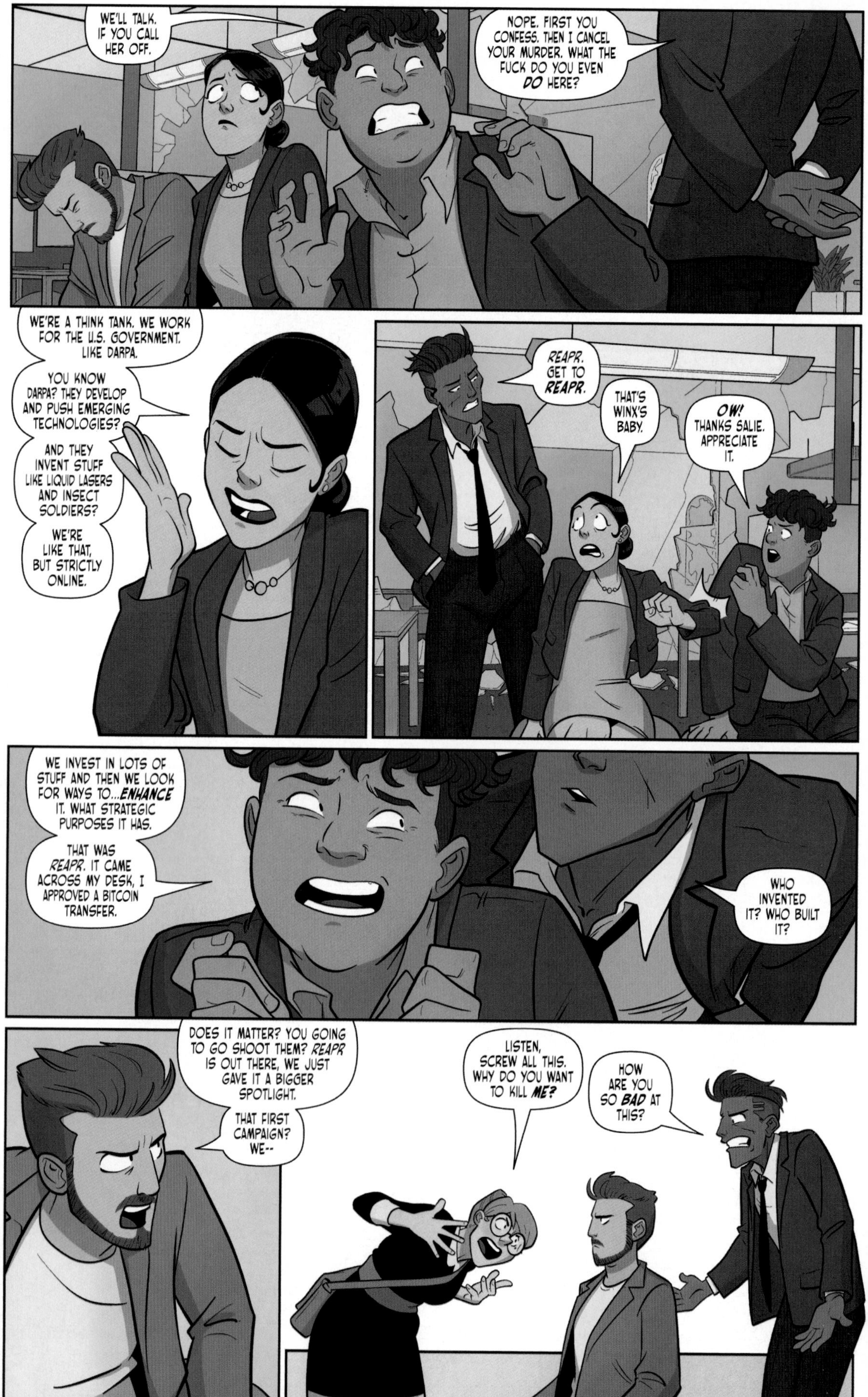
WE'LL TALK. IF YOU CALL HER OFF.
NOPE. FIRST YOU CONFESS. THEN I CANCEL YOUR MURDER. WHAT THE FUCK DO YOU EVEN *DO* HERE?
WE'RE A THINK TANK. WE WORK FOR THE U.S. GOVERNMENT. LIKE DARPA.
YOU KNOW DARPA? THEY DEVELOP AND PUSH EMERGING TECHNOLOGIES?
AND THEY INVENT STUFF LIKE LIQUID LASERS AND INSECT SOLDIERS?
WE'RE LIKE THAT, BUT STRICTLY ONLINE.
REAPR. GET TO ***REAPR***.
THAT'S WINX'S BABY.
OW! THANKS SALIE. APPRECIATE IT.
WE INVEST IN LOTS OF STUFF AND THEN WE LOOK FOR WAYS TO...***ENHANCE*** IT. WHAT STRATEGIC PURPOSES IT HAS.
THAT WAS *REAPR*. IT CAME ACROSS MY DESK, I APPROVED A BITCOIN TRANSFER.
WHO INVENTED IT? WHO BUILT IT?
DOES IT MATTER? YOU GOING TO GO SHOOT THEM? *REAPR* IS OUT THERE, WE JUST GAVE IT A BIGGER SPOTLIGHT.
THAT FIRST CAMPAIGN? WE--
LISTEN, SCREW ALL THIS. WHY DO YOU WANT TO KILL ***ME?***
HOW ARE YOU SO ***BAD*** AT THIS?

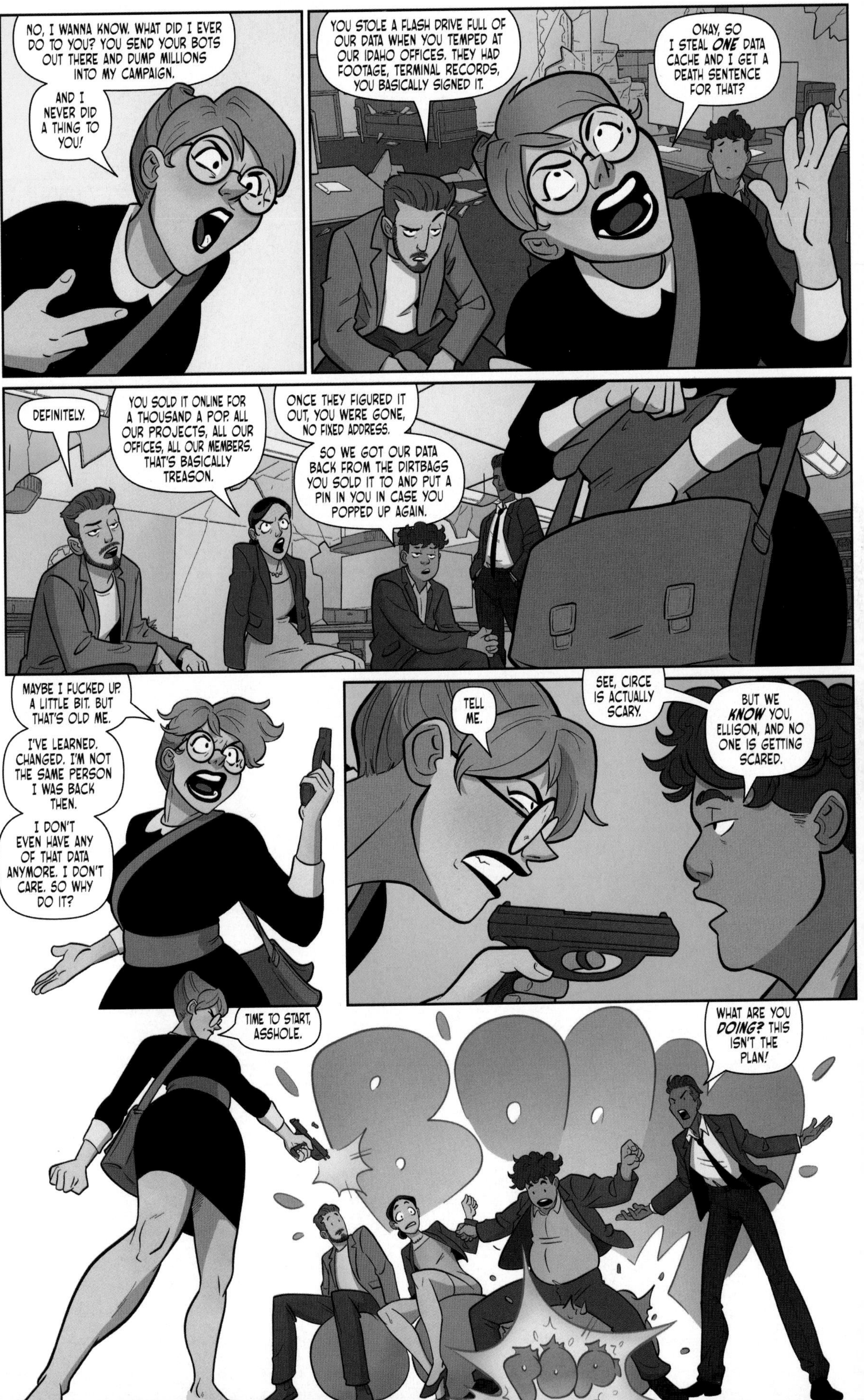
NO, I WANNA KNOW. WHAT DID I EVER DO TO YOU? YOU SEND YOUR BOTS OUT THERE AND DUMP MILLIONS INTO MY CAMPAIGN.
AND I NEVER DID A THING TO YOU!
YOU STOLE A FLASH DRIVE FULL OF OUR DATA WHEN YOU TEMPED AT OUR IDAHO OFFICES. THEY HAD FOOTAGE, TERMINAL RECORDS, YOU BASICALLY SIGNED IT.
OKAY, SO I STEAL ONE DATA CACHE AND I GET A DEATH SENTENCE FOR THAT?
DEFINITELY.
YOU SOLD IT ONLINE FOR A THOUSAND A POP. ALL OUR PROJECTS, ALL OUR OFFICES, ALL OUR MEMBERS. THAT'S BASICALLY TREASON.
ONCE THEY FIGURED IT OUT, YOU WERE GONE, NO FIXED ADDRESS.
SO WE GOT OUR DATA BACK FROM THE DIRTBAGS YOU SOLD IT TO AND PUT A PIN IN YOU IN CASE YOU POPPED UP AGAIN.
MAYBE I FUCKED UP. A LITTLE BIT. BUT THAT'S OLD ME.
I'VE LEARNED. CHANGED. I'M NOT THE SAME PERSON I WAS BACK THEN.
I DON'T EVEN HAVE ANY OF THAT DATA ANYMORE. I DON'T CARE. SO WHY DO IT?
TELL ME.
SEE, CIRCE IS ACTUALLY SCARY.
BUT WE KNOW YOU, ELLISON, AND NO ONE IS GETTING SCARED.
TIME TO START, ASSHOLE.
BOOM
WHAT ARE YOU DOING? THIS ISN'T THE PLAN!
POP!

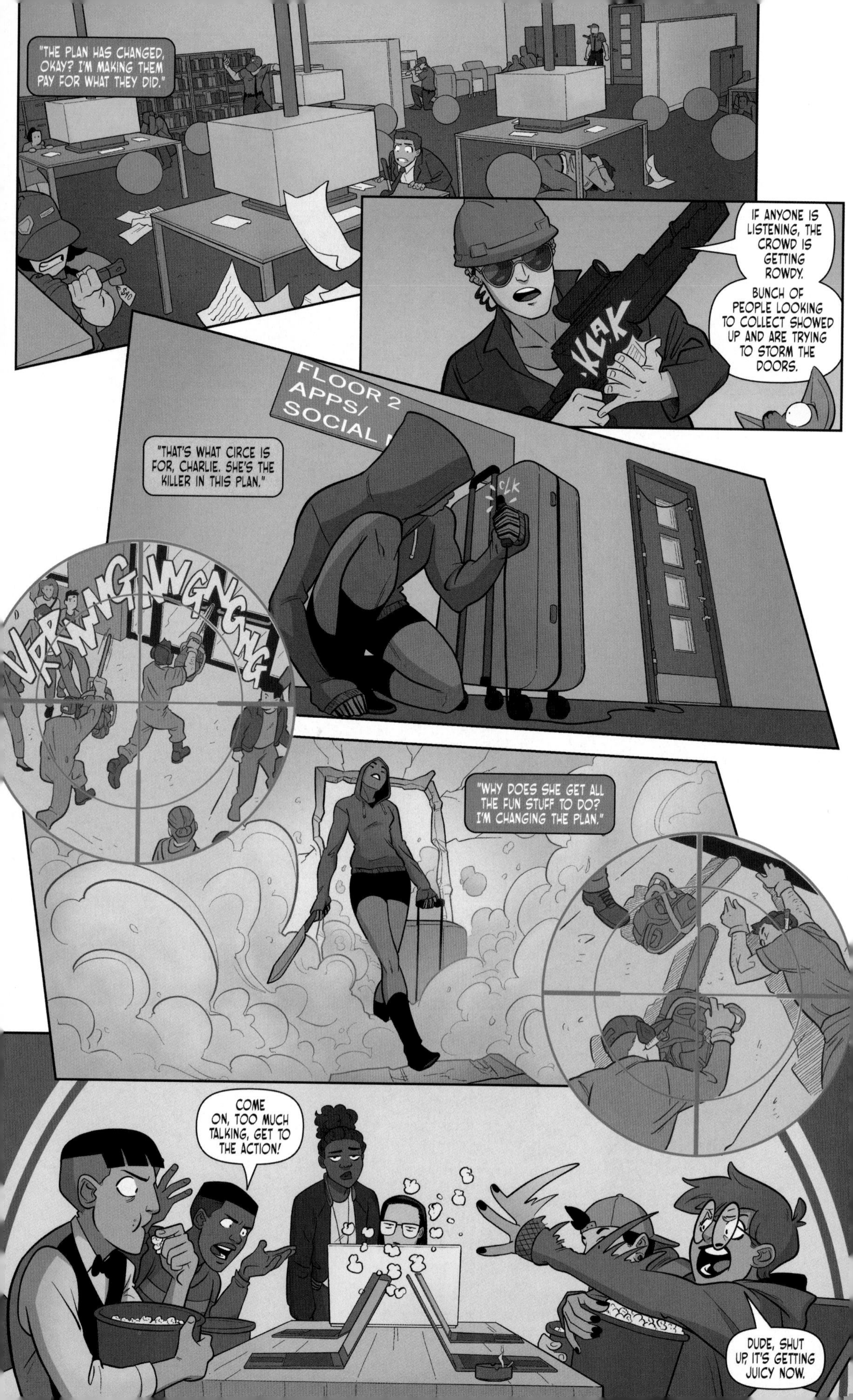
"THE PLAN HAS CHANGED, OKAY? I'M MAKING THEM PAY FOR WHAT THEY DID."
$40
IF ANYONE IS LISTENING, THE CROWD IS GETTING ROWDY.
BUNCH OF PEOPLE LOOKING TO COLLECT SHOWED UP AND ARE TRYING TO STORM THE DOORS.
KLAK
FLOOR 2 APPS/ SOCIAL
"THAT'S WHAT CIRCE IS FOR, CHARLIE. SHE'S THE KILLER IN THIS PLAN."
CLK
VRRANNGNNGNNGNGNGNG
"WHY DOES SHE GET ALL THE FUN STUFF TO DO? I'M CHANGING THE PLAN."
COME ON, TOO MUCH TALKING, GET TO THE ACTION!
DUDE, SHUT UP, IT'S GETTING JUICY NOW.

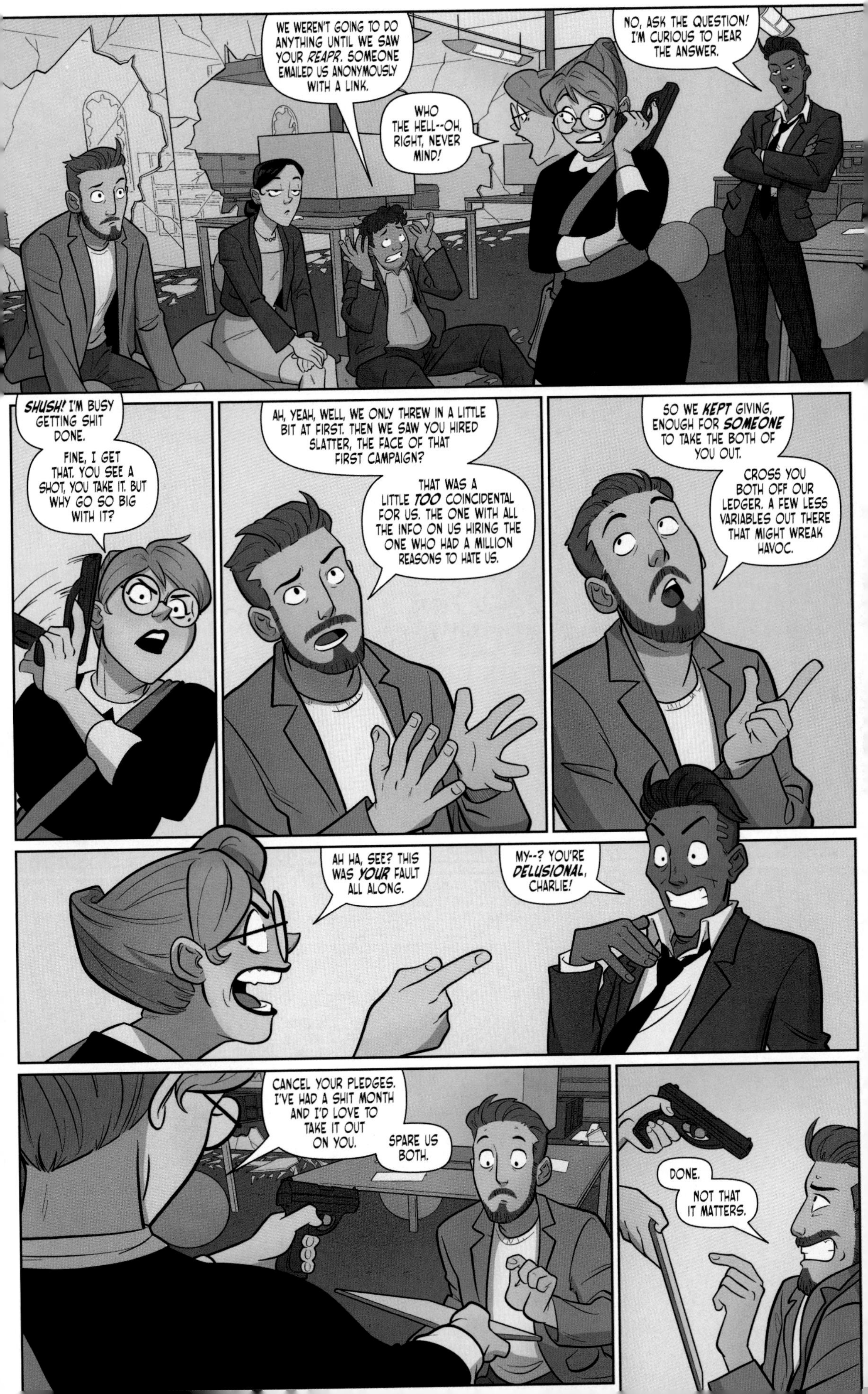
WE WEREN'T GOING TO DO ANYTHING UNTIL WE SAW YOUR REAPR. SOMEONE EMAILED US ANONYMOUSLY WITH A LINK.
WHO THE HELL--OH, RIGHT, NEVER MIND!
NO, ASK THE QUESTION! I'M CURIOUS TO HEAR THE ANSWER.
SHUSH! I'M BUSY GETTING SHIT DONE.
FINE, I GET THAT. YOU SEE A SHOT, YOU TAKE IT. BUT WHY GO SO BIG WITH IT?
AH, YEAH, WELL, WE ONLY THREW IN A LITTLE BIT AT FIRST. THEN WE SAW YOU HIRED SLATTER, THE FACE OF THAT FIRST CAMPAIGN?
THAT WAS A LITTLE TOO COINCIDENTAL FOR US. THE ONE WITH ALL THE INFO ON US HIRING THE ONE WHO HAD A MILLION REASONS TO HATE US.
SO WE KEPT GIVING, ENOUGH FOR SOMEONE TO TAKE THE BOTH OF YOU OUT.
CROSS YOU BOTH OFF OUR LEDGER. A FEW LESS VARIABLES OUT THERE THAT MIGHT WREAK HAVOC.
AH HA, SEE? THIS WAS YOUR FAULT ALL ALONG.
MY--? YOU'RE DELUSIONAL, CHARLIE!
CANCEL YOUR PLEDGES. I'VE HAD A SHIT MONTH AND I'D LOVE TO TAKE IT OUT ON YOU.
SPARE US BOTH.
DONE.
NOT THAT IT MATTERS.

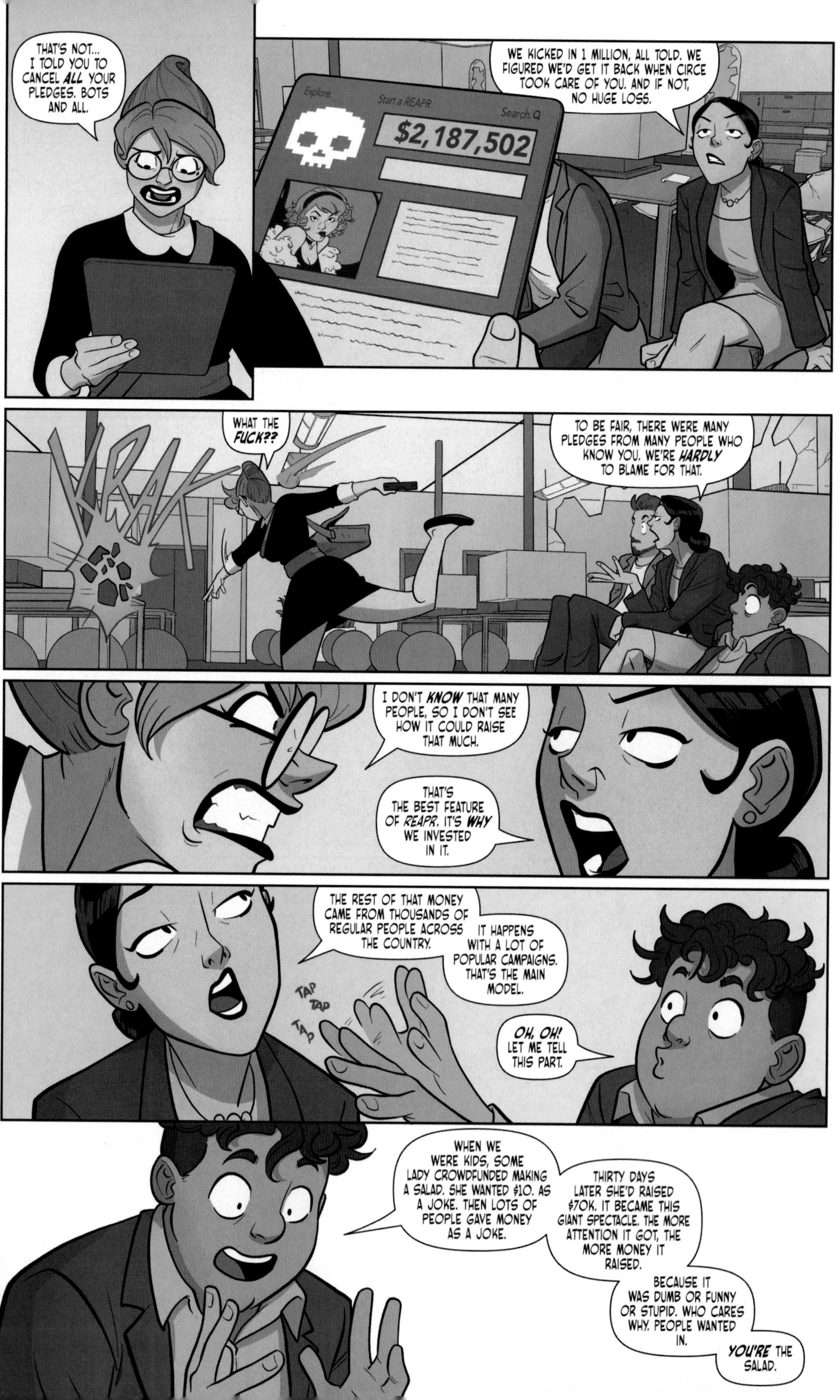
THAT'S NOT... I TOLD YOU TO CANCEL ALL YOUR PLEDGES. BOTS AND ALL.
Explore. Start a REAPR. Search. Q
$2,187,502
WE KICKED IN 1 MILLION, ALL TOLD. WE FIGURED WE'D GET IT BACK WHEN CIRCE TOOK CARE OF YOU. AND IF NOT, NO HUGE LOSS.
KRAK
WHAT THE FUCK??
TO BE FAIR, THERE WERE MANY PLEDGES FROM MANY PEOPLE WHO KNOW YOU. WE'RE HARDLY TO BLAME FOR THAT.
I DON'T KNOW THAT MANY PEOPLE, SO I DON'T SEE HOW IT COULD RAISE THAT MUCH.
THAT'S THE BEST FEATURE OF REAPR. IT'S WHY WE INVESTED IN IT.
THE REST OF THAT MONEY CAME FROM THOUSANDS OF REGULAR PEOPLE ACROSS THE COUNTRY.
IT HAPPENS WITH A LOT OF POPULAR CAMPAIGNS. THAT'S THE MAIN MODEL.
TAP TAP TAP
OH, OH! LET ME TELL THIS PART.
WHEN WE WERE KIDS, SOME LADY CROWDFUNDED MAKING A SALAD. SHE WANTED $10. AS A JOKE. THEN LOTS OF PEOPLE GAVE MONEY AS A JOKE.
THIRTY DAYS LATER SHE'D RAISED $70K. IT BECAME THIS GIANT SPECTACLE. THE MORE ATTENTION IT GOT, THE MORE MONEY IT RAISED.
BECAUSE IT WAS DUMB OR FUNNY OR STUPID. WHO CARES WHY. PEOPLE WANTED IN.
YOU'RE THE SALAD.

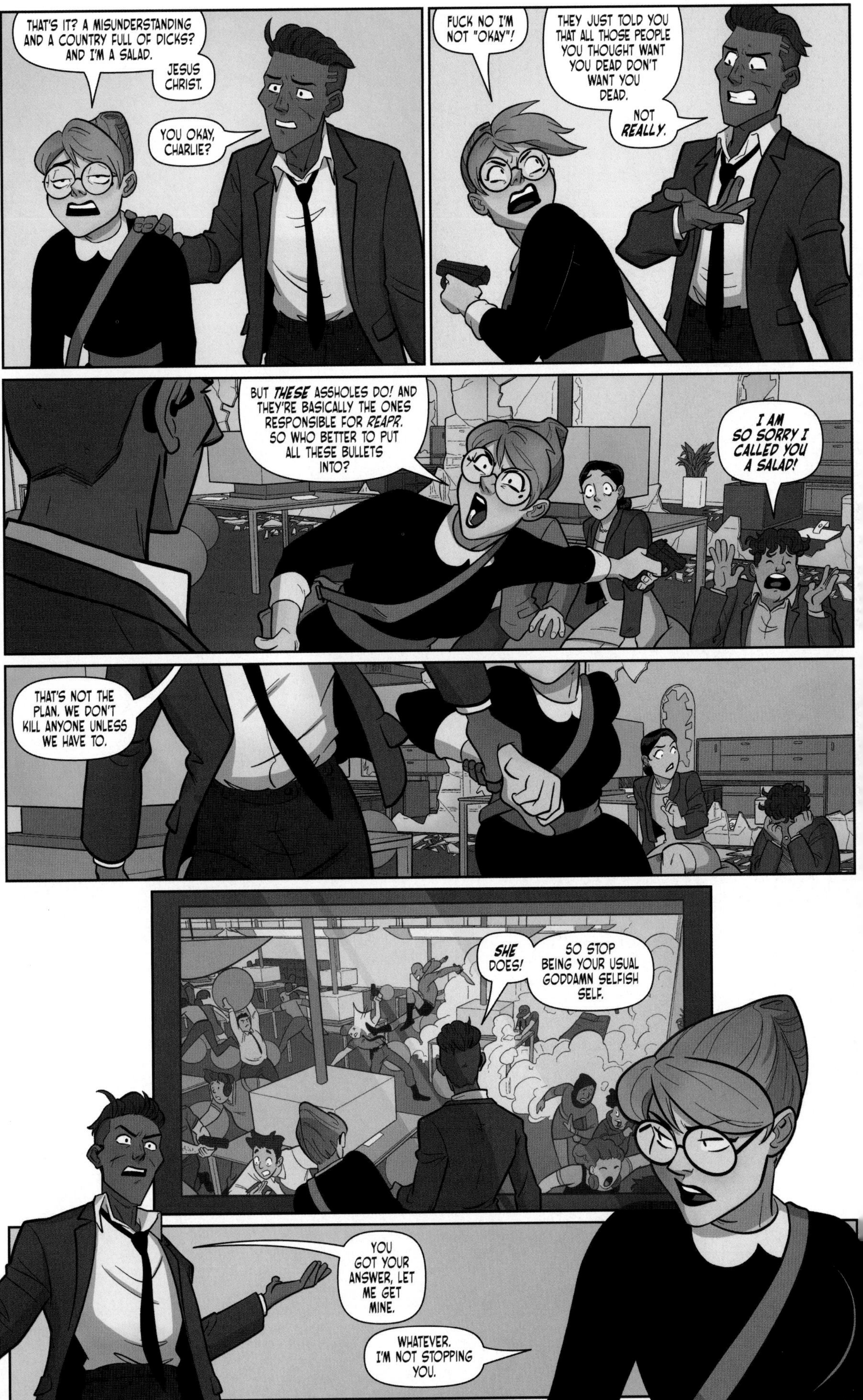
THAT'S IT? A MISUNDERSTANDING AND A COUNTRY FULL OF DICKS? AND I'M A SALAD.
JESUS CHRIST.
YOU OKAY, CHARLIE?
FUCK NO I'M NOT "OKAY"!
THEY JUST TOLD YOU THAT ALL THOSE PEOPLE YOU THOUGHT WANT YOU DEAD DON'T WANT YOU DEAD.
NOT REALLY.
BUT THESE ASSHOLES DO! AND THEY'RE BASICALLY THE ONES RESPONSIBLE FOR REAPR. SO WHO BETTER TO PUT ALL THESE BULLETS INTO?
I AM SO SORRY I CALLED YOU A SALAD!
THAT'S NOT THE PLAN. WE DON'T KILL ANYONE UNLESS WE HAVE TO.
SHE DOES!
SO STOP BEING YOUR USUAL GODDAMN SELFISH SELF.
YOU GOT YOUR ANSWER, LET ME GET MINE.
WHATEVER. I'M NOT STOPPING YOU.

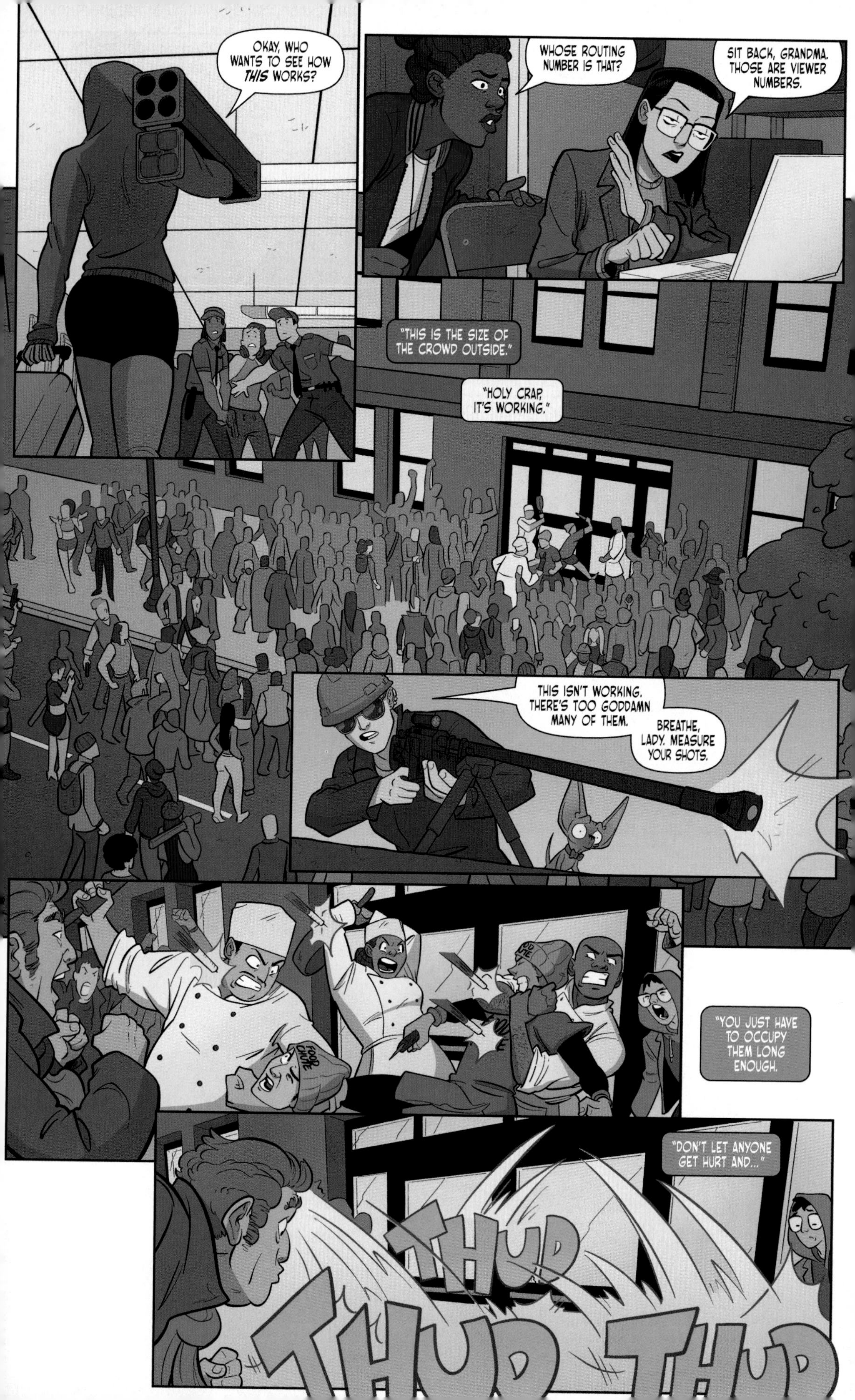
OKAY, WHO WANTS TO SEE HOW *THIS* WORKS?
WHOSE ROUTING NUMBER IS THAT?
SIT BACK, GRANDMA. THOSE ARE VIEWER NUMBERS.
"THIS IS THE SIZE OF THE CROWD OUTSIDE."
"HOLY CRAP, IT'S WORKING."
THIS ISN'T WORKING. THERE'S TOO GODDAMN MANY OF THEM.
BREATHE, LADY. MEASURE YOUR SHOTS.
"YOU JUST HAVE TO OCCUPY THEM LONG ENOUGH.
"DON'T LET ANYONE GET HURT AND..."
THUD
THUD THUD

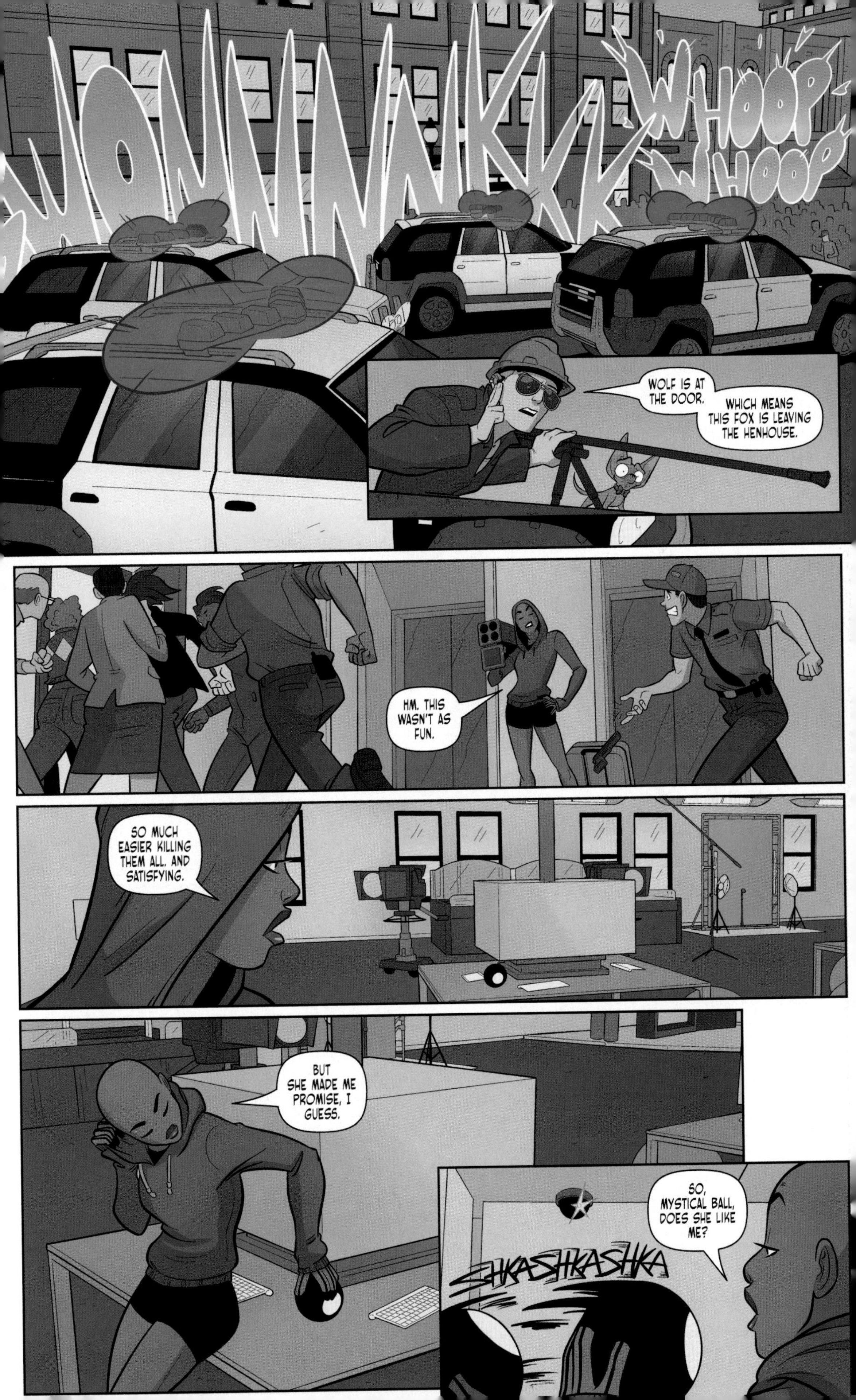

WHOMMMAKKK
WHOOP WHOOP
WOLF IS AT THE DOOR.
WHICH MEANS THIS FOX IS LEAVING THE HENHOUSE.
HM. THIS WASN'T AS FUN.
SO MUCH EASIER KILLING THEM ALL. AND SATISFYING.
BUT SHE MADE ME PROMISE, I GUESS.
SO, MYSTICAL BALL, DOES SHE LIKE ME?
SHKASHKASHKA

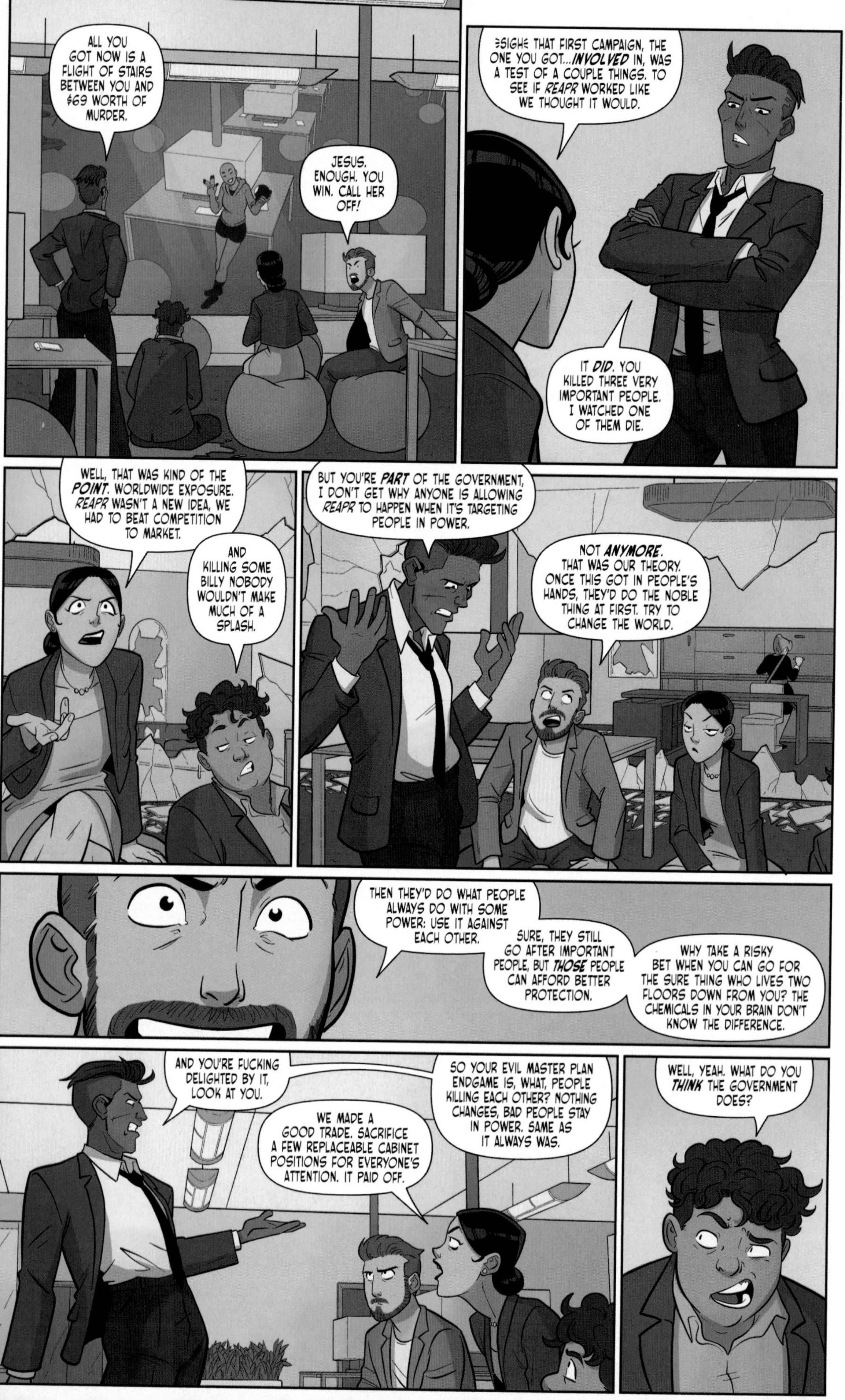
ALL YOU GOT NOW IS A FLIGHT OF STAIRS BETWEEN YOU AND $69 WORTH OF MURDER.
JESUS. ENOUGH. YOU WIN. CALL HER OFF!
=SIGH= THAT FIRST CAMPAIGN, THE ONE YOU GOT...INVOLVED IN, WAS A TEST OF A COUPLE THINGS. TO SEE IF REAPR WORKED LIKE WE THOUGHT IT WOULD.
IT DID. YOU KILLED THREE VERY IMPORTANT PEOPLE. I WATCHED ONE OF THEM DIE.
WELL, THAT WAS KIND OF THE POINT. WORLDWIDE EXPOSURE. REAPR WASN'T A NEW IDEA, WE HAD TO BEAT COMPETITION TO MARKET.
AND KILLING SOME BILLY NOBODY WOULDN'T MAKE MUCH OF A SPLASH.
BUT YOU'RE PART OF THE GOVERNMENT, I DON'T GET WHY ANYONE IS ALLOWING REAPR TO HAPPEN WHEN IT'S TARGETING PEOPLE IN POWER.
NOT ANYMORE. THAT WAS OUR THEORY. ONCE THIS GOT IN PEOPLE'S HANDS, THEY'D DO THE NOBLE THING AT FIRST. TRY TO CHANGE THE WORLD.
THEN THEY'D DO WHAT PEOPLE ALWAYS DO WITH SOME POWER: USE IT AGAINST EACH OTHER.
SURE, THEY STILL GO AFTER IMPORTANT PEOPLE, BUT THOSE PEOPLE CAN AFFORD BETTER PROTECTION.
WHY TAKE A RISKY BET WHEN YOU CAN GO FOR THE SURE THING WHO LIVES TWO FLOORS DOWN FROM YOU? THE CHEMICALS IN YOUR BRAIN DON'T KNOW THE DIFFERENCE.
AND YOU'RE FUCKING DELIGHTED BY IT, LOOK AT YOU.
WE MADE A GOOD TRADE. SACRIFICE A FEW REPLACEABLE CABINET POSITIONS FOR EVERYONE'S ATTENTION. IT PAID OFF.
SO YOUR EVIL MASTER PLAN ENDGAME IS, WHAT, PEOPLE KILLING EACH OTHER? NOTHING CHANGES, BAD PEOPLE STAY IN POWER. SAME AS IT ALWAYS WAS.
WELL, YEAH. WHAT DO YOU THINK THE GOVERNMENT DOES?

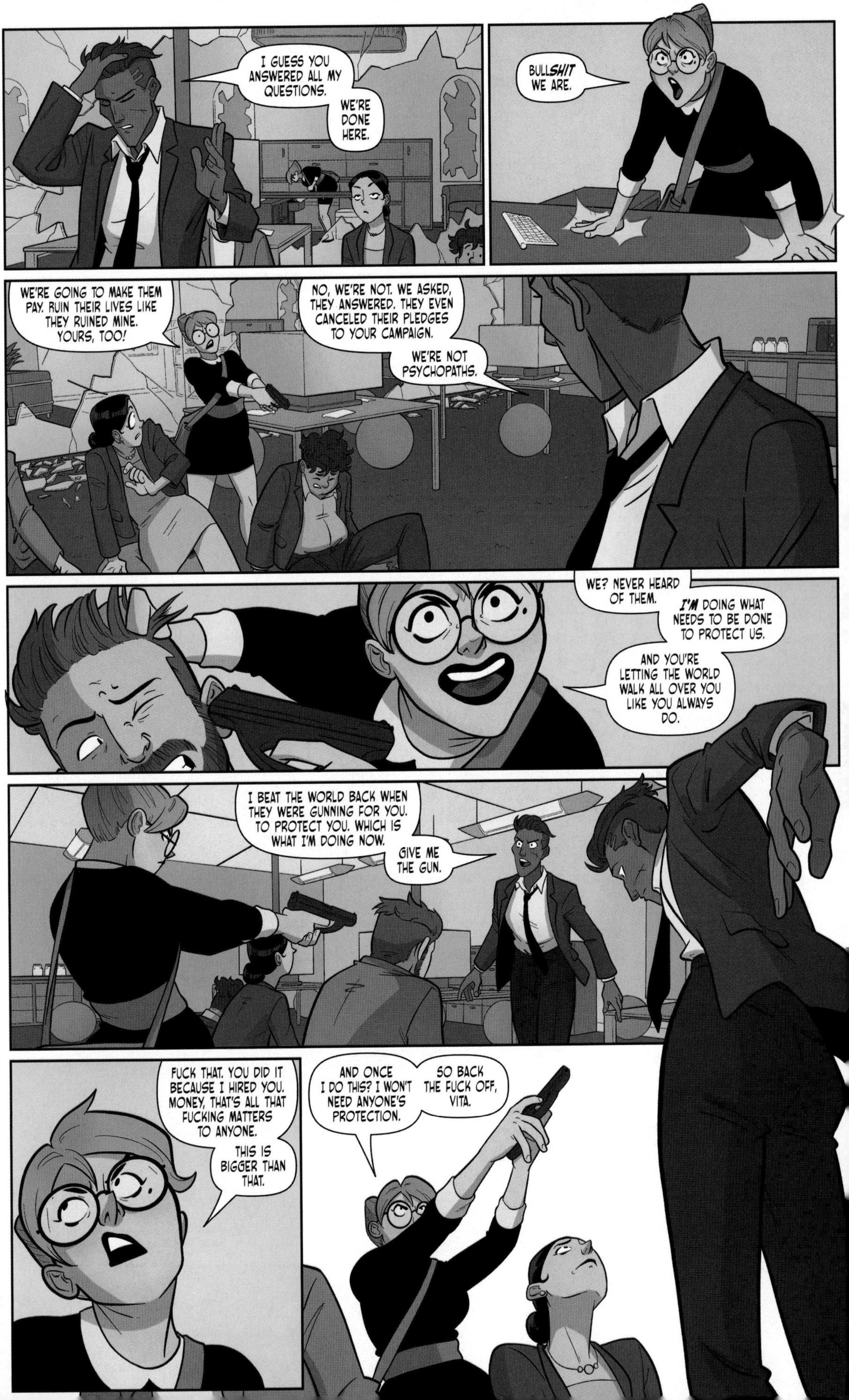

I GUESS YOU ANSWERED ALL MY QUESTIONS.
WE'RE DONE HERE.
BULLSHIT WE ARE.
WE'RE GOING TO MAKE THEM PAY. RUIN THEIR LIVES LIKE THEY RUINED MINE. YOURS, TOO!
NO, WE'RE NOT. WE ASKED, THEY ANSWERED. THEY EVEN CANCELED THEIR PLEDGES TO YOUR CAMPAIGN.
WE'RE NOT PSYCHOPATHS.
WE? NEVER HEARD OF THEM.
I'M DOING WHAT NEEDS TO BE DONE TO PROTECT US.
AND YOU'RE LETTING THE WORLD WALK ALL OVER YOU LIKE YOU ALWAYS DO.
I BEAT THE WORLD BACK WHEN THEY WERE GUNNING FOR YOU. TO PROTECT YOU. WHICH IS WHAT I'M DOING NOW.
GIVE ME THE GUN.
FUCK THAT. YOU DID IT BECAUSE I HIRED YOU. MONEY, THAT'S ALL THAT FUCKING MATTERS TO ANYONE.
THIS IS BIGGER THAN THAT.
AND ONCE I DO THIS? I WON'T NEED ANYONE'S PROTECTION.
SO BACK THE FUCK OFF, VITA.

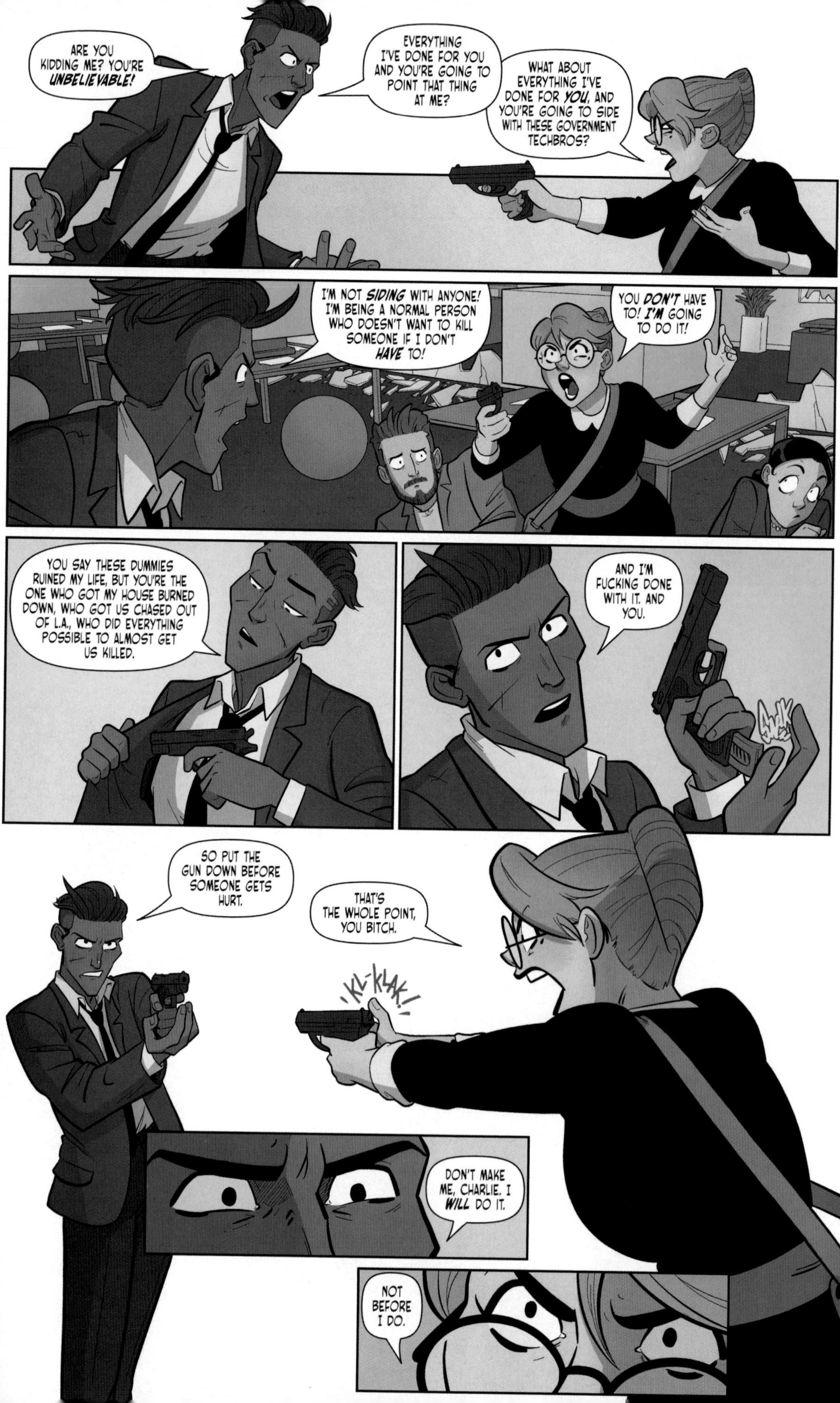
ARE YOU KIDDING ME? YOU'RE UNBELIEVABLE!
EVERYTHING I'VE DONE FOR YOU AND YOU'RE GOING TO POINT THAT THING AT ME?
WHAT ABOUT EVERYTHING I'VE DONE FOR YOU, AND YOU'RE GOING TO SIDE WITH THESE GOVERNMENT TECHBROS?
I'M NOT SIDING WITH ANYONE! I'M BEING A NORMAL PERSON WHO DOESN'T WANT TO KILL SOMEONE IF I DON'T HAVE TO!
YOU DON'T HAVE TO! I'M GOING TO DO IT!
YOU SAY THESE DUMMIES RUINED MY LIFE, BUT YOU'RE THE ONE WHO GOT MY HOUSE BURNED DOWN, WHO GOT US CHASED OUT OF L.A., WHO DID EVERYTHING POSSIBLE TO ALMOST GET US KILLED.
AND I'M FUCKING DONE WITH IT. AND YOU.
SO PUT THE GUN DOWN BEFORE SOMEONE GETS HURT.
THAT'S THE WHOLE POINT, YOU BITCH.
KL-KLAK!
DON'T MAKE ME, CHARLIE. I WILL DO IT.
NOT BEFORE I DO.

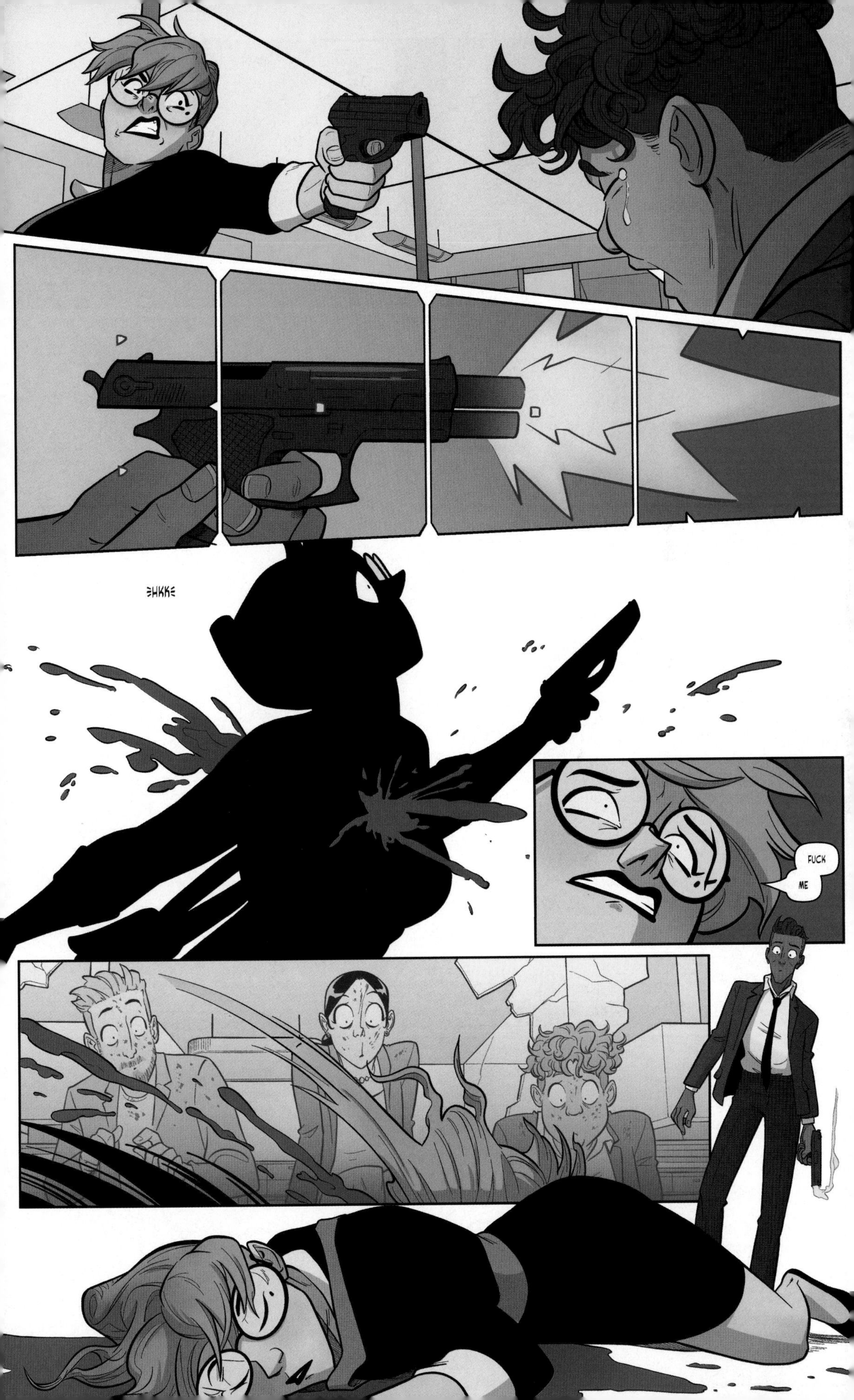
HKK
FUCK ME

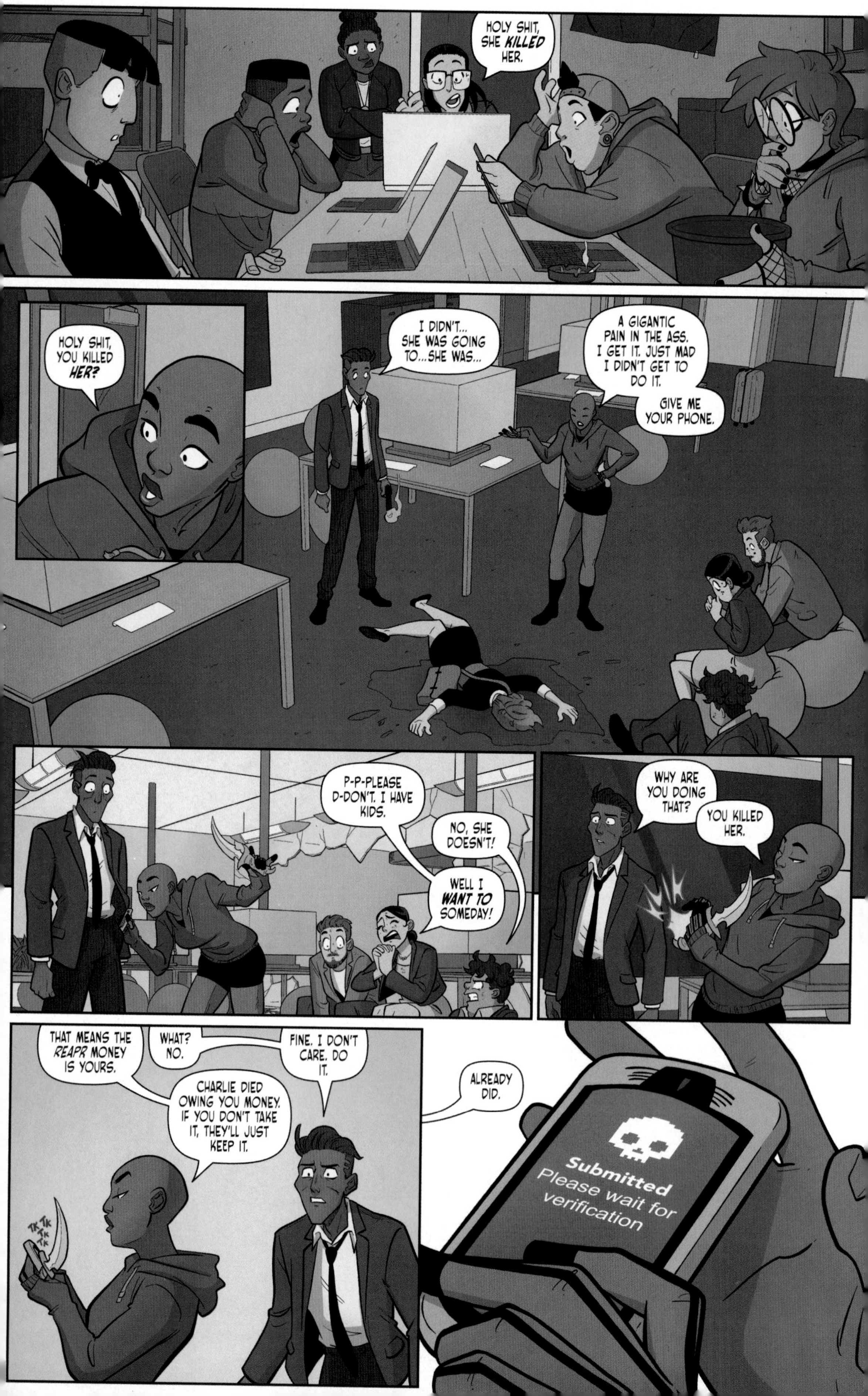
HOLY SHIT, SHE KILLED HER.
HOLY SHIT, YOU KILLED HER?
I DIDN'T... SHE WAS GOING TO...SHE WAS...
A GIGANTIC PAIN IN THE ASS. I GET IT. JUST MAD I DIDN'T GET TO DO IT.
GIVE ME YOUR PHONE.
P-P-PLEASE D-DON'T. I HAVE KIDS.
NO, SHE DOESN'T!
WELL I WANT TO SOMEDAY!
WHY ARE YOU DOING THAT?
YOU KILLED HER.
THAT MEANS THE REAPR MONEY IS YOURS.
WHAT? NO.
CHARLIE DIED OWING YOU MONEY. IF YOU DON'T TAKE IT, THEY'LL JUST KEEP IT.
FINE. I DON'T CARE. DO IT.
ALREADY DID.
TK TK TK TK
Submitted
Please wait for verification

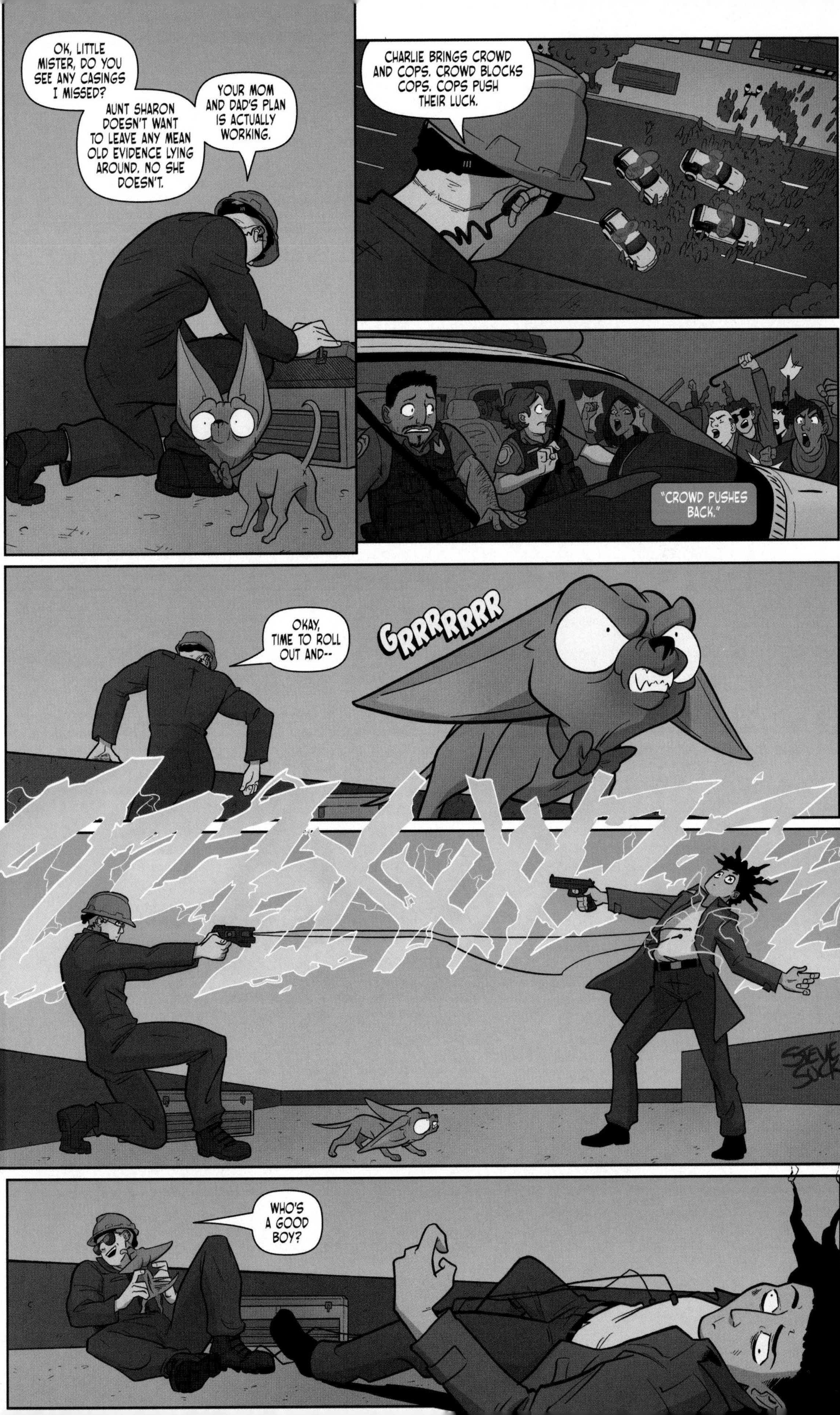
OK, LITTLE MISTER, DO YOU SEE ANY CASINGS I MISSED?
AUNT SHARON DOESN'T WANT TO LEAVE ANY MEAN OLD EVIDENCE LYING AROUND. NO SHE DOESN'T.
YOUR MOM AND DAD'S PLAN IS ACTUALLY WORKING.
CHARLIE BRINGS CROWD AND COPS. CROWD BLOCKS COPS. COPS PUSH THEIR LUCK.
"CROWD PUSHES BACK."
OKAY, TIME TO ROLL OUT AND--
GRRRRRRR
STEVE SUCKS
WHO'S A GOOD BOY?

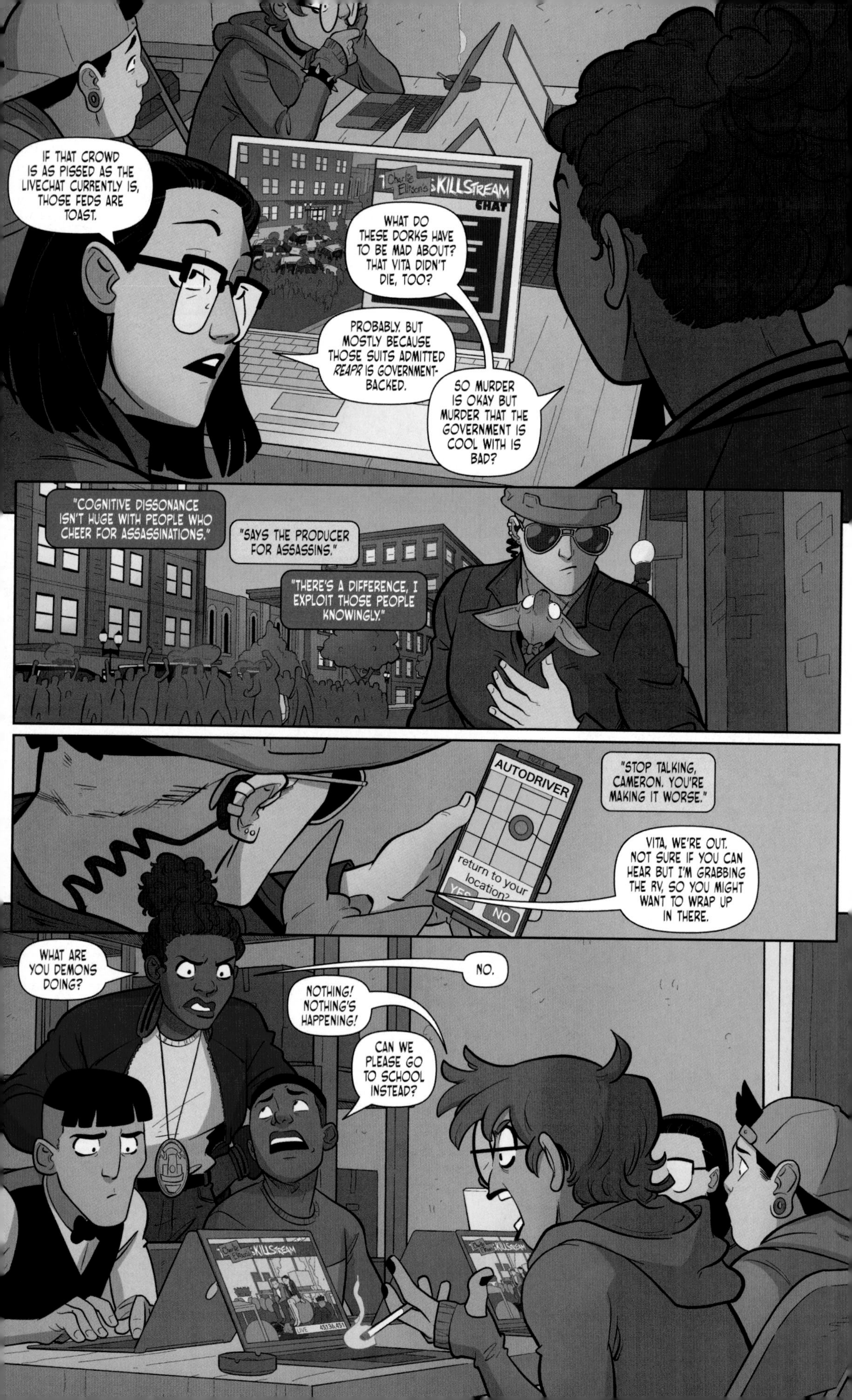
IF THAT CROWD IS AS PISSED AS THE LIVECHAT CURRENTLY IS, THOSE FEDS ARE TOAST.
Charlie Ellison's KILLSTREAM
CHAT
WHAT DO THESE DORKS HAVE TO BE MAD ABOUT? THAT VITA DIDN'T DIE, TOO?
PROBABLY. BUT MOSTLY BECAUSE THOSE SUITS ADMITTED *REAPR* IS GOVERNMENT-BACKED.
SO MURDER IS OKAY BUT MURDER THAT THE GOVERNMENT IS COOL WITH IS BAD?
"COGNITIVE DISSONANCE ISN'T HUGE WITH PEOPLE WHO CHEER FOR ASSASSINATIONS."
"SAYS THE PRODUCER FOR ASSASSINS."
"THERE'S A DIFFERENCE, I EXPLOIT THOSE PEOPLE KNOWINGLY."
AUTODRIVER
return to your location?
YES
NO
"STOP TALKING, CAMERON. YOU'RE MAKING IT WORSE."
VITA, WE'RE OUT. NOT SURE IF YOU CAN HEAR BUT I'M GRABBING THE RV, SO YOU MIGHT WANT TO WRAP UP IN THERE.
WHAT ARE YOU DEMONS DOING?
NO.
NOTHING! NOTHING'S HAPPENING!
CAN WE PLEASE GO TO SCHOOL INSTEAD?
Charlie Ellison's KILLSTREAM
LIVE 45136451

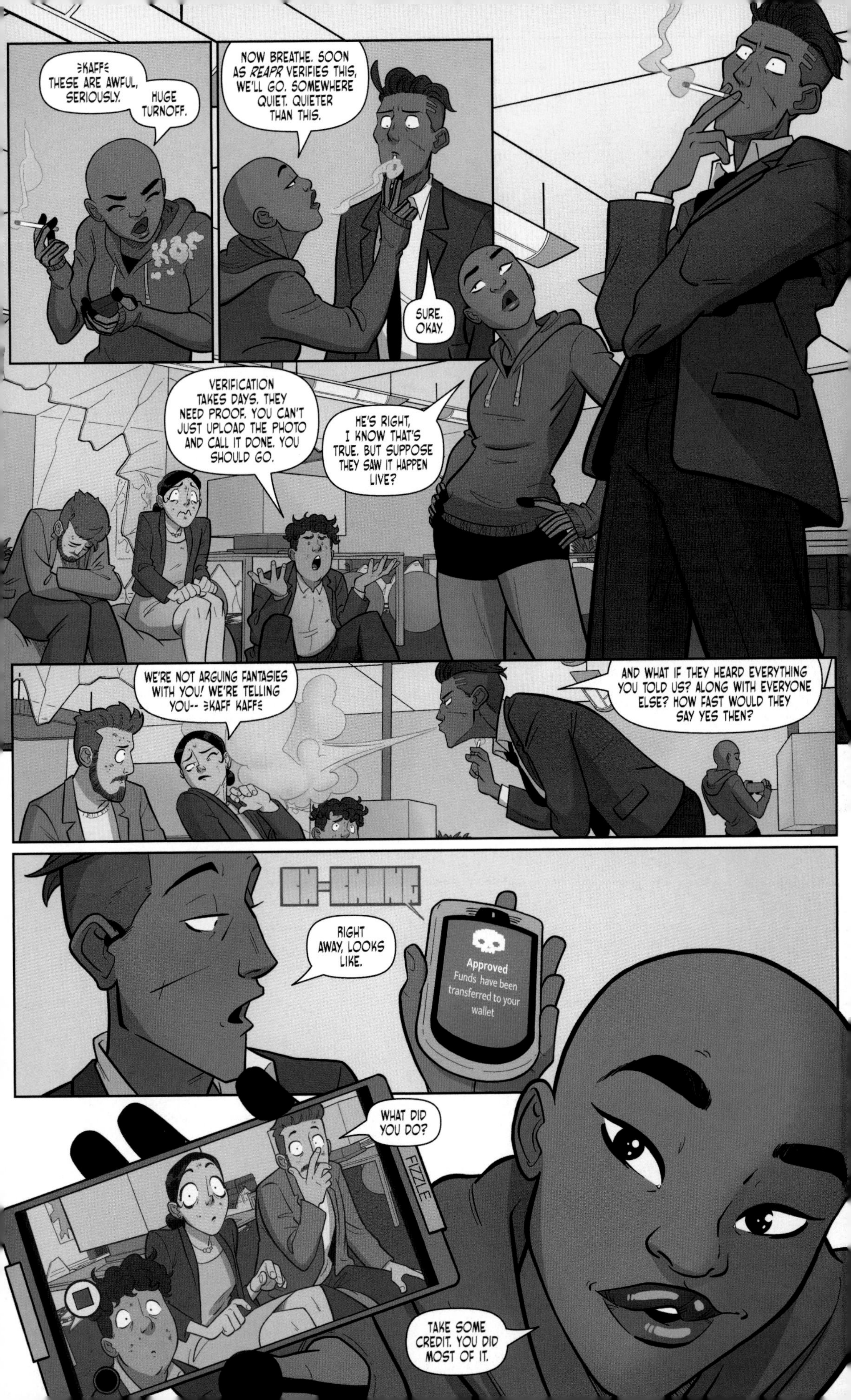

≡KAFF≡
THESE ARE AWFUL, SERIOUSLY.
HUGE TURNOFF.
NOW BREATHE. SOON AS *REAPR* VERIFIES THIS, WE'LL GO. SOMEWHERE QUIET. QUIETER THAN THIS.
SURE. OKAY.
VERIFICATION TAKES DAYS. THEY NEED PROOF. YOU CAN'T JUST UPLOAD THE PHOTO AND CALL IT DONE. YOU SHOULD GO.
HE'S RIGHT, I KNOW THAT'S TRUE. BUT SUPPOSE THEY SAW IT HAPPEN LIVE?
WE'RE NOT ARGUING FANTASIES WITH YOU! WE'RE TELLING YOU-- ≡KAFF KAFF≡
AND WHAT IF THEY HEARD EVERYTHING YOU TOLD US? ALONG WITH EVERYONE ELSE? HOW FAST WOULD THEY SAY YES THEN?
RIGHT AWAY, LOOKS LIKE.
Approved
Funds have been transferred to your wallet
WHAT DID YOU DO?
FIZZLE
TAKE SOME CREDIT. YOU DID MOST OF IT.

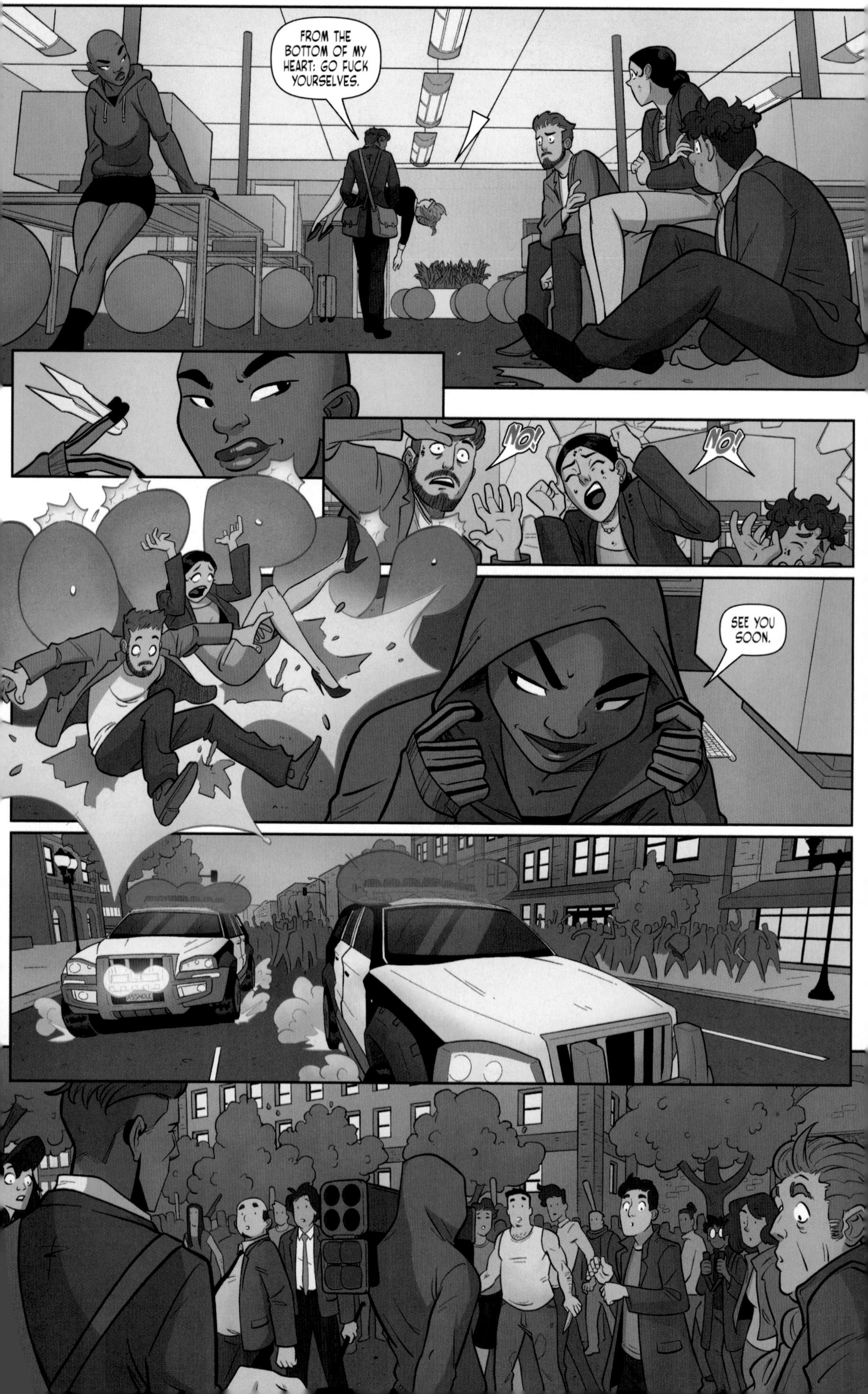
FROM THE BOTTOM OF MY HEART: GO FUCK YOURSELVES.
NO!
NO!
SEE YOU SOON.
ASSHOLE

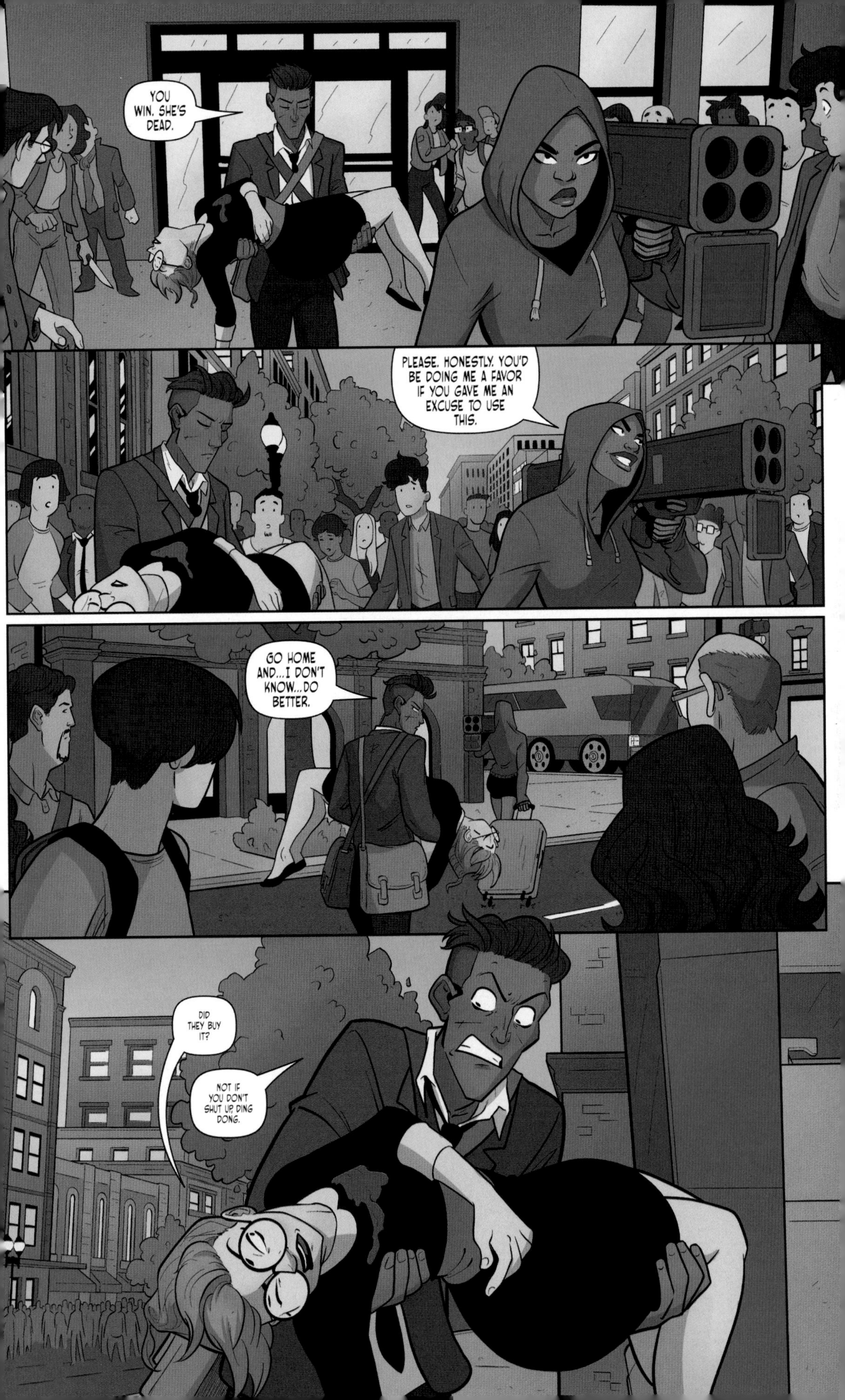
YOU WIN. SHE'S DEAD.
PLEASE. HONESTLY. YOU'D BE DOING ME A FAVOR IF YOU GAVE ME AN EXCUSE TO USE THIS.
GO HOME AND...I DON'T KNOW...DO BETTER.
DID THEY BUY IT?
NOT IF YOU DON'T SHUT UP, DING DONG.

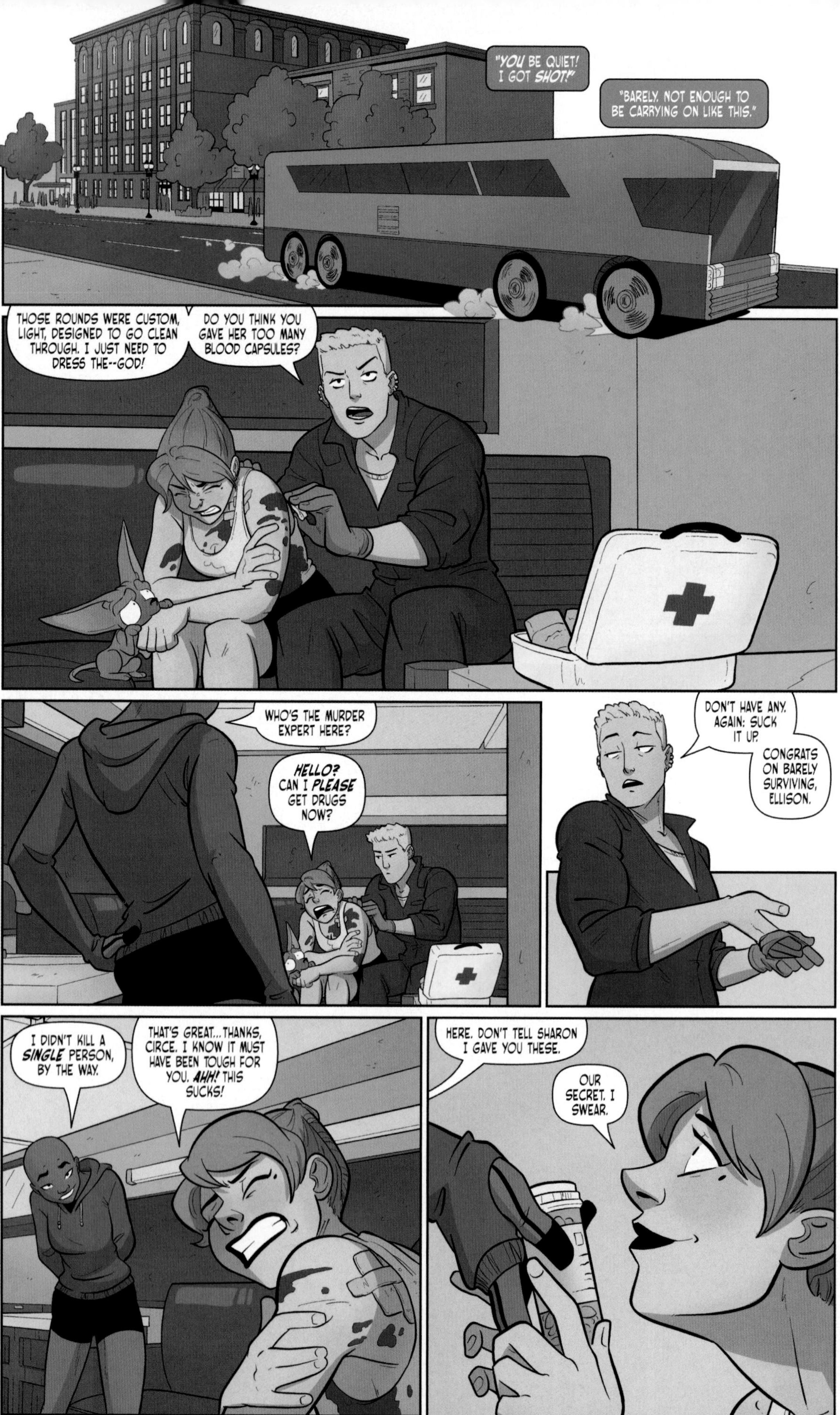
"YOU BE QUIET! I GOT SHOT!"
"BARELY. NOT ENOUGH TO BE CARRYING ON LIKE THIS."
THOSE ROUNDS WERE CUSTOM, LIGHT, DESIGNED TO GO CLEAN THROUGH. I JUST NEED TO DRESS THE--GOD!
DO YOU THINK YOU GAVE HER TOO MANY BLOOD CAPSULES?
WHO'S THE MURDER EXPERT HERE?
HELLO? CAN I PLEASE GET DRUGS NOW?
DON'T HAVE ANY. AGAIN: SUCK IT UP.
CONGRATS ON BARELY SURVIVING, ELLISON.
I DIDN'T KILL A SINGLE PERSON, BY THE WAY.
THAT'S GREAT...THANKS, CIRCE. I KNOW IT MUST HAVE BEEN TOUGH FOR YOU. AHH! THIS SUCKS!
HERE. DON'T TELL SHARON I GAVE YOU THESE.
OUR SECRET. I SWEAR.

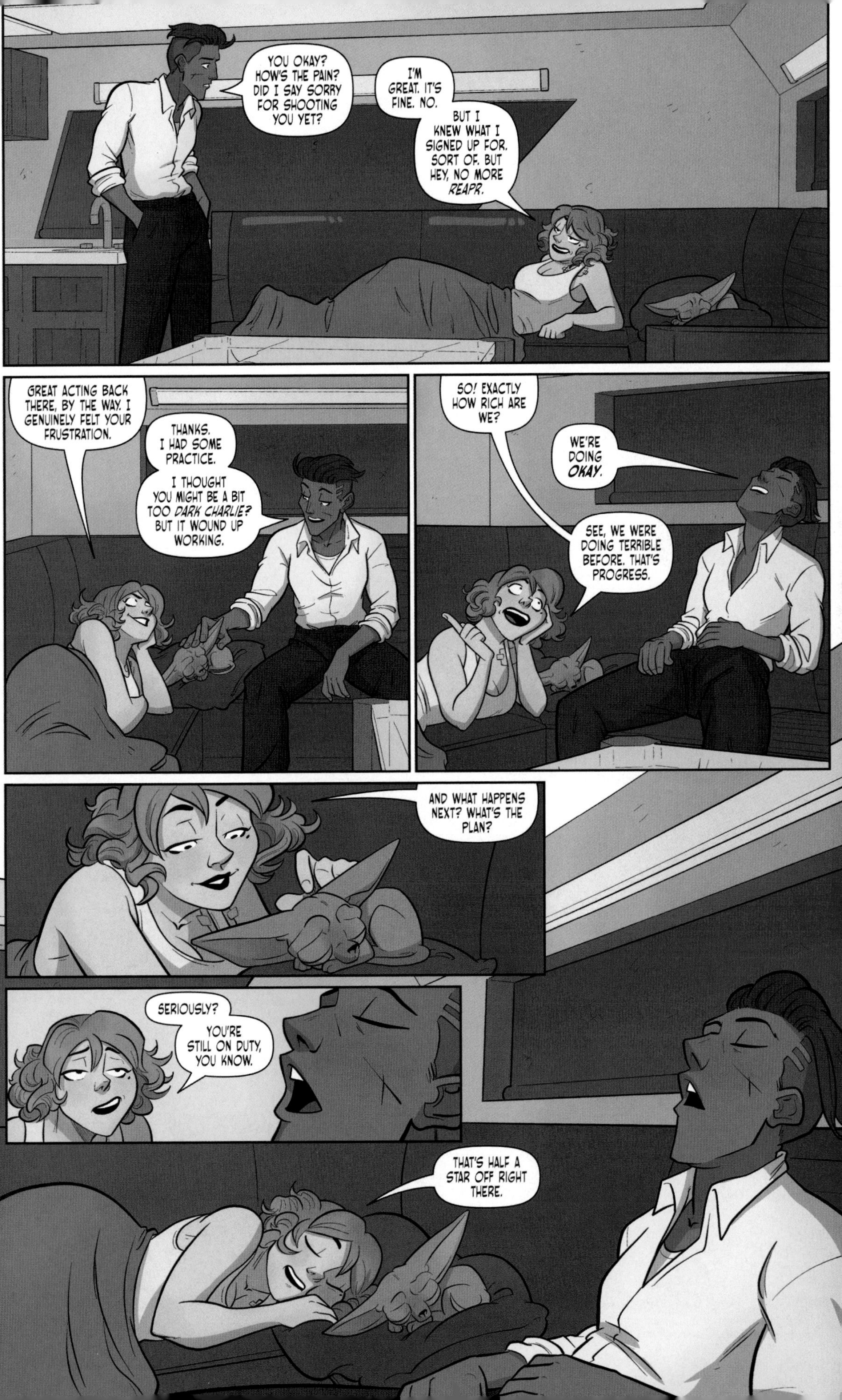
YOU OKAY? HOW'S THE PAIN? DID I SAY SORRY FOR SHOOTING YOU YET?
I'M GREAT. IT'S FINE. NO.
BUT I KNEW WHAT I SIGNED UP FOR. SORT OF. BUT HEY, NO MORE *REAPR*.
GREAT ACTING BACK THERE, BY THE WAY. I GENUINELY FELT YOUR FRUSTRATION.
THANKS. I HAD SOME PRACTICE.
I THOUGHT YOU MIGHT BE A BIT TOO *DARK CHARLIE?* BUT IT WOUND UP WORKING.
SO! EXACTLY HOW RICH ARE WE?
WE'RE DOING ***OKAY***.
SEE, WE WERE DOING TERRIBLE BEFORE. THAT'S PROGRESS.
AND WHAT HAPPENS NEXT? WHAT'S THE PLAN?
SERIOUSLY?
YOU'RE STILL ON DUTY, YOU KNOW.
THAT'S HALF A STAR OFF RIGHT THERE.

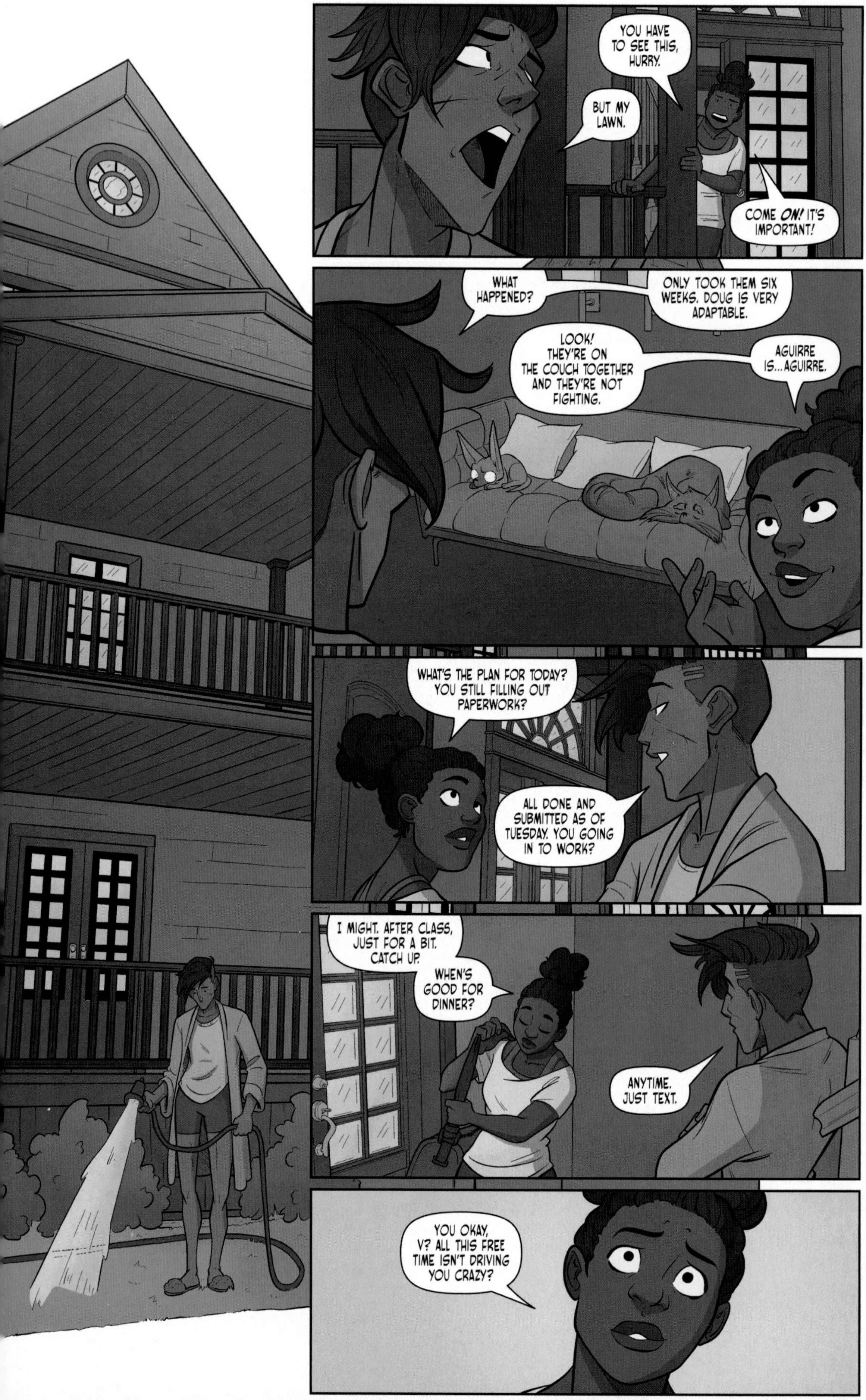

YOU HAVE TO SEE THIS, HURRY.
BUT MY LAWN.
COME ON! IT'S IMPORTANT!
WHAT HAPPENED?
ONLY TOOK THEM SIX WEEKS. DOUG IS VERY ADAPTABLE.
LOOK! THEY'RE ON THE COUCH TOGETHER AND THEY'RE NOT FIGHTING.
AGUIRRE IS...AGUIRRE.
WHAT'S THE PLAN FOR TODAY? YOU STILL FILLING OUT PAPERWORK?
ALL DONE AND SUBMITTED AS OF TUESDAY. YOU GOING IN TO WORK?
I MIGHT. AFTER CLASS, JUST FOR A BIT. CATCH UP.
WHEN'S GOOD FOR DINNER?
ANYTIME. JUST TEXT.
YOU OKAY, V? ALL THIS FREE TIME ISN'T DRIVING YOU CRAZY?

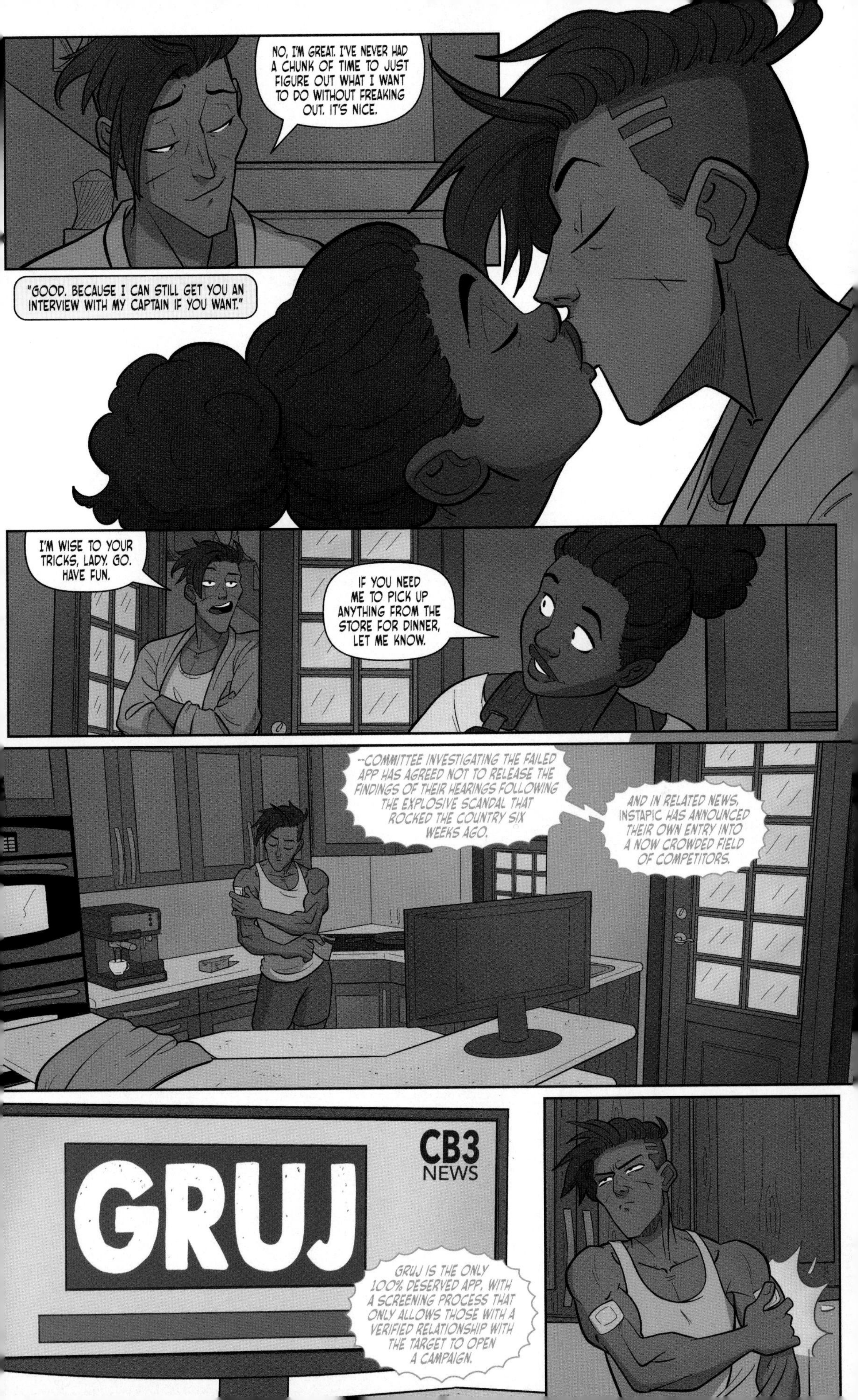
NO, I'M GREAT. I'VE NEVER HAD A CHUNK OF TIME TO JUST FIGURE OUT WHAT I WANT TO DO WITHOUT FREAKING OUT. IT'S NICE.
"GOOD. BECAUSE I CAN STILL GET YOU AN INTERVIEW WITH MY CAPTAIN IF YOU WANT."
I'M WISE TO YOUR TRICKS, LADY. GO. HAVE FUN.
IF YOU NEED ME TO PICK UP ANYTHING FROM THE STORE FOR DINNER, LET ME KNOW.
--COMMITTEE INVESTIGATING THE FAILED APP HAS AGREED NOT TO RELEASE THE FINDINGS OF THEIR HEARINGS FOLLOWING THE EXPLOSIVE SCANDAL THAT ROCKED THE COUNTRY SIX WEEKS AGO.
AND IN RELATED NEWS, INSTAPIC HAS ANNOUNCED THEIR OWN ENTRY INTO A NOW CROWDED FIELD OF COMPETITORS.
GRUJ
CB3 NEWS
GRUJ IS THE ONLY 100% DESERVED APP, WITH A SCREENING PROCESS THAT ONLY ALLOWS THOSE WITH A VERIFIED RELATIONSHIP WITH THE TARGET TO OPEN A CAMPAIGN.

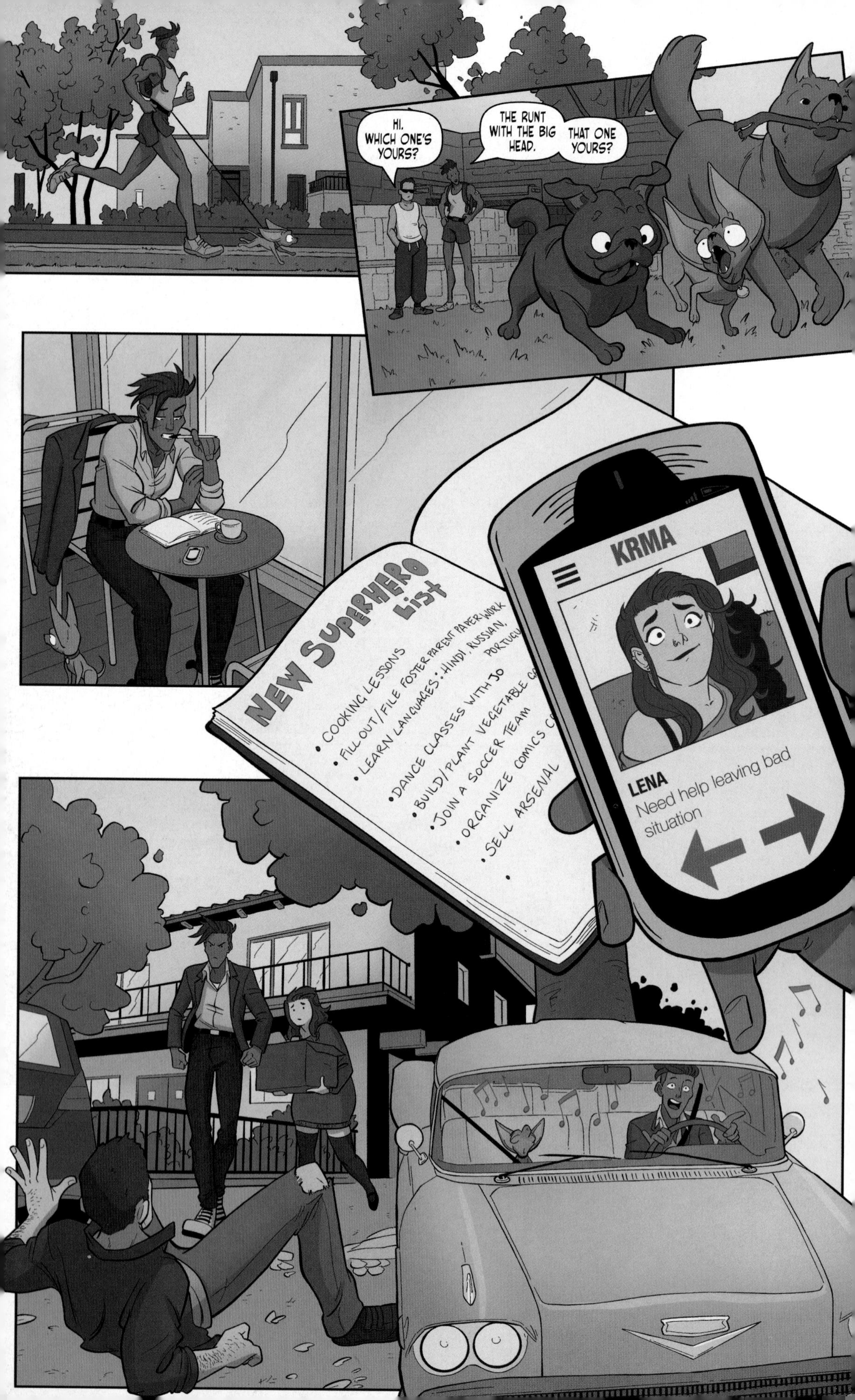

HI. WHICH ONE'S YOURS?
THE RUNT WITH THE BIG HEAD.
THAT ONE YOURS?
NEW SUPERHERO List
• COOKING LESSONS
• FILL OUT/FILE FOSTER PARENT PAPERWORK
• LEARN LANGUAGES: HINDI, RUSSIAN, PORTUGU
• DANCE CLASSES WITH JO
• BUILD/PLANT VEGETABLE
• JOIN A SOCCER TEAM
• ORGANIZE COMICS
• SELL ARSENAL
•
KRMA
LENA
Need help leaving bad situation

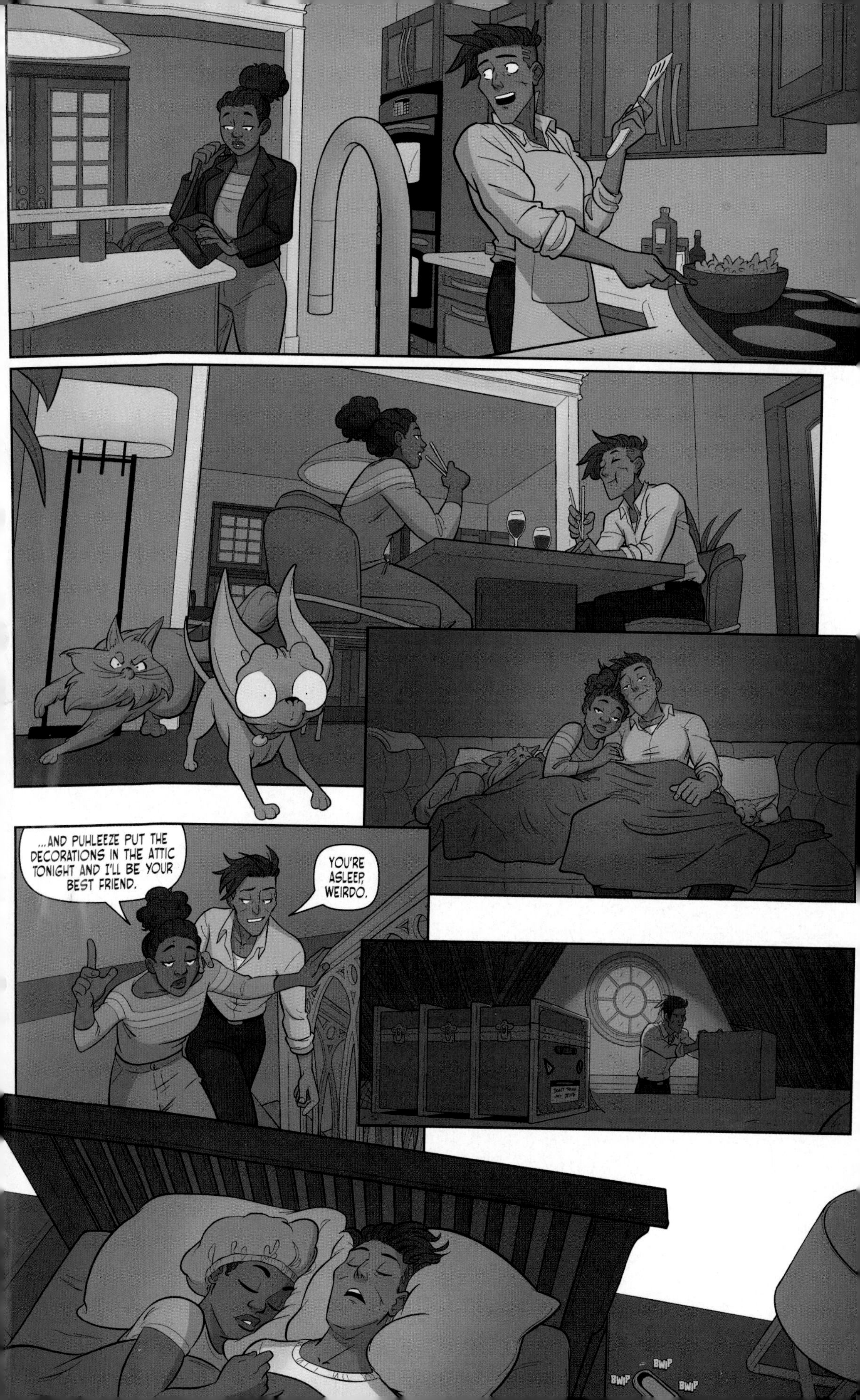
...AND PUHLEEZE PUT THE DECORATIONS IN THE ATTIC TONIGHT AND I'LL BE YOUR BEST FRIEND.
YOU'RE ASLEEP, WEIRDO.
DON'T TOUCH MY STUFF
BWIP
BWIP
BWIP

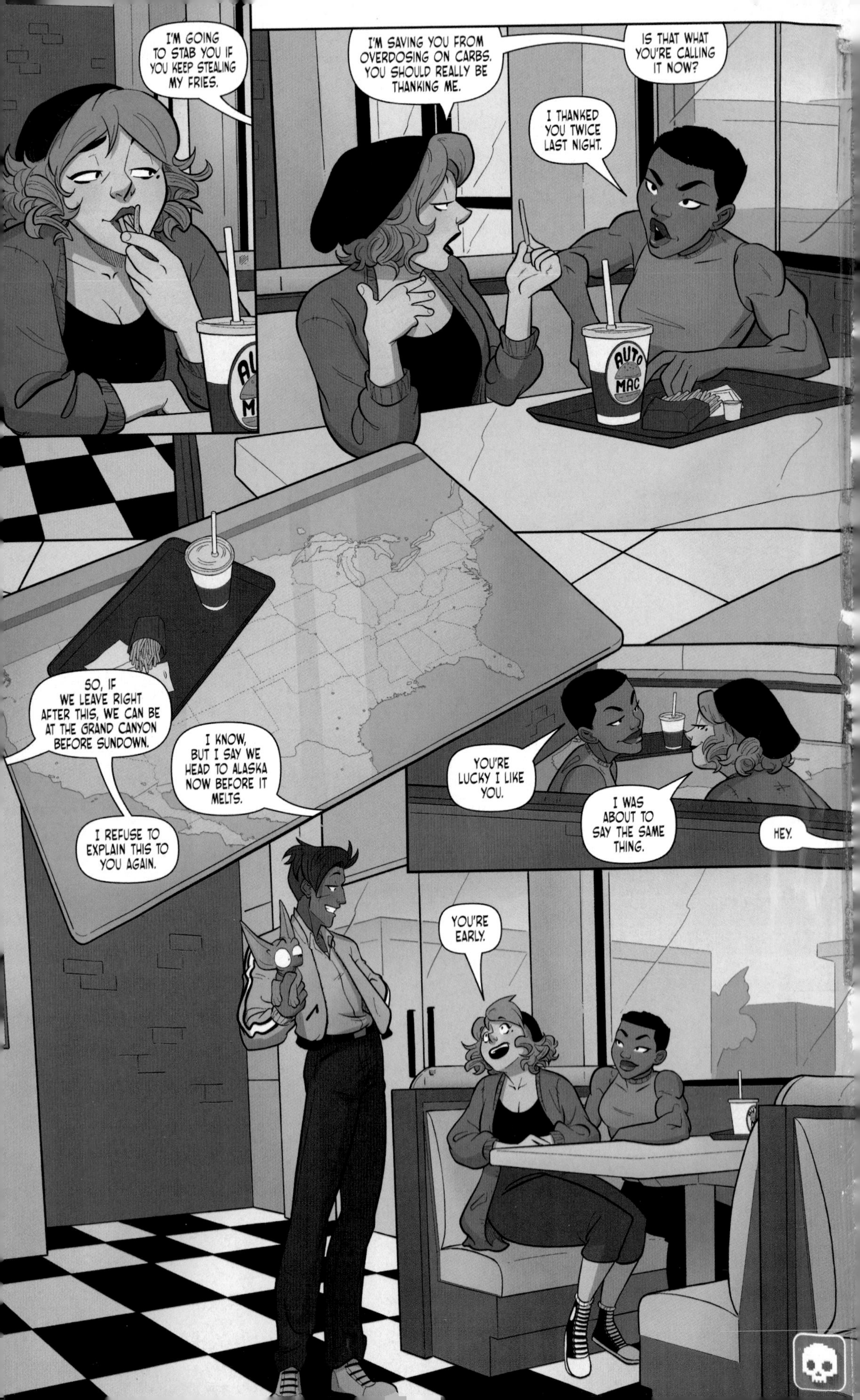
I'M GOING TO STAB YOU IF YOU KEEP STEALING MY FRIES.
I'M SAVING YOU FROM OVERDOSING ON CARBS. YOU SHOULD REALLY BE THANKING ME.
IS THAT WHAT YOU'RE CALLING IT NOW?
I THANKED YOU TWICE LAST NIGHT.
AUTO MAC
SO, IF WE LEAVE RIGHT AFTER THIS, WE CAN BE AT THE GRAND CANYON BEFORE SUNDOWN.
I KNOW, BUT I SAY WE HEAD TO ALASKA NOW BEFORE IT MELTS.
I REFUSE TO EXPLAIN THIS TO YOU AGAIN.
YOU'RE LUCKY I LIKE YOU.
I WAS ABOUT TO SAY THE SAME THING.
HEY.
YOU'RE EARLY.